LOVE AT LAST

"This is one hell of a place to . . ." Drake muttered, but his free arm came around her, drawing her to him. Their lips met in a heated kiss and the movement of their lanterns made the light dance, reflecting shadows on the walls.

Drake could feel her lips part beneath his, accepting at first, then returning the kiss with fire that ignited a force within him older than the place in which they stood.

When he released her, both were breathing deeply, completely shaken.

"I think it would be wise to get out of here," Drake said.

"I . . . suppose you're right," Caitlyn replied. She was still trembling from the passion that had swept through her and by her own crumbling resolve and lack of control. Her emotions were reflected in her emerald eyes.

"Caitlyn?"

"Yes?"

"I should say I'm sorry, but I'm not. The only thing I regret is the time and the place."

IF ROMANCE BE THE FRUIT OF LIFE—
READ ON—
BREATH-QUICKENING HISTORICALS FROM PINNACLE

WILDCAT (772, $4.99)
by Rochelle Wayne

No man alive could break Diana Preston's fiery spirit . . . until seductive Vince Gannon galloped onto Diana's sprawling family ranch. Vince, a man with dark secrets, would sweep her into his world of danger and desire. And Diana couldn't deny the powerful yearnings that branded her as his own, for all time!

THE HIGHWAY MAN (765, $4.50)
by Nadine Crenshaw

When a trumped-up murder charge forced beautiful Jane Fitzpatrick to flee her home, she was found and sheltered by the highwayman—a man as dark and dangerous as the secrets that haunted him. As their hiding place became a place of shared dreams—and soaring desires—Jane knew she'd found the love she'd been yearning for!

SILKEN SPURS (756, $4.99)
by Jane Archer

Beautiful Harmony Harper, leader of a notorious outlaw gang, rode the desert plains of New Mexico in search of justice and vengeance. Now she has captured powerful and privileged Thor Clarke-Jargon, who is everything Harmony has ever hated—and all she will ever want. And after Harmony has taken the handsome adventurer hostage, she herself has become a captive—of her own desires!

WYOMING ECSTASY (740, $4.50)
by Gina Robins

Feisty criminal investigator, July MacKenzie, solicits the partnership of the legendary half-breed gunslinger-detective Nacona Blue. After being turned down, July—never one to accept the meaning of the word no—finds a way to convince Nacona to be her partner . . . first in business—then in passion. Across the wilds of Wyoming, and always one step ahead of trouble, July surrenders to passion's searing demands!

Available wherever paperbacks are sold, or order direct from the Publisher. Send cover price plus 50¢ per copy for mailing and handling to Penguin USA, P.O. Box 999, c/o Dept. 17109, Bergenfield, NJ 07621. Residents of New York and Tennessee must include sales tax. DO NOT SEND CASH.

SYLVIE F. SOMMERFIELD

PROMISES OF LOVE

PINNACLE BOOKS
WINDSOR PUBLISHING CORP.

PINNACLE BOOKS are published by

Windsor Publishing Corp.
850 Third Avenue
New York, NY 10022

First Printing: December, 1994

Printed in the United States of America

Prologue

London 1892

The London night was shrouded in a grey, misty fog, through which the clop, clop of the horse's hooves on cobblestones carried with a hollow, echoing sound.

The rain that had fallen earlier in the evening had stopped, but a fine mist still filled the air and water glistened like silver beads on the stones.

The streets were deserted for the rain had driven all but the heartiest, or the most desolate, souls indoors.

The oil lamps that lined the streets sent eerie shadows dancing against the walls of the buildings as the lone carriage made its way through the narrow streets. The driver atop the box murmured an encouraging word to his horse through a scarf-muffled face and flicked his whip now and again, being careful not to touch the mare's gleaming, ebony-colored flesh.

Within the carriage sat a man, obviously deep in thought. He was a tall, slender, rather distinguished-looking man whose appearance belied his fifty-two years. His face was healthily tanned and his silver hair was thick and full; muttonchop sideburns matched its color, as did his full moustache. His deep blue eyes were alive with intelligent vitality.

The hands that rested on his gold-knobbed cane were

slender-fingered and strong. Overall, he exuded an aura of complete authority.

He was so deep in thought that he hardly realized the carriage had come to a halt until the door was opened and a voice brought him out of his reverie.

"We're 'ere, governor."

"Uhh . . . oh . . . yes." When he rose to exit the carriage, he moved easily and smoothly, as if his body were kept in an active and healthy condition.

He stepped down and gazed about for a few minutes as if to orient himself. The house had once been beautiful, but obviously it was slowly slipping into decay. It was a simple, soundly built brick structure, with well-made doors and windows. It was still one of the better houses on the street, for the others were small, dark, badly designed, and made of cheap materials.

There were all styles of houses, but this one was obviously Gothic, with porches, turrets, and plenty of fanciful decoration.

But neither the house nor the neighborhood interested him now. He paid the driver and waited until the carriage disappeared and the sounds of its retreat died away. He crossed the cobbled street and walked up the stone driveway. Looking about to assure himself that the street was deserted, he turned to the door and used his cane to rap solidly.

The door was opened by a small, mousy woman. Her rodent-like appearance was enhanced by the way her eyes narrowed and her nose actually seemed to twitch. Dark brown hair and a grayish cast to her skin made the comparison even more appropriate.

"Evening, sir."

"Mister Monroe is expecting me."

"Yes, sir. If you'll follow me. He's been waiting for you."

She scurried ahead of him toward a door at the far end of the entrance hall.

When she rapped lightly and opened the door, a wave of warmth and light met him and he welcomed it. He stepped inside and the woman pulled the door closed. He gazed across the room at the man who stood before the crisply burning fire.

Slade Monroe was not a large man and his bone structure seemed fragile. He was mild and ineffectual in appearance, which was his best camouflage, given his profession—that of a private investigator. His credentials seemed exemplary, and he had come highly recommended as a man able to accomplish more than the ordinary investigator. An extraordinary feat was needed now . . . in fact, had been needed for some time.

Even when he had first hired Monroe, the visitor wasn't sure this man could really be the qualified investigator he claimed to be. But his gentle manner and quiet exterior were soon recognized for what they were . . . a shield for a very clever and astute mind.

"Mr. Monroe?"

"Ah, come in, come in. Do sit down. Would you care for a brandy?"

"No, no, thank you. I've come because you sent a message." His voice sounded hopeful.

"Yes, I did," Monroe answered, satisfaction in his voice. "I'm sure you'll be very pleased with what we've found. It seems your long search is over."

"Ah . . . you've found her?"

"Yes . . . we've found her."

For a moment the visitor seemed stunned by the news, severely shaken. His face paled and he drew a deep breath and exhaled it with a ragged sigh.

"Please . . . do let me pour you a brandy," Monroe said as he took a step toward the visitor. "You look as if you need one."

"Maybe . . . maybe I will. Thank you. I'm afraid it's a bit of a shock. I thought I would never find her . . . never see her again."

Monroe urged him to a seat near the fire and gave him the brandy. The visitor took it with a trembling hand and took a deep swallow. After the glass was refilled, he sipped . . . and his color slowly returned. "How is she?"

"I'm afraid she's very ill, sir."

"Ill? How ill?"

"Well, from what I can find out, she has been told by her doctors that it would be very dangerous for her to leave the sanitarium. I'm afraid her answer was . . . she chose to die at home. I believe she'll be going in a day or two. The sanitarium is a few hours away—perhaps it would be best to wait until she's home."

"Then she's . . ."

"Terminal," came the abrupt reply.

"I see." The visitor sat thoughtfully, then leveled a penetrating gaze at Monroe. "How long . . ."

"I would say two days and she'll be home."

"I must see her," he said in a voice tinged with hope and desperation.

"I'll give you her home address, sir. I'm so sorry we did not find her in time. If you had only come to me sooner all might have been different. It's impossible to visit the sanitarium. They won't allow it."

"Please give me the address. I must go to her as soon as I can. You said she would be home in a few days?"

"Yes." Monroe jotted down the address on a piece of paper and handed it to his visitor, who looked at it closely. "So far . . . and yet so near. I never knew where she went all those years ago. Now it's too late . . . too late." He sighed deeply, put the note in his pocket, and rose to his feet.

"I appreciate your efforts," he said as he extended his hand to Monroe. "You're right. I'm sorry I didn't come to you sooner. I tried so many. You're the only one who's had any success. I'm grateful."

"I try to do my job to the best of my ability."

"I'll send round the balance of your fee tomorrow."

"Very good, sir." The visitor started toward the door and Monroe came with him. "Have you a carriage outside?"

"No."

"If you would like the use of mine . . . 'tis no night for any man to be out . . . and on foot."

"I need to walk, to think, to decide . . ."

"Whether to postpone your trip?"

"You knew of it?"

"The papers . . . you're somewhat of a celebrity. Your reputation makes it difficult to keep secrets. I understand you're to leave London in two days."

"My reputation . . . earned at a terrible cost. I am no longer sure it was worth it. Yes, yes, I sail in two days. Unless . . ."

Monroe said nothing. He escorted his client to the door and when he had disappeared into the fog he slowly closed the door.

His smile faded as he turned to see the woman standing in the arch of a nearby doorway. They remained silent, but the look they exchanged was one of complete understanding.

Late that night Monroe sat before his fire, engrossed in the newspaper. Finished, he laid the paper aside and reached toward a small table to slide open a drawer. From it he took something that looked, to the casual eye, like a rather rough-cut green stone.

He laid it on top of the folded newspaper. Then his chuckle gave way to deep, full laughter.

One

Eight Days Later

The room was semi-dark and so quiet that the ticking of the clock seemed to fill it. The woman lying on the bed stirred restlessly and muttered something, bringing the girl who sat curled up on a chair near the window instantly alert. She left the chair and in a swift, nearly silent, move, went to sit on the edge of the bed.

She took the frail woman's hand and watched her eyes flutter open. She smiled and murmured weakly, "Caitlyn?"

"Yes . . . are you in pain? You can have more medicine now if you like." Caitlyn Emmerson knew this wasn't so just as she knew it no longer mattered how much medicine was administered. She was going to make her mother's last days as peaceful and pain-free as possible.

She loved her mother deeply, and always pushed away any thought of the father who had deserted them so many years before. She had never seen him and her mother had never spoken of him, good or bad.

She had wanted to know about him, but time had passed, and for the last six months her still-young mother had been too ill to be pressed for information.

"No," Rose Emmerson said quietly. "I want to talk to you, Caitlyn."

"You must rest and regain your strength."

"Caitlyn, please. This is no time to play games. I don't want to leave you with any secrets between us."

"Don't . . . Mother . . ." Caitlyn's voice caught. She didn't want to face the truth . . . couldn't face it yet. "There's no secret that could be important enough to upset you."

Her mother squeezed her hand with sudden, surprising strength, smiling a smile that was both knowledgeable and loving. "It is time, Caitlyn. There's something I must tell you. You should have known it a long time ago. I have been unfair to have kept it from you for so long."

"There's nothing you *must* tell me except that you're feeling better."

"Please. It's not necessary to lie to each other. But there's one lie between us now and I want to clear it away. I haven't had the courage before. Now I must. I cannot rest because of it. I've cheated you out of more than you know."

"There are no lies between us," Caitlyn protested, "and I've never felt cheated even for a moment."

"Your father . . ."

"I don't think we have to talk about him, Mother. He's never been part of my life. I see no need to make him part of it now."

"You sound so like him," Rose said quietly.

"Mother!" Caitlyn protested. She didn't want to be compared to a man who seemed to think so little of her that he'd chosen to ignore his own family.

"You do. Don't you ever wonder why I was so shaken when you decided to study archaeology?"

"I thought it was because you agreed with my teachers that education wasn't necessary for a woman."

"Despite the fact that universities have been accepting

women since 1871, I didn't believe you would really go. Still, it was your choice of study that disturbed me."

"Archaeology? Why? It has always interested me. Of course, it really disturbed my professor. Oxford, he said, is no place for ladies. Thank heavens he was gentleman enough to change his attitude when he saw that my grades were high and I could do the work as well as any of the men. I'm glad he didn't try to stop me and I'm grateful to you for not trying, too."

"Could I have stopped you? I think not. You see, I think it's in your blood and I'm sorry I tried to smother it at first."

"I suppose you couldn't have. I know I'm slightly stubborn."

"Slightly?"

"Well . . . maybe a little more than slightly. Why were you so against it?"

"I never said I was against it. I only said that it was somewhat of a shock. I suppose it shouldn't have been."

"Oh? Why not?"

"Because it was what your father loved even more than he loved me."

"I don't understand."

"Do you recognize the name of Sir Richard Macdonald?"

"Do I recognize it! No student of archaeology would be worth their salt if they didn't know him. He's probably the best known authority in the field today. Why, his books have been my bibles. He's remarkable. Did you know him?"

"Yes . . . I knew him well."

"Mother?" Caitlyn suddenly knew what she was going to say and her heart began to hammer.

"Sir Richard . . . Richard," Rose said, her voice gentle, "is your father."

Caitlyn gasped softly. She might have expected a number of things, but this was not among them. It was so far beyond belief that she could not speak.

This man had been a god in her world. She had studied him carefully, read everything he had written. She had admired him above all others even though she had never had the privilege of meeting him.

She had seen vague, blurred pictures of him in newspapers taken at one dig or another. In 1875 in Egypt, in 1880 in Africa, and in 1889 in South America. The whole revelation was almost too much for her to grasp.

"I know how you must feel, how confusing this must be. I regret . . . I regret so much. Most of all, that I let my pride and jealousy separate two people who should have known each other. Oh, Caitlyn, will you let me tell you the truth? Will you listen?"

"None of this should matter now, mother. He deserted us when we needed him most. We've never had a shilling or a word from him that I can remember. Isn't it unimportant now? Obviously, he wanted nothing to do with us . . ."

"No . . . Caitlyn, it wasn't like that. If you must lay blame, please don't place it on him. It's not his fault."

"How can you say that? Desertion is a deliberate choice."

"Our situation *was* a deliberate choice, as you say, but it was mine . . . not his."

"I don't understand." Caitlyn wasn't even sure she wanted to understand. Her mother was very ill, dangerously ill, and she didn't see how these revelations could change either of their lives now.

"But I want you to," her mother said, anxiety making her tremble and cough harshly. "You *must* understand! Don't let my jealousy go on ruining your life. You could have so much more!"

"Don't, please," Caitlyn begged. "Don't try to talk. Rest, and I'll give you some medicine. Sleep a while. We can talk tomorrow."

"I don't want any medicine! I want to tell you now. I want you to find your father after . . . after I'm gone. I have written so many letters over the years. I never had the courage to send them. They're in the small chest beside my dresser. I want you to take them to him. You two should know each other. I owe him that at least."

"All right, all right. Don't get so upset. I'll listen. I'll even see that he gets the letters if that's what you want."

"You'll understand. Caitlyn, I was very young when I met your father, much younger than he. I was only sixteen. He was just beginning his career. Maybe I was fascinated by his budding reputation. He had dreams . . . so did I. But our dreams were different. I married him and only then did I realize that he wanted me to follow his dream and give mine up. We would have to live like gypsies, traveling to godforsaken places. Living in the wild . . . I . . . I wasn't strong enough to be the kind of wife he needed.

"Then . . . a wonderful opportunity came up. He was offered a chance to teach. We could have lived a calm, orderly life. He refused it. We had been having so many fights over this, but this was the worst. He begged me to understand that he could not be tied down to the life of a teacher. He begged me to stay with him. He promised me that the future would see all our dreams come true. My faith failed me, faith in myself and in him.

"You see . . . I was terribly jealous of the pleasure his work gave him. It took him from me. It would have been better if he had been having an affair. I could have done battle with another woman much more easily. Instead . . . I demanded he give up the only work he loved. *He couldn't.* He begged me to go with him. *I wouldn't.* Instead, I ran away."

"But surely he searched for you . . . and me."

"He never knew about you."

"Oh, Mother."

"It was so terribly unfair, I know, and I cannot justify it any more. I cannot lie, even to myself, any longer. For all these years I made sure we couldn't be found. I . . . I lied to you, not in words, but by saying nothing, letting you believe what you thought was the truth. First I went to Scotland, to a cousin I hadn't seen for years. You were born there. But I knew I couldn't stay there, so I returned to England and, you remember, we lived in Portsmouth for a while. But . . . I felt drawn to London. I wanted to be near Richard, to read about him and follow his career. I took another name and trusted it only to my parents. When they died . . . well, you were already making your own decisions by then. And you wanted to be . . . to be what your father was. I know how wrong I've been. I know that you must find him. I only hope you can forgive me."

"Don't speak to me of forgiveness. You've never given me anything but love. I love you, Mother, and you've paid more than a fair price for whatever you feel you might have done."

"Then you will find him? You will take him the letters and tell him . . . tell him how wrong I was? Tell him . . . that I never truly stopped loving him. My pride got in the way."

"I'll try, Mother. Honestly. But I think I read that he was going somewhere on a new project. He might not be in London."

"Find him, Caitlyn. Please. I knew him and I know you so well. You're so much alike. He can do so much for you now."

"I won't go to him out of a clear blue sky, asking for favors."

"No . . . maybe you'll be doing him a favor."

"Me? Do a man like him a favor? I don't see how."

"Maybe . . . maybe he's lonely, too. We . . . we were never divorced. There could have been no other children."

"You were lonely for him all these years? Mother, why didn't you just go back?"

"I couldn't, maybe because of my pride. Somehow, I couldn't. Now it's too late for me, but not for the two of you."

As if to emphasize her meaning, she began to cough raggedly again. Her body shook violently and Caitlyn rushed for the medicine and measured out an inch of the dark liquid into a glass. Caitlyn's hands were shaking badly and tears nearly blinded her. The combination of her mother's condition and the news she had just heard were nearly too much for her.

She carried the glass to her mother and helped her to drink it. The medicine was quick-acting—within minutes her mother relaxed into an induced sleep. Caitlyn returned to her chair slowly to think about the traumatic change a few words had made.

She had a million questions, but she couldn't put her mother through any more torment. She tried to think of the man who was her father, but it was still difficult to think that someone she had respected and admired for so many years, whose career she had followed so closely, was her father.

As a child she had always envied her friends who had loving, laughing fathers. She had felt a touch of disloyalty to her mother, who had given her such unreserved love.

She was excited and terrified at the same time. She had promised her mother so much, but could she do it? Could she just walk up to a man as important and powerful as he and say, 'Hello, I'm your daughter.' For twenty-two years she had been fatherless. Now it was almost too much to absorb.

"I'm Caitlyn Macdonald," she said aloud. "Caitlyn Macdonald." She rose and walked across the room to the mirror.

She looked into the brilliant green eyes of a girl she no longer quite knew. Her heart-shaped face was haloed by a mass of tawny gold hair and her complexion was like café au lait, tanned from the sun. Caitlyn was tall and boyishly slim yet completely feminine, a rare mixture that had taken some of her classmates by surprise. She could hold her own in the rough work of the field, digging and brushing with a delicate touch that had rescued many a piece of antiquated pottery. And she could dress in the latest frills and ruffles and carry it off with aplomb.

She had fought long and hard for her education in archaeology, but had never had an opportunity to go on a major dig with a man as respected as Sir Richard Macdonald.

"Look at you," she whispered with a soft laugh. "You're on a dig with the man already, and you don't even know if he'll speak to you, let alone invite you along."

She sighed and returned to her chair to continue her vigil. For now her mother was the most important thing. She tried to put this new knowledge in the back of her mind, but the long hours made it impossible to do anything but think.

In the next three days Rose's condition grew worse and worse. Five days later she died in her sleep. Caitlyn was devastated and the traumatic days until the funeral wiped everything else from her mind.

She was grateful for the friends who gathered to support

her during the funeral. That night her two closest friends remained at her home, not wanting to leave her alone.

"Caitlyn, why don't you come home with me for a few days?" Lettie Marsh suggested. "At least until you make plans and get your life in order. You've been nursing your mother for weeks, and now you're exhausted."

"She's right," William Holmes, Lettie's fiancé agreed. "You need to look after yourself now, my girl. You also need to make plans."

"You've both been so wonderful through all of this and I'm grateful. I don't want you to be angry with me, but . . . I really need some time alone to think."

"We're not angry with you," Lettie affirmed. "Bill and I just want to make sure you're all right. If you need to be alone, well, we can understand that, too."

Lettie and Caitlyn were so different that most people who knew them were often surprised that they were such good friends. Where Caitlyn was deep and serious, Lettie over-flowed with fun and humor. She had flame-red hair, a peaches-and-cream complexion, and eyes the color of a spring sky. Lettie always seemed to find adventure and pleasure in every day. She was several inches shorter than Caitlyn, and enjoyed being first with a new style. Her innovative char-acter was, in fact, the perfect buffer for Caitlyn.

"Just remember that we're right here should you need anything or anyone," Bill added.

"I know. Thank you, Bill. You, too, Lettie. If I need you I'll call on you both. I promise. For tonight I think I just need some sleep."

"Of course you do. I think it's been weeks since you've slept," Lettie agreed as she rose from Caitlyn's couch. "It has been a long, terrible day."

"Can you sleep?" Bill inquired gently.

"If not, the doctor has prescribed something. I'll be all right, really I will."

"Mind if we come around to look in on you tomorrow?" Bill smiled as he asked the question. "Just to make sure you're as fine as you claim to be."

Bill was a husky young man of independent means. He had sandy hair, deep honey-brown eyes, and a gentle disposition. Once he had been in love with Caitlyn, but, despite his intentions, their relationship only developed into a very close friendship. Then he had met Lettie and truly fell in love. The two of them had told her of their intention to marry, asking Caitlyn to be the maid of honor.

Bill was the link between Caitlyn and Lettie, for he understood and cared for them both completely.

Bill's parents had died when he was quite young and left him a vast fortune. That Bill needed their friendship both Caitlyn and Lettie knew, just as they knew that they would keep Bill from floundering. In this case, too much money at too young an age was more a burden than a pleasure.

"Being my big brother, Bill?" she smiled.

"You need one. You tend to overlook yourself."

"I'll be all right, really. Thank you both for your kindness."

"Well, no matter what you say, Bill and I are coming for you at the end of the week to take you to dinner."

"Fine. I'll be quite tired of eating alone by then and you two are the best company I know."

"Great. We'll see you then."

Caitlyn did not want to admit it, but when they were gone she was a little relieved. She truly did need some time alone.

She knew she had to make plans, but all her senses were numbed. She took some of the medication the doctor had given her and a half-hour later she was sound asleep.

* * *

The next day she woke very early, slipped on a robe, and made herself a cup of tea. She knew she would have to keep busy, so she decided to clean the flat she and her mother had shared for so long.

She gathered and folded her mother's clothes and packed them away. It was one of the most difficult things she had ever done. She wasn't quite sure what she would do with them. Perhaps, she thought, she might give them to the small church around the corner to distribute. Later she began to gather the clutter she had been ignoring for the past weeks during her mother's illness. Then she remembered the letters. She went to the chest and sorted through the contents until she found the bundle. There were at least twenty, tied neatly with a blue ribbon.

She sat with them on her lap for a long time, but she could not bring herself to open and read them. They belonged to someone else . . . someone she had not yet met. The name and address were clear and neat in her mother's handwriting:

> Sir Richard Macdonald
> 20 Surrey Place
> London, England

She put the packet in her handbag and continued to clean the flat until it sparkled.

Then she bathed and dressed carefully and went out to hail a carriage. When it came to a stop beside her she called out the address.

"20 Surrey Place."

"Yes, miss," the driver said and nodded.

When she disembarked in front of the house she stood and looked at it for a few minutes. It was a three-story Victorian and looked very grand. Lace curtains hung at the windows and the house was surrounded by a six-foot iron fence. The gate swung quietly on well-oiled hinges as she walked through, closing it behind her. She paused at the bottom of the three steps that led to the door, gathering her courage. This could have been her home. All this time he had been only an hour away. Sorrow at her terrible loss— and her mother's—filled her. She didn't really know what she expected to accomplish. She only knew that she had to meet him. She had to look in his eyes . . . and she had to let him know she was alive.

She walked up the five steps and across a wide porch to the door. After a moment's hesitation she knocked.

The door was opened by a rotund, cheerful woman who smiled pleasantly.

"Yes, miss?"

"I would like to speak to Sir Richard Macdonald, if I may. I'm an archeologist and I should like to ask Mr. Macdonald some questions. I'm quite interested in a dig he's planning."

"Lands, miss, Sir Richard hasn't been home for nigh onto eight or nine days."

"Not at home," Caitlyn repeated, deeply disappointed, "but . . ."

"He's gone for quite a long time, miss. I'm sorry. I was on holiday when he left, but the packing and arrangements had already been made."

"I remember reading something some time ago, but I wasn't sure."

"Sure there's been enough written about him to fill many

a book. We have the articles if you would care to read them again. It might refresh your memory."

"Would you please? I would be grateful. It is really important that I contact him."

"I'll show you the article, but I've doubts about contacting him. A letter would take such a long time . . . if it ever got there at all."

Caitlyn remained quiet. She had no intention of writing a letter. She had not really faced her intentions honestly, but now she did. She meant to find her father if she had to travel to the farthest corner of the world.

When she was ushered into a small library, she looked around her while the housekeeper left to get the material.

It was a comfortable room . . . filled with polished wood and huge chairs in which one could curl up to read on a rainy day. Books lined the walls from floor to ceiling. Beside one of the chairs was a table that held a book with a marker that looked as if the occupant would be back at any moment to pick it up. Beside it was a small rack of pipes and a jar of tobacco.

An Aubusson carpet covered the floor, and heavy drapes, that could be drawn to close out the world. It looked like a sanctuary and she could almost feel the presence of the man who lived here.

"Here you are, miss . . . I'm sorry, I didn't ask your name."

"Miss . . . Emmerson," Caitlyn replied, and wasn't sure why she didn't say she was Caitlyn Macdonald. It just seemed that the identity of her father was her secret for now . . . until she met him, knew him.

The housekeeper handed her a scrapbook filled with news clippings, and on top of it was a sheaf of articles she had not yet had time to put in the book.

She sat in one of the chairs near the fire and slowly turned the pages.

A man's entire career was here, between the pages. But it said nothing about the man himself, his likes and dislikes, his humor . . . nothing. Caitlyn could admire his accomplishments, but it was not enough. She began to feel a deep hunger to know the man.

Putting aside the book, she began to look through the articles. She recognized the last one, the same one she had read before her mother's poignant confession. But she read with newer meaning.

. . . leaves London for Bogota, South America, soon. He will authenticate, for the board of trustees of the Ziegler Museum, the finds of Mr. Drake Stone. Mr. Stone has held a grant from the museum for the past year. His theory that the Indians of Peru migrated further north than proven in past digs, and that the Indians of Colombia merged with them, will be tested by Sir Richard. Mr. Stone's progress, if his theory is proven correct, will be aided by a second grant from the museum that will enable him to continue his exploration of the territory for another three years . . .

The story went on to explain that Sir Richard would have the final word on the museum's position.

It was obvious even to Caitlyn, despite her inexperience, that her father could be somewhat of a threat to the archaeologist in charge of the Bogota dig. She wondered how this Drake Stone was taking it.

Of course, if she were the one working on a dig that could be authenticated by a man of her father's stature, she would be looking forward to it with excitement. But would Mr. Stone feel the same way?

Finished with the book and the articles, she lay them aside, realizing she had made a decision. She would go to Bogota, too. She had to meet her father.

The thought of working on a dig, shoulder to shoulder with him, was so overwhelming that she could hardly comprehend it. She would be working with the master, and meeting the man who was her father.

Then she was on her feet, thanking the housekeeper profusely, and out the door before she gave one serious thought to just how she would get from London to Bogota. She did not even have an idea of the cost or what the method of transportation would be.

But Caitlyn was not a weak woman and a challenge was always something that tended to stiffen her resolve.

When she arrived home she sat down at once to inventory her assets. Always careful with money and having a profession that didn't demand a huge wardrobe, Caitlyn had managed to gather some savings.

Once she had determined her resources, she set out to find the cost of her planned excursion along with someone she could convince that this trip would be the most exciting thing in the world.

Having no living relatives that she knew of, Caitlyn breathed a deep sigh of freedom. There was no one to tell her she could or could not do anything she chose.

Still, despite her ability to take care of herself, Caitlyn knew her womanhood alone would make her prey to all kinds of problems, the least of which would be the mistaken idea in every man's mind that a woman traveling alone was promiscuous. No, she needed a chaperone, preferably a

man, to travel with and she was determined to find one
even if she had to buy his services.

She thought first of Lettie and Bill. She was to have
dinner with them at the end of the week.

"Well," she murmured to herself, "this is going to turn
out to be the most exciting dinner you dear friends have
ever shared."

Caitlyn dressed carefully for dinner with Lettie and Bill.
When she met them at one of the restaurants that had been
a favorite of all three, her excitement must have shown in
her eyes. Bill was the first to mention it.

"Caitlyn, you not only look ravishing tonight, you look
like a kitten that's just lapped up the last of the cream. Is
there some secret you're planning to let us in on?"

"Very astute, Bill," Caitlyn said. "As a matter of fact, I
have a secret that neither of you will ever come close to
guessing."

"Whatever it is, you seem happy, and I'm glad for that,"
Lettie said. "My guess is you signed on to a dig in some
godforsaken place."

"Well, you're close."

"Caitlyn, come on," Bill urged with a grin.

"Well . . . you've both heard me talk about my chosen
profession so often . . . and you've been patient with me.
You've also heard me talk about Sir Richard Macdonald,
who's a giant in my field."

"Sir Richard Macdonald?" Lettie repeated with a frown.

"Yes," Bill added quickly, "I've heard his name rather
often. In your eyes I'm sure he's something of a saint."

"He's more than that, Bill."

"I don't understand and I'm most anxious to get to the bottom of this."

"He's my father."

For a moment both Lettie and Bill were stunned and they could only gaze at her in surprise. Then Lettie spoke.

"Oh, Caitlyn . . . how wonderful! But . . . I don't understand how . . ."

"How I know?" Caitlyn's voice grew serious as she explained what her mother had told her. "I was shocked at first, I admit. Then . . . then I really began to think about it. So . . . I went to his house." She went on to explain the scrapbook and the impression it had made on her. "So, I've made a decision."

"A decision?" Lettie repeated.

"Don't tell me . . . let me guess," Bill said. "Knowing you as well as I do, you've decided to follow him wherever in this world he decides to go. You're going to meet him and," he grinned, "your diabolical mind is telling you your daddy will let you work on some fantastic dig with him. Whereupon you'll become exceedingly famous and too rich to share dinner with two poor old friends."

"Bill, my darling, loveable idiot, you couldn't be closer to the truth. There's only one flaw—I'd never be too rich or too famous to have dinner with you two."

"You're serious, aren't you?" Lettie questioned.

"Yes, I am . . . and I need help from both of you." Caitlyn went on to explain about Sir Richard's latest trip. "It's a really fabulous chance for me to meet my father, and maybe get a chance to work as more than a fetch-and-carry girl."

"Caitlyn . . . you're jumping to conclusions," Bill said.

"Conclusions? No, I'm not taking anything for granted.

I don't know if he'll accept or acknowledge me, and I don't know if this Drake Stone will allow me to work."

"Sir Richard Macdonald's daughter and this nobody won't allow you to work?"

"It's his dig and, nobody or not, I can't do anything if he won't allow it."

"Maybe you should just wait until your father gets back from . . ."

"Bogota, South America," Caitlyn supplied, shaking her head. "I can't wait, Bill. I'm too impatient—and too anxious to meet him. We've missed so much."

"I can understand that."

"Caitlyn," Lettie said, "you have something else in mind. When do you need our help?"

"I've been trying to think up a way to explain that."

Bill sat back in his seat. He wasn't too sure he was going to like what he was about to hear.

Two

Drake Stone stood slowly and stretched his muscles. He'd been in the same position for what seemed like hours. He removed his wide-brimmed straw hat and used the crook of his arm to wipe the sweat from his brow.

His thick black hair was wet with the sweat that glistened on his tanned skin, drops of it dampening his thick moustache.

He inhaled the clear air and sighed deeply.

Sharp, silver-grey eyes surveyed the area about him, sparkling with pleasure. This dig had been a dream of his for so long that even after a year he couldn't quite believe it was happening.

For a second a smile flitted across his tanned face, turning rough-cut features boyishly handsome.

Drake was tall, fascinating the native men who worked for him and stood at least a foot shorter than his six foot, two. Thirty years rested gently on him. His shoulders were broad and his body was hard, well-honed muscle. But it was his hands that drew attention. They were large with long, slender fingers and they could be fierce or as sensitive as a woman's.

It was the mastering of a very delicate touch that had provided him the opportunity he was currently enjoying.

Fragile pieces of ancient pottery, gold, and silver had been rescued from oblivion by his patient, sensitive work. And more than one woman had responded to the same tactile talent.

The sun was nearly overhead, but despite his stomach's grumbling, he bent again to the task that had held his attention since just after dawn.

Delicately he dug around the object buried in the earth, using a small hooked tool, a brush and spoon, and, more often, his fingers. He was much too experienced to try and pull the object from the hard dirt around it, and much too patient not to scrape and brush the dirt away slowly until the earth revealed the treasure it had held for what could be centuries.

A raw excitement filled him. Slowly, laboriously, he worked, ignoring the heat and the sweat. Still it was another hour before the actual size and shape of the object could be discerned. His heart leapt.

All the pottery he'd dug so far had been fragments. This was an unbroken object, completely intact as far as he could see. He stood again and rubbed his dirty hands against the already grimy pants that clung like a second skin to his muscled legs.

"Lord," he muttered, "let it be what I think it is. Sure as hell I'll get drunk tonight."

"Talking to yourself nowadays, Drake?" came an amused voice from behind him. Drake smiled as he turned, recognizing the voice and the humor.

"Ethan, what are you doing up here this time of day?"

Ethan Marshall, the first and best friend Drake had found in South America, stood a few feet away, grinning broadly.

Then, when he'd gotten Drake's attention, he walked over to him and looked down into the small ditch-like hole. The two men were alike only in height. Ethan was blond and blue-eyed and lean and muscular from long, hard days of work.

"Discover some ancient king's tomb?"

"Nope, but maybe the key to his city."

"Looks like a jug to me," Ethan chuckled.

"A jug? You ignorant farmer. That's probably worth a knighthood in England," Drake said with a responding laugh.

"Well, you're not in England and it still looks like a jug to me. That reminds me, I came up here to drop off a letter."

"Letter? For me?"

"You, Tana, and Mendrano are the only ones besides me in these parts that can read English." He removed the letter from his pocket and handed it to Drake, whose puzzled frown remained intact. "Doesn't smell like it came from a lady," Ethan continued. "Old Stubbs dropped it by my place just in case I was coming this way. You know how lazy he is. Something important?"

Drake had torn the letter open and was reading intently his smile slowly growing wider and wider as he read. Finally he laughed aloud.

"Important! I'll say it's important. If I can get this . . . *jug,* as you put it, out and cleaned up and gather all the other things I've found I might just have a chance to have my grant renewed."

"I don't understand."

"Come on to my tent. I'll give you a drink and explain it."

Ethan followed Drake into a large tent a short distance away.

"I don't see why you stay in this tent when you have that little house down by the river."

"It's too far to go every day. Besides, I want to be close to the dig and when I go home, I like to put all this aside and relax."

"Come on. I've seen you 'relax'. You work as hard there as you do here. Keep in mind the old adage, 'all work and no play . . .' "

"You're one to talk. You've poured a lot of sweat into your place."

"Ah," Ethan laughed, "but I'm not giving it to some musty museum. It's all mine."

Inside the tent Drake poured some brandy into two tin cups and handed one to Ethan, who had found a seat on a small cot.

"I told you when I first came here that I had a one-year grant—one year to try and prove whether my theory had any grounds."

"Your theory that the Chibchas and the Peruvian Indians merged somewhere . . . that they had a contact that blended their cultures into something new. Right?"

"Right."

"So your jug proves it, I take it?"

"Well . . . no, it doesn't. But that doesn't make it any less true. I have to get the artifact cleaned and try and find which culture it fits into, along with all the others I've found."

"So, how do you prove it?"

"By finding evidence that the two cultures overlapped. My problem is that unless I can give the board some real good evidence, my grant runs out."

"From my calculations, your time is just about to come to an end."

"In two months. But now I don't have to worry about that."

"You deliberately trying to confuse me?"

"This letter is from Sir Richard Macdonald, probably one of the greatest authorities on ancient cultures ever to dig up a tomb. I did everything but crawl on my knees to get him to come here for a while . . . long enough to authenticate some of the pieces I've found."

"What if he can't?"

"Don't say things like that," Drake replied, smiling grimly. "I can't afford to think that way. He has to come. I'm inches from a great find. With another three years, I know I'll find it, I know it. I can taste it."

"You're putting a lot of faith in the belief that this man will come."

"Oh, but he is coming," Drake said. He removed the letter from his pocket and waved it at Ethan. "Here's his letter. He'll be arriving in a couple of weeks and will be my guest for the next six months. By that time I'll have proved my theory."

"You're sure?"

"I'd better, or I'll have to hire on someone else's dig until I can raise enough money to do it myself. The Ziegler Museum is generous, but they want results."

"Drake . . ."

"I know I'm walking a tight rope, but Ethan, I've got an instinct . . . a real feeling that something extraordinary is here. I just need time to find it."

"Like looking for a needle in a haystack."

"Sort of. But the looking is . . . is like nothing I've ever experienced before. Sort of . . . like reaching back in time and taking someone's hand. I don't know if you, or anybody, can understand how I feel."

"Maybe I guess I feel pretty much the same. Fountainhurst can sort of make me feel that way."

"Yes, I suppose it would," Drake answered as he paced the hard dirt floor. "God, I still can't believe he's actually giving me the benefit of the doubt and coming here."

"Don't get too worked up or you'll fall in one of those holes you've dug out there and old Macdonald will find your city instead." Ethan rose from his seat and tossed down the last of his drink. "Come down to my place tonight. I've invited a few guests for a late supper."

"Ethan . . ."

"Come on, Drake, you've been grubbing in the dirt without time off for weeks. One late supper's not going to break your stride."

"All right. I'll be there."

"Good. I'll see you later. About eight. You can stay the night if you like. It would be pretty dangerous to try to get back tonight."

"Sounds good. I haven't slept in a bed for weeks."

The two left the tent and Drake stood for a minute before he felt for the letter in his pocket, as if he still couldn't quite believe it. Then he returned to work.

But work proved difficult because, to his surprise, his hands were shaking. Richard Macdonald's name was probably one of the most prestigious in the field of archeology. Just the idea that he'd agreed to come the distance to the dig for a man as unknown as Drake was remarkable in itself. But the letter said he would stay six months. Drake grinned to himself. He felt he could conquer the world in six months.

Besides that, working with a man of Sir Richard's experience would be tremendous for Drake's credentials. He would never have a problem organizing another dig . . . anywhere.

There was a friendship between him and Ethan, but even

Ethan couldn't understand what the letter and its promise meant . . . maybe nobody could. Nobody except someone like Richard Macdonald, who had the same bond with the past as he did.

It was time to give up for the day anyway and go over his layouts and plans. He couldn't count the times he'd sat for hours looking at the landscape, planning and drawing until his own ideas were clear in his mind. Now, all he had to do was prove them right, find his city . . . and maybe add his name to the list of successful archaeologists . . . like Richard Macdonald.

Laying his plans aside, he walked to the narrow ditch in which he'd been digging. The dirt-clogged pottery lay less than half-exposed. There was no way of knowing *if* it were painted, *if* it carried markings, *if* it could be matched to any other and dated. He wanted to jump down in the ditch and jerk the pottery clear, but he knew that would only destroy it.

He was about to gather his nerve and give the unearthing a try when another voice broke his concentration. He turned to find the head man of his force.

"Mendrano, what is it?"

"Sir . . . must speak with you alone, please."

Mendrano was a strong, hard-working man, a leader among his people. If he wanted to talk to Drake alone it could only mean there was some kind of a problem he felt was too big for him to handle.

This was all he needed, Drake thought, some trouble to throw things off-track.

He studied Mendrano's face, but as usual it was inscrutable.

"Something is wrong?"

"It would be better if I spoke with you alone, sir," Mendrano insisted. He stood quietly, but Drake could sense he wasn't quite as calm as he appeared. His mahogany face was weathered and craggy. He was about five-feet-six, lean and wiry. He'd been Drake's best man for the whole year. They had learned to respect each other before Drake had worked with Mendrano less than a month.

"Come on," Drake said as he walked toward his tent. Inside, Drake turned to face him.

"Okay, what's gone wrong?"

"Nothing's wrong. I want to prevent something from going wrong. It's rather a difficult problem."

"Problem? What kind of problem?"

"I've been working the men on the far hill, the one near the foot of the little mountain."

"Yes."

"I dug a long trench. I was very careful. Just after the men stopped to eat the afternoon meal I was walking along it checking for weak points when I saw it. I was alone, so I went down into the ditch to look more carefully. I found the thing, and I know it will bring real problems if anyone else knows about it."

"I don't understand what you're talking about, Mendrano. What could you find that would bring me so much trouble?"

Mendrano looked at Drake for several moments, his dark brown eyes filled with worry. He was very fond of Drake. He reached inside his shirt and withdrew something wrapped carefully in a piece of dirty cotton.

He handed it to Drake, who felt the weight of it and slowly unwrapped the bundle.

For a minute he could only gape in complete shock at what lay in his hand. Despite the dirt that clung to it and the rough look to the stone that surrounded it, Drake knew

exactly what he was looking at, and he knew Mendrano
was right. It could mean trouble.

The 'green fire,' the natives called it. The white men
called it treasure. Drake stood, looking at the huge uncut
emerald in his hands. If his guess was anywhere near correct, the stone had to be close to a thousand carats. For a
stone like this many men would do a lot of things. For one
thing, if the word left his camp, in no time he would find
it aswarm with men in search of wealth. He could imagine
what historical finds could be destroyed by careless men
who put no value on such things. Worse yet, how could he
explain his own carelessness to a man as devoted to the
discovery of antiquities as Sir Richard Macdonald. The
thought was unacceptable. He had to do something.

"My God, it's the biggest emerald I've ever seen." He
inhaled deeply. "If word of this gets out . . . Lord, it would
ruin my dig in no time. I'd have . . . oh, great." He stood,
holding the emerald, his mind racing. "What the hell am I
going to do about this?"

"It would be better if you buried it somewhere, and we
pretend we've never seen it. And it's better we don't dig by
the little mountain anymore. If anyone else knows about
this, your city will never be."

"You couldn't be more right. Did anyone else see you
with this?"

"No, no one saw me . . . or it. I was very careful."

"It's not safe to take it out of this tent. If someone should
spot it and word got out . . . I'd hate to think of the consequences. And of all times, this is the worst."

"What are you going to do?"

"I'll bury it, all right, right here."

"You could talk about it . . . take the emerald and go
home. It would most likely make you a very rich man."

Drake contemplated Mendrano with a half-smile. "Yes, I could. I could give up my dream and just enjoy myself. But then," his smile grew broader, "I'd never know if my city was there or not, would I? I'd never . . . what is the expression I heard you use once about our profession . . . walk with the old gods? No, Mendrano, I think I would rather dig than retire."

"I thought you might," Mendrano said with a smile.

"You old fox," Drake chuckled. "Were you trying to tempt me or test me?"

"It is not my place to do either," Mendrano replied mildly.

"I'll take care of this. Thanks for keeping it a secret."

"I know how much the city means to you. It also means a lot to me. After all, it could be some of my ancestors you search for, and there is no doubt you search for the beauty in my culture. For that I am grateful."

"It could very well be. Let's hope we find them soon. By the way, Mendrano, I'm expecting a very important guest."

"A pretty lady?" Mendrano said with a hopeful grin and a gleam of amusement in his eyes. He would not be happy until he had Drake married.

"No," Drake chuckled. "Not a pretty lady, although that's not a bad idea. No, this is a very, very important man. He's the one who can help me the most. The museum will listen to anything he has to say. If I can show him an inch of proof we'll have this valley for another three years."

"Who is this 'very important man'?"

"His name is Sir Richard Macdonald. He's really an authority and I'm lucky that he agreed to come."

"You're a fine digger, you're a smart man, and you have a lot of experience. Why do you need this other man to tell you what you already know? Why do you have to prove what is true?"

"It's not me, Mendrano, it's the museum. A man with Macdonald's credentials will never be doubted. This is my first major dig. My credentials leave the big mucky-mucks with some doubts. If they're putting their money out, they need more assurance than just the fact that this is my dream and I know as sure as my heart beats that a great find is here."

"How will you prove to this Macdonald that it is there?"

"I'm hoping my last find works out and I can identify and date it, along with all the other pieces I'm trying to put together. I should be able to identify whether they're Chibchas or Peruvians . . . or combined, I hope."

"And if he doesn't believe you?"

"I'll convince him before he leaves here if I have to drag him down into the ditches with me."

"Tana said she broke a water jug today. It means something bad is coming."

"That's superstition, Mendrano. I thought you and Tana were more educated than that. A broken water jug is just that, a broken water jug."

"Maybe so . . . but it cracked from the bottom with four cracks. It mean four people see trouble."

"That's a lot of blarney. You can't believe in that gibberish," Drake insisted.

"Tana said . . ."

"Your daughter is too superstitious. They're old and foolish beliefs. I thought we were educating her. That's why I brought along the books and taught her to read. She's a sensible girl. Don't let her be caught up in things like that. You're her father."

"Nobody tells Tana how to think." Mendrano grinned. "Not even her father."

"Well if she's still hanging onto the old superstitions, she needs someone to tell her how to think."

"Tana needs a husband," Mendrano said positively.

"I don't think," Drake laughed, "that anyone can tell Tana how to think along those lines either."

Mendrano nodded with a wry grin. Obviously he had tried.

"Well, we'd best get back to work before the men begin to suspect there's something wrong."

"Where will you hide the stone?"

"I'll bury it here." He tapped the dirt floor with his foot. "I only wish I could make it vanish—it and every other emerald buried anywhere near here. But I'll have to settle for hiding it until I find a better way."

"Good. Do you want me to move the dig from the foot of little mountain?"

"Damn, that was a promising spot. But there's nothing we can do about it. I can't afford to have another emerald found . . . not yet, anyway." Drake walked to a low table and unrolled a hand-drawn map of the valley. Across the map lay a pattern of grids that divided the entire valley into sections. He tapped one of the small squares with the end of his pencil. "Here . . . begin a row of trenches here. If there's a city gate like I think there is, we ought to find some trace of it here. If the city lies beyond this spot there should be some sign here." There were entirely too many ifs to suit Drake.

"You want me to fill in the other ditches by little mountain?"

"No, it might arouse suspicion. Once I get the new find clear of the earth and cleaned and catalogued, I might go over there and take a look."

Mendrano nodded and turned to leave. When the tent

flap closed behind him, Drake sat slowly down on his cot. He held the emerald before him and gazed at it. Even in its rough, unpolished state it was still mesmerizing.

Once cut it would make a fabulous stone. He was sure his guess of nearly a thousand carats was close. He knew for certain there were men who would kill for such a thing . . . kill . . . or destroy his path into history. He just couldn't let that happen, especially not now when every instinct told him his dream was at his fingertips.

His tent was large, but only provided rough protection from the weather. It still had a hard-packed dirt floor.

Drake reached to the small table nearby, cluttered with maps and small digging tools, picking up a small, spade-like object. Then he went to his knees and began to dig.

When he had a sizeable hole, he put the emerald in it, still wrapped in the cloth. When he had filled all the dirt back in, he stood and began to pound the floor with his feet until he'd wiped away all signs that the earth had ever been disturbed.

He stood in the doorway of his tent for several minutes, surveying the land and the workers moving around on it.

Emeralds would, or could, make him a very rich man if he chose to dig for them. But Drake Stone had pursued his dream for too long and loved his work too much to be willing to put any price on it. He looked back over his shoulder only for a moment, then left the tent and returned to his labor.

That afternoon Drake took a dugout canoe from his house near the river and glided smoothly down to the docks at Ethan's plantation, arriving just after dark. As he moved around the last curve, he slowed his canoe and coasted, watching the main house appear out of the lush green jungle like a beautiful apparition.

He and Ethan had known each other for only a year, but it seemed to Drake they'd been friends all their lives. Ethan had greeted Drake when he'd first arrived since his was the only spot on the river that could supply a better map of the valley and a means to get there.

If Drake had worked hard to find his city, Ethan had worked even harder to carve his own dream, his plantation, out of a wilderness that could master any man who dropped his guard, even for a minute.

Ethan had worked side by side with the natives. Machete in hand, they had literally waged war on the jungle.

It had been half-done, the main house just a two-room affair, when Drake had come to the valley. But it had grown almost daily.

It was two floors now and built of heavy stone to keep out the heat. The first floor had been his residence for years and consisted of nine rooms. Only the year before had he added the second floor, when money became plentiful and he had time to design the nine bedrooms to his satisfaction. The roof was red and the walls were bleached white. The court in the back of the house had a stone floor, a fountain, and well-cultivated greenery.

The windows were bright with light and altogether the place looked comfortable and inviting.

Drake carried a rifle, a pistol, and a machete, but even that could never guarantee his safety. Ethan was the first to remind him when he arrived.

"Drake, I thought you'd be smart enough to get down here before dark."

"Sorry. I got caught up in something and I lost track of the time."

"You get down in one of those holes and you forget to eat."

"Come to think of it," said Drake, laughing, "I didn't have any lunch and I'm starving."

"Come on in. We've been waiting for you."

Drake walked with Ethan across the black polished stone floor. "Who are your other guests?"

"Mr. Girard from the British Embassy in Barranquilla, his assistant, Mr. Delvert, and Lieutenant Josiah from the military garrison."

"Boy, they've come a long way for dinner, haven't they?"

"Well, it's to be a week-long stay. I have a couple of business things I have to work out with them . . . and with you, too."

"Me? What business?"

"I'd rather explain it later, Drake. You don't mind?"

"No, of course not. Let's get to the food."

Ethan chuckled and the two entered the large sitting room to meet Ethan's guests.

As usual, the dinner was excellent, and by the time they were ready for cigars and brandy, all five men were in a comfortable, mellow mood.

"Much as I always enjoy your hospitality, Ethan," Rodger Girard said, "I have the feeling you have an ulterior motive."

Ethan's smile assured him he was right.

"I will defend myself by saying my ulterior motive has only the best of intentions. The three of you are pretty much the last authority here in Colombia."

"We are only the extension of her majestic arm, Ethan," Anthony Dilvert cautioned. He was not a man to deviate one iota from his responsibility.

"Of course. But I have no intention of usurping her majesty's laws or doing anything costly. On the contrary, I want to help with a problem."

"And thereby help yourself in some way," Emil Josiah added, smiling. He and Ethan had been friends too long for Ethan to take offense at words he knew were both accurate and not meant to offend.

"I'm afraid you're right, Emil. I'd like to discuss a project I have in mind. A project, I will admit at the start, that needs your approval before I can begin."

"I've seen your projects at work," Rodger said, "and I must say that most, if not all, have been both progressive and a boon for this area."

"Thank you, Rodger," Ethan said. "I hope you'll see this one in the same vein. This is my most challenging project, and I think it is also the best."

Drake was watching Ethan closely. He could not help but wonder how this 'project' could include him. But he kept silent and listened.

"You all know that in the two rainy seasons here the Magdalena River goes wild. So does the branch I live on . . . 'the Little Water,' as the natives call it. On the other hand, 'the Little Water' can come close to drying up when the dry season hits."

"Yes," Rodger agreed, "it was a terrible problem last year. Thirst and hunger. Destroyed fields and caused other problems. I've been searching for an answer, but . . ."

"But it's within our grasp to have some control over 'the Little Water'."

"How so?" Anthony questioned.

"A dam," Ethan replied quickly. "Look, I've laid out plans for a dam a few miles above my place. It would raise the water to just a few miles or so below Drake's dig. It would be too deep to dry up during the dry season and would control the water that goes into the Magdalena during the rainy season. We could eventually irrigate all the land below and above the dam. I can't see it as anything but beneficial to everyone in Bogota and the land around it."

"You've laid out plans, you say?" Rodger asked.

"Not only that," Ethan said. "If you gentlemen will join me in my study, I've made a model of exactly how the dam will look and work. I'll point out all the pluses," he said with a smile, "and I'll leave it to you gentlemen to find the flaws . . . if you can."

Ethan led them from the room, certain he could answer all their questions. Drake followed with a smile.

Three

By the time Caitlyn convinced Bill and Lettie about her reasons for wanting to go, and that an expedition to South America would be an adventure, she was already gathering equipment and acquiring the proper clothes. She knew she had to travel light. Although she packed sturdy skirts and blouses, pants, and two pairs of serviceable boots, she also, on a whim, brought two dresses and a pair of shoes that would hardly be worn at a dig. Still, it was difficult to leave *all* of civilization behind.

In her junior and senior years at college she had worked with Professor Graham and his wife on a dig in Egypt. Mrs. Graham, a teacher herself, had tutored Caitlyn in her other subjects and polished Caitlyn's Spanish and French until she was fluent in both. But it was the dig itself that had captivated her and although it was not renowned and publicized, it gave her two years of vital experience.

Also, in her senior year she had met and listened to lectures from the great Masperro, and had even been allowed to question him and spend hours digesting his theories.

Because of his wealth and generosity, Bill was able to arrange for an official guide who would be able to make the best travel arrangements once they reached Colombia.

He found a well-seasoned explorer who traveled and wrote articles for a botanical magazine. He was over fifty and looked as if he could not possibly manage the trip to the docks, let alone to South America.

His name was George Frasier. He was tall and rangy with a short white beard and intense eyes that were nearly black. His smile was quick and his vocabulary seemed inexhaustible. He assured them once they had reached Colombia that he knew exactly the men they would need.

"The map you have *is* accurate, is it not, Miss Emmerson?"

"Yes," Caitlyn said. "I finally convinced Sir Richard's housekeeper that it was really a matter of life and death. Then she was all atwitter, and I had no problem getting her to let me see a copy of his itinerary."

"Well, then, there's no problem. There's no place in that bloody area I can't get you to."

"Good. Then if we could, I would like to be on our way as soon as possible."

Bill and Lettie's informal wedding occupied everyone for several days and the newlyweds insisted the trip would make a fine honeymoon.

"It should be different and certainly exciting," Lettie said.

Bill agreed and Caitlyn was overwhelmed at the sacrifice she knew her friends were making.

"Caitlyn, you still have time to change your mind," Lettie said. "You could just write to your father and maybe he'd dash back home to meet you."

"And if he didn't, it might be years before I get to see him. No, Lettie, I want to go. Besides, if he's on a dig I might just get to work with him for a while. That's an experience I wouldn't want to miss."

"Umm," Bill muttered. "I hope this doesn't turn out to be more of an 'experience' than any of us is counting on."

"Bill, a dig is exciting. Just the thought of finding an ancient tomb, or a city. To be part of that would be worth almost anything."

"Well, old girl, we're off to find your city and your father."

At that moment the carriage came to a halt. They disembarked and stood in what to Caitlyn looked like total chaos. But George made it clear that it was organized confusion. "If such a thing is possible," he added. "If you'll come aboard, we'll be on our way in just a little over two hours."

"It . . . doesn't look very seaworthy," Caitlyn said hesitantly as she looked at the ship in which they would be crossing thousands of miles of the Atlantic Ocean.

"Ah, I've been aboard *Majestic* several times. She may not be a beauty, but she's seaworthy and surprisingly comfortable. Although," he turned to face her with a half-smile, his hands clasped behind his back, "you do not strike me as a lady who cannot . . . adjust to minor discomforts."

"I'm not, at least I hope I'm not. But by the time we get to Bogota you may wish you had never seen me."

"I hardly think so," he chuckled humorously. "Let us board, shall we?"

Caitlyn agreed, feeling a subtle pleasure at his obvious approval.

They settled in small cabins that were, to say the least, devoid of luxury. There was nothing but a hammock for each of them and a wooden wash basin with a chamber pot inside the cabinet door. They would wash from their basin and dress from their trunks.

True to George's prediction, almost two hours later they could feel the movement of the ship. Caitlyn was so filled with excitement that she was first on deck to watch London . . . civilization . . . disappear.

Late that night, when she was sure most of the passengers

and her friends were asleep, she went on deck. Standing at the rail near the bow she looked out into the distance. It was a balmy night and the stars seemed close enough to touch.

She let her mind drift, wondering about the father she had never known. How would he react to discovering he had a daughter? Visions of possibilities danced before her. She tried to imagine their conversation and realized that with so much in common they might become close. Caitlyn took a great deal of pleasure in the fact that she had chosen the same profession without ever having met him.

She heard no sound, so she was startled when a voice came from close behind her.

"Can you not sleep, Miss Emmerson?"

She turned to see George, a sympathetic smile on his face. She smiled in return.

"It's difficult. I guess I'm too excited."

"You're not seasick, are you?"

"Heavens, no. I'm too excited to be seasick."

"Quite understandable. A young, and may I say, very beautiful, lady does not choose to go to such a wilderness every day."

"A wilderness," she repeated softly. Then she turned to face him. "Tell me about where we're going. What's it like?"

"Well . . . that's a large question. Sometimes . . . no, most of the time, Colombia is quite difficult to describe," he replied. "Let me see. First we will go to Barranquilla . . . that is the front door to Colombia. It is a bustling town and has a collage of culture within it. Behind it are the steaming jungles and snow-topped mountains, the cities and plantations and endless empty *llanos,* or plains as we would say. And there's the coffee and gold of a country more than twice the size of France." He paused thoughtfully, "Bogota, the capital, was established high in the interior by Jimenez

De Quesada and his magnificent ruffians. It stands at the end of a river."

"Does it take long to navigate?"

"Depends on the season, the amount of water, and the ability of the pilot to dodge sand banks. Distances aren't always calculated in days, but often in weeks. When one goes to Colombia, one goes to another world. There is a timeless feeling about it. The jungle, the lonely rivers . . . it is magnificent in its own way."

"Why, George," Caitlyn said softly, "you sound like a romantic."

"Maybe I am, a bit. I do feel an extraordinary fondness for the place. A few months ago on a breezy terrace I dined on paté de foie gras, sole meunière, and boned squab, accompanied by properly chilled Traminer and much stimulating conversation. And I found myself remembering sitting on a bench outside a little 'dobe ranch house far up in the sierra, making supper from cocoa and cheese. On that evening the conversation was about crops and the possibility of unearthing worthwhile treasures. Both occasions were remarkably pleasant."

"Such a contrast."

"There are plenty of contrasts that are even more dramatic. For instance, you can be in a comfortable hotel in the morning and before noon be at a camp in the center of an almost unexplored jungle country inhabited by hostile Indians. I have done it." He paused and smiled at her again. "So, I've answered your questions. Colombia is a land of extremes and contradictions. There are towering mountains that march in tremendous columns three abreast, some of them snow-covered and eighteen thousand feet high; there are sunny jungles and fever-haunted swamps, where crocodiles slide into the shallow water and parrots scream from trees almost grotesque with orchids."

"You make it sound inviting and frightening at the same time."

"And that's just the contradiction that it is, inviting and frightening . . . all at the same time."

"You said you were there, in Bogota, discussing . . . what was it . . ."

"Crops and treasure."

"Treasure?"

"Well," George said, "the use of the word is rather ambiguous. *Treasure* means different things to different people. I have friends who consider this verdant land treasure enough. I also have friends who have left monetary treasures behind and come to Colombia to fulfill their dreams. Treasure, like beauty, is in the eye of the beholder."

"Yes, you obviously have a great many friends there."

"Oh, I do, I do. I value one young friend highly. He has scratched out a marvelous plantation near the river and is working like a demon to make it profitable. Matter of fact, we'll have to go there before we can go on to the dig. He's the one who'll supply us with equipment and transportation to make the last leg of the journey."

"Does he have a family?"

"No, and he has never dwelt long on stories of his past. Since he's so reticent, I hesitated to inquire too deeply. He seems to prefer the isolation."

"But it seems such a lonely life."

"Oh no, he has many people working for him and has made innumerable friends among the natives."

"George, have you heard of Sir Richard Macdonald?"

"Richard Macdonald! Of course. Who in the civilized world has not? I have never had the pleasure of meeting him personally, but I know his work. I've read every word he's written. He's a remarkable man."

"Yes, I've always admired him as well. I had hoped you had met him and could tell me more about him."

"I'm afraid not, my dear."

"Well then, you shall meet him, as well as I."

"Oh?"

"He left London some weeks ahead of us and is on his way to the same dig."

"How very fortunate. Is this why you're going?"

"For the most part. He's presumably going to authenticate the work of a rather unknown archaeologist. I believe his name is Mr. Drake Stone."

"You are well informed."

"Once his housekeeper began to talk, I could hardly get her to stop."

George grinned at her. "And you tried your best to do so, I expect."

"Well, not exactly," Caitlyn laughed. "I wanted to hear as much about Sir Richard and this dig as I possibly could. You see, I've been studying for years and this could be a tremendous opportunity. I only hope Mr. Stone doesn't object."

"Why should he if you're well educated?"

"Archaeologists can be somewhat . . . possessive about an area where they hope to make a great find. He may willingly accept Sir Richard Macdonald, but he might not be so willing to accept Caitlyn Emmerson."

"You're most charming. I cannot see this Mr. Stone resisting for long."

"That's exactly what I don't want. I don't want him to tolerate me as a . . . charming lady. I want him to accept me because of what I could contribute."

"I see," George repeated. "I suppose everyone has to prove

themselves at one time or another. I have a feeling I was right about you. You're one to adjust to circumstances . . . and accept a challenge. I wish you good luck, Miss Emmerson, and success."

"Since we are to be together for some time I do wish you would call me Caitlyn."

"Thank you, Caitlyn," George smiled. "I'm honored. Now I think I shall take myself off to bed. Good night."

"Good night, George . . . and thank you."

"For what?"

"Oh, for your encouragement, support, and kindness."

"It's truly not kindness, Caitlyn. I really believe you're a rare young lady and I do wish you well. Good night."

When George left she turned again and rested both arms on the rail. Such a combination of emotions filled her that it was hard to separate them. She was excited, thrilled . . . yet she was, in an odd kind of way, scared to death.

Caitlyn inhaled deeply of the soft night air. The expedition had begun and she wouldn't stop it even if she could. She had a big dream . . . and she intended to follow it.

Drake hadn't been able to stand the waiting much longer, so he arrived at Ethan's earlier than planned. It had been weeks since he had received word that Sir Richard had agreed to come. Now, he would soon be here and Drake was impatient.

Ethan had sent a messenger to Drake, telling him the boat bringing Sir Richard was on its way upriver. No matter how long he'd been in this country, Drake could still be amazed at how fast word spread. A man could take one step out of Barranquilla and the natives miles away already knew it. In fact, he didn't think they missed a thing that went on in the huge, sprawling wilderness.

"Drake, come and have a good, hot breakfast. If we leave now we'll be pacing the dock for hours, and we'll be in the way of my workers. So let's relax and have some coffee."

"You're right, Ethan," Drake agreed. "I just can't stay still much longer. I know I've been driving Mendrano and his men mad. Not to mention Maria. She's tossed me out of my own house twice in the past two weeks."

"Wise woman," Ethan said with a grin.

Drake followed Ethan into the spacious dining room where they were served a large breakfast, to which both men did justice.

The sun was up when they mounted and rode the hour to the river, taking along two mules and another horse for Sir Richard. Ethan had built his own docks in several strategic places and found them quite useful.

They stood on the dock, looking downriver. In the distance they could see the boat approaching as dark puffs of smoke came from the stack and they heard the huff, huff of a laboring motor.

As it neared they could make out the tall, distinguished man standing in the bow.

Drake was surprised at his sudden calm. He had to make a good impression. This man was much too important to start off on the wrong foot. When the boat bumped the dock, a wooden gangplank was lowered.

Richard Macdonald strode down the gangplank with a vigor that impressed both men. He extended his hand to Drake first and his words took both men by surprise.

"Mr. Stone, I presume?" His voice was deep and mellow. Drake took his hand in a firm grip.

"How did you know which of us was which?"

"Ah, my friend," he said, his voice filled with humor. "You have the intense, brooding look of a colleague. And you, sir," he said, turning to Ethan, "have the look of a planter, of a man who needs the sun, the air, and the earth. You are Mr. Ethan Marshall, are you not?"

Ethan shook his hand and he, too, was taken by surprise. "You're correct, Sir Richard. This," he waved his hand to the land around them, "is my plantation, Fountainhurst."

"Sir Richard, it's a great honor to welcome you to Colombia."

"I thank you, Mr. Stone."

"Please, sir . . . it's Drake."

"Drake. Is your dig some distance from here?"

"It would be best if you had dinner and stayed the night. We can be on our way first thing in the morning. We go part way by boat and the rest on a very dangerous trail. I'd hate to have you in those hills after dark. In fact, most of the seasoned travelers don't enter the jungle after dark if they can help it. It isn't exactly safe," Drake replied.

"Predators?"

"Of all species," Drake laughed, "including human ones."

"I have somewhat lost track of directions."

"We'll be traveling north to south," Drake said as they walked back toward the horses. "It's a good thing we're not going west to east or reverse."

"Why so?"

"Colombia is an obstinately perpendicular country," Drake began. "Crossing it from west to east presents a really dizzy variety: sea level to eight thousand feet, down to three thousand, back up to ten thousand and all in a little over two hundred miles. Down between the mountains along the river it's insufferably hot. In fact, the coastal jungle belongs in the steam-cooker class. But Bogota is cool even at midday, and can even be penetratingly cold at night."

"Sounds as if there's very little change of seasons."

"Twice a year it's rainy," Ethan added. "We call it winter; and twice a year there's a dry period."

"And that's your summer," Sir Richard said. "It's quite different in Bolivia, Venezuela, and Peru."

"So, Sir Richard," Drake said as the three mounted, "was your journey very difficult?"

"It was nothing more than I expected," Sir Richard replied. "I have crossed some rougher seas, but I expect your jungle might prove to be a problem."

"Well, it's stubborn," Ethan agreed, "and it refuses to be tamed. Nature here is not meek and submissive. It is extravagant and demanding, fantastically generous, and stubborn. It's a violent and magnificent creature to be courted like a lover, and vanquished like an enemy."

"And you sound as if you love it."

"That I do, Sir Richard, that I do. Mother Nature and I have been fighting and loving for three years."

"And you, Drake. Do you love as strongly?"

"I believe so, but maybe in a different way."

"How so?"

"I am a more . . . casual visitor. Mother Nature need not fight me so hard because I only want to share her secrets. I guess I would be labeled more a groom than," he smiled at Sir Richard and winked, "a seducer, like my friend here."

"A seducer?" Ethan protested with a laugh. "To get the earth to relinquish what you want is the height of seduction. Nature usually guards treasures fiercely."

"Treasure?" Sir Richard questioned.

"His reference to artifacts," Drake said. "He's sure I'll

find a hoard of gold and precious stones. I keep telling him he doesn't understand what treasure is."

"I take it you two have had a similar argument before."

"Every time we have one too many," Ethan said, "or he runs across an old bone or piece of pottery."

"Or you get your crop half-drowned in the rainy season."

"I should like to be around when the . . . discussion is settled," Sir Richard responded with amusement.

Both men laughed and Sir Richard joined them. As they continued their ride, Drake, who was riding to the left and slightly behind Sir Richard, had an opportunity to study him. He was a tall, slender man, tanned, with silver hair and a moustache. Drake knew his age to be over fifty, but he certainly didn't look it. His eyes were blue, inquisitive, and Drake could see he missed nothing.

Still, a vaguely uncomfortable feeling plagued him. He wondered if it was a premonition. This man could effectively keep the promised hope of a career leap from ever happening. So far he had been kind and polite. But would that change? What if he couldn't prove he was on the verge of a huge find? Where in God's name would he find the means to continue on his own? The thought was sobering.

As they jogged along a trail that was rapidly becoming more rugged, conversation became more difficult so they continued the balance of their ride in silence. The mules, carrying Sir Richard's equipment and personal items, would follow at a leisurely pace.

It was obvious to both Drake and Ethan that Sir Richard was well used to riding. He offered no excuses and kept pace with the two younger men.

When they arrived at Fountainhurst, Ethan had one of his servants show Sir Richard to his room, with an invitation to join them later for drinks. He agreed.

Drake and Ethan walked into the large living room.

"Well, Ethan, what do you think?" Drake asked as he found a comfortable seat in a large wing backed chair.

"It's not what I think, it's what *you* think. You've got something on your mind, my friend. What's wrong?" Ethan sat down in a chair opposite Drake so he could watch his face. He'd begun to be able to read Drake's moods.

Ethan had poured them both a drink before he sat down, and now he waited while Drake took a sip and contemplated his answer.

"Outside of the fact that this man holds my future in his hands . . . I don't know."

"I've never seen you so unsure of yourself . . . or are you unsure if it was the right decision to ask him here?"

"Maybe it's because there's so much at stake. I'm jumping at shadows. I haven't given him much of a chance, have I? It's just . . . he's so . . . powerful. And I know . . . it would only take a few words from a man like him to make . . . or destroy my chances."

"Drake, let him get a good look at what you're doing before you jump to conclusions. By the way," he added, grinning to ease Drake's mood, "did you get your jug out of the dirt?"

"Yes, I got my jug out of the dirt."

"You don't sound happy about it."

"Disappointed a bit maybe. It's not convincing proof, at least not as convincing as I'd hoped. I think I've got it dated all right and culturally placed, but my theory needs hard evidence of two *mingling* cultures. I know it's there. Damn it, Ethan, I know it's there."

"Well, this might prove to be the best piece of luck you've ever had. All you have to do is convince him the way you're convinced. There must be something in your mind that made you feel this was true . . . so make him believe."

"I'm sure going to try."

The sound of footsteps on the stairs put an end to their conversation and drew their attention to the large doorway in which Sir Richard appeared.

He accepted Ethan's offer of a drink and found a comfortable seat to await dinner.

"Shall we be leaving early tomorrow?" he inquired.

"I would like to get started early," said Drake. "It's not an easy trip to the dig. We'll go upriver by boat for some distance, then it's mules from there to my camp."

"I'm quite prepared."

"We'll go on ahead," Drake continued. "Ethan will have your baggage delivered to us."

"Good," Sir Richard said as he leaned back in his chair and put all his attention on Drake. "So tell me a bit about your dig. What have you found so far, and what is it you're searching for? I heard you make mention of a theory of sorts. I should like to hear more."

Ethan had to smile at the contained excitement that lit his friend's eyes. Drake set his glass aside and bent toward Sir Richard, resting his elbows on his knees, as if he wanted his words to have more force.

"You know that Don Gonzalo Jimenez De Quesada led an expedition into Colombia," Drake began.

"Yes . . . yes."

"I'm sure when Quesada led his bedraggled remnant of a conquering army over the Andes into Bogota, even the magnificent superiority of the Conquistadors was a little shaken to find it studded with villages, crisscrossed by well-worn roads, patched with cultivated fields. Towns, built in geometric patterns that had steep, thatched roofs and bright, flying flags. They discovered this with eyes long accustomed to the lonely savagery of hostile jungles. They looked out over a plain called 'The Valley Castles'.

The people who lived there had been there so long they did not even have a dim memory of migrating. Now most authorities agree they must have come down from the north, through Mexico. Surrounded by mountains, jungles, and savage neighbors, they lived in what I refer to as a relatively advanced state of civilization . . . that all-embracing word which means everything and nothing. Self-contained and apart."

Sir Richard had been listening intently, occasionally nodding his head. Ethan, as he always was when Drake expounded on his theory, was caught in a rare kind of magic. It was as if through Drake's eyes and imagination, he could lift away a veil and see a magnificent panorama of the past.

"But your theory is not to justify this?"

"No . . ." Drake inhaled deeply. "My theory is they came down from the north . . . and were met here by the migrators from Peru . . . and that this is where the two cultures overlapped, where they blended."

"And do you have any proof?"

"Not conclusive," Drake admitted reluctantly. "But you would have to see the puzzle as a whole, as I do. You fit the pieces together first visually . . . then physically. I believe very firmly that with enough time I can prove this. I feel as if I almost know these people."

"I can understand how you feel. The days I spent in Peru were almost as consuming. Sometimes I grew so involved I found I would often forget to eat and would have to be reminded by my head man to drink before I dried up into a mummy."

"That is one of the reasons I've asked you to join me

here. You, of all people, will recognize the integration of foreign cultures much more quickly than I. I may already have evidence I don't understand."

"I'm quite honored and I hope I can contribute something positive. These people are called Chibchas, I believe."

"You're right. Some evidence points to the title *Muyscas* . . . people. But Chibchas is more relative." Drake was relieved to see Sir Richard already had a working knowledge of his position. "By the time the Spaniards came to the land of the Condor, the Chibchas had not only a religion of some nobility and a moral code, but an established body of laws. Homicide, incest, robbery, untruthfulness, and treason were crimes; industry, cleanliness, charity, and courage were enjoined by their faith. We can't do much better in our . . . civilization."

"You have some refined conclusions there."

"They aren't conclusions. I've found written laws . . . evidence of their moral and social code. But I haven't found the answer to my questions—did the two, or maybe even three, cultures meet and overlap here? Did they share tools and weapons and history until they melded into one? That's the answer I'm searching for."

"You've bitten off a monumental task. It's wonderful that you've found all you have. That alone is enough to establish you."

"It might be enough to establish me, but it isn't enough to satisfy me."

"It seems you have a dream, Drake," Sir Richard said gently.

"Yes . . . a dream. I know how the procedure went for the burial of a king. Somewhere in the valleys and mountains here, concealed in caverns or the beds of streams, there are still the inviolate tombs of the lords of Bacata, as the natives once called Bogota. The places of burial were secret, though they were fixed by the high priest the day the ruler ascended the throne and took in his hand the golden scepter of Muequeta. When Zipa, one of their strongest rulers, became chief of chiefs, he ruled well. When he died, the body lay in state for six days while the city rang with stories of his power. Then, wrapped in mantles painted with designs of rank, it was laid in a casket made of a hollowed palm, lined and covered with plates of beaten gold. Then Zipas's choicest possessions and rarest jewels were placed beside him. His favorite concubines and slaves, drugged with *borrachero,* were killed and buried in the same pit." Drake's voice grew deep and intense. "Even the intense greed of the Conquistadores did not enable them to discover one of these concealed sepulchers. King after king lies in private, little specks of dust enclosed by vast fortunes. Nor have the hidden treasures that escaped the conquerors been unearthed. Oh, great amounts of loot were taken from a few, but many were never found."

"So it's treasure you seek as well?" Sir Richard questioned.

"No . . . not treasure . . . information. The *Muysca* strain had *not* been lost. The two cultures *met,* and I want to be the one to prove it."

"I'm glad to hear that. Great treasures have been sought and found among other cultures, and have been quite thoroughly stripped. I've heard of other treasures and now I'm hearing stories of yours. There's a vague rumor that this is where the stone the natives call 'the green fire' was once found."

He watched Drake's eyes closely. Despite the fact that he kept control of his features, and, with great effort, held his hands and body stiff so he would not react, something flickered in his eyes . . . and Sir Richard did not miss it.

"I've been digging here for over a year and I've never seen such a stone," Drake said. Although it was the literal truth, since Drake did not *personally* dig up the stone buried beneath his tent, he still felt nervous. One hint to this man that it was treasure he really wanted, or finding 'the green fire', and his future as an archaeologist might come to an abrupt end. No. As far as he was concerned, he wanted no hint of the presence of emeralds to surface and he'd do everything in his power to make sure it didn't.

"Well, maybe it was just that . . . a rumor. I know how they can get out of hand, especially in our field. I had heard that the natives found, cut, and wore emeralds as part of their finery and had them buried with them."

"Unless we find the grave sites of some very important people, it's unlikely that we'd know the truth. By then, I hope everything is authenticated and we have guards to protect us."

"You have no armed guards now?" asked Sir Richard.

"Not at the moment. There's little to guard. I have only about twenty men myself, and they just do the rough work. I'm doing the actual digging myself. It's slow, but I have control. If I discover anything of financial value, I'd hire some of the more trustworthy men from the village as guards."

Ethan, who had been listening to the conversation in interested silence, interrupted. "I have arms and men if Drake should need them. My men are trustworthy and trained to use guns."

"We might not need them. My men are all pretty trustworthy and I'm looking over their shoulders all the time as is Mendrano, my head man. He's about as solid as a rock."

"Well, time will tell about that," Sir Richard said. "Things often seem to work well until a tomb or something of real value is discovered. Then, if you're careless, the whole dig can fall apart."

"There'll be two of us for a time. If you decide my work is worthwhile, then I'd be glad to make use of any advice you have to offer."

"I hope your discovery turns out to be all you want it to be. The museum will be most grateful . . . and well-off, if it is. I would be most honored to put my expertise at your disposal."

Drake was about to answer when a servant appeared in the doorway to call them to dinner.

During the meal Sir Richard asked a great many questions about Ethan and his plantation, as if to balance his earlier lack of interest.

It was a relaxed dinner and soon both Drake and Ethan had Sir Richard laughing as they recounted some of their adventures in Colombia.

Due to his exhausting journey, Sir Richard decided to go to bed shortly after dinner. "As you said, we should get an early start and since I'm not as young as I used to be, I'd better get some rest."

They bid him good night, then Drake and Ethan decided to enjoy a nightcap before they, too, sought their beds.

"So, Drake, it looks like you have a very sympathetic ear in Sir Richard. I think he wants you to find your answers almost as badly as you do."

"It's heartening, isn't it?"

"You were a little shook up there for a minute, weren't you?"

"Me?" Drake questioned guiltily. He should have remembered how well Ethan knew him.

"When he was talking about finding some kind of treas-

ure, and especially when he brought up the subject of emeralds. I thought you were going to jump out of your skin."

"Was it that obvious?"

"Not to him, but I know you pretty well. It touched a
nerve somewhere."

"Yeah, it did."

"What's up, Drake?"

"You have to keep this a secret, Ethan. My dig and all
my future plans are at stake."

"All right. It's just between us."

"I've found . . . no, Mendrano found an emerald big
enough to choke a horse."

"Good Lord! Did he say anything to anyone else?"

"No. He brought it straight to me."

"What did you do with it?"

"Buried it." Drake said firmly.

"Someone will sure as hell run across it."

"No, not this time. I buried it in the dirt beneath my tent.
No one knows and no one would think to look there if they
did."

"What are you going to do if someone runs across another one?"

"Hope it doesn't happen soon . . . I'll cross that bridge
when I get to it."

"That's a big chance. What if someone does dig up another one, though? How are you going to prevent it?"

"I've moved them away, more out on the valley floor
where it's less likely. In the meantime, I'm starting to work
on the mound itself. If I can strike a burial site I'll have to
send for armed guards. Your offer stands, doesn't it?"

"Of course."

"Then I'll just cross my fingers and hope I'm lucky enough
to keep it under control until I find what I want. Thank God

I don't have any students or amateurs on the dig like some do. One of them would want to track his own idea and sure as hell they'd run across something I *don't* want found."

"Well, good luck. You know if you need any help all you have to do is call."

"Thank's Ethan."

"For now I'm going to bed. Don't worry, Drake. I won't say anything to anyone."

"I appreciate that."

"You'll be running on raw nerves for a long while. I don't know if you can, but you'd better try to get some sleep yourself."

"I will. But first, I'm going to finish this drink."

"Okay, see you in the morning."

When Ethan left him, Drake walked out on the stone patio and stood, sipping the last of his drink and looking up at the star-studded sky.

He had no reason for the strange, anxious, excited feeling. But it was as if fate, in some way, was about to tap him on the shoulder.

Four

Barranquilla was a gleaming, busy city sprawling in hot sunlight just east of Panama, where the Rio Magdalena emptied into the sea.

Scanning the city, Caitlyn felt both bewildered and excited. She turned to George, Bill, and Lettie, who stood at the rail with her waiting to disembark.

"How extraordinary, George—modern and ancient, all at once."

"Yes. There are Indians of all kinds here, from the *Putumayans* to the shy tribes who burn their villages and move back into the jungle when the canoes of the outlanders become too numerous. There are servants and medicine men, statesmen and aborigines, poisoned arrows and sacred lakes. All are, to varying degrees, the essence of Colombia."

"Sort of hard to put in simple words," Bill said. He was amazed at how much he was enjoying the new adventure. And George was the most excellent of guides—it seemed to the three that he knew everything there was to know about Colombia.

"That's right, young man. There's no neat definition. Colombia will not wrap up into a tidy parcel. When one attempts to combine all the ingredients, the result is a bulky bundle of odd angles that refuses to conform to any established formula. But it is physically magnificent and end-lessly interesting."

"You're not a bit prejudiced, are you, George?" Caitlyn teased.

"Perhaps, a bit," George conceded with a smile. "But I believe you three will feel the same way by the time you leave here."

"How do we continue our journey from here?" Bill inquired.

"Travel is limited. You could cut your way through the jungle with a machete . . . or you could be taken upriver. If you were to decide on the jungle, there are occasional bits of level land. But these are just happy accidents. You'll run across all kinds of reptiles, great and small, from croco-diles to the deadly coral snake; there are tapirs, tigers, mon-keys, ocelots, wild pigs, and animals whose names mean nothing to English ears. Worst of all, there are insects of every description, all of which bite, some painfully and some even fatally."

"You make me want to turn right around and go home," Lettie announced firmly. "I think you'd better tell me some-thing nice about this country."

"And I think," Caitlyn smiled at George, "you're trying to test us to see how faint-hearted we are. Well, my friend, you can't scare us away."

"Believe her, George," Bill chuckled. "She's not easy to scare and where she has the nerve to go, we go."

"Then I shall tell you something nice about this country."

"It's about time," Lettie said, mustering a smile. "I thought you were trying to fox us somehow."

"Dear lady," George protested, "I was only presenting the facts. The worst first so the rest would be easy."

"Very clever," Bill said. "Now let's hear the good part."

"Let me see," George pondered. "The mountains . . . the magnificent, awe-inspiring mountains. You cannot stand anywhere in the length and breadth of the land and not see them. Soon you'll be seeing them much closer. They hold great wealth and defy man to pass. There is your challenge, your adventure. Your map leads you to an amazingly beautiful valley, surrounded by these majestic mountains. You'll find great pleasure there, I promise you. It's a place where one can almost reach the stars."

"And still reach into the past?" Caitlyn asked softly.

"Yes, a past rich in so many things."

"How long will it take us to get to our destination?"

"Well, the journey from Barranquilla would take about a week. But . . . we will not go directly to Bogota. Instead, we will go upriver to Ethan Marshall's plantation. That will take as long as providence and the state of the channel decrees."

"Then it's just one more long boat ride to this . . . plantation?" Bill said.

"Long," he agreed. "If the water is low it could take a week."

"That long?" queried Lettie.

"Don't be alarmed. The water is not low. It should take less than that."

"We'll take sheets and blankets, lots of mosquito net, plenty of tinned food. I also have a supply of bottled drinks to cheer us. Yet . . . the long days moving quietly upstream, the green banks and villages, the star-filled nights, and above all, the magnificent sunsets compensate for every moment of discomfort."

"So tell us, George, what are the Colombians like?" Caitlyn urged. "I want to know all I can before I get there. At least I want to talk to everyone as if I cared enough to find out about them and their homeland."

"You're insatiable," George laughed.

"Yes, I am," Caitlyn admitted happily. "I shall be asking you questions until the very last minute."

"Well, they do present a unique picture. When you talk to a professor or a dry goods merchant, the differences are only of character and outlook, but when you talk to a peasant high up in the Andes or the Putumayo, you enter other centuries and touch history. Colombians are usually divided by this question with amusement and exasperation. *'Mas sabor han de tener las cosas ocultas que las destapadas.'* Freely translated, it means 'a deep dish pie is more exciting than an open tart'."

"And we . . . civilized English . . . are open tarts," Bill added with an amused laugh.

"Precisely," George responded with a grin.

"What does a Colombian look like?" Lettie wanted to know.

"In the largest sense of the word, a Colombian may have any of dozens of physical characteristics. He may be tall, blond, and blue-eyed or small, brown, and Asiatic-looking, or he may be black. He may be dressed, or favor the least common denominator . . . a loincloth. He may read or write or hunt jaguar with a spear. The fierce *caribs,* whom other tribes from sad experience decided were descended from a tiger, used to say superbly, *'Ana carina rote—Only we are people.'* In Colombia as elsewhere, the upper and middle classes are the people, the *gente.* There is nothing picturesque about an eminent lawyer or banker or businessman, nothing especially romantic about import and export merchants. The Indians and peasants are far more magnetic and interesting."

A million other questions were begging to be asked, but the time to disembark had finally come.

They walked down the gangplank into the bustle of the busy city, eyes wide with interest and enthusiasm. George had made all the arrangements for their stay, but none of them wanted to go to a hotel—not yet, when there was a multitude of new and very exciting things to see.

By the time they did allow George to hustle them into the hotel, it was nearing dinnertime. The meal they ate in the hotel dining room was excellent, and after Bill and Lettie retired for the night, Caitlyn and George talked.

"George, please go on telling me about this place . . . these people. I feel so . . . so compatible."

"I believe you are. I've never seen anyone *want* to know so much and adapt so completely."

"Then tell me what else you know."

"Colombians," he sighed and sat back in his chair, "are generous, proud, and sensitive; they love ideas and respect those who have them and enjoy a . . . sort of 'spiritual agility'; they have a keen and very adult sense of humor, a tendency to chips on the shoulder, an innate and effortless courtesy, and an enviable level of culture. Their family feeling is strong, but they're intensely independent, an attractive trait that has its social drawbacks. They are loyal friends and hearty enemies. Make friends of them, Caitlyn," he added quietly. "Give them your honesty and your respect. Honor their beliefs and their way and you'll find what you seek here."

"What I seek?"

"I have a feeling you are searching for more than even you know. I hope you will find it here . . . and I hope it makes you happy."

"Thank you, George. I'll try to remember all you've told me. I'll try to be worthy of my quest."

"I'm quite sure you will. Now, it is best you take your

pretty self to bed. You'll be on your way by the time the sun comes up."

Caitlyn rose from her chair, went to George's side, and bent to kiss his cheek. "Thank you," she said quietly. Then she went to her room. To her surprise she had no trouble going to sleep and awoke at the first sound of a knock on her door.

They strolled through the narrow streets of rough stone and hard-packed dirt, through the bustling, noisy market-places. They passed the old Spanish houses with their se-cretive walls and barred windows; just beyond they could see the stucco adaptation of French and Italian architecture and beyond that the towers of the colonial church and the earth-brown tangle of thatched roofs. Canoes carved from a single log moved past the bigger ships in the harbor. Peo-ple on diminutive burros, riding high on loads with their feet crossed scissor-like on the animals' necks, jogged along the sides of the road toward the marketplace.

The three new visitors gazed about them with wide eyes filled with wonder and pleasure.

Soon they reached the dock and the three huge flat-bot-tomed boats that would pole them up the Rio Magdalena to Ethan's plantation. Arrangements would be made from there for transportation to the dig site.

One look at the jungle, and hearing the cacophony of sounds that surrounded them as they began their journey upriver, made the travelers quite happy that they were trav-eling by river.

All three wore serviceable boots and pants. Both women wore white cotton shirts and carried wool jackets that George assured them they would eventually need.

Caitlyn had braided her tawny gold hair and wrapped it in a circlet about her head, taking George's advice quite seriously. She didn't want some flying object to get entangled in it. Her green eyes were alight with interest and fascination.

To their surprise, Bill and Lettie were enjoying the journey almost as much as Caitlyn. As for George . . . he was enjoying watching their first glimpse of this fascinating land.

Either Caitlyn or Lettie would point . . . a fabulous colored bird, a strangely twisted tree, the long, brownish objects that slid so ominously into the water as they passed by . . . and George would name and explain as best he could. Their enthusiasm often made him laugh. He assured them that no one ever really could begin to understand the country if they hadn't traveled it by river.

"Will we stop along the banks to sleep at night?" Caitlyn asked.

"Not unless you want a croc or a stray tapir to enliven a mosquito-haunted night," George replied. "No, we will, believe it or not, anchor in the shallows that form huge inlets here and there. It's much safer and you won't be eaten alive."

They continued to watch in fascination until the inlet where they would make their first stop was reached. After they had anchored and consumed a light supper, George assured them they were in for a sight that would make them belong to Colombia forever.

He made each of them find a seat at the back of the boat and continued to talk while he waited for what he knew would be a breathtakingly beautiful sunset.

"Tomorrow will also be an experience," he went on. "You will awake to a singing day of summer, a morning where the air is chilly and sweet and clear as the sound of a flute, the indescribable goodness of sunshine. And a scented breeze to stir the heart."

"Oh!" Caitlyn exclaimed. She actually rose from her seat for a moment, then slowly sat back down. George knew he would not have to say any more.

The sun was disappearing behind a lush, vividly green landscape and bathing the world in a purple and red glow. The golds and mauves blended with white clouds, giving a painter's palette so intense the viewer could nearly feel and taste it.

"I've never seen anything so beautiful in my life," Caitlyn said, completely awed.

"It's like a touch of heaven," Bill agreed.

Caitlyn was finding it hard to breathe—she longed to capture this panorama forever.

Even when the sun was gone they all sat in a kind of breathless silence. In fact, they remained so until George quietly suggested they should all get some sleep as they would be moving before dawn. "You will want to be up then, because it's just as spectacular," he added.

"That's pretty hard to believe," Bill said. "I don't think I've ever seen anything quite as breathtaking. For that, if for nothing else, I'm glad I came."

"I thought you might be."

"Good night, George," Caitlyn said quietly.

The natives who poled the boats, George, and his three guests went to sleep, still overpowered by a rare and barely believable beauty.

George had been right about sunrise—it was an awesome thing to see the huge red sun rise from behind the mountains. They were already well on their way.

Five more days of traveling finally brought the group to

a bend in the river where a long plank dock extended into the water.

"This dock belongs to Ethan Marshall," George said. "I wouldn't be surprised if by the time we land he isn't there to meet us."

"How would he know?" Caitlyn questioned.

George chuckled. "My dear, he heard of our approach many miles back. Word travels much faster here than our small boats could ever hope to. He will be there."

In the distance the dock still seemed deserted, but moments later two men on horseback rode out of the jungle. They dismounted and strode out onto the dock, looking in their direction.

The road from Ethan's plantation to the docks was lovely in the early morning, when the light was soft and shadows fell long and transparent across his fields. He rode along slowly, thinking how peaceful it was. Little adobe *ranchitos* dotted the valley slopes. Slow bullocks lurched docilely along the furrows; burros, their packs swollen with covered bundles, shuffled delicately along the road in their typical serious well-intentioned manner.

Occasional groups of peasant women in dark, shapeless clothes and straw hats walked single file, the spindle swinging as their busy fingers rolled the thread they would later weave at home.

Little puffs of yellow dust rose up from his horse's feet as Ethan rode along. He passed his workers' houses, built of dry mud on a cane or sapling frame and topped by heavy thatched roofs. Usually they consisted of three to four rooms with a patio or veranda, but always, however simple, there were flowers.

The air was sharp and hard in the vast blue sky, everything sharply etched in the clear light. Behind him, in the distance, the bare mountains lay like sleeping animals in long, tawny rises.

As always, Ethan felt a wondrous pride that this was his, carved with his own sweat and determination. He loved what he had and where he was. If, occasionally, he was a bit lonely, he ignored it. In time he would leave his world and find the right woman to share it with him. A woman of refinement, who could bring culture to his house and make it truly the home of a gentleman. He knew the kind of woman he would need, but for now, he was utterly content.

Caught in his thoughts, he didn't realize someone was calling out to him until he heard the sound of hooves. He turned to look behind him and saw one of his head workers coming his way in a great hurry. He reined in his horse beside Ethan who was quick to ask anxiously, "What is it, Perez, what's wrong?"

"Senor, the boats are coming upriver."

"Boats? I wasn't expecting anyone. How far?"

"Nearby great bend in river. They be here pretty quick. Best maybe you come see."

"Yes, that's a good idea. All I need right now are a houseful of unwelcome guests. How many boats?"

"I count three."

"Must be a good-sized party. I wonder what would bring strangers here."

Perez shrugged. If Ethan didn't know who was visiting, surely he wouldn't. Perez knew few people outside the plantation workers and his own family. Secretly he liked it that way—the fewer visitors, the more smoothly his life would run.

Ethan and Perez rode toward the dock. When they arrived, the three boats could already be seen in the distance. Ethan stood in his stirrups and shaded his eyes, but he did not recognize the boats. Besides that, the figures were only shadowy forms.

They dismounted, tied their horses, and walked to the end of the dock to wait. When the boat bumped against the dock, George was the first one to step out. Ethan smiled and walked toward him, hand extended.

"George, you old mountain goat, I thought I'd never see you around these parts again. From the moaning and groaning I heard the last time, I thought you'd be in your rocking chair."

"Would have been, Ethan," George said smiling, "but I had to rescue a few journeyers in distress." He turned toward the boat and put out his hand to help Caitlyn and Lettie. Ethan's appreciative eyes had already discovered two pretty faces.

"Ethan, let me introduce my friends. This lovely lady is Caitlyn Emmerson and next to her is Lettie Marsh, or rather Lettie Holmes. The young man behind them is her husband, William Holmes. My friends, this is a companion and a very good friend, Ethan Marshall."

"How do you, Mr. Marshall," Caitlyn said.

"Mr. Marshall," Lettie repeated sweetly.

"Hello," Bill added, extending his hand to Ethan.

"Hello to you all. I'm sorry not to have welcomed you more appropriately, but I had no idea it was George who was on his way, much less bringing such attractive guests." He smiled at Caitlyn and Lettie.

"Actually, we won't be intruding on you for long, Mr. Marshall," Caitlyn replied. "We're on our way elsewhere."

"Elsewhere?" He cast a puzzled look at George. The only 'elsewhere' anywhere near was the small town of Giradot a few miles beyond, or . . . he looked quickly at George, who confirmed what he saw in Ethan's eyes with a short nod.

"I'm taking these charming people to an archaeological dig some distance from here."

"It's a dig being excavated by a Mr. Drake Stone," Caitlyn added quickly. "If I'm not mistaken, I believe another man passed this way a few weeks ago on his way to the same location.

"Sir Richard Macdonald," Ethan said. "Yes, I took him up to Drake's dig. It's been almost three weeks."

"Is it possible to procure transportation from you, Ethan? I'd like to get these people up to the dig as soon as possible."

"Of course. You can have boats to get to Drake's house. From there it's not far to go on up the dig. In fact, I'll ride with you. I wouldn't miss this for the world," Ethan chuckled. He turned to George before the questions on the tip of Caitlyn's tongue could be verbalized. "George, why don't you all come on up to the house? It'll be midday before long and I'm sure you must be thirsty and hungry. Let me offer my hospitality."

"We'll be glad to accept. We've been on the move since before dawn—I'm sure the ladies would appreciate it." He said the words to Ethan, but he was looking at Lettie and Caitlyn.

"I for one would like to sit down to a meal on something stationary," Lettie said.

"I believe Lettie has a point there." Caitlyn smiled warmly, gaining Ethan's rapt attention. "We certainly appreciate your kindness, Mr. Marshall."

"The name is Ethan. With nothing but jungle around us, formalities seem a little unnecessary, wouldn't you agree?"

"Absolutely," Caitlyn said with a smile that Ethan found mesmerizing. Then he turned to Perez.

"Go on up to the house and tell Ama to prepare lunch for five. Then bring the horses back with you."

"Yes, sir," Perez called as he mounted and rode away.

"Can we not walk from here?" Caitlyn inquired.

"I'm afraid it's a bit far—the walk would be more tiring than you know. You're quite a way above sea level and a walk like that would tax your lungs and heart before you've become adjusted to it."

"I see," Caitlyn nodded.

"Drake's dig is also quite a distance. Might I hope you would all honor me by staying out the day as my guests? A good dinner and a restful night will make tomorrow's trip much easier."

Caitlyn was about to protest, knowing her father was just a few miles away, but George, Lettie, and Bill were already accepting enthusiastically. She could do little more than agree as graciously as possible, but impatience was gnawing at her.

Baggage was unloaded and stacked on the docks and less than an hour later, the boats were pushing away and heading downriver.

Caitlyn stood and watched them go, feeling as if she were cutting away her old life and beginning anew. It excited her . . . and Ethan could see the excitement dancing in her eyes.

What a lovely creature, he thought at first. His second was more penetrating. What was a beauty like this doing here . . . at the edge of the world . . . where danger was present at every turn? In fact, what connection did these three have with Drake Stone? Drake had never said he might be expecting guests, so obviously he was in for a surprise. He wanted to see Drake's face when someone like Caitlyn Emmerson walked into his world.

She had asked about Sir Richard Macdonald. What was

he to her? And why, if they were friends or colleagues, did he not mention her at all? It was a puzzle . . . and Ethan Marshall was always drawn to puzzles.

Lettie, Bill, and Caitlyn had a multitude of questions about Ethan's plantation and the environment in which he lived. He was more than pleased to elucidate on the place he called home.

"You're very proud of it," Caitlyn said. "I'm looking forward to this."

"I guess I am. It's not all I hope for yet, but it's coming along."

"And your wife, does she enjoy living in such an isolated place?"

"There is no wife, Caitlyn. Until it's what I want it to be I wouldn't ask a woman to share it."

"That's a little unfair, isn't it?" she said teasingly.

"Unfair?" he asked in surprise.

"Wouldn't you think it unfair to want to do everything yourself and not give the lady of your choice a chance to be part of it?"

"I hadn't thought of it that way," Ethan answered with a grin. "Are you politely telling me I'm selfish?"

"A bit." Caitlyn's smile matched his. "If I loved a man I would want to be part of the battle and not just the one to come in and claim all the glory."

"Very interesting premise. I shall have to give that some thought. Maybe we can discuss it further after dinner."

Before Caitlyn could answer, George called their attention to the fact that Perez was returning. Behind him were the saddled horses and several men on burros to bring the baggage to the house.

* * *

Caitlyn's first glimpse of Ethan's home took her by surprise. "Why, Ethan, it's beautiful."

"Does that surprise you?"

"I suppose it shouldn't, but I'm afraid I let the isolation and the fact that there was no woman's touch influence me. I'm sorry."

"Don't be. I'm pleased you like it. I'll have your baggage taken to your room, then, if you like, I'll give you a guided tour."

"I'd love it, thank you."

"And you, Mrs. Holmes?"

"I'd really prefer a hot bath and a little rest before we eat, if you don't mind."

Ethan didn't want to admit that he was glad to have Caitlyn to himself for a while.

Settled comfortably in their rooms, Lettie drew a tub while Bill and George enjoyed cool drinks on the veranda.

Caitlyn was captivated by the civilized beauty with which Ethan had surrounded himself. The floors were of highly polished wood and the stone walls a soft cream color. The house was filled with sturdy wood furniture that Ethan had assured her had all been built on the premises. Splashes of color in the handwoven rugs, wall hangings, and plants made the house warm. What really surprised her was the grand piano in a large room near the dining room. For a minute she could only pause in the doorway and stare. She heard Ethan chuckle softly." You have no idea what it cost in man hours and money to drag that thing here."

"Can you play it?"

"No." He smiled again at her puzzled look. "But I love music, so I bought it just because . . . because I wanted it and . . . one day I hope a lady will come along who can play it."

"You have so much to offer that lady. I hope you find someone who can appreciate it."

"I might take your advice and start looking *before* the place is completed."

"Very wise of you," Caitlyn said with a laugh.

"Caitlyn, are you staying long at the dig?"

"I hope so. It depends on a lot of things over which I have very little control."

"Oh, Drake *is* a little possessive of his dig, but I'm sure you'll be made welcome. Now I'd better give you a chance to get some rest."

"I really don't need . . ."

"Caitlyn, don't underestimate this country. It can wring everything from newcomers before they know it. The altitude takes some adjusting to and tomorrow you go even higher."

"Well, then, I guess I'd better take your advice. But before I do—" She paused and he waited expectantly, but she did not continue. Instead she walked to the piano and sat down. First she touched a chord or two, and was pleased to find the piano was well tuned. Then she began to play.

Ethan said nothing; resting an elbow on the piano, he listened for a while, then smiled. "That's Debussy's 'Claire de Lune,' isn't it?"

"Yes. I thought you didn't play."

"I don't, but I do appreciate good music. My mother used to play. It's nice to hear music in this place."

"I used to hate taking lessons when I was a child. Now I'm glad I did."

"You'll have to come back here often . . . to play for me."

"My pleasure," she said, smiling up at him. She finished the piece and rose.

"Come on, I'll show you to your room. Playing the piano entitles you to the best room in the house, and I intend to tell my cook to make tonight's dinner very special."

"Thank you."

They walked upstairs together and when Caitlyn closed the door, she realized she really was tired.

It both surprised and pleased her to find a tub of steaming water and a supply of fresh towels. She didn't know when Ethan had had time to see to her comfort, but she realized his home was run with impressive efficiency.

She took a leisurely bath, then, dressed only in her chemise and petticoat, she lay across the bed. After a few moments, she drifted off to sleep.

Ethan sat before the piano and very lightly touched the keys. He had been anxious since Drake had told him about the huge emerald and his fear that rumors would bring predators. It could seem very strange, having all these visitors at such an opportune moment.

How could the rumor have gotten out? Was more than one emerald found and did someone spread the news without telling Drake?

There were a million questions that he had no way of answering. One thing he did know: Drake should be warned.

He went to his desk and sat down to write a message to Drake. When he was finished he sent for Perez.

"Get a runner and have this message taken to Drake Stone," he instructed.

"Yes, sir."

"Tell him to hurry. I don't want any accidents. If he leaves now he can get there by nightfall. If he stays the night he can come back in the morning. What's most important is that Drake get this message tonight."

"I will send our best man. He will get the message before he sleeps tonight."

"Good," Ethan handed him the folded note and watched him move rapidly away.

Maybe his visitors were exactly who they said they were. For his sake, and the attraction he felt toward Caitlyn, he hoped so. But for his friend's sake he knew he couldn't take any chances. He, above all, knew how important this dig was to Drake.

Once the servant was gone, Ethan started out to see the afternoon's work. As he crossed the room he paused near the piano.

The strains of Caitlyn's music still lingered in his mind. He hoped that she was who he thought she was.

He was certain, in his heart, that her beautiful face was not a mask. Yet he couldn't jeopardize Drake's future.

"Well . . . time will tell," he said half-aloud. "Time will tell."

Ethan closed the piano and left the room.

Five

Drake and Sir Richard stood shoulder-deep in a long, narrow ditch which graded downward until the deepest end was about eight feet. It was approximately four feet wide and the two men had been working there for over three hours.

"I believe your theory has some merit, from the logical direction of your presentation," Sir Richard was saying, "but to prove the two cultures were here at the same time we have to have more conclusive evidence."

"I know," Drake replied. "You can see the number of levels here." He pointed to the side of the wall that revealed time by the differences in color and structure and the various objects found at diverse spots. "I would estimate about . . . maybe fifteen hundred years."

"And you found the water jar at this level?" He pointed to an area less than two feet in depth.

"Yes, and the large clay jar. You could see its simple lines and the subtle modeling of the features of a nearly life-size face. I'd say it depicted a noble who lived about 400 A.D. It's a masterpiece and a sample of the best Moche art."

"And distinctly identified and dated?"

"Yes, but at a later date than I want to confirm. We need to date something about two thousand years . . . then match it in the same time period with the Peruvian and Incan cultures."

"You're being too optimistic. You've found nothing written?" Sir Richard questioned.

"Nothing definite, although it's not the written word I need. The ancient Peruvians had no written language, but they left a vivid artistic record of their culture and mores in beautifully molded and painted ceramics and exquisitely crafted metal objects." Drake wiped his dirty hands on his pants and turned to look at Sir Richard. "But the Inca had a recordable kind of language and so did the Chibchas."

"Umm . . . so we begin with the pottery . . ." Sir Richard mused.

"Two-piece molded pottery," Drake countered firmly and pointedly with a laugh. "That's the Moche for you."

"You can feel it, can't you?" Sir Richard replied with a smile.

"That I can," Drake rubbed his thumb and fingertips together. "Right on the tip of my fingers."

"I thought we were going to look at your new site."

"We are. Right now." Drake heaved himself up out of the ditch, then reached a hand down to help the older man. "Ready to take a little walk?"

"You asked me to come down to this place *for a minute,* and that was three hours ago. I'm not too sure what you mean by a *little* walk."

"We could take a burro."

"Perish the thought," Sir Richard said with a chuckle. "I'll walk."

"I thought you might."

They stood in the heat of the midday sun and surveyed the area. A string grillwork had been laid out in squares in one area and in each small section a digger worked slowly, carrying what he had dug up, in a bucket, to a sifting place.

Each load was carefully run through a fine mesh screen in a search for pieces of pottery or any other significant objects.

Not too far in the distance, groups of men dug shafts into the earth, hoping to discover a hand-placed block that could mean a walk or a wall.

On the sides of the hills men scraped away at the earth like a multitude of diligent ants.

Drake pointed some distance away. "There," he said, "do you see? If you stand exactly right and look carefully you can see that that huge hill does not look like the rest of the area."

"And?"

"And I think it could be one of two things. A pyramid or . . . a tomb, if I'm real, real lucky."

"You have your maps?"

"Yes."

"Let's take a closer look at this valley before we go strolling all over it."

"Good idea."

They went to Drake's tent where, on a rough plank table, he rolled out several hand-drawn maps, one atop the other.

"Fine work," Sir Richard said as he gestured toward the meticulously done maps.

"Thanks. I did them myself. I walked this valley for weeks before I chose this place."

"And I know what made you choose it."

"Oh? What?"

"Plain, pure, gut instinct."

"I couldn't have put it better myself," Drake said, smiling. "Now," he said as he put his finger on a spot on the map, "here's the hill in question. You can see . . . it's different, both in size and form."

"Obviously too even and slightly level on top, like . . ."

"Like an Inca pyramid," Drake said quietly, "or Egyptian."

"You believe there's a link there, too?"

"I do. Pyramids can only be pyramids, no matter where they are. But the men who built them must have had some connection. God, I'd love to be able to prove *that*."

"Columbus should have had you along. There would never have been a question about the shape of the world."

Drake laughed. "So I get carried away sometimes."

"I think you ought to try to prove one thing at a time. Let's take first things first, and find out about the Indians who passed through this valley. Ready for that walk?"

"Yeah, let's go."

Drake walked purposefully out of the tent and Sir Richard followed. He'd encouraged the younger man every chance he'd had.

They walked slowly along a path Drake had made. He'd visited this particular site several times in the past month, trying to decide just where and how to begin to dig.

It was hard to get to the top and when they did, they found it amazingly and hearteningly flat. They stood looking out over the valley. Drake handed Sir Richard his canteen. "It's best you drink as much as you can. This kind of heat is deceiving—the altitude plays havoc. Stop and rest when you can."

Sir Richard drank and handed the canteen back. Then both men stood in silence while they carefully studied the mound, its relationship to everything around it, and the expanse of valley lying below.

"Look," Sir Richard said. "There are several other mounds not quite as high as this, but as flat. It does give a lot of credence to the idea that there was a large and busy culture here."

"I'd say a nice sprawling urban center that could have supported fifteen . . . maybe twenty thousand people."

"Well, your enthusiasm seems to be contagious." Sir Richard smiled. "What do you say we get up a crew and begin to dig here?"

"Sounds like a first-rate idea."

"Then let's get started."

They headed back toward the main camp.

"I notice you have only hired workers here, no students, no volunteers trying to learn."

"God forbid. I don't need either. These men do what I ask, are loyal as hell, and I don't have to argue the quality or quantity or the historical value of what I find. It helps me do good work with no interference. I hate the idea of arguing over every piece. I also find I have no trouble researching and cataloguing myself."

"Most archaeological sites are forced to put up with them. You know the rules."

"Yes. If I'm funded by a museum, I have to make room for a certain number of students."

"How did you manage to get out of it?"

"I don't know why, but the original announcement about the dig didn't get announced publicly until I was well on my way," Drake said, his eyes sparkling with humor.

"A shame," Sir Richard said mildly.

"Yes, wasn't it?"

Sir Richard had to laugh and Drake soon joined him.

The majority of the men were to remain working where they were. Drake and Sir Richard chose eight men and instructed them to bring shovels and picks. In the meantime both of them had decided they would work beside the men, so they picked up the necessary tools and the entire group moved out to the hill.

Four men were to dig a shaft from the top and the second four were to start one on a slant from the side. As they began to dig, Drake unrolled his maps again and he and Sir Richard studied them carefully.

"Temples," Sir Richard finally said.

"What?"

"A series of small temples. Look, they form a semicircle around this one. It's pretty clear. This is either a tomb or the main temple. If there's anything Incan about it, I expect to find a sun god somewhere inside and an altar for human sacrifices."

"If that's true then my city is here."

"I agree . . . in theory and expectation. It could have sprawled out over half the valley. Later I'm sure we'll find roads. Right now, let's find it."

Drake threw himself into his work with renewed enthusiasm. He'd been excited before, but this encouragement from Sir Richard put new vigor in him.

It was late afternoon when they stopped. Drake sent the men back to the main camp while he and Sir Richard rested before they started back. Drake was reluctant to leave the site—he felt as if he were about to make a momentous discovery.

"Tired?" he asked Sir Richard.

"A bit. I'm more hungry than tired, though."

"By the time we get back, supper will be ready."

"And I think I'll find my bed early. It's been a while since I've worked this hard. I think you're too young for me. Maybe I'll have to limit my hours of physical activity."

"I'm sorry. I haven't been a considerate host. If you agree just to examine what I find, I'll be more than happy to take care of the work part."

"That's a deal."

"Fine. So let's get back so we can feed you. Besides that, I have a bottle of brandy just begging to be sampled."

"Ahh, now we're speaking my language."

The walk back to the dig was done without much conversation. After dinner, the brandy made them relaxed and comfortable.

Sir Richard did go to bed early, and Drake took a walk by himself and stood alone on an outcropping of rock. The stars seemed close enough to touch. He found it hard to understand his feelings—it was as if he stood on the edge of something vast. It was a little frightening, yet exhilarating. His dream of the city was so vivid that he could actually imagine it before him.

Suddenly Drake realized he wasn't alone. He turned to look behind him and saw Mendrano.

"Something wrong, Mendrano?"

"I don't know. Maybe you will believe so. Tomorrow we have visitors. I didn't tell you of the message until your guest went to bed. I wasn't sure what you would want to do."

"What kind of visitors?"

Mendrano handed Drake the message from Ethan. Drake unfolded and read it carefully. Then he cursed as he angrily crumpled it and tossed it aside.

"Why now?" he muttered. "Why the hell now? Of all the times for me to get overrun with some tourist amateurs. Why did it have to be now, when I'm so close?"

"Maybe they might go quick. Maybe they are just friends of Ethan and he is bringing them up only to meet you."

"Unlikely—Ethan would have said so. He said they were on their way here." Then another thought struck him and he turned to Mendrano. "Good God, Mendrano, you don't think . . ."

"That word of the green fire has gotten out somehow?

It is possible, but I don't know who or how. I could swear it was not one of our people. No one has left this dig from the day I found the stone."

"I don't believe this. If they're looking for emeralds we have to keep a close watch and make sure they don't find anything," Drake said firmly.

"We'll watch them . . . closely," Mendrano responded with conviction.

"The note said there were women in the party?" Drake inquired.

"Yes, two women and one man, plus the men they have hired to make the journey with them."

"A large group to watch."

"Don't worry, we will watch them."

"I need women here like I need a bucket full of coral snakes. What kind of woman wants to come out to a place like this, anyhow? Probably an old maid who can't find a place in some man's kitchen."

Mendrano laughed aloud at this and then Drake laughed with him. "If they are ladies from the city they won't like it here. There's not much in the way of comfort so they'll most likely run for home. It might prove to them where a woman's proper place is," Drake said.

"It might," Mendrano agreed, "and if any place in the world is uncomfortable for a city woman, this would be the one."

"Ethan's note didn't say how long they planned to stay?"

"Perhaps," Mendrano suggested, "we can hope that their stay is a short one."

"Mendrano," Drake said with a grin, "I would be grateful if the stay was very short. We can hope."

"Yes . . . we can hope."

"Good. Good night, Mendrano."

"Good night."

Mendrano walked away and Drake was left with the realization that whoever their guests were and whatever it was they wanted, they were not likely to find it. Instead they would find all the choice discomforts this rugged country could offer.

Mendrano Chavez, tired from a day of hard work, returned to the home he shared with his daughter, Tana, and his son, Antonio.

He had built his house a little more substantially than most, because it would be permanent. He knew and admired Ethan as well as Drake and when the work on the dig was over Mendrano meant to turn the area into a farm. He was saving all the money Drake paid him and had Ethan's assurance that he would give him all the help he needed.

Since the death of his wife several years before, his children and his work were his entire life.

He thought of Drake more as a second son than as an employer and would have done just about anything Drake needed short of murder.

He'd liked Drake from the first moment they had met. Drake was *sympatico* to his people and his country and that was rare. Drake respected his culture and his ancestry and in return Mendrano respected him.

Mendrano's son, Antonio, had arrived home a short time earlier and was scrubbed and awaiting his father's return for the evening meal. A handsome boy of twenty-three, Antonio was an enthusiastic worker. Mendrano was proud of the boy.

Mendrano washed away the dirt from the day's work and took his seat at the head of the table with his son and daughter on either side. Tana had prepared the meal and set it on the table, then slid into her chair. Mendrano smiled at her, always aware when he looked at her of the absence of the wife Tana so resembled. At twenty she had become a beauty.

"You have had a hard day, Father?" she questioned in her velvet-soft voice.

"No harder than usual," Mendrano replied.

"Senor Drake has not found what he seeks?"

"No, Tana. But I am certain he will."

"Only yesterday," Antonio added, "Louis found the jar with the face on it. Drake was so excited he almost dropped it. He gave Louis a handful of coins as a reward for finding it without damaging it," Antonio said excitedly. "It has made everyone careful. No one wants to break anything."

"It is an exciting thing when something like this is found," Mendrano replied. "One cannot blame him for needing careful men."

"I must go to Senor Drake's house tomorrow to help Maria clean it," Tana said. "He spends so little time there, and the house is so nice."

"He wants to be on top of his work at all times in case something of importance is found," Antonio told her.

"But . . . he has no time for anything else," Tana argued. "A man needs more than his work to keep him happy."

"I think he is happy," Mendrano said with a frown. "Why do you think otherwise, Tana?"

"I did not say he was not happy, but . . . he used to laugh more often and not work as many hours as he does now; and he used to have guests . . ."

"Ah," Antonio's eyes lighted with wicked humor. "It is not really Senor Drake that our little Tana worries about."

"Oh?" Mendrano looked from his son to his daughter.

Her face was flushed and her eyes flashing with annoyance. "And who do you worry about?"

"I think maybe it is Senor Ethan that has our little Tana's attention," Antonio chuckled. He was teasing his sister in fun and was not prepared for her reaction.

"You need to join the women at the well, Antonio! You fill your ears with gossip and spread it just as carelessly!"

Antonio, who adored his sister, was stunned into silence and even Mendrano, who long ago knew an inherited temper lay behind her sweetly smiling face, was taken by surprise. But an astute look into his daughter's eyes was enough. He turned to Antonio. "It is enough, Antonio. Eat your meal and do not tease your sister."

Antonio was contrite. He bent over his dish and ate.

The rest of the meal was eaten with only a smattering of conversation. When the men were finished Tana gathered the plates, washed the dishes, and tidied their small kitchen.

"I'm going for a walk," Tana said to them and left the house. Antonio, still uncomfortable with her anger, followed her.

"Tana," he called when she was only a few feet from the house. When she turned to face him he ran to her side. "Do you mind if I walk with you?"

"No," she answered quickly and began to walk again.

"I'm sorry, Tana. I didn't know my careless words would upset you so much. I was only teasing."

"I know, Antonio. I am not angry with you. I guess maybe I am more angry at myself."

Antonio cast a sideways look at his sister. He had always thought her beautiful—even for a sister, he thought with amusement, and he knew the other men looked at her with hopeful eyes.

But he also knew that Tana looked at one man only and

he was pretty certain Ethan Marshall was out of Tana's reach.

"Tana," he said quietly, "sometimes dreams are too far away to touch . . . like the stars."

"My brother has become a poet."

"I'm serious, Tana."

"I know." She stopped walking and turned to face him. "My mind knows . . . but my heart asks why. Am I so unpleasing to look at? Can I not make him happy?"

"It's not that. Of course you are pretty. Even if they are careful around me I hear the men sigh when you go by. But . . . you should choose one of your own and not a man who does not even know you are alive."

"How can one do that, Antonio?"

"What?"

"Make yourself want someone else when all the time you can only think of belonging to one person."

"You have to accept the difference between what is real and what is a dream. You are worlds apart and your world and his do not mix. You would be out of place in his house. I think, little sister, that he may have dreams of his own. Maybe, where he came from, a woman waits."

"Then . . . she can't love him very much."

"I don't understand you."

"Why does she let him come here alone, be lonely and build his fine house for her? Why does she not come with him if she loves him? No! She is a selfish woman, and I have begun to hate her."

"The way you think is only a woman's way. Maybe she wanted to come and he wouldn't let her."

"Then she doesn't love him!"

He laughed and threw up his hands in a gesture of helplessness. "You have always been so stubborn." He put his arm across her shoulder. "Come, let's go back in the house. It is too dangerous to be walking around out here."

Tana knew he was right—and about more than just the dangers of the night. She walked back to the house with him.

Mendrano sat inside, his hands busy carving a wooden figure with a small, sharp knife. Had Drake been there he might have observed an ancient artistry that had been handed down for hundreds of generations.

Beneath dark brows Mendrano studied his daughter.

She was small of stature, but it was obvious to him that in the past few years she had developed a woman's body. Her almond-shaped eyes were amber in hue—wide, deep, and observant. Her skin was a mixture of ivory and copper, glowing with youth. She was the flower of his life and he did not like the idea that she had cast her eyes on one of two men in the area it would be useless to pursue. He had to find out for himself.

"We received a message from Senor Ethan today."

"Oh?" Tana seemed uninterested, but Mendrano had sensed something more. "Senor Drake will be making his house ready."

"I wondered when he would decide to move back into it. It is much better than living in a tent."

"I am afraid that is not so. He is preparing it for guests."

"Guests?"

"Yes."

"Who are they?"

"Strangers to him as well as to us."

"Why would," she paused thoughtfully, *"how* would strangers come here?"

"Senor Ethan will bring them, of course."

He watched her turn from him, but not before he saw

the glow in her eyes or the look that spoke a million words. What her brother had said in jest had been true.

"They . . . they come tomorrow?" Her question was spoken breathlessly.

"Yes . . . tomorrow, after the midday meal."

He stood up, then walked across the room to stand close to her. "I expect you to return to the house *before* the guests arrive. There is no need for you to be there."

"But . . ."

"No, my word you will listen to. I do not want you to be there when they arrive."

"It is my job," she protested.

"No, it is Maria's job!"

She looked up at him with no fear in her eyes. She knew him much too well for that. "I am not a little girl anymore, Father."

"No, you are not. You have outgrown your little girl's body, but it seems you have not outgrown a childish dream. You need to think with the mind of a woman. And that should be clear. This man is a good man, I think, but I do not want to test that. I do not want you hurt."

"You, of all people, should know that what the Gods choose to happen, will happen. What is meant to be will come to be."

Antonio, who had remained silent, merely shrugged when Mendrano cast him a pleading look. Mendrano began to really worry.

Dawn breaking over the rugged peaks of the Andes was a sight that Drake seldom missed. The workmen were moving about in the light of the rim of a bright red sun. Sir Richard was not up yet, but Drake was patient.

Today they would begin to dig at a site about which he felt exceptionally optimistic. What did dampen his spirits temporarily was the thought of the uninvited guests that were most likely on their way by now.

The best that he could hope for was that their reasons for coming was not the green fire that lay buried somewhere between here and the river. But no matter what they came for, they were leaving with nothing, and they were leaving fast.

Sir Richard exited his tent and inhaled deeply of the clear, crisp air.

"Good morning, Drake. Sorry I slept so late. I see we are all ready to begin."

"Just waiting for you."

"Well, let's get about it," Sir Richard said. The group began to move after a gesture from Drake. Mendrano led the workers and Drake and Sir Richard followed.

For over an hour Sir Richard and Drake measured and marked the area, conferred with Mendrano, then marked their map. Still, it was nearing nine o'clock when Drake gave the order to begin digging.

Drake was not a man to observe or stand around while others did the work. Shovel in hand, he began to dig. Sir Richard was also caught up in the buoyancy that seemed to permeate the atmosphere.

There was a kind of humming expectation. Shovels were lifted, tossed, and pushed into the ground rhythmically.

The sun moved higher, but the digging remained a steady, flowing thing. Men began to sweat, then to breathe deeper. Muscles grew taut, but still the driving energy was uninterrupted.

Drake had twisted his handkerchief into a band to tie about his head, and rolled his shirtsleeves above his elbows.

Men passed continually with buckets of water that had been carried from the main camp.

Sir Richard stopped to rest on his shovel for a while and Drake did the same, breathing hard but satisfied at their progress.

He was surprised to see the sun nearly overhead. He took his watch from his pocket and snapped it open. "Eleven-fifteen. Lord, I didn't realize how much time had passed. Are you hungry, Sir Richard?"

"I thought you were never going to ask." Sir Richard laughed.

"Well, if we start back now we'll probably be just in time to find them putting out the food."

"Then I suggest we do just that before you forget and get busy again."

Lunch was eaten amid much discussion—Sir Richard could clearly see Drake was in a state of high excitement.

"I hope this site is all you expect it to be," he said to Drake. "I would hate to see you disappointed."

"Well, if the *Huaqueros* haven't been here before me, and if this turns out to be a tomb, which is my fervent prayer, I won't be disappointed."

"Huaqueros?"

"Grave robbers. It's one of our major problems. Someone local, knowing a bit about his own history, finds a likely spot and sinks a shaft. If he's lucky, he finds a grave and robs it of just about everything of value. He sells it, and by the time someone like me comes along, the tomb is pretty well stripped. Worse yet, things are destroyed by carelessness—things of far more value than they sell for."

Drake was a little surprised that Sir Richard didn't already know this, but his excitement was too overpowering to question it.

"You have quite a command of the ancient cultures here."

"It's like coming home," Drake admitted with a smile. "As a boy I spent time with a friend of my father's who had a special love for the *Moche* life and battle scenes. This fascination stayed with me all the time I was a student."

"And who did you study under?"

"I was lucky to find a place with Dr. Schliemann for a while when he led the dig to find Troy, and later with Flanders Petrie. He was responsible for the digs at Thebes and the finding of that royal burial site along the western bank of the Nile. And you know how good they are."

"Yes, yes, I do. You certainly have impeccable credentials. That find was remarkable."

"It was exciting. There was a shaft seventy-four meters long that led to the sepulchral vault that measured seven meters by four. When we went in there were thirty-six mummies, including more than twenty kings and queens besides princes, princesses, and high priests; to say nothing of an immense store of sacred vessels, funeral statues, alabaster vases, and precious objects in glass and bronze. It was, to say the least, breathtaking. But my credentials are nothing to compare with yours," Drake said. "I can't begin to tell you how grateful I am to have you here."

"Say nothing more about it, my boy. It's my pleasure. I wouldn't have wanted your find to be lost to society because I chose not to make the trip. Besides, I'm enjoying myself. And," he smiled, "I don't have to do the work."

"Well, no matter. If I conclude this as I hope to, and publish my work, I want you to share the find with me."

"No, no, that's not necessary. I assure you it is enough just to be here. Besides, you have, if you do strike something now, a good four to five years of work ahead of you."

"Four to five exhilarating years."

"Most definitely." Sir Richard paused. "Drake . . . don't you . . . well, you're a young man. Don't you feel the need of civilized society now and again?"

"Of course I do. Once I get this find going I can take time now and again. But for now I couldn't be happier than right where I am doing what I'm doing."

"Ahh . . . how good it is to be young. Sometimes I feel the ticking of the clock."

"I guess that's one of the reasons I like what I do."

"How so?"

"When you reach back like this and touch the past it gives you a feeling of timelessness. I guess it's my way of slowing the clock."

"Speaking of clocks, don't you think it's time we got on with it?"

"I certainly do."

The entire group made the trek back to the site. The sun was just passing its zenith, the heat bringing the sheen of sweat to the workers' skin.

Engrossed in their work and being a good distance from the site of the main camp, neither Drake nor Sir Richard was aware of the arrival of the expected visitors. Drake had pushed the thought of them as far to the back of his mind as he could.

A runner was sent from the camp at once to inform Drake of the arrival.

Then several things happened at once. The runner arrived at the site, breathless, but before he could announce that Drake had company, another voice was heard—much closer and much more excited.

At the sound of the words Drake jerked himself erect in the shallow pit.

"What is it?" Sir Richard asked quickly, puzzled by Drake's reaction.

"I think . . . good Lord!" Drake's face broke into a broad grin and he nearly leapt from the pit. Sir Richard struggled up beside him. They stood for a moment looking toward the spot from which Drake was certain the call had come.

"What has happened?" Sir Richard asked again.

"Tumba! Tumba!" It was the excited voice of a digger working on one of the narrow ledges that circled the site. His shovel had grazed the edge of a mummy bundle, breaking through the decomposed textile shroud to expose the skeletal hand of a human.

Drake cast his shovel aside and raced to the area with Sir Richard close behind. The evidence that lay before him caused a surge of wild joy in Drake. For a few minutes he could only stand and look at it.

"The first sign," Sir Richard said quietly. "Whether we've found a cemetery or a tomb remains to be seen but . . . you have found something."

"It's like nothing I've ever experienced," Drake murmured. He was in a state of euphoria.

But from there he was drawn back abruptly to the present when the runner stopped at his side again.

"Senor Drake?"

"What is it?"

"You have visitors in the camp."

Sir Richard and Drake exchanged looks. The last thing Drake wanted was to leave here and he muttered a curse at the interruption. He was excited and nervous, dirty and hot, and he was annoyed that intruders were there at all.

"Your find will still be here," Sir Richard cautioned. He could clearly see the annoyance in Drake's eyes.

"I'll go back," Drake said grimly, "but if a couple of giggling female students think for one minute they're going to poke around here and get in my way they have another think coming. I'd better make the situation clear right now. Maybe they'll leave."

"Drake, don't be too angry." Sir Richard smiled. "I've learned from experience that amateurs can be very sensitive—and very verbal when the newsprint comes out."

"Don't worry," Drake said firmly. "I'll find a way to get rid of them as quickly as I can. I think," he added, "they're going to regret this trip."

Six

Caitlyn, Ethan, George, Lettie, and their group dismounted and stood looking out at the grandeur of the valley spread before them. Caitlyn was so filled with excitement she was unable to speak. All of this beauty, plus the almost overwhelming thought that she was going to meet, and with any kind of luck have a chance to work with, the extraordinary man who was her father had rendered her speechless.

Ethan had asked about Drake's whereabouts, then sent a runner to inform him of their arrival. He walked over to Caitlyn, who was gazing out over the valley.

"It is beautiful, isn't it?" he said as he stopped beside her.

She turned to look at him and he had to smile at the warmth and enthusiasm he saw in her eyes.

"Yes, it is. This is like a dream."

"Caitlyn . . . you never really told me what brought you here. I mean . . . well, this is a pretty godforsaken part of the world for a beautiful woman."

"Oh no, it's not. I'd rather be here than anyplace else right now." Caitlyn didn't really want to tell Ethan about her relationship with Sir Richard until she spoke to her father first. "I've been studying archaeology for some time now and when word filtered back about this dig . . . and the fact that Sir Richard Macdonald was going to be here . . . well, I just had to come. I know it's funded by the museum, so I'm sure it's open to students."

Great, Ethan thought. Drake is really going to love this. Ethan wanted to believe her, but he was worried. If they'd come for emeralds, then her excuse to dig would be a reasonable one . . . and Drake would have to be very careful.

"I'm afraid there are no other students. There are only the locals that Drake has hired and a few men he's trained himself."

Caitlyn was quick to see that Ethan was laying the groundwork for Drake's refusal, even if she was qualified.

But Caitlyn wasn't one to be pushed aside so easily. There were certain rules governing digs and she meant to make use of them. Of course, she thought, a mention of her parentage, once Sir Richard was told, should have some effect. But this annoyed her as well. She was a legitimate student and she had rights, and Sir Richard or not, she wasn't about to give them up. She made her decision firm. No one would know who she was until she felt the time was right.

"This Drake Stone, he sounds rather . . . selfish. What he . . . we . . . do, is for the good of the world, not for personal motives."

"Oh, no, Caitlyn, I didn't mean to sound that way. Drake's not like that." Ethan smiled. "He's just kind of caught up in his work."

"And he thinks anybody else would interfere."

"You're putting words in my mouth. Drake is a nice guy and he likes what he does. He gets pretty wound up in it and, I guess, when you're as intense as he is it's hard to move over and make room."

"I'll try not to cause him a problem," Caitlyn said as she returned her gaze to the valley. In the distance she could see the vague shapes of men moving in their general direction. She was reasonably sure one of them was Drake Stone. Her resolve began to solidify and unconsciously she began to build a resistance. She meant to stay, Drake Stone or no Drake Stone.

Tea had been prepared and they were made as comfortable as possible, but Caitlyn was aware of the surreptitious looks cast in her direction.

They had planned to put up a tent but Ethan was informed that Drake's house had been prepared for guests. Their baggage was still packed on the burros, which two men led away.

"How far is Mr. Stone's house from here?" Caitlyn asked.

"Not far. It's an easy trail and," Ethan shrugged, "maybe an hour's walk or a short ride by horse or burro. Once he got my message, I'm sure he set about getting his house ready."

"I hate to put him out of his house. We'll be comfortable in our tents," she remarked.

"Myself, I'm going back to Ethan's at once," George laughed. "I like comfort when I can get it."

"Actually, Drake very seldom uses the house," Ethan said. "He prefers to be right on the site. He built it the year before he began the dig and he has a housekeeper take care of it. I think he plans to enlarge it if the backing for the dig is renewed. I don't doubt he'd choose it as a permanent place even after the dig is finished. At least I hope so. He's a neighbor I'd hate to lose."

Caitlyn really wanted to ask more questions, but she restrained herself. There would be time when she'd gotten permission to stay . . . *if* she got permission to stay.

Lettie and Bill began to ask Ethan questions and while the three were involved, Caitlyn drifted toward the closest digging area. Eventually they decided to return to Ethan's with George. Ethan had nearly insisted and both Lettie and Bill agreed it would be more comfortable.

She found the ditch in which Drake and Sir Richard had been digging earlier. Casting a glance back toward the tents, she could see the three were still in conversation, so she jumped easily down into the ditch and began to examine it closely. After a few minutes, as it always did, the past slid tendrils around her and drew her into its web of forgetfulness. She never knew when Drake and Sir Richard arrived at the camp.

Ethan was the first to greet a hot, sweaty, and not-too-amused Drake.

"Drake," Ethan said, "I've brought you some company. This is Bill Holmes and his wife, Lettie, and you remember George Frasier." He looked about him a little surprised. "Well . . . there is a fourth party—I just don't know where she is at the moment."

Drake acknowledged the introductions as did Sir Richard . . . but he had a deep suspicion about where the fourth party might be.

"So," he directed his question at Bill, "you're students of archaeology?"

"Me?" Bill laughed. "I have enough trouble handling the present without digging around in the past. It's not Lettie and me . . . we just came along with Caitlyn. She's the one who's knee-deep in old cultures."

"Caitlyn?"

"Caitlyn Emmerson."

"And just where is Miss Emmerson?" Drake asked in a voice that barely contained his irritation.

"I swear she was here a minute ago," Bill answered. "If you like, I'll look . . ."

"No, don't bother. I'll find her." Drake walked away from

the camp toward the dig. Bill and Lettie watched with puzzled eyes as did Sir Richard . . . Ethan kept close control of his amusement, but he had a feeling Miss Caitlyn Emmerson was going to get her ears singed.

Deeply involved in examining the walls of the ditch, Caitlyn was quite unaware of Drake's approach until, standing at the edge of the ditch, his broad shoulders blocked the sun and cast a shadow. She looked up in surprise.

From her position her first impression of Drake Stone was that he was extremely tall and very large. Then she realized her perspective was out of kilter. She smiled up at him and extended her hand.

"If you'll be so kind as to pull me up I'll apologize for trespassing and introduce myself."

The hand he reached down engulfed hers and with a strength that surprised her he pulled her up in one fluid movement to stand close to him. Then she came face to face with a pair of grey eyes that gleamed almost silver with barely controlled anger.

"I take it you're Miss Emmerson?" Drake said sternly.

"Yes, I am."

"Well, Miss Emmerson, if you've studied archaeology for very long I'm sure you know that protocol demands you at least ask permission to dig at a site that does not belong to you."

"Ah . . . yes . . . I'm sorry. But I . . ." Caitlyn began contritely. The last thing she had wanted to do was cause this kind of reaction.

"But you just felt you could do as you choose?"

Caitlyn's temper was slowly beginning to overwhelm her guilt and good manners.

"And you, I take it, are Mr. Drake Stone?" she asked, her voice growing chilly.

"I am."

"Well, Mr. Stone, I do know the protocol, just as I know good manners. I apologize for treading on your sacred ground, but I *am* qualified to do so. I hope that this boorish behavior is not something you save for the female members of the archaeological society."

For a second Drake was taken by surprise. He'd expected retreat, not attack. Besides that, he knew he'd been hasty. He intended to handle the situation, he just hadn't intended to handle it so bluntly.

"I'm sorry, Miss Emmerson, I guess I'm a little off stride. It's a long walk from where we were, and I had just run across a pretty good find."

Her smile reappeared in a very disturbing way. It surprised Drake with its sudden warmth. "I can certainly understand how you feel. I once threw a rock at a friend who'd interrupted me when I was digging up a piece of pottery."

Drake smiled. "Did you hit him?"

"Absolutely." She laughed softly. "No one should be allowed to get away with such a thing."

He was forced to laugh, acknowledging to himself that she was an exceptionally pretty girl. But he still didn't want an amateur getting in his way. He just had to find a smoother, easier way to rid himself of his unwanted guests.

"Well, if you'll come back to camp with me I'm sure we can make your *short* stay comfortable."

Caitlyn heard the stressed word, but she didn't want to test his anger again; besides, she was anxious to meet her father.

"Thank you," she said, trying to act demure. "I've been told you have another guest . . . a very prominent one."

"Sir Richard Macdonald, yes. But he's much more than

a guest. He contributes a great deal to the quality of any dig."

Caitlyn clenched her teeth. They walked along in silence, but she was seething. Sir Richard was a contributor, while she, without him knowing a thing about her, was relegated to nuisance status . . . a guest he was forced to tolerate.

It brought up every ounce of her fighting spirit, yet she never let it show. She simply continued to walk beside him. There would be time to straighten out Mr. Drake Stone, because he didn't have the power to throw her out. If it was the last thing she did, she was going to make him rue this day. For now there was something—and someone—more important.

As they neared the tents Caitlyn's heart began to pound. She was about to meet him, the man who'd given her life. The man who was most likely responsible for her love for the past and the career she had chosen. A man larger than life and much more romantic. She could feel her nerves tense. How could she tell him . . . how *should* she tell him? She couldn't just blurt out, *Hello . . . I'm your daughter.* No, she had to wait until they had a moment alone and for that she had to stay . . . and to stay she had to get past Drake Stone.

He walked beside her, slowing his stride to match hers and she became deeply aware of his powerful aura of masculinity. He was better than a head taller than she, and when he was no longer angry she had to admit that he was very handsome.

They could see the others standing in a group. At their approach, all eyes turned toward them.

Caitlyn's eyes were on one man only. He was handsome, too—tall, his hair silver-white under the bright sun. As they grew closer, she was surprised at her first thoughts. His eyes were grey, too . . . but a completely different tone from Drake Stone's.

"I see you found her," Ethan said. "Have you been introduced or do we have to make it formal?"

"We introduced ourselves," Drake conceded. He directed Caitlyn's attention to Sir Richard. "But you've not met my honored guest. Miss Emmerson . . . this is Sir Richard Macdonald. I'm sure you recognize him . . . if you have any knowledge of archaeology at all."

Caitlyn tried her best to ignore another jab at her credentials. She smiled and extended her hand. "It's an honor, Sir Richard. Of course I know who you are. This is really a privilege. I've always wanted to meet you."

"I'm quite flattered, my dear. It is rare to see a lovely lady like yourself interested in such a field."

"Interested! I love it, and you're somewhat responsible for that. Your books have been my bibles."

"Again, I thank you."

Caitlyn wanted so desperately to find the love she'd lost so long ago. She wanted to cry out, *I'm part of your flesh and blood!* She knew when she touched her father's hand and looked into his eyes she *had* to stay.

Drake was deeply frustrated—it was clear that they had to at least stay the night. No one would send a group like this, excluding Ethan and some of the natives, back through a dangerous jungle at night. But Ethan and his men would be up and gone by the time dawn broke the next morning—and the others would stay.

"Well, you ladies try to make yourselves comfortable," Drake said. "But please, don't wander too far from the camp. It's imperative that Sir Richard and I return to the site. We'll be back by supper."

"You've found something interesting?" Caitlyn asked.

"Quite," Sir Richard said. "It's either a cemetery or a tomb. It will take quite a while to discern which."

"Oh, may I please come? I won't interfere. But just to see . . ."

"I don't see why not," Sir Richard smiled. "Such enthusiasm should be rewarded. But, of course, it's not up to me."

Both Caitlyn and Sir Richard looked at Drake, who, despite his urgent desire to throw Caitlyn from a cliff, could hardly find it in him to argue with Sir Richard.

"Of course . . . come along." He turned and started toward the digging site. Sir Richard and Caitlyn followed while Ethan, Lettie, and Bill exchanged looks but remained silent.

Drake, Caitlyn, and Sir Richard walked toward the site and despite his anger at her, Drake soon found himself caught up in the discovery and forgetting all about Caitlyn. The three of them were transfixed as the remains were very gently unearthed. But Drake soon had to make a decision: it had to remain where it was until he found a safe way of carrying it back to camp without causing the delicate object any harm.

The next morning Ethan, Lettie, Bill, and George left for the plantation. It was a hard day's travel as Ethan had decided they would not camp for a night as he usually would. George could handle it fine, but he was not too certain about Lettie and Bill.

For the next two weeks Drake concentrated . . . or tried to concentrate, on his work. It annoyed him that he was so physically aware of Caitlyn. He tried to focus his mind on everything else.

Caitlyn made every attempt to keep some distance between them, but it really taxed her because she wanted desperately to share the excitement of a find.

Sir Richard gave her what attention he could. Drake wouldn't let him dig during the midafternoon heat, so there was time to talk to Caitlyn. They soon found they could do so very easily. The rapport between them gave Caitlyn the confidence she needed.

She sat silently, her knees drawn up, her arms wrapped around them. For some time Sir Richard didn't interrupt her thoughts. It was Caitlyn who spoke first.

"I don't understand why Drake is always so annoyed. All of us . . . in our field . . . we all work for the same goal, to give the world knowledge about the past."

"I don't believe he's angry at you, my dear."

"What, then?"

"I don't know. It's more like . . . over-protection."

"Over-protection of what?"

"His valley . . . his dig . . . maybe his dream. He's a young man who's dreamed for a long time. Now, when it's at his fingertips . . . well, maybe he's a little afraid."

"What does he have to be afraid of?"

"I . . . I don't know." Sir Richard's voice sounded as if he were giving the idea some thought.

"I want to work on this dig with you and . . . him. I'm good. Please believe me when I say . . . I'm not just bragging. I'm proud that I was second in my class at the university, and I've worked on a dig every summer. I was careful and reliable. I don't want to interfere . . . I just want to help."

"Give him time . . . give him time. If you do stay for a

while he'll see your qualities for himself. He's an intelligent man."

Caitlyn looked at him for a long moment. This was the best time to tell him who she was.

"Sir Richard?"

"Yes."

"I . . . there's something of utmost importance I have to tell you."

"Me?"

"Yes. It . . . it's my real reason for being here."

"Then tell on, my dear."

"I've followed your career very closely and with deep admiration."

"Thank you."

"But I had other reasons."

"Oh?"

"You see . . . I followed your personal life, too. In fact, that was most important."

Caitlyn realized Sir Richard was startled, yet he remained quiet as she went on.

"In 1868 you married a woman named Rose Davidson."

"Yes, I did."

"You were separated in 1869 and you never saw each other again."

"I don't understand your interest in my life. But, yes, I was married and yes, my wife left me. I've devoted my life to my work since then."

"I know that. Your success has been remarkable."

"That doesn't tell me why you're so interested."

Caitlyn was quiet for several minutes. Then she said, "I'm more than just interested." She turned her head to look at him. "My mother was Rose Davidson. I was born in 1870. You . . . you are my father, and I have come all these thousands of miles just to meet you. I wanted to . . . to know you, maybe even to work with you. And more, I . . . I wanted to tell you how much mother regretted leaving you. She told me so before she died."

Sir Richard looked at her in utter amazement. He was so totally stunned he was speechless. Finally he seemed to choke out the words.

"My . . . my daughter . . . Rose . . . our daughter . . ."

"I know this is hard for you. Please, don't think I'm lying or that I've come to you just because you have such a reputation. I have my mother's letters to you, my birth record, and your marriage certificate. My only purpose was to meet you and talk to you and . . . to tell you who I am."

"I never knew."

"I know. Mother wanted to tell you. Oh, it's so terrible to let pride stand in the way of happiness. I . . . I don't want anything from you. Can you understand? I just want to know you."

"Of course I can understand. I'm sorry if I have seemed so . . . so uncaring. It has been a shock. It's not every day a man finds out he has a daughter like you. You'll have to forgive me if it takes me some time to gather my wits."

"I know how it must seem. But . . ."

"No buts. I believe you," he smiled and reached out to touch her arm. "Does that surprise you?"

"I suppose. I do have the letters. She wanted to mail them but never did."

"And so you followed my career."

"Very closely. From the minute I became interested in archaeology, you were my idol. I never knew until a few months ago that you were my father as well."

"And . . . you came here to work with me, did you?"

"No . . . well, maybe that was part of it. But not the main reason."

"It is quite a compliment. It will be interesting to get to know one another, and working together is one way to do it. Once I tell Drake who you are, he'll put aside all his objections and . . ."

"No, no, please don't tell him who I am."

"Now I really don't understand."

"If you tell him, then he'll have no choice but to let me stay. His admiration and respect, not to mention his need for you, will prevent him from doing anything else. He'll also never see me for who I am. I will always be Sir Richard Macdonald's daughter. I want to be like you one day . . . on my own. And I don't want any special consideration from Drake Stone."

"But Caitlyn . . ."

"There's only one way. If you tell him who I am, he'll put up with me with resentment. I can do it. All I need is for you to say you want me to stay. Just . . . give me the chance."

"Consider it done. He will not know your true identity from me. But what about your friends? Does Ethan know? He and Drake are the closest of friends."

"Ethan doesn't know, and my friends will never say a word. If, by the time you want to leave, I haven't proven myself . . . then I'll go, too."

"All right, that's a deal."

"Thank you," Caitlyn said, her eyes misty.

"You're more than welcome. I hope in the next few weeks you and I shall get to know each other."

Caitlyn was about to speak again when she saw Drake approaching. Ignoring her completely, he dropped to his knees before Sir Richard and held out a dirty hand that contained an even dirtier object.

Sir Richard looked closely at the object, as did Caitlyn. It took a few minutes for both to realize it was a small, delicately carved mask.

Drake rubbed the dirt with his hand and the burnished gleam came clear.

"It's gold," Caitlyn said, "and it's . . . it's not Chibcha . . . it's Peruvian."

Both Drake and Sir Richard cast her a quick, startled look, but it was Sir Richard who spoke first. "She's right. It's distinctly Peruvian."

"I'd thought so," Drake grinned. "But I was too excited to trust myself."

"It's a replica of the altar mask of the Inca temple of the sun, the place called *Corieancha* or 'place of gold'," Caitlyn said as she reached to touch it lightly.

Again Drake looked at her closely. He had thought the same thing, but it surprised him that Caitlyn knew it.

Neither paid attention to the momentary frown on Sir Richard's face. It was gone by the time Drake turned to him. "She's right. You have quite a discovery. If you like I'll take it back to camp and see that it's cleaned properly and then I'll research it. I'm sure you want to continue digging since it looks so promising."

"It's a doorway, isn't it?" Drake breathed as if afraid the possibility might fade away."

"I would say it definitely is. But it's still not conclusive enough. One piece . . . it could have been lost, stolen, or traded. We must find something that could not have been brought here by accident."

Caitlyn could see the excitement dancing in Drake's grey eyes—it welled in her, too.

Sir Richard stood up and Drake and Caitlyn followed. Drake handed the find to Sir Richard, almost as if he were reluctant to let go of it.

"I should have an answer by the time you return to camp." Sir Richard turned to Caitlyn, "would you care to come with me?"

"No. If you don't mind I'd rather stay here. I might be of some help." She looked at Drake, whose brows had drawn together in a dark frown.

"This is not exactly the place for an amateur," he said.

"And I'm not exactly an amateur," Caitlyn retorted. "You have been too . . ." she meant to say something stronger but realized it wouldn't help her argument, "*busy,* to even consider my credentials."

"Again, I repeat, this is not the time for it. Besides, you should have applied through proper channels."

"I'm afraid, my boy," Sir Richard interjected, "that was not possible. You do remember telling me that you left before the proper announcement could be made. She has told me her qualifications and they are very impressive."

Drake could have done battle with Caitlyn, but it was nearly impossible to do so with a man who held his future in his hands . . . a man of Sir Richard Macdonald's stature.

"All right," he surrendered with as much grace as possible. "You can stay as an observer for now. We'll discuss any further involvement later."

The words on the tip of Caitlyn's tongue were hardly flattering and there was no doubt Drake was well aware of the anger in her eyes. She wanted to tell him he was an arrogant, selfish egotist, but, out of respect for her father, she bit back the words. She turned to Sir Richard instead.

"Thank you for your kindness and consideration."

"You're quite welcome. Now, let me go back and clean this. I'm most anxious to know its origins."

"I'll see you back at camp."

Drake and Caitlyn watched Sir Richard leave, and the silence between them grew. Caitlyn turned to Drake.

"I'm sorry you feel as you do, Mr. Stone. It seems to me it would be advantageous to take help when it's offered."

"This is not exactly the place for a woman." He fell back on man's ancient argument . . . the only one left to him since she had such illustrious support. "It's hard work, and . . ."

"I'm not afraid of hard work. I may not be able to handle the weight that you can, but I'll wager I can dig and brush with a more delicate touch than you'll ever have."

"Most women I know hate to get their hands dirty." He grinned with aggravating calmness.

"You've known the wrong ladies."

"Come on, Miss Emmerson. This is not a game. Find some other hobby to pursue and . . ."

"Hobby!" Her temper had taken just about all it could stand. "I don't know where you get your arrogant, superior attitude since you've not accomplished much more than I have. But I'll have you know I've studied for four years under some of the best people in the field, such as Maspero and Amelia Edwards. At the university I was second in my class and I'll wager I can do anything you can, and I know my historical background. Did it not register in your ego-swollen mind that I was the first to identify the mask?"

Drake's anger was beginning to grow as well. "This is still my dig!"

"And you're a coward!" she stated angrily.

"A coward?"

"Certainly. You're afraid I'll be able to do exactly what I said I can do and . . . maybe find . . ."

"Now just a minute."

"Well, are you afraid?"

"I've nothing to be afraid of."

"Then why not give me a chance?"

Drake gazed down at her thoughtfully. He was very aware that her blazing eyes and flushed cheeks only enhanced her beauty. If he was wary of more than her ability he brushed the notion aside.

Besides, it was the nagging thought that emeralds meant more to her than a historical find that made him nervous. It occurred to him that to keep an eye on her might be the best way. He had to know. If it were true that emeralds were really what she and her friends were after, just how had the word gotten to her? And worse, was it someone in his camp?

"All right," he said, almost casually.

"All right?" Caitlyn's anger and preparation for continued battle was brought to an abrupt stop. "What does *all right* mean?"

"It means we'll see what you've really got."

"You'll let me work?"

"That's what it means," he said. But his thoughts were more grim. He fully intended to push her a step further than she could go. "On one condition."

Caitlyn paused and eyed him suspiciously. She had come up against male dominance at every dig and in every classroom. She was wary of conditions.

"Just what do you have in mind?"

"That I'm the boss."

"And?"

"And, that when you decide to quit, you leave the dig altogether. No questions and no excuses."

"And you think I'll want to quit?"

"I do. The first time things get tough."

"Really," she looked up into the silver-grey of his challenging gaze. There was no way in the world she would back away. "As far as I can see it's a little one-sided. Why don't we make the contest a little tougher?"

"How so?"

"I work at whatever you say. No complaints, no problems."

"And my side of the bargain?"

"If I find anything of real value, I get the credit for it."

"Credit for it! Come on . . ."

"Can't you take the pinch when the shoe's on the other foot?" she asked with a too-sweet smile.

She watched the muscle in his jaw twitch and she could almost feel his anger. Her smile grew broader.

"Too much for you?" she taunted.

"No. I see no problem. *If* you find anything of value the credit will be yours."

She hesitated for a minute. His eyes had begun to twinkle and that made her nervous, yet she couldn't afford to back down now.

"And," he added with a tormenting grin, "I'm the boss. You follow my orders."

"Only during working hours," she added cautiously.

"Only during working hours," he agreed amiably.

Every sense was screaming that a trap lay ahead, but for the life of her she couldn't see it.

"Well?" he urged.

"All right. It's a bargain."

"And when does the bargain begin?"

"Why not right now?"

"I don't see why not." His smile was white against his tanned face. "Well, then as the latest . . . employee, you, of course, start at the bottom of the heap."

"What does that mean?"

"You see those men carrying buckets to dump?"

"Yes."

"That's your job for today."

"But I want to dig! I've already . . ." she stopped and clenched her teeth.

"Ready to quit already?" his voice dripped amusement.

"Hardly. I've spent more than one summer doing menial work. I can handle it. But it's not fair if that's my only job."

"I agree," he chuckled. "When you've done that for a week or so you're promoted to another one."

"Which is?"

"You can work with me . . . hand me my tools and take notes on findings." He watched her eyes smolder, yet she smiled and he had to give her credit for that. "After all, every little piece needs to be catalogued."

"And that should definitely be a woman's job, right?"

"Right."

"And after that?"

"Maybe some minor digging."

She had to agree or leave, and she didn't intend to give him that satisfaction. Besides she had the consolation of having her father to spend time with, to learn from, and best of all, to talk to. He would make it all worthwhile.

"I think," she said, her chin high, "that I'd best get about my work." She watched his smile widen. "Who knows? In all that dirt I might find something of real value . . . and you said it was mine, didn't you?"

Her mind was on a precious artifact, but his leapt at once to the secret of the emeralds. His smile faded and she walked away in satisfaction.

He watched her join the line of very surprised men. She

picked up a bucket of dirt and hauled it to the sifter and dumped it in, then returned for another.

He went back to his work, but kept an eye on her. After a while he could see the evidence that she *had* done this work before. She paced herself, moving her body carefully and rhythmically.

The men cast puzzled glances at him, wondering why he would assign this kind of work to a woman.

But Caitlyn smiled at them and after a while she began to sing and it shocked the men to hear a rhythmic chant from their own culture. Before too long they had joined in and to them the work seemed to move a little faster . . . a little smoother. The satisfied look that Caitlyn cast Drake did not go unnoticed, and did not soothe his annoyance one bit. It was much like rubbing salt in an open wound.

Drake had been so certain that an hour or so of the work he'd given her would be enough to make her back down, that he found it hard to concentrate on what he was doing.

From where he was, he could see every move she made. He watched the setting sun catch her tawny hair and make it gleam like gold. He watched every lithe move and it annoyed him even more that he found a part of himself responding in a way he had definitely not anticipated.

When the day's work was over, Drake began to gather his tools. He saw the workers in a clustered group, prepared to go back to the main camp and supper.

He heard Caitlyn's soft laughter and the men's response. He felt the tug of an emotion he hadn't felt for a long time.

His brusque order to the men that it was time to return to camp surprised them . . . but not Caitlyn. She had won round one . . . and she and Drake Stone had a long, long way to go. He was sorely in need of a lesson . . . and she intended to see that he got it.

Seven

Beneath a black canopy of sky filled with a million gleaming stars, small campfires dotted the site and groups of men sat about eating the evening meal. For Drake, Sir Richard, and Caitlyn, a wooden table was provided from the work tent along with two benches.

The food was much better than Caitlyn had thought it would be, and the conversation was interesting.

"Sir Richard," Drake inquired as he filled his plate and found a seat at the table, "what did you verify about our find today? Was the mask all we hoped it would be?"

"It was. It took me a while to get it cleaned and an even longer time to match it. It must have been part of a large piece of jewelry, like a belt or a necklace of some sort. You can see that it was broken away and had to be attached to something much larger . . . as a decoration."

"Maybe a shield?" Caitlyn asked.

"No, I think not. I'm more inclined to see it as an accessory, probably worn by some very wealthy lord."

"But it was distinctly Peruvian?" Drake asked.

"Oh yes. There's no doubt about that. Drake, what progress have you made in bringing that body out whole?"

"We got the bundle free, but there will be problems bringing it back. It's very delicate."

"Why not make a mesh bed and slide it under," Caitlyn

asked. "I've seen it done at . . ." she paused as she realized Drake had cast her a quick look of annoyance.

"A mesh bed?" he questioned. "And just where do we get such a thing? Miss Emmerson, this is South America, not London. One doesn't just trot off to the store."

Caitlyn regretted bringing up the subject . . . then it began to annoy her as well. She lifted her chin and held his eyes with hers.

"We didn't have any comforts in Egypt, either, and I never suggested *trotting* to the store. But a good archaeologist can improvise. What," she asked coolly, "is the matter with mosquito netting?"

For several moments there was silence; then Sir Richard spoke.

"By George, I believe the lady has come up with a rather novel and workable idea."

"If it works," Drake said.

"It will work," Caitlyn replied.

"We'll find out tomorrow."

"You'll try it?"

"Why not? I'm all for improvising, and I'm not stupid enough to discard an idea that might work."

"I never meant to imply . . ."

"Caitlyn," Sir Richard interrupted, "the meal was excellent. Would you care to take a short walk? I'm afraid I'm much too full to sleep."

"Yes, I'd like that." Caitlyn knew he was rescuing her before she said enough to make Drake really angry or to make him change his mind about letting her stay.

"Don't wander too far," Drake cautioned. "This is not the safest place in the world."

"We'll be careful, I assure you."

It was a magical night. Diamond-bright stars gleamed in

a midnight sky, dominated by a huge yellow moon. Night sounds from the hills surrounding them supplied a strange kind of jungle music. The darkness was pierced only by a few low-burning fires.

"I'm sorry," Caitlyn said softly.

"For what?"

"I didn't mean to create a problem."

"You didn't, but it may be hard for him to understand your feelings right now. However, he did accept your suggestion. Maybe not as graciously as he could have . . . but he did accept it. He even agreed to your help."

"He really can be obstinate, can't he?" She laughed. "But obstinate or not, he's stuck with me."

"Stuck with you?"

"We've made a . . . sort of bargain."

"Just what kind of bargain?"

Caitlyn explained the conversation and consequent deal with Drake.

"Why that's preposterous! I won't have him treating you like a common laborer. We'll have to put an end to this.'

"No, we won't. Don't worry so. I don't mind the work and this way I can prove myself to Drake Stone. When I get him to admit that I know what I'm doing, then I'll tell him."

"My," he smiled down at her, "what a little fighter I have on my hands." His eyes grew serious. "You are so like . . ." He paused. "What a treasure I've found."

She smiled in response. They continued to walk in comfortable silence for a while.

"It's like . . . watching the beginning of the world," Caitlyn said.

"Yes, it is an exceptionally beautiful place."

"You've been to so many beautiful places."

"Every place is unique, every place has its own treasures."

"I've never been able to think of a find as treasure."

"And how do you think of it?"

"As adventure."

"I don't think you'd better let our very serious Mr. Stone hear you say that," Sir Richard laughed.

"No, and I don't think I'll refer to *treasure* in front of him either."

"This is an extraordinary experience. I can't believe I'm talking to my daughter. What a pity that we never knew each other before."

"I feel that way, too, but at least we have a chance now. It will be such an experience—and a privilege—working with you."

"Well, I shall be with you if you need me. You never know, you might find the best treasure of all."

They were so intent on their conversation they didn't hear anyone approaching until Drake's voice came from behind them.

"I'm sorry to interrupt but we'd all better get some sleep. It's late and we've got a lot to do tomorrow."

"I think bed is the place for me," Sir Richard said. "I'm not as young as I used to be and the day has been, to say the least, exciting. If you don't mind, Caitlyn, I'll see you in the morning." He brushed her cheek with a light kiss and Caitlyn, in return, put her arms around him in a spontaneous hug.

"No, of course I don't mind. Good night. Sleep well."

"Good night, Drake."

"Good night, Sir Richard."

When Sir Richard had left, Drake and Caitlyn found it a little difficult to find something to say.

"Are you tired?" Drake asked.

Caitlyn wasn't sure he wasn't being facetious and she answered warily.

"I am, a little, but the night is so beautiful I hate to go to bed."

"I know what you mean," he said, moving to stand beside her. "When I first came here I was so stunned by how beautiful it was that I spent hours out here."

He stood almost touching her, his attention seemingly on the huge moon. Then he spoke. "I could see that you get safely down to my house tomorrow."

"I don't see how I can work every day and make the trip back and forth. I'll stay here in the tent. I've slept in a tent before and never had a night so uncomfortable that I couldn't sleep. I'll be fine and quite capable of a good day's work tomorrow."

He turned to look at her. "Do you really intend to go on with this?"

"Most certainly. I think you're about to discover something very valuable. I want to be one of the first to see it. You're not going back on our bargain?"

"No, but I hate to have you sleeping in tents."

"Don't let your concern for my comfort stand in the way. It's a small thing compared to the excitement I feel about working again."

"You," he said gently, "are one of the most . . . unusual people I've ever met."

"Why? Why do you think I'm unusual? Just because I enjoy what you consider a man's work? Why do you feel you have a right to search for the past and I don't?"

"Maybe it's because I'm not certain your search is only for the past. Are you looking for something else, Caitlyn Emmerson?" he added softly.

"What else is there to search for?" she countered.

In the light of the moon her hair had turned to spun silver
and her eyes reflected the glow. She was a beautiful emer-
ald-eyed threat—to his work and to his peace of mind.

Caitlyn, too, felt something she didn't want to face. Her
world and her goals were too well planned for her to fall
prey to a man whose motives, she was certain, were to
charm her out of her plans and out of his life's work.

"Nothing, I suppose," Drake had thought her reaction
might reveal something but it hadn't. She registered only
curiosity and interest. "I guess we'd best go back to camp.
Dawn comes early here."

"Dawn?"

"That's when we start." His eyes sparkled and he smiled.
Caitlyn had to laugh in response.

"You don't really think that's going to stop me, do you?"

Drake shrugged, but his silence told her he had hoped
for exactly that.

"I'll be ready."

"Fine."

They walked back to the camp together. It was very quiet,
with all the workers asleep. Drake walked with her to her
tent.

"We'll be able to do better by tomorrow," he said quietly.

"Thanks, Drake. I'll see you in the morning. Good night."

Caitlyn turned and went inside and drew the tent flaps
closed. In the darkness she could make out a cot and a
small table beside it. A lantern swayed gently from the ceiling brace. Its wick had been turned down, so it shed very
little light.

Caitlyn turned it up a bit until the tent grew lighter, not
realizing the effect it would have against the utter darkness
outside. She slowly began to undress.

Drake had walked a short distance away, his thoughts on

Caitlyn. He turned to look at the tent and what he saw took his breath away.

Caitlyn's shadowed form was clearly outlined against the mellow glow. One by one, slowly . . . almost sensually, she was removing her clothes.

Drake felt a flush of guilt for watching but for the life of him he could not pull his eyes away.

She reached up to unpin her hair and let it fall about her, running her fingers through it.

Drake could imagine her, tall and cool, her naked body brushed by the glow of the lanterns, her tawny gold hair falling about her and those emerald eyes, heavy-lidded with sensuousness. His heart began a rapid beat and he felt as if a flame had been ignited deep within him.

Finally Caitlyn reached to dim the light and her body, poised like a goddess, slowly melded with the darkness. Drake wondered if he would ever be able to get that vision out of his mind. He went to his tent and despite his determination it was quite some time before he was able to go to sleep.

True to her word, Caitlyn was up and dressed and prepared to walk to the dig while the sun was still a narrow rim on the horizon.

It was the beginning of a week of very hard work. Sir Richard watched with great interest while Drake attempted to prove to Caitlyn that the work was too much. She worked with a grim determination that matched Drake's move for move. True to his word, even though it was reluctant, he had to upgrade her position as she proved herself at each job.

By the end of the three weeks Caitlyn was ready to speak with Drake about having fulfilled her end of the bargain. It was over the morning meal and more than one pair of eyes watched with interest. Mendrano found the situation difficult to comprehend—and somewhat amusing. He had been watching Caitlyn and had developed respect for her attitude, ability, and easy way of working with the men. Besides, he was enjoying the war of wills between her and Drake.

Sir Richard watched as well. It was obvious that Drake was hoping Caitlyn would fall on her face, and there was the other obvious fact he knew Drake would never admit: he was more than attracted to Caitlyn.

"I'm looking forward to working with you today," Caitlyn began. Drake looked at her across the table in feigned surprise.

"With me?"

"Don't tell me," she said with a smile that was hardly friendly. "That you're not a man of your word. How disappointing. I'd expected more of you."

Sir Richard smiled to himself and listened with the utmost attention, eyeing Drake's discomfort.

"Of course I remember our bargain, but it should wait a few more days. We've been sinking a shaft and it's almost ten feet. I'm going down today. I just don't think it would be wise . . ." But he left the sentence unfinished when he saw the glow of excitement in Caitlyn's eyes. He sighed. He'd made a bargain and she meant to call him on it.

"All right," he agreed reluctantly, "but it's narrow, dark, and dirty."

"In the past few days, after what I've been doing, that's nothing new. You," she grinned again, "have no complaints about my work, do you?"

"No," Drake admitted. "If anything, you worked harder than most."

"If you're going down the shaft today it must mean you've found something interesting."

"It could be."

"What is it?"

"We're not quite sure. Maybe the foundation of a building . . . or a wall."

"A wall," she breathed softly. "That could mean . . ."

"It could mean that if we break through, we could find nothing . . . or we could find a room leading . . . almost anywhere."

"Then this could be a tomb."

"Or a temple," Drake added, "or the kitchen of some peasant's house."

"But it *is* exciting," Sir Richard interrupted.

"You want to join us today, Sir Richard?" Drake questioned.

Sir Richard had spent his days studying the mummy Drake had finally, thanks to Caitlyn's suggestion, gotten safely back to camp. He'd worked alone in a tent Drake had set up for this purpose.

"No, I think not. I have some very important work to do today and I want to keep at it. If you do make a breakthrough, every detail will be vital."

"Well," Drake said, looking at Caitlyn, "we'd better get a move on." Caitlyn stood up and prepared to go, but before they could leave Mendrano made a motion to Drake that meant he wanted to say something in private.

"If you'll excuse me for a moment," Drake murmured.

Both Caitlyn and Sir Richard acknowledged his request.

"It should prove to be a very interesting day for you, Caitlyn," Sir Richard said.

"I'm so excited. I pray it's a room and not just the foundation of something."

"I have a feeling you'll be lucky today."

"You're sure you don't want to go along? I can't imagine you not wanting to be part of what could be a tremendous find."

"Try to understand it this way, Caitlyn. This is Drake's dig. If I'm there . . . well, I'm afraid I have to admit that my name is a little better known than Drake's. The papers and journals, not to mention the archaeological society, might take it in their heads to give credit where it isn't really due."

"I see." Caitlyn smiled fondly. "I should have known you would be so considerate. You really are wonderful and I'm so proud to be your daughter."

"Thank you. I'm rather proud of you myself. You've done a great deal of very hard work in the past few days. You've more than earned your right to work with Drake. I wish you good luck."

While they talked, Drake crossed the open area of hard-packed ground to where Mendrano stood.

"What's wrong, Mendrano? Trouble?"

"I don't know, senor. Something was brought to my attention a few days ago. I watched very carefully and find out that what was told to me was true."

"What is it?"

"It is the gentleman," he said, motioning toward where Caitlyn and Sir Richard were standing. "He has been leaving the camp . . . sometimes for several hours a day, sometimes only for a short time."

"Leaving? I don't understand. He's not that familiar with the area. Where could he go?"

"I don't know."

"It could be he's just checking out the area carefully so he can map out better places to dig. He's very good at his profession and has a much more experienced eye than I do. It's strange, I'll admit, and I would question anyone else's motives—but not Sir Richard's. The last thing he would do is cause any difficulty. I wouldn't worry about it, Mendrano."

"It will be however you say," Mendrano replied.

Drake walked back to join Sir Richard and Caitlyn, pushing what Mendrano had said from his mind. There was no way he would even consider questioning the motives or actions of a man like Sir Richard.

"Ready to go?" he asked Caitlyn.

"As ready as I'll ever be."

"Then let's get a move on—the sun's almost up."

They walked together toward the site and neither spoke much. The momentous idea of what they might find filled them with a kind of overwhelming tension.

Sir Richard watched Drake and Caitlyn disappear. Even after they had vanished from sight, he stood for quite some time. Then his eyes moved to Mendrano, who was packing up more equipment to carry to the new site and giving orders to the men who were to remain and continue to dig.

Mendrano felt his eyes on him and looked up. Sir Richard did not move for several seconds, then turned and walked into his tent.

Mendrano stared after him for a while, fighting the strange feeling for which he had no name. Drake trusted this man . . . so why did Mendrano feel this way? He shook his head and returned to his work, but the nagging feeling continued to plague him.

Even when he and several of the men hoisted the bundles on their backs and started toward the new site, the feeling oppressed him. He had the distinct idea that he should remain in the main camp, or . . . that he should have Sir Richard watched. Drake would be angry should Mendrano suggest such a thing . . . but Mendrano would make his plans in private and never mention them to Drake . . . unless he was proved right, and the necessity rose to do so.

Caitlyn and Drake arrived at the mound where diggers were working like busy ants. They came to the tip of a shaft dug on a slant through the hard earth to about ten feet. It was over four feet wide and abutted a rough stone wall. When the diggers hit the wall they had immediately stopped and waited for Drake.

Drake and Caitlyn stood at the top of the shaft, exchanging a look of shared emotion.

"I guess we'll never know if we don't get down there and find out," Caitlyn said.

"You sure you don't want to change your mind? It could be dangerous?"

Caitlyn looked up at him with a smile. "Not on your life."

"All right, then let's go?"

Drake started down the slanted shaft slowly, carrying a small lantern that sent shadows leaping and dancing against the hard-packed walls. Caitlyn followed close behind.

When he reached the barrier wall Drake stopped and set the lantern aside as Caitlyn moved up beside him. Both gazed at the wall for a minute.

"To think," Caitlyn said softly, "this wall has been here for . . . maybe two thousand years."

"And behind it," Drake added, "might be a million secrets of the ancients. It has a way of making you feel inconsequential, doesn't it?" He paused to look at her, "Sort of like a speck in the eye of God."

"Yes."

"Shall we begin?"

Caitlyn could only nod. They set their tools down and started to study the wall. As they began the work of opening it, Drake took the time to watch Caitlyn. Whether he wanted to admit it or not, she was self-assured and in complete control of what she was doing.

It was slow, laborious work, and the heat, cooler in the shaft than above, was still intense. The heaviness of the air made breathing difficult. Still, their concentration closed their minds to discomfort.

The wall itself was made from flat, oblong stones, roughly made and about eighteen inches thick. There was no sign of any type of mortar around them other than dry, packed earth. At the places where the stones joined they dug . . . carefully.

Caitlyn was so intent that she did not realize Drake had stopped until he put a hand on her arm. Then she turned to look at him in surprise.

"It's time to go up for a while."

Caitlyn realized she was damp with sweat and her breathing had become labored. Still she was so caught in the excitement she didn't want to quit.

"We're almost through."

"I don't want to leave your body down here as some kind of gift to the gods. We need fresh air and rest. It's been three hours and that's almost too long. Come on, we're going up. You can leave your tools here. An hour or so and we can come back."

Reluctantly Caitlyn agreed. But when she came up from the shaft she was surprised to find how tired she was.

"You can't play games with the altitude here. You're not accustomed to it yet so be careful. Come on, there's a nice grassy spot over there. Let's relax."

She followed him to an area a short distance from the

dig. Gratefully, Caitlyn sat down and drew in deep gulps of the clean, sweet air. Drake sat beside her and even though he was more accustomed to it than she, his breathing was deep.

With a sigh Caitlyn lay back against the soft, grassy earth warmed by the kiss of the sun. She looked up at an azure blue sky filled with clusters of white clouds.

Drake turned to look down at her. Her hair curled damply on her forehead and her skin had a fine sheen that drew his attention.

He lay back on one elbow and looked at her, returning her smile when she turned her head to look up at him.

"Tell me, Caitlyn . . . what really made you decide to come here, I mean, to pick this particular place out of maybe ten current archaeological expeditions?"

"You want the real truth?" She laughed softly.

"Absolutely."

"Sir Richard Macdonald."

"He invited you?"

"No. I read that he was coming here. I just couldn't resist . . . especially when I realized you would have a difficult time throwing me out. Sir Richard is a very charming and logical man and besides," she smiled, "he likes me."

"Very clever."

"Don't pretend to be angry," she laughed. "In the short time I've worked with you I've begun to understand you a bit. You're an enterprising man. If you'd been in my shoes I have a suspicion you would have done the same thing. How many chances like this do you think I would get?" She sat up to face him. "You really don't want to admit that you know by now I'm not a bumbler or an amateur. I know you've worked hard . . . and that this could be your dream come true. I just want to help," she finished.

Drake didn't want to believe her. He didn't want to be interfered with . . . but he couldn't honestly deny what she said.

He was too professional not to recognize how good she was. Besides that, her excitement was obviously genuine.

"All right. Maybe I made a mistake. From all I've heard in the past few weeks and from watching you, I can tell how you feel about the work. The idea of using mosquito net was pretty good, and today your enthusiasm pretty much matches mine—and I know what it can do to me. Why don't we just call a truce?"

"Then I don't have to . . ."

"No, you don't have to hold my equipment," he grinned, "but I'm still the boss."

"Oh! I wouldn't . . ." she began, then she realized he was laughing.

"Let's get to work."

He rose and reached down to help her up. The contact was almost electrical. Caitlyn withdrew her hand at once. This was no time for physical attraction. Then he would certainly be suspicious.

They descended the shaft again and began to work.

Excitement began to course through them as they slowly worked one of the huge, flat stones free. It took both of them to wiggle it from the wall. It was heavier than Caitlyn had thought it would be. They set it aside to return their attention to the opening in the wall, hoping it would provide a clue as to what might be inside. But the black void could not be penetrated yet—it would require the removal of several more stones. There was no hesitation. Both could feel each anxious moment as if it were an hour as they attempted to work the second stone free. It was a little easier, and the third a little easier yet.

There was enough room now to work their way inside.

"Let me hold the lantern inside first and see if I can make out anything," Drake said.

He extended his arm inside the dark cavern and moved his head and shoulders cautiously.

"What do you see?"

"Not much. It looks like a rather small anteroom or something. Wait here, I'm going in."

"Let me . . ."

"Just wait there," Drake said firmly. She waited as he vanished inside, moving cautiously. After a few minutes his head reappeared and he was smiling broadly. "Come on. But be careful, the floor's not too even."

Caitlyn quickly climbed through the narrow passageway to find herself in a small room about twelve by fifteen feet.

The glow of the lantern light cast her shadow against a wall, creating an eerie apparition. She looked up to see that the ceiling was quite high, nearly eight feet.

"It's empty," she said.

"It is now, but I don't believe it always was."

"How do you know?"

"I'm not too sure. We'll have to examine the place more carefully, but I think this is just a small section. If we can find the entranceway to the other levels . . . I think we're in a tomb and this is only one level . . . most likely the top of maybe five or six. If we can find our way through we might just be lucky enough to have found the tomb of a lord."

"I can't believe it," Caitlyn said as she looked about her with awe. Drake moved close to her. "I don't see any kind of entrance to another level," she added as she surveyed the room.

"It's here," Drake said. "It's here somewhere. We just

have to find it. I have a feeling . . ." He held the lantern high and began to move around.

"What are you looking for?"

"Maybe this whole structure isn't just one tomb . . . it could be several. Sometimes the ancients did it that way. There was a burial . . . then a second, so they simply added another layer. As time passed the layers grew. I think we're on the smallest one since the overall shape is like a flat-topped pyramid. If we can find the way from this level to the next, I'll bet we run across corridors and steps."

"Then let's get busy."

"No. This is as far as we're going for today. I want to go back to camp and study my maps. I have a few ideas I'd like to look up. Besides, I need to ask Sir Richard a few questions."

"Like what?"

"Like how he found the passageways in the tomb in Egypt and what we can look for here. The information might make it a whole lot easier tomorrow. Come on, let's go up to the top. The air is getting pretty thick in here."

They left the room, dirty and tired but elated.

The first thing Drake did was to put several trusted men around the shaft as guards, with instructions that no one but he, Caitlyn, and Sir Richard were allowed to go down. He ordered the others to return to camp and relax for the balance of the afternoon.

Neither Drake nor Caitlyn realized how tired they were and the long walk back to camp did not help. Both were ready to wash away the grime and begin to work on the next day's problems.

As Caitlyn disappeared into her tent with a large bucket of water, Drake hunted for Mendrano. When he found him, Mendrano was deep in conversation with a small group of men. Drake was rather surprised that he failed to recognize some of them—Mendrano must have sent for more help.

Mendrano left the group and walked toward Drake.

"How are things going here, Mendrano?"

"Very good. The digger ran across more small pieces. They've been put in your tent. You have discovered a temple?"

"We're not sure what we've discovered. I want to talk to Sir Richard about it."

"He's not here."

"What?"

"He has been gone since this morning. I was just asking about him, but no one seems to know where he is."

"It's damn dangerous for him to be drifting around alone!" Drake said in alarm. "Some kind of serious accident could happen. Send men out to scout him up."

"I have already done that. They will leave now . . ."

Before he could finish, Drake heard his name and turned to see Sir Richard walking toward him. Mendrano wandered back to join his men.

"Drake, you're back early, aren't you?"

"Sir Richard, you've given us all quite a scare. Mendrano was just about to send someone to scout you out. It's really dangerous to leave the camp alone, even if you're armed. I wouldn't want you to run into trouble."

"Don't worry about me, Drake," Sir Richard smiled. "I've taken care of myself in more than one dangerous place. I'll be careful from now on though and try not to worry you. You've found something important, haven't you? I can see it in your eyes."

"Yes, we have some real good news."

"You've really got hold of a tomb?"

"I don't know if it's a tomb. I'm hoping. I'd like to discuss a few things with you."

"Of course."

"If you'll give me a few minutes to get cleaned up, then come to the main tent, I'd like to get some advice."

"I'll be glad to help in any way I can."

"Be out in a minute," Drake called as he went into his tent and took as little time as possible to clean up and change his clothes.

When he joined Sir Richard again he carried his maps and a sketch pad. They found some space among the artifacts on the table and spread out the maps. Then Drake took his pencil and sketched out the mound and the shaft. He also described the empty room.

"It's obvious you've penetrated the top burial site, and I agree that there might be as little as two or as many as six or even seven layers below."

"One of which might hold the key I'm looking for."

"It wouldn't surprise me."

"My only problem is this. Is there an entrance to the next layer or must we sink another shaft? To sink another shaft would prove to be pretty difficult and we might do damage."

"There might just be a way to get in. With your permission, I will accompany you tomorrow."

"I was hoping you'd say that."

"From what you say," Sir Richard said, "I believe you and Caitlyn have settled your differences. That pleases me as well. I have begun to think the young lady is quite good at her chosen career."

"We've buried the problem and I'm quite willing to let her work."

"That calls for me to open my one and only brandy tonight after dinner so we can share a toast."

"That sounds interesting," Caitlyn's voice came from behind them.

"Caitlyn, come join us. We're talking about celebrating your marvelous find."

She walked to them, feeling welcome for the first time.

Dinner was a very enjoyable affair. Even the worker's voices could be heard at their campfire singing softly.

When Sir Richard brought forth his bottle of brandy his eyes met Caitlyn's over the table. He smiled and winked.

"I believe," he said to her, "it's time for a toast. Don't you agree, Caitlyn?"

She knew what he meant and agreed. It was time to tell Drake exactly who she was.

"Yes, you're absolutely right. If you gentlemen will agree, I would like to give it."

"Very apropos," Sir Richard agreed.

He opened the brandy with a flourish and poured three glasses. He handed one to each of them and picked up his own.

"The floor is yours, my dear."

"Drake," Caitlyn said, "First, I want to propose a toast to you for accepting me. I'm very grateful for the opportunity."

Drake bowed his head slightly and smiled.

"And I want to toast you and the marvelous results I know you're going to have here. Then, I want to toast a very special man, Sir Richard Macdonald . . ."

Drake clinked his glass against the other two, but he stopped in total surprise at the last words of the toast.

"My father . . ."

PROMISES OF LOVE

Eight

For a minute Drake couldn't believe what he had heard.

"Your what . . . what?" He looked from Sir Richard to Caitlyn again, as if one of them would laugh it off as a joke. But neither did. Instead, Caitlyn held his eyes with a calm, steady gaze.

"Sir Richard is my father."

"But . . . Caitlyn *Emmerson?* I don't understand. I thought I knew all about Sir Richard. I never heard of a daughter."

"You're not alone, my boy. Before Caitlyn arrived I never knew I had a daughter either. Now, I'm very pleased, and very proud."

"It makes no sense." Drake was half-angry. "Why let me believe all along that you were . . ."

"I'm afraid Caitlyn's pride has a bit to do with that," Sir Richard chuckled. "Your attitude was, to say the least, somewhat . . . aggressive. Caitlyn wanted to prove herself. She wanted you to accept her for herself and not as Sir Richard Macdonald's daughter. I had to agree, because I knew how she must have felt. In fact, if you examine your own feelings I'll wager you could understand as well. Have you not wanted to prove yourself at times?"

Caitlyn watched Drake's face, praying he would take the

news in stride. Her father's words had some impact on Drake, who smiled a little ruefully. "I think I need this brandy. This has been a bit of a shock. I'll bet no other archaeologist ever dreamed of two Macdonalds."

"Believe me," Caitlyn replied, "I cannot dust my father's shoes yet and I know it. I *am* here to learn, Drake, and I expect to carry my own weight. Can you consider me just a willing worker?"

"I can try," Drake smiled. "But if you're your father's daughter," he inhaled deeply, "I'm going to expect remarkable things from you."

"I'm not prepared for remarkable things yet. But I am prepared to contribute as much as I can to any remarkable things you do."

"Nicely said, my dear," Sir Richard chuckled. "I, for one, expect remarkable things from both of you."

"Then let's have one more toast," Drake said as he raised his glass. "To whatever we find beyond the room tomorrow. When *we* open it."

Caitlyn raised her glass to touch his. "Thank you," she said softly.

"I think I'll retire for the night," said Sir Richard. "Tomorrow should prove most exhilarating for all of us. Good night."

Caitlyn and Drake bade Sir Richard good night and remained silent as he walked to his tent and went inside.

"I'm too excited to sleep," Caitlyn admitted with a quick smile. "I think I'll go for a short walk."

"I'm not about to let you wander around alone. I warned you before—this place wasn't safe. Looks like I'll have to go along," he grinned. "Just to make sure the prize pupil doesn't get into any trouble."

Caitlyn laughed. It looked to her as if it were the end of all their difficulties. The future looked bright indeed.

Mendrano sat before the smoldering campfire. Any other time he would have gone home to his comfortable bed, but tonight was different. He had to wait, because he had to talk to Drake and he had to talk to him alone. This time he didn't want any of the visitors to see him going to Drake's tent.

He watched the three who had shared supper together. He heard their laughter and he waited.

After a while he watched Sir Richard walk to his tent and still he waited. Surely the woman would be going to her tent soon and he would have the chance to talk to Drake.

But he was disappointed when Drake and Caitlyn walked away from the camp. He clenched his teeth in grim determination. He would go on waiting. They had to come back soon.

Drake and Caitlyn walked slowly, and without speaking. Beyond them the mountains rose to breathtaking heights. The air was clear and still warm from the heat of the day.

The floor of the valley was shrouded in darkness, and the combination of mountains and shadows gave a vastness to the place.

"Ethan said something before about you choosing to live here permanently?" Caitlyn asked.

"If I don't, it's not because I don't want to. I built a house like an optimist, hoping Sir Richard would get me the time I wanted. But even if he does, I guess it wouldn't be too wise to plan so long a stay."

"Especially if you get caught up in another dream." She stopped walking and turned to look up at him, "And you will, won't you?"

"You make that sound wrong somehow, yet I believe you'd do the same."

"Not wrong. I just wondered . . . if that's all you want out of life."

"I'm in no position to want more right now. You'd be the first to admit I don't have a whole lot to offer a wife, and you certainly can't raise children here . . . no doctors, no schools, no friends. I'm afraid I have to stick to dreams for a while."

He paused, "And what about you? There's . . . no one special? No one who wants you to settle down in a cozy cottage somewhere?"

"No. There's no one special. I guess, like you, I just haven't had the time."

"That's . . . rather unusual."

"Unusual? How so?"

"Most women . . ."

"Mr. Stone," she said teasingly, "your . . . experience with *most women* does not apply to me. I distressed my mother her entire life because I haven't been *most women*. I know what I want. I've studied hard to get where I am."

"And . . . your father?"

"I never knew him until I came here. Of course I admired him, as hundreds of others have. But I only found out he's my father recently, when my mother was dying. If you think I intend to use his name as some kind of leverage, you're mistaken. To the world I'll be Caitlyn Emmerson . . . until I can stand on my own. But I'll work with him every chance I get."

"You've already proven your point to me, and I don't

blame you for wanting to work with him. I feel pretty much the same way. You know, when I first wrote to him to explain what I'd found and what I hoped to find and asked him to come here, I really didn't think I stood even a slim chance."

"He's an archaeologist first, and a famous man second. I can't imagine him not wanting to come."

"Now that I know him, I can't either, and now that I know you're his daughter I can see why you stuck . . . even despite my prejudice."

"You were so sure you could scare me away."

"I tried," he chuckled, "but your ability comes through when you need it, I guess."

They had come farther from the camp than either had realized. Now they found themselves in an indented space between two walls . . . even with the number of people in the camp nearby, they were totally alone. Both were silent for several minutes. Caitlyn stopped and turned to look at Drake.

"Do you ever get lonely here?" she said softly.

"Sometimes, but those times, balanced against every thing else, like today . . . well, it's really no contest."

"The excitement does overpower anything else, doesn't it?"

"I was watching your eyes today, when you stood in that room. They were glowing."

Caitlyn laughed softly and Drake found himself enjoying her laughter.

"You didn't exactly look unimpressed yourself."

"And that's my reaction to an *empty* room. You won't believe it if we find rooms that aren't empty." He chuckled. She look up at him in response, their eyes met . . . and held.

Between one breath and the next, something intangible

seemed to swirl about them and neither seemed to be able to back away.

In the wash of white moonlight Caitlyn seemed to reflect its brilliance. Her hair was like strands of silver and her green eyes reflected the moon's glow.

To Caitlyn, Drake suddenly seemed to be a force stronger than the mountains around them. His dark, almost Spanish, looks made him appear as if he belonged, like a Conquistador of centuries old. And his grey eyes were magnetic in contrast to his tanned skin.

He was a definite threat—a threat she had not planned on. She hoped he couldn't tell the effect he was having on her.

But Drake was caught in his own dilemma—he wanted to take her in his arms.

Drake braced one hand on the wall beside Caitlyn. She didn't move, because she knew she wanted him to kiss her, and her own honesty wouldn't let her deny it.

"You're very beautiful, Caitlyn."

"It's the moonlight," she said huskily, "or the atmosphere."

"No, I don't think so," he murmured as he moved closer. "I think the magic is you."

Caitlyn could feel a shiver of expectancy course through her. His hand rested lightly on her waist, but he didn't pull her to him. Instead he bent his head and touched his lips to hers lightly . . . gently . . . tentatively.

At first it was a taste, an exquisitely sensual touch, as his lips lingered against hers. Caitlyn moved first—she slid her arms about his waist and moved into his arms.

Drake lost himself in a sudden burst of desire that was so alive it temporarily blocked all reason. Her mouth was soft and giving beneath his and she seemed to fit against him perfectly, as if they were two parts of one whole.

When the kiss ended Caitlyn was quiet, only because she was shaken by an uncertainty she couldn't quite understand.

Drake had taken no advantage. She had wanted him to kiss her, and she had moved quite willingly into his arms.

"I was right," he said.

"About what?"

"The magic *is* you," he grinned. "Archaeologists are not supposed to be beautiful and exciting. And don't say it's because I've been in the jungle for a year. There are a lot of pretty girls between here, Bogota, and Barranquilla. I'm beginning to get the feeling you're special in a whole lot of ways."

"Don't you think it would be wise to test that theory over a period of time?" She smiled up at him. "You might find it's a passing thing."

"Now you misjudge me," he chuckled. "I'm a man who makes quick decisions. I hate wasting time."

"But I'm very cautious. Besides," she laughed softly, "I've been on several digs and I've decided archaeologists are a very dangerous breed."

"How so?" he asked innocently.

"About the time you think you have their complete attention some Roman lord or ancient Greek princess comes along, or better yet, in your case, an Inca Goddess, and you feel their attention disintegrate."

"Doesn't that apply to female archaeologists as well?" he retorted. "Some ancient Greek god or feathered warrior comes along and I'll bet your attention drifts, too."

"Sounds like we're two of a kind. I admit I am a bit in love with my work."

"Ah, then . . . the time has come, the walrus said . . ."

"To speak of many things," she finished for him . . . "of shoes and ships and sealing wax, and cabbages and kings."

"And that mystic word you just referred to . . . *love*."

"One doesn't just speak of love, one also doesn't fall in love just like that."

"You've had experience in falling in love?" he chided with amusement.

"No, just a little experience with reality. We both have goals. You know that and so do I. It's a little too soon to let the subject of romance interfere with everything we have planned."

"Well," he said, his voice tinged with humor, "why do we have to let anything interfere? We can work together and enjoy it. If romance rears its head . . . we have a lot of time to make decisions about it."

Caitlyn was stimulated by his give-and-take. She was enjoying sparring with him. She wanted to ignore everything else, but she found herself watching the moonlight reflected in his eyes . . . his long, slender fingers . . . the lines of his mouth. She discovered, to her surprise and in spite of everything they'd just said, that she wanted to be kissed again and that was the most upsetting thought of all.

"If you find what you hope to find tomorrow, my father . . ." She paused. "I still can't get used to calling him that. Anyway, I'm sure he's really as anxious to find something as you."

"I'm sure. I just wonder if he's planning to stay and go on working with me."

"I can't see him wanting to leave. But . . . if he did decide to go," she began, "I . . ."

"I'd like you to stay," he said quietly.

"Not to make up for our . . . differences?"

"No, because I think one day, you're going to be as good as your father."

"Thank you," she said, looking somewhat surprised.

"That surprises you?"

"Yes, it does."

"What happened to that confidence I heard in your voice last week? And the girl who worked so hard to prove it."

"I was afraid, if my father left, I'd have to find a nearby valley to dig on my own." She didn't literally mean what she said, but Drake believed it.

"Dig for what?"

"Oh, I'm sure there's treasure in various places around here."

Caitlyn was teasing, but the word *treasure* meant more than one thing to Drake. He just wasn't too sure of what it meant to Caitlyn. He wondered suddenly if he had begun to trust a bit too soon. After all, Sir Richard had not been with Caitlyn when she was growing up. He had no real way of knowing that she wasn't aware of Sir Richard's reputation all along and had found his presence here to her advantage. Other thoughts began to crowd into his mind.

Sir Richard seemed to be a very trusting man, and it occurred to Drake that despite his physical attraction to her and her obvious knowledge of her field, she could be a fortune hunter after all. The thought annoyed him. He knew Sir Richard believed her and he wanted to believe, too . . . but something vague and disturbing plagued him. It could be costly to believe . . . just as it could be a tremendous loss not to.

"We'd best get back to camp. It's pretty late and tomorrow's a big day."

Caitlyn wasn't quite certain why she felt as if she had said or done something drastically wrong, but with Drake deciding to return to camp she couldn't very well say *No, don't go yet, I would really like you to kiss me again.*

The walk back to camp was puzzlingly silent for Caitlyn

and when they reached her tent, Drake only spoke a few words. "Good night, Caitlyn. Sleep well." Then he was gone.

Caitlyn watched after him, completely unable to grasp the sudden change. Then she sighed and entered her tent.

Drake walked slowly to his tent, angry at himself. He wasn't one to lose his head easily, but he had to admit Caitlyn had sent his senses spiraling and his common sense down the drain.

He knew there had always been the chance that the secret of the emeralds had filtered out of his dig. He'd been prepared for a lot of things, but not a sweet-faced, green-eyed girl seeking the stones.

What bothered him even more was the chance that he could be wrong and she was exactly what she said she was. In that case, he was pushing away the one woman who had pierced his protective shell.

He had his work, and the need for occasional physical relief came easily with one of the girls in Bogota. He didn't mind paying; it left no strings attached, and as a matter of fact, he was welcomed by several girls who'd shared passion with him and enjoyed it enough to coax him back.

He went inside his tent and reached up for the familiar lantern. But before he could grasp it to light it, a voice broke the silence with a rasping whisper.

"Don't light the lantern, Senor Drake."

"Mendrano?"

"Yes, senor. Please keep your voice quiet. I wouldn't want anyone to overhear us."

"What's wrong? Why all the secrecy?"

"I am worried."

"About what? Mendrano, this is certainly not like you. What's gotten into you, anyway?"

"I have been thinking of how Sir Richard has been acting and I decided it would be wise to watch him . . . and to speak to you."

"So?"

"So I did not succeed. After you and the lady left I kept a close eye on his tent. But so much time passed that I began to worry, and I went to his tent. He was not there."

"Maybe you weren't watching as closely as you thought. He must have been nearby. Maybe in one of the other tents."

"No, senor. He left his tent from the back."

"As if he deliberately didn't want you to see him. Come on, Mendrano, this is ridiculous. Sir Richard is a man whose reputation and honor can't be in question. Number one, he's very wealthy, and number two, he doesn't need my dig for anything. *I need him.* If word of the emeralds had gotten out, and if that was his motive for coming here, he would have come on his own before I even had a chance to invite him. Invite him, Lord, I begged him."

"Senor . . . three of our men are gone as well. I don't know how long they have been gone, I only know they were here when Sir Richard came."

"Now, that, my friend, is really jumping to conclusions. We've been deserted before. If a few deserted us again it's most likely because they're tired of working. Do we have any shortage without them?"

"No, senor, but . . ."

"Then it's not really a problem. The secret of those emeralds is safe with the two of us. And I don't have time to waste suspecting a man who has nothing to gain. Something like this would ruin his reputation forever and he's not a fool. He's worked thirty years to establish himself. I'm sure he doesn't have the slightest idea there are emeralds here. You'd better get some sleep. We have a hard day ahead of us."

"Si, senor." Mendrano rose from Drake's cot and started toward the door.

"Mendrano."

"Senor?"

"I'm grateful for your dedication and your loyalty, believe me. It's just . . . we're jumping at shadows because we're afraid this secret will get out. We have to stop that and go on with our work."

"Si, senor."

Mendrano left the tent, but Drake was certain he hadn't paid much attention to anything Drake had said. The whole situation was getting out of hand. There was no way of knowing whether he should suspect anyone, or if they were all innocent and he was letting his imagination and his fears get the best of him.

Drake undressed and stretched out on his cot, but it was a long time before he slept.

When Drake left his tent the next morning he was a little surprised to find Caitlyn and Sir Richard already waiting. It was hardly light enough to make out each other's features.

"Good morning. Looks like I'm the last up."

"You'll have to excuse our excitement," Sir Richard said, "but one doesn't have the possibility of opening a tomb every day. I think my daughter and I were much too excited to lie abed any longer."

Drake was smiling, but he was watching Caitlyn and Sir Richard closely. He just couldn't see any kind of family resemblance. And he had a few questions he would like to have asked them both.

"Caitlyn, Mendrano is going ahead with our equipment. I'd like you to go along with him and start setting up so we can clean and catalogue right there instead of dragging everything back."

"All right. As soon as I gather up my things I'll be ready to go." Caitlyn didn't question Drake's orders.

When they watched Mendrano, Caitlyn, and several men leave the camp, Drake turned to Sir Richard.

"Before we get on our way there's something I would like to discuss with you, if I may."

"Of course, my boy. What is it?"

"I hate to ask personal questions but a couple of things have been bothering me. You didn't seem too surprised when you found out Caitlyn was your daughter. You'd never seen her before?"

"No, I'd never known about her at all. My wife and I separated after only a year or so. I was surprised when Caitlyn first told me, but later that night she gave me a packet of letters her mother had written to me. She also gave me the marriage certificate. There was no doubt in my mind that Caitlyn was my daughter. She looks exactly like her mother and not a bit like me. Drake . . . I don't understand."

"I'm sorry. It's just . . . well, when you have a dig of this importance you don't want any problems to arise."

"Caitlyn is a novice, but her qualities are so pronounced that she would be an asset to any dig."

"But all the years she was growing up you never knew her? You had no idea . . ." He shrugged.

"Drake, I don't know what your point is . . . or whatever it is you suspect. But I believe Caitlyn is a person of integrity and is seeking only to increase her knowledge. What other reason could she have for leaving behind the comforts of civilization? Caitlyn is my daughter and I look forward to sharing many years with her. If you want her to go . . . then I shall have to go with her."

"I never meant that, Sir Richard," Drake said quickly. "I was only thinking of you. It would not be hard to understand someone wanting to take advantage of you. I didn't know you had so much proof. I'm sorry."

"Consider it forgotten. And," Sir Richard smiled, "I have no intention of discussing this with Caitlyn. You and she have made peace and for your good as well as mine I'd like to see it remain that way."

Drake felt really rotten. His suspicions were groundless. Obviously, Caitlyn really was Sir Richard's daughter and just as obvious, Sir Richard had begun to love her. Caitlyn was indeed good at her profession. Drake had no leg to stand on, but he had the deepest feeling that something, somewhere, was very definitely wrong.

When they arrived at the site, Caitlyn had it bustling with activity. Drake could see the flash of excitement on her cheeks and the glow in her eyes. She could barely wait.

Drake, Sir Richard, and Caitlyn walked to the shaft and descended carefully to the wall. With Drake in the lead, Caitlyn in the middle, and Sir Richard behind her, they worked their way through the small opening and into the room. Once inside, they stood and looked around carefully.

"There are no markings on the walls or floor," Sir Richard said. "Nothing to tell us who might be buried here."

"Then do you think it's a tomb?" Drake asked.

"There's only one way to find out," Sir Richard replied.

"Start to dig again," Caitlyn urged.

"I think not," Sir Richard said.

"Why not?" she asked.

"He thinks there's a stairway somewhere near," Drake said.

"Right," Sir Richard concurred. "I would suspect this serves as a cap to the passages below. Obviously, the creators meant to do more to it, but something happened and it was left as you see it. But there's no doubt there's a stairway nearby. We need only find it."

"Then we must dig down to the next level," Caitlyn argued.

"No, we might cause some sort of cave-in chain reaction. It's best we begin with the walls and look carefully for some sort of doorway," Drake said, as he set his lantern aside and moved toward a wall. Slowly, he rubbed his hands over it, seeking an indentation or sign.

Quick to follow suit, Caitlyn moved to the opposite wall and began to look. Sir Richard went to the third. Slowly they moved over the walls, brushing the walls with sensitive fingers.

For a while there was nothing but the sound of their breathing in the confined space, and the rough sound of their hands moving on the stone.

Then Drake, who was coming to the edge of his wall with no results, turned to Sir Richard and Caitlyn. A thought had occurred to him.

"Stop looking for a doorway as tall as we are. Try lower on the wall. It was an entrance they didn't want anyone to find . . ."

"Of course," Sir Richard said at once. "A doorway in the most unlikely place."

Again, slowly, laboriously, they went back over the walls, this time dropping to their knees to feel all the way to the floor. It was Caitlyn who found it.

"It's here! I've found it, it's here!"

Drake and Sir Richard rushed to her side and knelt. Feverishly Drake felt along what appeared to be a slight crack between wall and floor. The outline of the door was so fine and so well placed that it took several minutes, but his fingers finally outlined a square about four feet high and three feet wide.

He took a knife from a sheath on his belt and probed the outline again until it was well defined.

"It's a doorway, all right. But how do we get it open? It doesn't look like it's hung on any kind of a hinge."

"Maybe it slides," Caitlyn offered.

Drake braced himself on hand and knees and put his shoulder against the slab. But despite his efforts it didn't budge an inch.

He sat back on his heels, "Well, by God, someone came out of here and closed this behind him."

"There has to be another way," Sir Richard said.

"A lever . . . or something that makes a mechanism work," Drake said thoughtfully. "But what kind of lever . . . and where?"

Drake stood and examined the room again. The walls seemed bare of any object that could be connected to the door. He retraced his steps to the opening they had come through and resumed his examination.

Neither Sir Richard nor Caitlyn made a sound or a movement to distract him. They, too, were studying every facet of the seemingly empty room.

Just when Drake was about to give up he paused, then gazed raptly at the floor. While the walls seemed to be smooth, huge slabs, the floor was made of many large squares.

Very slowly he began to move from one stone to the other, placing his foot in the center of each. Caitlyn laughed softly as she and Sir Richard came to realize what he was doing. They remained still while Drake moved across each stone. Up . . . and back. Up . . . and back, until he stood only a couple of feet from the small door itself. He started up the pathway of stones that passed the little door, bracing his hands against the wall as he moved.

A short distance from the door he put his foot on a stone and knew at once something was different. Cautiously he put his weight on the stone, feeling it slowly began to give. He wasn't too sure it wasn't going to give completely.

He began to sweat a little as he put more weight on it and the stone moved deeper, an inch or so. More weight . . . and then a low rumble came from behind the wall. Taking the final chance, Drake put his entire two hundred and ten pounds on the stone. It slowly receded into the floor until Drake was sunk to his knees, but at the same time the small door had slid back, exposing a dark opening. For a while the three could only look at each other. Then Drake regained his control.

"We need to know if it will stay open." Gingerly he stepped up out of the hole—and slowly the door slid closed and all sign of it was hidden again. It was obvious that unless the weight remained the door would close.

"We've got to find a way to keep it open. I wouldn't want to be closed up in there. I have a feeling the air wouldn't last too long. No one's going inside until we understand how this thing works."

"I heartily agree," Sir Richard said. "If we find a way to keep the pressure on it we can keep it open while we examine what's below."

"I've never seen anything like this before," Sir Richard said. "It poses a rather dangerous problem. We have to be extremely cautious. There may be no way of opening that door from the opposite side."

"Took a very clever mind to work that out," Drake added. "I wonder what other little secrets lie in store. This doesn't look like just any tomb. I'd say someone or something of decided importance is buried here."

"Again I agree," Sir Richard replied. "What are your plans?"

"I'm going in," Drake said calmly.

"No!" Caitlyn blurted. Drake turned to look at her. Her face was white and she looked as if she were scared. "You can't take a chance like that. What if the door closes?"

"Sir Richard, would you go back up and tell Mendrano to come down here? I have something I want him to do." Drake really wanted help from Mendrano, but he wanted to talk to Caitlyn alone as well. He'd seen fear in her eyes for the first time and it had shocked and worried him.

Sir Richard nodded and went to the exit. When he was gone Drake turned to Caitlyn again. "Caitlyn, centuries ago, someone came and went through here. If we're careful we can do the same. If it upsets you, Sir Richard and I will go down. You wait outside. That way you can catalogue what we send up."

But Caitlyn had regained her composure. She could not tell him that it wasn't fear for herself but the thought of him trapped in some dark, airless place that had caused her reaction.

"No, I'm going down with you and my father."

"Caitlyn, come on. It's not necessary and it . . ."

"You were going to say it's too dangerous. Well, I can't see it being more so for me than for you. I'm going."

He knew her stubbornness by now and he wasn't too sure Sir Richard wouldn't agree with her. "All right, but I have to figure out some safety thing first, and I want to scout out what's there *before* you go in."

"Okay. Why do you suppose they built something so elaborate?"

"Protection . . . I'm just wondering what it was they thought needed such protection."

"Maybe . . . it was to protect others from what's down there."

"That's a novel idea. I'd never thought of it like that. So what were they protecting us from?"

"I don't know. But . . . it frightens me a little."

"Whatever was down there has been dead for over two thousand years. I don't think we have a great deal to worry about."

Caitlyn remained silent but Drake had the feeling he hadn't convinced her.

They could hear Mendrano and Sir Richard coming minutes before Mendrano stuck his head through the rough-cut doorway.

"You wanted me?"

"Yes," Drake said. "Go back up and get a sack or container of some kind. Load it with some of those large stones and come as close to my weight as you can. Bring a few extras back in case. Then I want a strong brace, possibly a timber about four feet long. Make it sturdy. Weight or no, once we get that door open we're using a strong brace to hold it that way."

Mendrano left as Sir Richard entered the room.

"The air in here is not the best. You hardly realize that until you go outside," he chuckled. "Too bad we don't have a vent of some kind."

"I couldn't agree more," said Caitlyn.

"It might be a good idea if we go up for a while while

Mendrano has his men get things prepared," Drake said. His mind was on Caitlyn, who still looked a little too pale to suit him. "Come on, apprentice, you first. Out of here. And that's an order from the boss." He smiled, easing his words. "I won't have any arguments. I think we both need some fresh air and a cool drink."

Caitlyn wasn't about to argue. She had no idea why, but her nerves seemed to be stretched tight. She felt a strange kind of primeval fear and couldn't find a single reason for it. Tombs had been opened for nearly a century and no one had died from it . . . in fact, there'd never been an accident that she'd heard of. Yet she *was* afraid, and the feeling was new to her.

Caitlyn left the small room just ahead of her father and Drake. As she neared the top of the shaft she inhaled a deep gulp of fresh, clean air.

She walked some distance away and sat on a huge outcropping of rock. Then she bent her knees and put her arms about them, looking out over the valley.

It was silly! It was ridiculous! She scolded herself, but she could not push the feeling away.

Drake and Sir Richard exited the shaft and stood for a moment together.

"Caitlyn seems unusually quiet," Sir Richard said.

"It's still a little new to her, I think," Drake said, not too sure he believed it himself. "Once we make a find of some kind the excitement will overcome the nerves and she'll be all right."

"I'll go and talk to her."

"No, it's best I do. We don't want it to look to like she's getting pampered, do we?" Drake grinned. "She doesn't take to that very well."

"I suppose you're right," Sir Richard smiled in return.

"Being a father is a little new to me. I can't treat her like a little girl, can I? Somewhat confusing."

"I imagine it would be. It's a shame the two of you never knew each other."

"Well, that's half the reason she came here. I suppose we'll just have to work at it. At least we have archaeology in common."

"Well, let me go talk to her."

Sir Richard watched Drake walk toward Caitlyn, his face unreadable. And from the entrance to the shaft, Mendrano watched him.

Drake walked to Caitlyn and sat down beside her. She spoke first.

"I feel foolish."

"Why?"

"I . . . I was actually scared."

"First-time jitters. It happens to all of us. The first time I went down into a tomb I ran a fever and became ill. Took me . . . and everyone who's ever done it, a while to get used to it."

"Drake . . . it was more than that," she said quietly.

He turned to look at her. The lines of her face were clean and perfectly proportioned. Her hair caught the sunlight. In all, the effect was enchanting and Drake wanted to watch her for a while. But she turned to him and there was something in her eyes he couldn't understand.

"You can stay up here. At least until we get down and see what's there. Then the men can . . ."

"No, this is foolish and if I'm going to overcome it I have to go back. I'll be all right."

"You don't have to do this, Caitlyn."

"Yes, I do. Not for my father or to prove anything to you. I have to do it for myself. Can you understand that?"

"Of course I can. Take it easy for a while. We'll see how the mechanism works and how we can control it. Then we'll stop for lunch and go back down again. I think it would be nice to have you beside me when we go in."

"Thank you," she said, smiling at his understanding. He smiled in return and rose to go back to the work site.

Caitlyn's smile faded. She had not told him the truth because she knew he couldn't believe it. But, not for a moment had she been afraid for herself. Her fear, for a reason she could not understand, was that Drake was somehow in grave danger. She did not question her motives. She only knew she was going to be beside him when they did find whatever secrets lay in store. Somehow, she knew she should be.

Nine

Ethan whistled softly to himself as he crossed the wide front veranda and entered the front door of his house. The message he had just received had brightened his entire day. It seemed the powers that be had pulled every political string possible and given the okay to building his dam.

He was going to have a party, a celebration, and make it a memorable one. He would go up to Drake's and make the invitation personally, since he had already invited his friends from Barranquilla and all the authoritive figures involved who had helped him.

He walked into his study for another look at the scale model of his proposed dam. It covered a table about six feet by four and was an exact replica of the structure and the area around it. He felt a surge of pride. Not only would the dam help him, it would be a blessing for everyone who had to suffer through the dry season hoping they would have enough water in the well for their fields and animals.

Ethan turned at the sound of a rap on his door and smiled as his overseer, Perez, entered.

"All is ready, Senor Ethan."

"Good. Let's get going. As it is we'll have to camp out tonight since we're getting such a late start. I don't really like taking this trip on horseback, but since I've sent the men by boat up to the dam site to look the area over, it's the only transportation we have."

"The men are prepared. We should get at least halfway by nightfall, and the rest of the way to Senor Drake's camp before midday."

"Right. Let's go."

The almost unseen trail that Ethan and his men followed threatened every day to surrender to the jungle. Still, expert eyes found a way that only those few who had traveled it often knew.

They moved at a steady pace single file, and covered a surprising distance before deepening shadows warned them to stop before nightfall made travel more dangerous.

Camp was made, a meal was cooked and eaten, and soon all but Ethan were rolled in their blankets to sleep.

The night sounds of the jungle were symphonic, filling the air with the music of the predator and the prey. Ethan had become so used to it that he wondered if he would be able to sleep without it if he ever went back to civilization.

Civilization . . . the civilization he knew had no qualities to lure him anymore. He had run from it and found contentment.

He thought of Caitlyn and her suggestion that a wife should be a woman who would build his little empire with him. It was the first time since he arrived in South America that he'd considered that part of his future. It had been enough to build his empire.

Still, Caitlyn's words had opened a door he preferred to keep closed. To secure the lock he kept on it, he put his thoughts on Caitlyn.

She was an enigma. A beautiful woman who seemed to be quite capable of dedication, ambition, and that subtle thing that drew admiration from a man, even if reluctantly.

He wondered how she and Drake were hitting it off. He knew Drake had been less than happy about her arrival, and he had half-expected to see her back. He was a little surprised when the days passed and Drake had not found a way to send her packing.

He poked the fire with a stick and then tossed it aside. It was time to sleep. They would be on their way at dawn. He rolled in his blanket, feet toward the fire, and soon drifted off into a dream-filled slumber.

At dawn he groaned himself awake—when his shoulder was shaken, he felt as if he hadn't slept at all.

"Senor, it is time to go."

"I swear," Ethan laughed, "you and the sun run on the same clock. You both get up at the same time."

The man chuckled and proceeded with their preparations. They were on the move in no time.

When they rode into Drake's camp there was only a skeleton crew and Antonio was among them. Ethan questioned him quickly because he knew Antonio would most likely know more than anyone else.

"Senor Drake and all the others are there," Antonio said as he pointed into the distance, "on the high ridge."

"What are they doing there, Antonio? I thought he was finding everything he needed right here."

"They have found something new. Senor Drake is very excited. They have been working since yesterday."

"Well . . . maybe I ought to take a look." He dismounted, adding, "And it looks like I have to go on foot from here."

"Si, senor," Antonio grinned amiably, "you must walk."

Ethan chuckled, handed the reins of his horse to one of the other men, and started toward the latest dig site. Mendrano was the first to see him coming. He was in the process of lifting a bundle to carry to Drake when he saw Ethan. He waved and waited for Ethan to get close enough to talk.

"Senor Ethan. It is good to see you again. There is no problem that brings you here so soon?"

"Just the opposite, Mendrano. I've come to share some good news. Where's Drake?"

Mendrano motioned toward the shaft. "He is down there, with Miss Emmerson and Senor Macdonald. They have made a very interesting discovery."

"Well, then. It looks like Drake and I both have something to celebrate."

"Not yet, Senor Ethan. There has been nothing but an empty room found so far. In fact, Senor Drake is working on the problem right now."

"Think he needs a hand?" Ethan grinned.

"I do not think he would be too upset at another strong arm."

"Then let me help you carry that load and we'll go down and see what we can do," Ethan replied as he reached down to help lift the bundles Mendrano was moving. "Good Lord, man, what's in this?"

"Rocks," Mendrano answered mildly.

"Rocks? You're carrying rocks down into a hole it probably took a week to dig out? That makes sense."

"It will only make sense when you see what Senor Drake is using the rocks for."

"Intriguing. Let's go. I'm interested now."

Ethan followed Mendrano as he walked down the shaft. A man who enjoyed the brilliant sun, clean air, and growing things, Ethan was not one to like going deeper and deeper into the earth. He suffered a claustrophobic moment that made him a bit breathless for a few minutes, but he regained control quickly.

Drake was silently impressed with the room they entered as he remembered that the room itself was thousands of years old.

He was kneeling before the small inner doorway with the upper part of his body inside holding a lantern aloft and examining the area carefully. Caitlyn was close by on her knees and Sir Richard was holding the door open with his weight on the stone.

"Well," Ethan's voice echoed in the empty room, "I always knew you'd find a tomb. Looks like you did it, all right."

Caitlyn and Sir Richard turned to face him and Drake withdrew from the entranceway so quickly he bumped his head on the stone. He bit back a curse and looked askance at Ethan.

"So far we've found an empty room, but there's a promise of a lot more." He motioned to the dark opening. "There's a flight of steps going down. They look like they're in reasonably good condition. I don't see cracks or crumbling, but then I can't see too far, but I have a feeling it's like we thought. It looks like it leads to another level." Drake frowned, "What are you doing here—something wrong?"

"Something's right. Very right, and I need my friends to help me celebrate."

"I take it you've heard from the authorities?"

"That I have."

"Authorities?" Sir Richard questioned with a puzzled frown.

"I'll explain it all at the party. I'm throwing a big bash

and I want you all there." Ethan looked at a rather disheveled and slightly dirty Caitlyn. "I hope you brought a party dress, little lady. This is the time for dancing."

"I never thought I would need them, but I did bring a couple. I think Lettie brought a while trunk full. Her trousseau, to be exact." Caitlyn smiled up at Ethan.

"Just when are you planning on having this party?" Drake questioned.

"Day after tomorrow. Why?"

"I need tomorrow here. I want to get down on the next level and see what we've got and where we go from here."

"All work and no play, and so forth," Ethan chuckled. "Is that the secret of the rocks?"

"It is. I need to displace my weight to make sure this door stays open. Come and look. This is an ingenious affair. The man who invented this could have a lot of little tricks up his sleeve."

Ethan examined the unique entranceway and was as fascinated as Drake had been. "So, if you place your weight on the stone it should keep the door open."

"It should. But I'm not taking any chances. I'm putting a brace to hold the door open as well, and Mendrano is going to be the door watcher when we go down. Want to join us?"

"Lord, no," Ethan said firmly. "This is as deep in the ground as I'll go. In fact, it's one level too deep. If you all don't mind, I'll go up top and wait for you."

"If you don't mind, Drake," Sir Richard said, "I shall also leave this find to you. I'm afraid I'm not as equipped as I used to be to handle this."

"Are you all right, Sir Richard?" Drake asked anxiously.

"I'm fine. A little breathless and somewhat tired. I'll just go up and chat with Ethan while you and Caitlyn go on down."

Sir Richard was quite unaware of the intense scrutiny Mendrano, who was standing some distance away, was giving him. Despite everything Drake had said, something . . . no, everything, about Sir Richard Macdonald did not ring true.

"Of course," Drake said, "you and Ethan can relax and talk. Mendrano, you keep an eye glued on this door. If it shows one sign of movement, yell your head off."

"Si, Senor Drake," Mendrano said reluctantly. He would rather have gone up with Ethan and Sir Richard, but there was no choice between that and Drake's welfare.

Ethan helped Mendrano and Drake measure out Drake's approximate weight, replace it in a bundle, and center it on the floor stone. Then the wedge of timber was forced against the far wall and the door.

"Well, I guess we're ready to give it a try." Drake said. Despite the danger, Caitlyn could see the excitement dance in his eyes when he turned to look at her. She had to admit she was both scared and thrilled. Drake reached out a hand to her. "Ready?"

"Yes." She said the word quickly and firmly and was rewarded by Drake's conspiratorial smile. They were sharing a unique thing . . . just the two of them, which excited her as well.

"This is no time for chivalry," Drake said. "I'll go first. If there's any problem at all I want you to back out of there as fast as you can. Is that understood?"

"Yes . . . boss." Caitlyn smiled at him and Drake wondered how obedient she would be if danger presented itself. He had a feeling it would take an awful lot to make Caitlyn run.

"Here, we'll each take a lantern." Drake inhaled deeply as he handed a lantern to Caitlyn. "Let's go."

Drake had to bend low to get through the door because the timber took some room, but he was inside in minutes. Without hesitation, Caitlyn followed.

Ethan and Sir Richard exchanged glances, then turned to go back up. Mendrano was torn. He would guard the door, but his mind was with Sir Richard Macdonald. If Drake hadn't put his trust in him he would have gotten one of his men to guard the door. But if anything went wrong he would never forgive himself.

Drake and Caitlyn stood together on the stone floor at the top of a flight of steps carved centuries before out of heavy gray stone that would most likely last until the end of time.

Their lanterns reflected only a short distance before them where the steps disappeared into inky blackness.

Caitlyn could feel the strength of Drake's hand as it enclosed hers and realized she felt a sense of security. She also knew she would rather be in this dangerously exciting place with Drake than anyplace else with any other man she had ever known.

They moved down the steps, careful to watch for crumbling stone or cracks that might make a step give way.

His eyes missed nothing, from the gleam of walls that seemed to have been polished smooth before being sealed away forever to the accurate carving of the stone steps. Not knowing why, he counted the steps as they descended.

"Thirteen," he said softly as they reached what appeared to be a solid floor.

"What?"

"Thirteen steps," he chuckled. "I wonder if those who built this were superstitious."

"Are you?"

"Nope. Thirteen is just thirteen," he said, but the memory of Tana and the broken jug flitted through his mind.

They stood together and held their lanterns aloft as the light brought the area into hazy view.

The room was several feet larger than the one above, confirming Drake's idea that the entire place was one tier built upon the other, the largest on the bottom and each tier growing progressively smaller. Along the sides, about three feet from the floor, a shelf protruded from the wall, running the entire length of the room. On it, in measured spaces, lay bundles that were, to the trained eye, the remains of humans who had walked this place so many years before.

"It's an honorary guard room," Drake said. "I'll bet we'll find armor and weapons."

"I'd agree. With this kind of a guard, can you imagine the position and power of whoever might be buried here?"

"A king of sorts . . . *El Viejo Senor* . . . the old lord, as the natives would say. Stand still and let me walk off a measurement. If we stay at opposite ends we can light the area better."

"Be careful. If one stone can move a door that weighs as much as the one above us does, who knows what they've cooked up for this room."

"Don't worry, I'll be careful."

Caitlyn held her lantern up, shedding as much light as possible, and Drake did the same as he moved ahead of her. When he released her hand and moved away, Caitlyn felt the loss of his touch like a tangible force. She was shaken and fought the urge to go to him.

When he'd completely traversed the room he returned to her side. "I counted it fifteen feet by eighteen. And there are . . ." he paused, looking a little surprised, "thirteen bodies," he added softly.

"Somehow, thirteen seems to have significance here."

"Maybe. There's also a doorway at the other end with a stairway leading down to the next level."

"Are we going down?" If her voice trembled a bit, Drake pretended not to notice. He was shaken, too, and he respected how she must feel.

"No. First we're going to have to lay some pipe for air, at least to the top level. The air on this level is really bad, but there's no way to run a pipe here without the risk of damaging something. I can imagine how the air will be below. While Mendrano and his men make some air vents, we'll start storing these until we can do some detailed work on them. I'm looking forward to seeing if I'm right."

"How long will it take Mendrano, do you think?"

"About three or four days. I want an air shaft to the room above. We'll worry about the other rooms when we find them. At least that will give us enough air to work with. It won't be the most comfortable affair."

"Then we'll start work on the mummies right away?"

Drake looked down into Caitlyn's eyes. She had a lot of courage, and this pleased him. But there was no sense pushing her courage too far.

"What do you say we go to a party while the men get those shafts dug?"

He watched the smile brighten her face. For a moment their eyes met and their bizarre surroundings faded as a current flowed between them.

"I think that would be fine," Caitlyn breathed softly. Her whole body seemed to come to life.

"This is one hell of a place to . . ." Drake muttered, but his free arm came around her, drawing her to him. Their lips met in a heated kiss and the movement of their lanterns made the light dance, reflecting shadows on the walls.

Drake could feel the warm, moist, willing lips part beneath his, accepting at first, then returning the kiss with a fire that ignited a force within him older than the place in which they stood.

When he released her, both were breathing deeply, completely shaken.

"I think it would be wise to get out of here," Drake said.

"I . . . suppose you're right," Caitlyn replied. She was still trembling from the passion that had swept through her and by her own crumbling resolve and lack of control. Her emotions were reflected in her emerald eyes.

"Caitlyn?"

"Yes?"

"I should say I'm sorry, but I'm not. The only thing I regret is the time and the place." His eyes held hers, forcing her to see the truth in what he said. His voice grew to a velvet-smooth whisper. "I want to make love to you, Caitlyn, and that's the honest truth."

Caitlyn felt suddenly breathless. She could lie and say she didn't want him, but she sensed he knew the opposite was true. And she found she did not want any lies between them.

"I won't deny that I feel the same way," she answered honestly. She watched the pleasure dance in his grey eyes.

Drake pulled her against him again, savoring for one more moment the feel of her soft curves. She, in turn, clung to the iron-hard strength of him. "Ah, Caitlyn, Caitlyn," he breathed softly just before he took her mouth with his in a deep kiss.

"I've got to get you out of here before what little control I have left is gone. You're much too special for it to be anything less than perfect."

Caitlyn's heavy-lidded gaze was the only answer he needed. He took her hand in his and started for the stairs.

Ethan and Sir Richard had found a comfortable grassy spot and sat down side by side to wait. To all outward appearances Sir Richard seemed relaxed and just mildly curious as he questioned Ethan, who was quite unaware that the questions had more importance than he knew.

"I didn't know you had so much contact with the authorities in Barranquilla from here."

"Most of them have been friends of mine since the day I came here five years ago."

"I see."

"There's not too much goes on in Colombia that isn't known. We might be at the end of the world, but we keep in closer communication than most would imagine."

"I understand," Sir Richard said gently, then he changed the subject. "Your party sounds very inviting. I think your friend does need relief from the pressure he puts on himself."

"Drake is really devoted to his beliefs," Ethan agreed, "but he's really easy-going and fun once you get him away from a dig. I suppose you, of all people, would understand that."

"I certainly would. That's why I think your timing is so wonderful. You said you were celebrating a special occasion?"

"Well, pretty special for me, anyway."

"I don't see the connection between your special occasion and the authorities . . . you did say the authorities were involved?"

"In a way. I had to have their permission for a project—a rather ambitious project—I have in mind."

"I see. You're quite good friends with all the authorities from Barranquilla then."

"Pretty much so. I've been dealing with them for some time."

"Sort of keep you in touch with the outside world more or less."

"More or less."

"And Drake has the same kind of relationship."

"Oh, he had to have their permission to dig, and if he makes a big discovery he has to inform them. I'm sure the museum here will get a healthy part of the find. After all, it is their country. But Drake . . . well, he hasn't gone to Barranquilla more than a few times since he's been here, and that was mostly for supplies. He's a single-minded man," Ethan laughed. "I wouldn't want to stand between Drake and what he's got his mind on. He can be as tenacious as hell."

"The project, is it a secret you can share?"

"I suppose it won't be a secret long, but I'd like to keep it a secret until the party. That way I can show you as well as tell you. I think you'll be surprised and pleased."

"I'm sure I will be." Sir Richard hid his curiosity behind a smile, and shifted the conversation to other subjects.

Mendrano sat cross-legged on the floor a short distance from the door through which Drake and Caitlyn had gone. His background, steeped in the ancient beliefs, made him nervously aware that he could be sitting on the tomb of an ancient lord. No matter how much Drake had tried to educate him, the old superstitions still clung. He wasn't sure this particular tomb should have been disturbed.

He was also aware that Drake respected his feelings and

did not disturb the ancient ones for profit, but to make the world understand the pride and glory of his ancestry. He knew there were others who would care little for the almost holy place where he sat and would plunder it carelessly if given half a chance.

This brought his thoughts abruptly to Sir Richard Macdonald, whom he not only disliked, but distrusted. He couldn't say why and he knew how much he meant to Drake. Still, he felt as if something was drastically wrong and he meant to do everything in his power to protect Drake and the tomb of his ancestors.

He thought of the brilliant green stone buried beneath the earth under Drake's tent. It worried him that another could be found at anytime. Was this the reason so many outsiders had seemed to arrive so suddenly?

He sighed deeply. Life had been so good before the finding of the stone—it seemed that from that moment on things had gotten more complicated.

He would be patient. He was quite used to that. But he would also be on the alert.

He was caught in his thoughts, but not so deeply that he didn't hear Drake and Caitlyn ascending the steps.

When they climbed through the small doorway Mendrano was standing beside it.

"Mendrano, when we get back to camp I want to lay out an air shaft and have your men sink it. It should only take a few days."

"Si, senor."

"And don't forget to place guards every night. Be extremely careful that no one . . . absolutely no one comes down here."

"You will not be here?"

"Caitlyn and I and Sir Richard have been invited to Fountainhurst. Ethan is having a celebration party. We should be back in a couple of days."

"I will be very careful."

"I've no doubt about that. Come on, Caitlyn, let's go up and see what Ethan's plans are."

Caitlyn walked up the hard dirt shaft beside Drake. "Do we have enough horses to ride down to Ethan's?"

"We won't go by horseback this time. We're only a couple of miles from the river when we get to my house. We'll go by boat."

"Why didn't we come up by boat?"

"Against the current? Makes it difficult when you're carrying baggage. This way we sort of float down. We won't be carrying any supplies on the way back, so poling against the current won't be so hard. It's a nice trip downriver and even if we leave tonight we won't have to worry about company. I've taken the trip by boat a hundred times. It's really easy."

"I'm looking forward to it."

"I'm a little surprised."

"At what? That I'm looking forward to it?"

"No," he chuckled, "that you brought a dress. You are, to say the least, enchanting in that outfit, but I really find it hard to wait to see you all dressed up. It's downright exciting."

"It's a woman's natural instinct," she replied. "Silk, satin, and perfume are almost necessities." She gave him an arch look. "One never knows what one will run across, even in the jungle. It's wise to be prepared."

"You're looking forward to the trip," he said as he paused before they reached the top. He turned to her and reached out to brush her cheek lightly with his fingertips. His eyes warmed to the point that she could feel the heat of a matching flame deep within her. "I'm looking forward to it, too." He bent, brushed her lips with his, and before she could respond, took her hand and drew her into the clear sunlight.

"Well, gentlemen," Drake said as they approached Ethan and Sir Richard. "What plans have you made?"

"We think it's better to go downriver first thing in the morning," Ethan said.

"Then we have time for a meal and a good night's sleep before we go," Drake replied.

Ethan and Sir Richard were both aware, as the late afternoon and evening went on, that Drake was in an exceptionally good mood. Caitlyn laughed easily and it set a comfortable tone for the evening.

The meal was studded with animated conversation, mostly archaeological. Ethan laughingly complained it was unfair since he was outnumbered three to one, yet he expressed curiosity and interest.

From then on the conversation drifted to tales of the surrounding area and Drake captivated Caitlyn's interest with a romantic legend.

"For hundreds of years this region has given birth to magical stories," he began, "of white Indians and hidden cities, of diamonds and strange beasts, of rivers that ran uphill. Anything seemed possible. Imagine sitting beside a stream with a half-moon bright enough to turn the water to silver. The kind of night you hear about in legends. Let me tell you the legend of the lake of Guatavita.

"The story of Guatavita is a story of gods and demons," Drake began, his eyes glittering with pleasure at Caitlyn's rapt attention. "And of an enchanted princess, a very human prince, and fabulous riches. It had been a sacred lake from the beginning of time and because the wife of the lord of Guatavita was lovely and faithless, the little lost lake contained riches beyond Scheherazade. It's called *El Dorado* and it means exactly that . . . the golden man. Very long ago, so long that names are forgotten, there was a lord of Guatavita who had a wife more proud and beautiful than any other. She was so aware of her own beauty that she sought continual confirmation of it. She betrayed her husband with a noble of a court. The only thing was she didn't keep it enough of a secret and her husband found out about it. The lover died by torture, but the lord's pain was so great he sought to punish his wife, not by death, but by having her name and the story of her dishonor continually sung . . . in palaces, taverns, and courtyards. The princess, since she could not escape the punishment, decided to escape life. She climbed to the holy lake, taking her daughter with her, and threw herself in. In mortal anguish the prince begged the gods to give him his wife back, promising he would punish her no more.

"They say," Drake added softly, "that at night, if you wander by the lake you can still hear his mournful cry. It is also said that for years he threw great riches to the gods of the lake in the hopes of getting his lost love back. You see, the demons of the lake had told him she still lived in the lake, forever young and fair in an enchanted palace. The lord of Guatavita lived the rest of his life without consolation."

"What a terribly sad story," Caitlyn exclaimed.

"The natives have a story for any and every occasion," Drake chuckled, "some sad, some happy, all having to do with riches."

"Do you believe any of them?" Caitlyn inquired.

"I don't know," Drake said with a shrug. "It might be quite an adventure to find out, wouldn't it?" He laughed softly "If half of the stories are true . . . if a man found truth in a single legend, he could be rich beyond his dreams."

Caitlyn's eyes held Drake's and she smiled and spoke softly. "But it's not the riches you would search for, is it, Drake? It's the legend itself."

"I suppose. Goes to show you how hard-headed and single-minded archaeologists can be." He grinned. "Be they male or female."

Everyone laughed as the meal ended—and Sir Richard suggested they prepare what little they intended to take along.

Tana had watched the preparations for the trip and was almost overwhelmed with jealousy. Caitlyn was so beautiful and Ethan was so . . . she could not bear to think of the attraction Caitlyn and Ethan could have for each other.

Caitlyn was much more a part of the life and the world that Ethan had come from, that he was so much a part of. She would be able to fit into Ethan's world so well.

She wanted to hate Caitlyn, but that wasn't possible either; her frustration was almost overpowering.

She remembered well when Ethan had come to the small village between his plantation and Bogota with the idea of carving out a working farm between Bogota and the river. He had hired her father as one of his foremen and her brother as a worker.

At fifteen, Tana was quite conscious of the fact that she was becoming a woman. She could see it in the eyes of the men of her village, and in her father's reaction.

But she had no intention of marrying anyone just for propriety's sake. She wanted a man as strong as her father, handsome as a prince, someone she could love. Then Ethan had walked into her life.

She had loved him almost at once. But she knew he was so caught up in his plans that he was hardly aware of her as anything but Mendrano's little girl.

She had carried Ethan's meals to him in the fields. He'd smiled, thanked her, and concentrated on his work.

He'd seen her only as Mendrano's child, Antonio's sister, another pair of willing hands to help with the work. He'd been good to her, kind and gentle, but the years that separated them seemed to be too wide a gulf to bridge.

She knew the times he'd gone to Bogota to 'relax' and wished she'd been the woman he'd been with.

She would see his quick smile in her dreams and often she would watch him at work, his body bronzed by the sun, admiring his long-legged stride. She'd hear him laugh or give crisp, no-nonsense orders, and her heart would heat with the need to touch him.

Many nights she cried herself to sleep, but she knew that would do little good. She prayed to all the saints and gods and that did no good either. Now . . . now she was nearing a time of decision. She could not stand it much longer. Maybe honesty would be the best thing. Maybe, her hopeful heart decided, it was because Ethan was so involved he just hadn't had time. Maybe it was because she was Mendrano's daughter. Tana finally had to make Ethan open his eyes and see her for herself. She began to make plans of her own.

The brief journey downriver was made in a sturdy launch made of stout, protective wood and seats running along either side. Caitlyn sat near the back and the men gathered to talk. The journey was also unbelievably beautiful.

On either side of the river the jungle rose a hundred and fifty feet, so dense the eye could not penetrate more than a foot or two beyond the bank. The water was alive with fish, egrets, and snakebirds by the hundred perched along the shallows looking for a meal. Crocodiles lay in little coves like logs in the sun, sleeping or guarding eggs their casual wives refused to care for.

For a long while Caitlyn was captivated by the immensity and the beauty around her. Drake and Sir Richard were in conversation about some artifact or other and she let her attention drift.

Caitlyn was so absorbed in her thoughts that she didn't realize that Drake had left the other men until he sat down beside her. She turned to look at him.

He smiled, his eyes warming as he looked at her, and she could feel that warmth within her, stirring her. She was totally aware of him in seconds. It amazed and somewhat shocked her that just the vivid memory of their kiss in that secluded stone room could heat her blood and make her feel so . . . expectant.

Caitlyn was much too strong to deny that she felt like a simpering schoolgirl. She wanted Drake with so much depth of emotion that it shook her a bit to realize how much of herself was dammed up, waiting to be released. No other man had ever affected her so powerfully.

The others were just far enough away that Drake's voice didn't carry as he bent toward her.

"With the sun on your hair like that a smart man wouldn't have to search for El Dorado's treasure. It looks like spun gold. You're so beautiful, Caitlyn."

She wanted to say he was beautiful, too, and she laughed to herself. The silver of his eyes in his deeply tanned face made them vivid and deep—she felt bathed in flame as she immersed herself in them. His thick ebony hair caught the morning sun and gleamed with life.

She could feel the vitality, the immense strength of him and if others had not been present she would have moved into his arms and kissed that sensual mouth with all the fervor in her heart.

She turned her gaze to Drake, filled with this wordless, exultant thing and Drake felt it to the center of his being. He drew in a deep breath and fought valiantly the need to hold her. But he had to touch her. His hand rested gently on hers in a moment of mutual promise.

Ten

They arrived at Ethan's plantation just before dusk, hungry yet brimming with enthusiasm. Ethan ordered their baggage taken to their rooms.

"Tomorrow night should be fun," Ethan said. "I've certainly got a lot planned."

"And you don't intend to announce the reason for the surprise party until then," Sir Richard said. "The suspense might prove too much for us to bear."

"Well, my friend," Ethan's smile was broad as he clapped Sir Richard on the back, "the bunch of you will just have to prove your stamina, because you can't pry the truth out of me until tomorrow night."

"What a hard man you are," Lettie said, laughing.

Supper was a fun-filled affair, with everyone trying to coax the reason for the party from Ethan, who laughingly defended himself. To divert their attention Ethan begged Caitlyn to play some songs for him. She smiled as he escorted her to the piano.

"It'll take their attention from me," Ethan grinned, "and it'll give me a great deal of pleasure at the same time."

To the delight of all, Caitlyn played a few songs, then enticed them into gathering around the piano to sing. She could see the relaxed pleasure in Ethan's eyes when she finally claimed exhaustion.

The group dissipated just after eleven o'clock to find their way to their rooms and bed.

Caitlyn was tired, yet sleep seemed elusive. The house had grown quiet so she slipped a robe over her nightgown and walked downstairs out onto the back patio.

The breeze was cool and she was grateful she'd thought to bring a heavier robe. Nights in this area seemed much colder than a newcomer would expect them to be.

The fountain had its own music, accompanied by night sounds from the surrounding jungle.

She walked to the fountain, sat on the narrow edge, and trailed her hand in the water. It rippled the reflection of the moon and the stars.

The water stilled and she looked down at her own reflection. She had loosened her hair so it glistened in the moonlight.

Then another face appeared beside hers in the water. She smiled and turned to look up at Ethan. The moonlight softened his blue eyes and glazed his blond hair to a bright gold.

"Can't sleep?" he questioned.

"I suppose I could if I tried, but the night is so beautiful I decided to enjoy it for a bit."

"Are you cold?"

"Not really. But the temperature does change a lot between sunset and sunrise."

Ethan smiled and came to sit beside her. "It surely does. It gets colder than this," he paused to look at her closely. "What ever made a beautiful woman like you become an archaeologist? I mean . . ."

"I know what you mean, Ethan." Caitlyn smiled, too. "And I'm sorry I don't fit into the picture you have of young ladies."

"You surely don't. But then it's always the one that doesn't fit the mold that's the most intriguing."

"That goes for a man, too." She studied him. "You don't fit the mold, either."

"Oh? How so?"

"Well, the handsome, young, and reasonably wealthy men of my acquaintance," she said, pretending an aristocratic attitude, "don't head for the wilderness to carve out a life for themselves. Most of them arrive after empires are already built and they just buy them. It makes you rather unconventional."

"You could tell I had money before?"

"Of course."

"How?"

"Ethan," she said teasingly, "you know good wine and good food. You set your table with fine china and silverware. Your home reflects your taste. So many reasons, but the main one is just you. You . . . you walk and talk with an assurance that requires a good education and more experience than you could possibly have at your age. I would say it goes back several generations."

"An archaeologist," Ethan said in wonder. "You picked the wrong calling. You could have run Scotland Yard. Okay, it's true my family has more money than it knows what to do with. I have over two million in a trust right now."

"Then . . . what are you doing here?"

"I . . . I needed to find something meaningful to do. I don't know if I can make you understand. I just couldn't live a life that was . . . empty. I wanted what I had to be something I built myself. I had my share of traveling, wine, women, and song. In fact, I had my share of everything. But it was all like . . . shadows. I needed something substantial that I could say was mine . . . not what my father had left me."

"And what makes you think I can't understand that? It's the same with me. You just answered your own question. That's why I became an archaeologist. You see . . . I don't want to be *just* someone's daughter, or *just* someone's wife. I . . . I want to be something on my own."

"You're are a most interesting woman, Caitlyn. I don't believe I've ever met anyone quite like you."

"I'm flattered." Caitlyn smiled.

"I should like to see much more of you, here . . . in my home."

"Ethan . . . I . . ."

"I didn't mean to make it sound so . . ."

"I have so much I want to do . . . to accomplish. I don't want . . ."

"I know I sounded a bit oppressive. I'm sorry. Will you at least agree to come here often?"

"Yes, I'll be happy to do that."

"Good, and I'll visit you, too, so I expect you and I will see a lot of each other."

Caitlyn didn't want to give Ethan the impression she was prepared to make their relationship anything more than a friendly one, at least not at the moment.

"I think I'd best go to bed now. I'd like to see your whole plantation tomorrow, if you have time."

"I'll make time. First thing after breakfast?"

"Depends on when breakfast is."

"Mine is at five-thirty."

"Heavens . . . how about eight?"

"That's almost the middle of the day," he said cheerily, "but eight it is. Good night, Caitlyn."

"Good night, Ethan. She rose and walked away and Ethan

remained seated, watching her go. Until Caitlyn's coming he hadn't realized how alone he really was. Finally he rose and went inside to bed.

Caitlyn walked to her room slowly, thinking of Drake and of Ethan. Both excessively charming men. She knew that she and Drake had been poised on the edge of something, but now she was uncertain.

Was it their excitement over the discovery combined with that star-filled night? Did that weave a kind of spell around them?

A frightening thought came to her—was this some kind of game with Drake? She knew her father was valuable to Drake and he didn't want to lose his influence. It startled her to think that Drake had to know if she were to leave, her father would most likely go as well. And Drake couldn't afford that.

He wanted to make love to her, he had told her so, and she had known that she had wanted him, too. But now, away from the aura that surrounded their remarkable find, she wondered if she hadn't lost control. She would have to be with Drake again . . . away from that atmosphere, and find out for herself.

Her dreams were strange that night, filled with objects that looked like ancient Egyptian artifacts and faces she could not identify.

The next day, as Ethan had predicted, Caitlyn enjoyed the ride around the plantation. He was a witty and interesting guide.

When they returned they discovered the arrival of the other guests.

Caitlyn was quite aware of the intensity of Drake's gaze as she and Ethan returned and introductions were made.

But if he felt any annoyance at their jaunt, he showed no sign of it.

Drake was quick to realize that the guests were Rodger Girard and his wife, Sophie, Emil Josiah and his fiancée, Anne, and Anthony Delvert and his wife, Carol. That meant that Ethan's dam project had been accepted and that the surprise celebration was to announce it.

Drake found no occasion to get Caitlyn alone for the balance of the day.

Dinner was to be a formal affair and Caitlyn was relieved that she had decided to bring along the dresses. Lettie came to her room while she was finishing her preparations. "You look stunning, Caitlyn."

"Thanks. I'm glad I thought to bring this, although I'll never understand what made me do it."

She gave herself one last look in the mirror and was satisfied. The dress was ivory lace draped enticingly over pale green silk. It enhanced the color of her eyes. She had drawn her hair back severely in a chignon, adding a strand of pearls and a drop of perfume.

Caitlyn and Lettie came downstairs and walked to the doorway of the large living room where the rest of the guests had gathered. They paused in the doorway and the guests turned to look.

Caitlyn's gaze had found Drake at once, standing with his shoulder resting against the fireplace and a glass in one hand. Her breath caught slightly. If Drake was attractive in his rugged daily wear, he was heart-shattering in dinner clothes. He looked almost dangerous, and she knew she was more than vulnerable. She would have to be cautious because falling into Drake Stone's arms would be very easy and she was no longer sure of his motives.

But if Caitlyn was captivated, Drake was downright

stunned. She had walked into the room and suddenly it seemed brighter. He didn't move, merely stood and watched her come toward him, no longer quite aware of the flow of conversation around him.

The girl who had joyfully dug in the dust and dirt with him now seemed like a vision.

He remembered vividly the feel of her in his arms and the taste of her mouth and at that moment had the distinct urge to grab her up in his arms, carry her to his room, and remove her clothing one piece at a time, very, very slowly and . . . all except the pearls, he thought, he'd leave the pearls . . . then he would make love to her until this burning desire was spent . . . if it ever could be.

He was tied in knots with a combination of desire and jealousy. He was surprised to admit it to himself. He'd never felt an emotion that remotely resembled it before. He wanted to be back at the dig . . . where he and Caitlyn could be alone.

A kind of excitement permeated the atmosphere during dinner, for each of them looked forward to Ethan's announcement.

Drake sat next to George and across the table from Caitlyn, who was seated between Rodger Girard and Anthony Delvert. He found it difficult to concentrate on food when he could watch her in animated conversation with both men. Occasionally her eyes would meet his and he could feel the electrical contact.

He'd planned these two days much differently, but Caitlyn suddenly seemed as elusive as a firefly. The previous night he'd seen Caitlyn and Ethan by the fountain. Then he rose the next morning, and by the time he came down for breakfast he found that Caitlyn and Ethan had already ridden out for a tour of the plantation from which they did not return until noon. As far as Drake was concerned, things had gone from bad to worse—he found it impossible to get Caitlyn away from the group.

He watched her across the table, at the same time trying to be attentive to Mrs. Gerard and Mrs. Delvert, who were on either side of him. It was utterly frustrating.

By the time dessert was over and they were enjoying coffee, Drake was giving some deep thought to the novel idea that Caitlyn had deliberately slipped through his fingers. He wondered if she were a bit afraid of him . . . or if she was playing some kind of game. He didn't want to consider what that could be, but the emerald buried beneath his tent was the first thing that came to mind.

Well, he thought as he forced himself to calm down, two can play that game, my dear Caitlyn.

His attention was drawn back by the fact that champagne glasses were being filled and Ethan was rising, holding his.

"Well, ladies and gentlemen, it's time to reveal a well-kept secret. I want you to have the pleasure of sharing a new, and, I hope, rewarding project for us all. A toast."

The others rose and lifted their glasses toward Ethan expectantly.

"It's been my dream to build a dam along the Little River to help control damage during the rainy season. Now that dream is coming true. With Mr. Delvert, Mr. Girard, and Mr. Josiah's blessing . . . and Drake's, since the water will rise to within a few miles of his dig, I have seen that dream come true at last. The dam will be built during the coming year. We begin work in less than a month."

"Here, here," Anthony said.

The others joined in congratulating Ethan. No one noticed that Sir Richard's face had grown pale and the hand that held his glass trembled. Only when the glass slipped from his hand and splintered against the table did the others react.

"Oh, good heavens," Sir Richard said apologetically. "I'm so very sorry. How clumsy of me."

"Don't worry," Ethan said with a smile. He ordered another glass. "No problem. I'm sure the news made us all a bit shaky."

Caitlyn rose to help cover the uncomfortable situation. All eyes turned to her as she raised her glass.

"I would like to propose a toast as well. I have some news I would like to share with the rest of you since Drake already knows. I want you to join with me in a toast to a man whom I've admired all my life and who, I have recently discovered, is my father, Sir Richard Macdonald." She raised her glass and the enthusiasm and joy changed the situation swiftly from embarrassment to happiness.

Everyone cheered enthusiastically, everyone except Drake who was regarding Sir Richard with a puzzled frown.

Little pieces of the mystery seemed to shift around in his head, but none fit well enough to give him a clear idea of what was plaguing him. But they made him uneasy. It was as if something lay clear before his eyes and he just wasn't seeing it.

For some reason Mendrano had had misgivings about Sir Richard. The idea was farfetched and he didn't want to believe it. Besides, if he accepted the fact that there was some problem surrounding Sir Richard . . . what about Caitlyn, the daughter Sir Richard had never known? He drank his champagne. For now the puzzle was too much. He had another, more interesting, subject on his mind at the moment, and it sat across the table from him.

The dinner concluded and Ethan invited everyone out on

the patio. Music and dancing and more champagne were to follow.

Comfortable chairs had been set at random spots. Caitlyn headed for one, only to find a strong hand taking hold of her arm. Caitlyn wondered why she didn't resist when Drake took her hand and they walked down the walk to the deeper shadows of the trees. She had just warned herself about how dangerously exciting Drake Stone could be.

"It's a beautiful night," Drake ventured.

"We'll be missed."

"Not until the entertainment's over . . . an hour or so. Caitlyn, I want to talk to you."

"That's pretty obvious," she said as she smiled. "What was it you wanted to talk to me about?"

He wanted to say, *you . . . you and the sudden change.* But he didn't.

"I'm going back up to the dig early in the morning."

"What do you mean by early?"

"As soon as the sun gives us enough light."

"Oh."

"Are you coming?"

"What gave you the idea I wasn't?" Surprise was heavy in her voice.

"I'm not sure," he said. "It seems you're pretty attracted to the plantation life."

"Now what is that supposed to mean?"

"I . . . ah . . . stopped by your room last night."

"I was . . ."

"I know."

"I couldn't sleep so I took a walk."

"By the fountain on the patio. I know that, too."

Caitlyn was quiet, watching the controlled look on his face. Then she smiled. "If you saw me, why didn't you join me?"

"I didn't want to interrupt anything . . . special."

"Why, Drake," her voice was touched with amusement. "You sound . . . almost jealous."

If he was annoyed or embarrassed, he gave no sign of it.

"Not jealousy . . . I don't have any right to be jealous. But it would help if you knew what you wanted. Or . . . maybe you've found something that offers more . . . substantial rewards than digging for artifacts."

The slap was an angry reaction and Caitlyn regretted it the moment she did it.

"I'm sorry. I didn't mean to do that, but I resent your attitude. I thought we'd . . ."

"Maybe that's what I thought, too," he said quietly. He reached out and took her wrist with a hold that was not painful, but firm enough for her to know she couldn't pull away easily.

"I'm the one who's sorry, Caitlyn. What I said was pretty stupid." He drew her to him. "And I'm damn jealous." His voice softened. "I can't get you out of my head or off my mind. Last night was one of the worst I've ever spent. I guess I let my imagination run wild."

"Nothing happened last night," Caitlyn said softly. "I wish . . ."

"What?" he whispered as he drew her against him, "what do you wish?"

"I'm not sure," she was suddenly breathless under the intensity of his gaze. He put his arms around her and held her close enough so she could feel the solid thud of his heart. "Drake . . ."

"I don't know what you feel, Caitlyn. I wish I did. I wish I knew I was making you feel what I feel." He turned slowly, so the shadows across her face were washed away with the pale light.

She knew what the light must be revealing. She could feel her pulse racing and the heat uncoiling within that made her tremble. Her breath seemed caught and she parted her lips to inhale deeply, and Drake took her parted lips with his in a kiss that rocked the foundation of her world and sent her senses spiraling out of control.

Their mouths fused, hers opening to accept him, feeling his tongue taste the inner recesses of her mouth, demanding all. And she gave all, molding her body to his, feeling her own will demand that she give more . . . and more, until she eased the fiery need that boiled within her.

When the kiss ended both were breathless and Caitlyn could only cling to him because her legs were weak.

"I sure pick the wrong times and the wrong places," he muttered. "Another wish. I wish we were up there on that grassy plateau away from everyone. Where the stars are so close . . . where . . ." He crushed her against him and she had no doubt that his need matched hers. "I told you once before . . ." She placed her fingertips against his lips to stop the words. Words he had once said and words that now, in complete honesty, she wanted to say.

"I want . . ."

"There you are!" Lettie's voice came from the pathway. Both Drake and Caitlyn turned at the sound. Drake could have happily drowned Lettie at the moment and it would have surprised Lettie to know that Caitlyn's sentiments were much the same.

"Lettie," Caitlyn said, "is the entertainment over already?"

"Just about. It's getting a bit late. In fact, I've seen some uncomfortable men yawning behind their hands."

"This climate is conducive to early retirement," Drake said.

Caitlyn smothered a laugh.

"Well, I'm going to bed," Lettie claimed. "It's after midnight and Bill told me you said we were going back first thing in the morning."

"At dawn," Drake verified.

"Dawn! Good heavens."

"I have a job, Lettie," Drake grinned, "and there's a lot of work to be done. If you'd like to stay on here I'm sure Ethan would be glad to have you. He could send a guide to bring you back when you're ready."

"Well . . . I wouldn't mind . . . Caitlyn?"

"Go right ahead. You and Bill stay as long as you like. I'll be so busy working that I'd most likely be very neglectful."

"Good, then I'll stay. Mrs. Girard is the most interesting person and I love gossip," Lettie sighed. "Anyway I came to find you two because the entire group is breaking up. I thought," she grinned amiably, "I'd best be the one to come after you."

"Lettie!"

"I'm afraid Lettie is right. We'd best join the others," Drake said. "Dawn comes faster than you can imagine."

They could do nothing but accompany Lettie back to the group.

Ethan was not exactly overjoyed that Drake had decided to go back to the dig so quickly. He tried to coax them to stay a few more days, but succeeded in getting only Bill and Lettie to agree. Drake claimed his new find made it necessary to return to work. Sir Richard agreed and Caitlyn's enthusiasm over the find was clear to Ethan. By one o'clock the entire party was settled in for the night . . . except Caitlyn.

She had prepared for bed, but she could not seem to calm her senses to the point where sleep could be possible.

Never one to ignore reality, Caitlyn faced the truth. The

flame Drake had ignited pulsed within her, waiting to be stirred to life. It wouldn't go away. She wondered at herself, realizing that she wished Drake were here with her, knowing she would not resist.

She tormented herself with the thought of how wanton her emotions were. Her skin felt hot and too tight to contain her. Her blood seemed to bring every nerve to life. She wished her mother were here. She always seemed to give good advice, and that was what Caitlyn needed now.

For a while she simply paced the floor, with no way to ease the ache. She had been on the edge of telling Drake that she wanted him to make love to her and she wondered how the night would have ended had Lettie not interfered. Would she be in his arms now, releasing these pent-up feelings?

She had never felt this way in all her life. It was as if every part of her was vitally alive, expectant, prepared.

She could not bear it much longer. It was time to decide just how far she was willing to commit herself. She walked to the door, knowing Drake's room was not that far from hers.

Reaching for the door handle, Caitlyn was startled to hear a soft tap. Drake! The idea of his presence on the other side of the door was, to say the least, overwhelming.

She opened the door and was taken totally by surprise to find her father.

"Father! What's the matter? Are you ill?"

"No, Caitlyn, nothing like that. I know the hour is terribly late, but I wanted to talk to you privately and there has been very little chance to do that for the past few days. May I come in for a minute?"

"Of course," she said as she stepped aside and let him pass, then closed the door slowly, trying to grasp what could be so urgent.

"There's nothing wrong?"

"No, child," he smiled a bit self-consciously. "I'm afraid I'm at a loss as to how to explain why I'm taking the liberty to . . . give a little fatherly advice."

"Fatherly advice . . . I don't understand."

"May I sit down?"

"Please," she said as she motioned to a chair. He seemed a bit uncomfortable.

"I . . . I have realized there is a certain . . . relationship developing between you and Drake. I know I have come into your life late . . . and that maybe I have no right to interfere. Being a father is rather new to me. But I have memories, memories of a terrible mistake I made. I have so many regrets, Caitlyn . . . so many."

Caitlyn's heart went out to him, and she realized he was trying in some way to make up for all the lost years. Sir Richard could read the understanding in her eyes.

"Up at the dig we were in a unique circumstance," he went on. "It was exciting, but . . ."

"But excitement and shared enthusiasm is not enough to build a lasting relationship."

"I'm only saying that I want you to be happy in every part of your life. Drake is completely caught up in his work. Relationships could run second to his ambition. I made that mistake. I don't want to see the daughter I'm just beginning to know . . . and to love, make the same mistake." He reached out to take one of her hands in his. "Caitlyn, you're a very lovely woman—intelligent and level-headed. I know you've paid for the mistake your mother and I made as much as we did. To let passion rule above all other emotions can be most deceiving."

"You regret meeting . . . knowing Mother?"

"No, I regret allowing it to be less than it should have been. But I'm afraid Drake is just as blind. He is an ambitious man." His eyes held hers and she knew *all* that he was implying. The questions were as clear in her mind now as in his.

Could Drake be romancing her to further his own career? Was she a step up the ladder? He became attracted to her almost at the same moment he'd discovered she was the daughter of a prominent—no, eminent—man in his field. Linking their names together could only help give Drake the credibility and stature a man with his ambition would want.

Sir Richard saw the impact he'd had on her, and was satisfied that he had planted the seeds of caution.

"You're not angry with me?"

"No, of course I'm not. I know you have my best interests at heart. I just cannot believe Drake is such a . . . devious kind of person." She said the words, but her thoughts were deep in reality. Drake had never professed to love her. He had said clearly that he wanted to *make love to her.* There was a monumental difference, yet he had not lied to her, nor had he professed more.

"I didn't say he was. I have worked beside him and I respect him as a colleague. He is excellent at what he does. And I admire his intelligence. If it were to be fated, I would welcome him as a son-in-law. But I am not you. As a woman, with her life . . . and her own career, at stake, you have much to lose. I want you to be very careful, that's all. Don't grow as old as I am with the heaviness of regret in your heart. I . . . I don't ever want you to have those regrets," he added in a soft voice. "Or alone, as your mother was. Can you understand, Caitlyn? Can you understand an old man's heartache and a new father's words of caution? Can you understand that I want to make up for what we've lost?"

Caitlyn could have wept with the pain she sensed he was

feeling. All the lost years weighed so heavily on his heart and he was afraid she was going to end up the same way.

"Of course I understand," she said gently, her eyes glimmering with tears. "I promise I'll be very careful with my life. I'm . . . I'm so very grateful that I found you. How I wish Mother could have been here."

"I, too," he whispered as he patted her hand. "I, too." His voice was husky, as if he couldn't say more without losing control. "Caitlyn . . . if Drake feels . . . well . . . there's plenty of time for decisions. Make your own, without anyone's needs but your own to consider. Be happy, and remember, I'll stand by you no matter what choices you make."

He rose and Caitlyn stood beside him. Then she put her arms about him and rested her head against his chest while he embraced her, rocking her gently in his arms as one would a child.

"I'd best let you get some sleep. Dawn will be here long before we're ready for it. Good night, dear Caitlyn . . . sleep well."

"Good night . . . Father." She said the word for the first time and realized she really meant it.

Caitlyn watched him walk to the door and leave quietly. She stood in the center of the room, deep in her thoughts.

Some part of her ached with a need as old as time, while a subtle thing within her cautioned her that she could be hurt in a way that could mean disaster for her heart, her pride, and even her future.

She realized that the magnetism between her and Drake was too great to ignore and too dangerous to continue. She was suddenly afraid. Not afraid of Drake . . . afraid of herself.

As if he were there, in her room, Caitlyn could feel his presence. The taste of him was still on her lips, and the feel of his hard, lean body could still make her come alive with a sensual expectancy that made her shiver.

If he came to her at this minute, even with the danger foremost in her mind, she wondered if she could deny him.

As if in self-protection, she went to her door and turned the key. Then she turned out her lamp. Crossing the room, she opened the windows to let in the breeze, closing her eyes as it cooled her fevered flesh. Then she went to bed, aware that sleep was going to be difficult.

Sir Richard left Caitlyn's room and walked to his. Once inside, he closed the door and slowly began to undress for bed. He was satisfied that he had made Caitlyn understand just how vulnerable she was. She would be extremely careful before she trusted Drake . . . and her concentration would be on the dig, and not on anything that might impede progress.

Drake Stone was, as Sir Richard had pictured him for Caitlyn, a very dangerous man. He was smart, very smart. But his concentration would be divided, too.

He had seen the look in Drake's eyes when he looked at Caitlyn and he knew that explosive thing was reined in with forced control. Well . . . Caitlyn was duly warned . . . and Drake Stone was in for a surprise.

Drake had impatiently waited until the house was settled for the night. He had to see Caitlyn. Something very vital lay unfinished between the two of them.

He had known what she meant to say in that heated moment before Lettie had come along, and he wanted to hear her speak the words.

He hadn't crossed paths with a woman quite like Caitlyn

before. He hadn't thought of any relationship as permanent until she had come along. Now he found visions dancing before his eyes that surprised him and would probably shock Caitlyn.

Lord, he thought, she burned inside him like a dormant volcano. Jealousy of Ethan had been an ugly, surprising thing he still found hard to believe. He'd never suffered that emotion because of any woman.

But when Caitlyn had denied that anything existed between her and Ethan he had believed her, and her kiss had pushed any other doubt from his mind.

He moved down the long hall quietly and paused before Caitlyn's door. He raised his hand to rap lightly, then paused as he heard the sound of muffled voices. He was thunderstruck.

Obviously Caitlyn had a late visitor and it stunned him to think of who that visitor might be. He rested his hand lightly against the door for a moment, quite unable to believe his own reaction.

Then he turned away and went back to his room.

Eleven

The ride back to the dig was a quiet one . . . too quiet. Caitlyn could feel a heaviness in the air, but Drake said nothing so neither did she. Even Sir Richard seemed to be engrossed in his thoughts.

When they arrived at the dig it was nearing nightfall and Drake went off at once in search of Mendrano. He had told Caitlyn before he left that they would not start back to work until the next morning. She was reasonably sure he wanted to see what had been done and talk to Mendrano alone.

Caitlyn and Sir Richard sat on low stools before her tent and drank tea. But Sir Richard was quite aware that Caitlyn's gaze kept turning in the direction of Drake's departure.

"Drake is an excellent leader," Sir Richard said conversationally. "He doesn't rest until the plans are made and every string is thoroughly tied up."

"If I'm not mistaken," Caitlyn smiled, "in your last book, *Kings and Queens of the Nile,* you stressed the importance of doing just that. I believe," she teased, "that he's trying to follow in some very big footsteps."

"Why, thank you, my dear. I've always tried to be a worker, not an observer."

"He has a very good man in Mendrano."

"I agree. Maybe," his eyes sparkled, "if I go off on another dig I might just try to entice him to work for me."

"You can try. To tell you the truth, I think Mendrano would walk across the desert in his bare feet for Drake. I don't think anyone has enough money or influence to get him to leave."

"I suppose you're right." Sir Richard set his cup aside. "But that's in the future, anyway. If Drake finds all he wants . . . or thinks he's going to find, he'll be tied up for quite some time." Caitlyn remained quiet. "Caitlyn . . . do you plan to stay for the length of the dig?"

Caitlyn considered this, then nodded. "If Drake agrees, I'd like nothing better. I have so much to learn and I . . . I feel so . . . so . . ."

"Attached?"

"Yes." She turned to look at him, "Do you believe in fate?"

"I've always felt that what was meant to be will be."

"Well, I feel like that. It certainly seems fatalistic that my search for you brought me here. It could have happened so many other ways."

"I suppose you're right," he said as he patted her hand affectionately. "I hope fate doesn't disappoint you."

"That's too much to ask . . . I expect I'll be disappointed often in my life. But not now, not here, and not . . ."

"Not with Drake," he added gently. "Well I hope for nothing but the best for you both."

Caitlyn smiled. She realized that her life was very good, and it looked as if it was going to get better every day . . . at least in regard to her work. But as far as Drake was concerned . . . she was unsure.

Drake found Mendrano busy supervising the last details of the air shaft that had been dug into the mound. It was about six feet in width and shored up by heavy timbers cut from nearby trees. They would assure those who worked in the first two layers below some reasonably clean air, and at the same time function as an exhaust for the musty air.

"Mendrano, how are things going?"

"Fine, Senor Drake. The shaft is almost finished. If you would care to go below and work tomorrow you will find the air most satisfactory."

"Good. I think I'll go below for a while and look around."

"You would like me to come along?"

"Yes. By the way, how does the weight on the stone hold that door?"

"It works fine," Mendrano replied with a grin. "As soon as I gathered enough stones to match your weight. You are not exactly a small man like me."

Drake chuckled. "Come on, let's take a look."

"The door has remained open since you left. The weight of the stones must be right, for it has not budged an inch."

"I don't doubt it for a minute," Drake said as he moved down to the small entrance. He climbed through and stood in the small room.

The excitement was still there, he thought as he examined the inner door and the weight of stones in the sack that held it open.

"Well, it's pretty obvious it won't move. With you guarding it, I guess we can go down tomorrow."

"You go alone?"

"No, I'm sure Caitlyn and Sir Richard want to go along, or at least Caitlyn. Sir Richard is still trying to be considerate of my amateur position." Drake glanced at Mendrano, whose face seemed to be struggling not to reflect either disapproval . . . or something deeper.

"You still having a problem with Sir Richard?"

"I am sorry, senor," Mendrano said, but there was no regret in his eyes.

"But you have no real reason to make you feel like this."

"I know," Mendrano said quietly.

"Doesn't change your mind a bit, does it?"

Mendrano lifted his eyes and met Drake's gaze. "No."

"Anyone ever tell you you were stubborn?" Drake grinned.

"Si, senor . . . always."

"What is it, Mendrano?" Drake asked seriously. There was too much trust between them. He had to take Mendrano's attitude and feelings into consideration.

"I don't know. A feeling, something I can't touch with my hands or my words, but can feel in my soul. Something is wrong."

"You have the same feelings about Caitlyn?"

"No . . . I don't. I cannot see how the same blood flows in the two of them."

"But it does."

"As you say," Mendrano replied so complacently that Drake had to laugh.

"To tell you the truth, Mendrano, I'm having a few problems myself but I can't put my finger on anything." He went on to tell about Sir Richard's reaction to the building of the dam. "Now I can't see why that dam should affect him at all, yet I'm certain the news upset him."

"With your permission, I would like to take one of the men and look at the area where the water will be. Maybe there is an answer there."

"We're talking like the man is guilty of something. I don't like all this suspicion, Mendrano. He's done nothing but come to help me. That doesn't show much gratitude on my part. No . . . let it go—there's nothing to it. Let's concentrate on why we're here. We've got enough work to take up all our time without creating problems."

"Si, senor," Mendrano agreed amiably, but Drake wasn't sure he didn't have some ideas of his own.

"Let's go up. We'll start to work first thing in the morning. It's time we see what's down there . . . what's been so carefully guarded all these centuries."

"It almost takes a man's breath away to consider that we will be the first men in there since the ancient kings of my people," Mendrano said thoughtfully.

"By this time tomorrow we'll know what lies down there. You're right. It is kind of awesome." Drake stood up and dusted his hands. "Let's go see if supper's ready."

"I'm sure something will be prepared," Mendrano said, smiling. "You are turning the cook gray with these late meals. He likes to work with very strict time. Before your guests came you were easier to provide for."

Drake cast Mendrano a quick glance, but could read no other meaning to his words. The two men went up into the fresh air and walked back to the camp in silence.

Mendrano seemed to have vanished by the time a very late evening meal was served. Sir Richard, Drake, and Caitlyn shared it with a minimum of polite conversation that focused on questions about the next day's work.

Drake could still feel Caitlyn's presence like a dammed-up force and he found it very difficult to handle. He was stupidly and needlessly jealous and he knew it. And he wanted Caitlyn, which didn't improve his mood.

By the time the meal was ended, Drake insisted both Caitlyn and Sir Richard get some rest.

"At daybreak, I'd like to be leaving camp. We'll be going

in tomorrow and being tired won't help matters for either of you."

"It gives me something to dream about," Caitlyn said happily. "Truthfully, I can't wait to see what's there. For your sake, Drake, I hope it's all you want it to be."

Drake was caught off balance again. Caitlyn seemed like mercury, unable to be captured and held, but with an attraction so magnetic it was impossible not to reach out and try.

"Thanks. I hope so, too."

His gaze followed her as she walked to her tent and disappeared inside—he was totally unaware that Sir Richard was watching him intently.

Sir Richard's voice interrupted Drake's thoughts. "I guess I'll find my bed as well. Good night, Drake."

"Good night, Sir Richard."

Drake watched Sir Richard, all too aware of the strange wariness he had begun to feel. Then he walked to one of the dying campfires around which a group of the men sat, having their last smoke before bedtime. Antonio was among them.

He squatted down close to the fire and looked around. "Antonio, have any of you seen your father in the past hour or so?"

There was a slight stir and the men regarded one another and waited for Antonio to answer. He replied almost at once. "Si, Senor Drake. He has gone to his bed. He was very tired and he knew you wanted to start early tomorrow."

Drake knew he was being lied to, just as he knew there was nothing he could do about it. Mendrano was his own man, and since Drake had no demand on his free time he could not question what Mendrano did with it.

He engaged Antonio and the men in conversation for a while, unaware that Caitlyn stood just within her darkened tent and watched him.

The light from the fire danced across his face, revealing a steady strength. She watched as he stood, stretched, and said something to one of the men, then walked into the darkness.

But he was not going to his tent—she knew exactly where he was going. Even if she had questioned herself about why she followed him she would not have been able to answer.

Her father had warned her, every sense she had had warned her. Still, there was that mystical thing that drew her from her tent. It was a force that was like no other.

Drake found his favorite spot and sat looking out over the valley. Here in the mountains, he wondered at the moon that seemed large enough and close enough to touch. Its light made the area seem washed in gold.

This place always seemed to ease him before, but tonight was different. The moonlight, the diamond-bright stars, the cool breeze all brought Caitlyn vividly to mind. Try as he might, here, alone, he could not lie to himself. He wished she was here . . . he wanted her with an urgency that filled every corner of his being.

He heard her laughter, saw the way she tilted her head when she listened to something that interested her. He remembered the way she made that soft sound deep in her throat when he kissed her and even more vividly he remembered the way she felt in his arms . . . as if she belonged there forever.

A sound behind him made him turn abruptly . . . and suddenly Caitlyn seemed to take form out of the mixture of shadow and light. He wasn't really sure if she were truly here or if his yearning had created her.

* * *

Caitlyn had been right about Drake's destination. Was it her own will or some other force that drew her to him? She seemed suddenly attuned to the phenomenal power of nature surrounding her. It was primeval, and logic and reality had no effect.

She hadn't spoken a word but Drake sensed her presence. He turned, then slowly rose to his feet.

"Caitlyn," he said softly, as if afraid she would disappear. He held out a hand toward her and she put her hand in his.

There were so many things she wanted to say, and so many that he, too, wanted to say. She wanted to tell him of a fear she could not name and he wanted to tell her of the certainties he sensed . . . but they said nothing. It was something so deep and primitive that neither could question it.

He drew her slowly to him, until their bodies barely touched. For a long moment it seemed as if they could not get their fill of looking at each other.

Caitlyn lifted her hands to thread her fingers through his hair, feeling its thick fullness, then gently drew his head down to hers. Their lips met and she pressed close to him, aching to be absorbed by him.

She gasped at the flow of raw pleasure that swept through her as his mouth took hers, smothering all sound and drawing her breath from her body.

She wanted him . . . and he wanted her . . . wanted her with a ferocity that staggered his mind. It was a near-violent passion. Desire had lain dormant for so long—now it burst into bloom, making her feel incredibly strong yet weak at the same time.

He bent slightly, his arms lifting her up against him, and she felt the satisfying pressure of his mouth on hers as he kissed her deeply, drawing from her feelings she had never known before.

She felt her insides grow meltingly warm, as if she could flow around him, enclose him, make him part of her. So many feelings filled her that she did not try to sort them or examine them, but only savored them. His deep and hungry kiss released all the pent-up hungers and exposed the depths of her passion.

For a moment they paused to look at each other, conscious of the matching beat of their hearts.

He reached to work the buttons of her blouse while she feverishly unbuttoned his shirt. When the heat of his hands touched her skin she pressed close, feeling her breasts flatten against the hardness of his chest. She pressed her lips to his throat and tasted the salty, warmth of his skin.

She shivered with expectancy, knowing exactly what she longed for. There was a power in his hard, muscled body and a wild strength in the arms that drew her down to the grass-covered earth.

Again he kissed her, long and deep, and she made a soft sound—half-groan, half-cry—as the kiss drifted from her mouth to her throat and from there to the rigid peak of her breast. The curling heat unleashed itself and produced an ache that started so deep within her the source seemed to be her soul.

He could hear the depth of her sigh, taste the moans on her mouth . . . and heard her plead for the torment to cease. At this moment and in this place she belonged to him and he belonged to her. That was the only certainty.

He felt her shudder as he came into her and her breath caught on his name as she felt him fill her. She was hot and moist and as she wrapped her legs around him it robbed him of all thought but her softness. Like the fury of lightning, the wind of a tornado, and the heat of a desert, the pressure built and then burst in a torrent that swept them away. They could only cling together, wrapped in each other's arms as everything exploded around them.

The world righted itself slowly. Slow breathing eased into soft sighs and contentment. She lay in his arms, close to his side, and they were still—bathed in the nearly miraculous beauty around them.

Drake had never known such power or such humility. For Caitlyn it was the knowledge that they had become one at that moment when they had moved together in rhythmic harmony.

She stirred and leaned on an elbow to look down at him. He smiled and reached to tuck a strand of hair behind her ear.

"You're not sorry?" he questioned gently.

"No," she said and smiled. "You told me once you wanted to make love to me. I never got the chance at the party but I meant to say the same to you. I wanted you to make love to me, Drake . . . and I don't regret a second of it."

"I also said you were an extremely interesting woman, and you are."

"Why? Because I don't hide what I feel? Do men have a monopoly on honest emotion?"

"I think so, in terms of this. I guess they don't expect women to have feelings of passion."

She chuckled. "If you think I'm about to propose to you just to make an honest man out of you, prepare for a disappointment. There was no bargaining as I remember." Her voice became serious, "Drake . . . I don't know . . . I mean, this is a beginning."

"And you don't know where it's destined to go."

"No."

"We talked about love once before, and you said no one fell in love just like that. Maybe you're right, even though

I don't think you are. Don't you think, that we deserve a chance to see where it goes?"

"I suppose we do. I just don't want you to believe that there is . . . some kind of debt . . ."

"We owe each other nothing but a chance. A chance to see if what I *know* I felt is the same thing you're so unsure of. I have a feeling I'm walking way ahead of you, Caitlyn, but I'm willing to wait."

"We have time."

"All the time in the world," he said gently as he turned to her. "And I don't want to rush a minute of it. I want to know you, Caitlyn . . . I want to know what makes you happy or sad . . . what makes you cry or laugh. I want to talk to you and listen to you. I want to know how you think and what you think. I want to share so much with you that I have no idea how I could ever fit it in a lifetime."

"A lifetime," she repeated.

"Does that scare you?"

"A little."

"Why?"

"I had a long talk with my father while we were at Ethan's."

Drake chuckled.

"What's funny?"

"Nothing, really. I just can't picture you seated docilely before a father who's lecturing you about life's pitfalls."

"It wasn't actually like that. He . . . he's been so unhappy, and finding out about Mother's death and me all at one time was a bit of a shock. I guess he feels a little delayed responsibility."

"So he warned you . . . about what?"

Caitlyn laughed softly. "About archaeologists and their dreams, which I quite understand . . . and about finding myself before I found someone else. He just doesn't want me to end up like my mother."

"It wouldn't be that way."

"No?"

"No. You're you, Caitlyn, not your mother. You have your dreams and I have mine. I can't see why they can't come true for both of us. We're lucky—we can share a world we both love and understand." He kissed her lightly. "It has nothing to do with either of your parents, and it's a great deal more than just this." His eyes gleamed with humor. "Of course I, personally, could exist on this for a long, long time."

"It's not bad fare," she laughed and moved against him. His arms tightened as he kissed her. "I suppose we should go back."

"I suppose," he agreed, but he didn't release her and the kisses were growing warmer. "Caitlyn . . . I don't want to make you unhappy or take anything away from you. But you can't let your mother's memory or your father's fears run your life."

"If I planned on doing that I wouldn't be here."

"Well," he said as he feathered soft kisses over her cheeks and pressed his lips gently to the pulse at her throat, "I'm glad you're here. This is a night to forget everything else."

"It is remarkable, isn't it?" she said huskily. "I've never felt anything so . . ."

"So perfect," he finished. "So let's not ask questions now—there's time . . . lots of time."

"I hope it's true . . ." she whispered, almost too softly for him to hear.

He silenced her doubts with a long, deep kiss. For this moment she cast aside everything but the amazingly vital thing that consumed them both.

* * *

It was two hours before they came back to camp. At her tent Drake took her in his arms again and kissed her good night.

"Tomorrow should be an exciting day," she said.

"Tonight wasn't half bad, either," he replied with a smile. "Caitlyn . . . think about us. I want you to know you're not making a mistake. We have a long way to go . . . but I'd like to make it together."

"I will," she smiled up at him, "I don't think my father will be reaching for his shotgun yet."

"He doesn't strike me as the type."

"Oh, you mean my honor wouldn't be avenged?" She pretended dismay.

"Oh, yes. But he's more the type to pull the rug out from under me, then squash me like a bug."

"He's really a very sweet man. But if he frightens you . . ." she began teasingly.

"Caitlyn," Drake chuckled, "the worst terror in the world couldn't keep me away from you. You're the only one who could do that, and even you would have one hell of a fight on your hands."

"Seriously, Drake, maybe we should keep . . . us a secret until you've gotten your grant. After that," she shrugged, "we would have at least four or five years here to finish the job. There would be no problems."

"I have a hunch keeping my feelings from showing would be pretty difficult. He'll be able to read my face every time I look at you."

"Oh, Drake, you know how devoted he is. The work has him entranced. He has his mind on a lot of other things, too."

"What about his little warning at Ethan's?"

"He was away from the dig and concentrating on me. Up here . . . well, he'll get engrossed and forget to be so fatherly."

"Speaking of Ethan . . ." Drake began.

"What?"

"If I seemed a bit obnoxious it was because you had me tied up in knots. I never felt that way before and I didn't handle it well."

"How flattering. Ethan and I talked . . . as friends. It never went beyond that."

"Don't get me wrong, Ethan *is* a good friend. He's the kind to play fair . . . but this isn't a game . . . and I have too much at stake."

"I'm glad you feel that way."

"Are you?"

"Yes, I am. I only suggested we keep our secret for the good of our work."

"I guess you're right. But it's asking a lot."

"Oh?"

"You don't have any idea how hard it is not to reach out and touch you. There are times . . . like that day down in that room, when I had to fight harder than you'll believe. It's going to be pure hell. When you laugh I want to take your hand. When you're all dusty and concentrating, and those eyes of yours are far away, I want to kiss you so badly it hurts. This isn't going to be easy."

"Then . . . we'll have to find time to be together because . . . I'm not sure it's going to be so easy for me either."

"That's good news."

"Drake . . . we'll take one day at a time. You're right, we both have a great deal at stake here. I'm sure everything that happens in the next few weeks will have more effect

on our lives than we can imagine. We'll find time for us . . .
we have to. Every day, every night is precious. Let's grab
every moment . . ."

He had been drawing her tighter to him as she spoke and
now he finished her sentence with a deep kiss. When it
ended she could see the silvery fire in his eyes.

"If I don't let you go now, I won't be able to let you go
at all."

"Then, I'd best say good night." He heard her soft laugh
as she put her arms about his neck, pressed herself against
him, and kissed him feverishly until his world began to tip
precariously. Then suddenly she was gone and he had to
inhale deeply to regain enough control to walk to his
tent . . . a very empty tent.

Mendrano had not gone to his house, although he had
made it appear so. He had left the camp, circled around,
and found a place where he could watch.

With satisfaction he saw Caitlyn follow Drake from the
camp. There was no doubt in his mind about the attraction
between these two and as far as he was concerned Drake
deserved all the happiness he could find.

He liked Caitlyn . . . felt her to be the perfect companion
for a man like Drake, who could become obsessed with his
work and forget there were other things in life. Caitlyn
could make him smile, relax, and enjoy himself.

Again he pondered the fact that as much as he liked
Caitlyn . . . and trusted her . . . he disliked and distrusted
her father. He felt there was too much secretiveness about
him. There were shadowy places in the man, and it made
Mendrano curious. How could such a father have such a
daughter?

He knew Drake might be upset so he felt it wise not to inform him of how close a watch he kept on Sir Richard Macdonald.

It was a long, quiet time, with no stir in the camp at all, and Mendrano was growing sleepy. He argued with himself—maybe Drake was right and his suspicions were groundless; maybe it was just the differences between him and Sir Richard that made Mendrano feel the way he did.

Another half-hour, he promised himself, another half-hour and he would give up this idea and go to bed.

He scooted into a more comfortable position, slowly beginning to resign himself . . . reluctantly . . . to the fact that he might be wrong, and had wasted half the night finding it out.

A half-hour later he was ready to surrender to much-needed sleep, when the almost imperceptible movement of Sir Richard's tent flap drew his attention. It took concentration to discern the movement amid the shadows, but slowly he saw a dark form leave the tent and cross the area to the place where the jungle bordered the clearing.

The man was coming in Mendrano's direction, following the almost nonexistent path. He would have to pass within a few feet of Mendrano, who remained breathlessly still.

Once Sir Richard was several yards past him, Mendrano rose and followed stealthily. It was difficult and if Mendrano had not been alert and adept at jungle travel he would have lost track.

He was following as silently as he could and almost burst upon him before he realized the man had stopped.

It was a small clearing, and only now, in the moonlight, did Mendrano see Sir Richard's face. He was standing absolutely still in the center of the clearing, and Mendrano knew he was waiting for something.

He didn't have long to wait before he saw two men break from the opposite side of the jungle and join Sir Richard. He would have given anything to be able to hear what they were saying, but it would have to be enough for now that he recognized the two men. They were two of the ones who had deserted the camp earlier.

The three stood in deep, animated conversation. Then one of the men withdrew something from inside his shirt and handed it to Sir Richard. It surprised him that Sir Richard immediately put it inside his jacket, as if he didn't want to take the time to look at it there.

The conversation continued, with gestures that told Mendrano Sir Richard was enforcing a point. The other two seemed to be arguing, but it was soon evident that Sir Richard dominated.

After a while he clapped one of the men on the shoulder and spoke to him swiftly. The man nodded . . . paused . . . nodded again. Then, as silently as they had come, the two men vanished into the jungle.

Sir Richard remained standing in the center of the clearing as if he were deep in thought. After a few minutes he withdrew the object from his jacket and stood looking down at it. Again, Mendrano would have given a great deal to see what it was.

The object returned to his pocket, Sir Richard turned and walked back toward the camp. Mendrano did not have to follow him now, but could return at his leisure.

Tomorrow, when Sir Richard was involved in the exploration of the tomb, Mendrano planned on doing some exploration himself. He would search Sir Richard's tent until the mysterious object was revealed.

When he arrived at his house it was quiet and dark, and

he was grateful. Now was not the time for explorations. He found his bed, and went to sleep immediately.

Drake spent a restless and surprisingly uncomfortable night. He could not shake the feeling that something portentous was about to happen. Was it the beginning of a new discovery? Was that why the heavy feeling hung over him and prevented sleep from coming?

It was Caitlyn . . . because he felt a certain kind of security there. He knew how he felt, and he was sure after tonight of how she felt. Of course, they had a lot to work out, and he was more than willing to give it his best effort.

He thought about her idea that they should keep their relationship a secret from her father for a while. If a questions presented itself subliminally he chose to ignore it. Caitlyn was right. He needed her father's unbiased opinion.

He pushed away all negative ideas and thought about Caitlyn and the kind of future they could share. They had so much in common—a love for the kind of work they did, and a chance to do that work together. They spoke the same language physically and mentally. He allowed the comfort of this to soothe him to sleep.

For Caitlyn the night was just as full of questions. She had gone to Drake, he had not come to her, and there was no denying the fact that she had enjoyed being with him. She had walked into it willingly, with her eyes wide open.

She had not made promises and neither had he. She told herself she didn't need promises, that having their freedom was the best way to hold them together.

But she, too, felt the vague unrest, the kind of feeling one got in the silence before a storm.

She recalled her father's words and the unrest grew. It confused her and she rose from her bed. Silently she left her tent and made her way to her father's.

She stood inside until her eyes became used to the dark. It was only then that she realized that her father was not in his bed.

Twelve

No one seemed to have the time or the desire for breakfast the next morning. Mendrano already had the men moving toward the tomb, while Drake, Caitlyn, and Sir Richard gathered what personal tools they felt they needed. The three of them walked together, caught in their own thoughts.

Drake was running over plans of exactly how far he would go and who else was going. Sir Richard had been very observant and considerate, helping only when needed, and Drake was grateful.

"Drake?" Caitlyn said, breaking into Drake's thoughts.

"What?"

"You're bringing several lanterns. Is there a reason for that?"

"Sure. I don't know what we'll find or how deep we're going today, so I want lanterns placed all along our way. I want plenty of light. This deep darkness can make a person claustrophobic or worse. I've seen men panic underground when the light goes. I've been pretty close a few times myself."

"I see."

"Besides, we might run across anything—caved-in walls, broken floors, or a fabulous discovery. And I don't want to find anything we can't handle because there's not enough light."

"I certainly hope it's a fabulous discovery and nothing more."

"Tension does get to you, doesn't it?"

"I keep imagining all the things that could be there . . . things I hope are there."

"I've come prepared to research whatever you may find in the room below," Sir Richard said. "If you don't mind, I'll set myself up in the entrance room and make ready to work on what you send up."

"That's a good idea. I'll look it over first, then if there are things to be sent up I'll take a couple of men down and they can bring them to you."

Mendrano, who had been listening as he walked, was more than satisfied. With Sir Richard below ground and busy, he might have just a short time to slip away.

At the site, Drake examined the air shafts carefully.

"You did a real good job, Mendrano. We shouldn't have a problem with air at least for the one level below." Drake inhaled deeply. "Well, let's get to it."

Going first, Drake moved slowly with Caitlyn following him, Sir Richard behind her, and Mendrano bringing up the rear. In the small entrance room Drake again paused to examine the doorway and the weights that held it open.

"This has shown no sign of moving so we ought to be fairly safe. Each of us will carry two lanterns," he said to Caitlyn. "I'll leave one at the top of the stairs and one at the bottom. We'll need the other two to work with."

"Don't worry," Sir Richard said, "I'll keep a very close eye on that door and those weights. One little tremor and I'll shout."

"Okay," Drake said, turning to Caitlyn. "Ready?"

"Whenever you are," she replied firmly, although she was

a bit pale. Drake could see the hands holding the lanterns tremble a bit, but she had the light of excitement in her eyes.

"Then let's go," Drake shouted, leading the way to the small doorway. He reached in and set one lantern deep inside on the top step. Then he maneuvered his large frame carefully through the door and in minutes he stood on the top step.

He held the second lantern aloft but the light did not extend far and the steps disappeared into black oblivion. The stairway itself was only three feet wide. As Caitlyn handed the third lantern in, he set it aside, took her hand, and soon she was standing beside him.

"It's not exactly roomy," Drake said. "I'll go first—you stay close behind and watch for crumbling steps."

A lantern on the top step illuminated the small open doorway. Holding his lantern aloft, Drake moved down slowly, one step at a time, and Caitlyn followed.

"I wonder just how far down it is," Caitlyn asked.

"No way to tell," Drake replied. "I hate to count," he chuckled, "if it's thirteen again I might begin to wonder."

One step at a time, carefully, Drake picked his way down. Subconsciously, as Caitlyn had done as well, he had counted. Thirteen . . . and the floor leveled before them. Neither mentioned it.

"Stand still," he told Caitlyn as he took one of the lanterns from her and set it on the last step. Then he lifted the third lantern as high as he could and moved forward.

The room was several feet longer and wider than the one above and at first seemed empty . . . until the light reached the farthest corner. Drake and Caitlyn stood in heart-pounding wonder as they gazed at several large, rather squat-looking pottery jars in a cluster against the wall, as if they had been forgotten there.

They looked at each other in hopeful surprise. Then Caitlyn started toward the jugs, but Drake's hand on her arm stopped her.

"What?" she said.

"Just because man hasn't been in here for centuries doesn't mean something else hasn't. You have to be careful."

The thought of some poisonous crawling or slithering thing made Caitlyn shiver. They both approached cautiously and Drake drew his pistol.

When they came within inches of the first one he handed the lantern to Caitlyn, then reached out tentatively to grasp the top of one of the jars and carefully tip it on its side. When he did some of the contents spilled out, causing them both to jump. Caitlyn gasped, for even in its corroded state, gold was easily recognized.

The metal had been formed into a multitude of different objects they soon recognized. Sea birds, crayfish, land snails, iguanas, and spiders. Some, nearly eight inches wide and five inches high, were made of hammered gold and silver.

"Well, one thing's almost a certainty," Drake said.

"What?"

"Someone very important has to be buried here."

"Oh," Caitlyn breathed softly, the thrill of it filling her. She reached down and picked up one of the ornaments. Its weight told her it was not plated with gold, but completely solid. It was one of a pair of ear ornaments with running figures made of precious stones and shell. "They're more exquisite than most things you could buy today . . . and certainly more valuable than anything I could afford."

"Well, before we check all this out we'd better examine the rest of the room. I have a feeling there are a lot of levels below us. If this has been untouched . . . Lord, I can only imagine what could be right under us."

The rest of the room seemed to be empty, but what they did find was the steps that continued down.

"You game to go down another level?" Drake asked. "You can't expect the air to be very good, but I hope it's breathable."

"I'm right behind you."

"We only have two lanterns. We'll leave one a couple of steps down and take the other with us."

At the top of the steps Drake took the lantern and when he had descended a step or two he set it close to the wall. To Caitlyn's relief he reached for her hand in a firm, comforting grip. Together they moved down the stairs slowly. Neither wanted to count the steps, but it seemed almost impossible not to . . . thirteen.

In the room above Mendrano and Sir Richard waited with the other two workmen. Their purpose, once Drake and Caitlyn had come up, would be to help carry whatever was found.

With pilfering so easy, none of the workmen would carrying anything up until Mendrano had catalogued each piece.

Mendrano squatted on his heels near a wall and watched Sir Richard, who had brought a portable camp chair. He was deeply engrossed in a small notebook that Mendrano would have given anything to read.

A heavy silence seemed to echo among the ghosts that lingered there. Mendrano had no idea that Sir Richard was well aware of his close scrutiny. He was a thorn in Sir Richard's side, and his continual dark eyed gaze was making him quite sure that for some reason, Mendrano did not like or trust him.

He was tempted to ask him, but he didn't want any overt breach between them. Mendrano carried too much weight with Drake, and the last thing Sir Richard wanted was Mendrano saying anything to Drake that could strain their relationship.

But his irritation was growing and he felt it necessary to relieve the situation, at least temporarily.

"Mendrano?"

"Si, senor?"

"I wonder if you could do me a favor."

"If I can, of course."

"Drake has a book in his tent . . . an archaeological research book. It's larger than the rest of his books, and it has a dark blue binding. Could you fetch it and that small table outside my tent? It might be wise to do some work right here . . . as Drake and Caitlyn bring things up."

Mendrano didn't want to appear relieved that he had found a way to move without being questioned, so he rose slowly and walked to the exit. But once outside he loped toward Drake's tent. He found the book at once, then quickly covered the distance to Sir Richard's.

He set the book on the cot and began a quick search, being very careful not to disturb anything.

Not sure where to look but reasonably sure that whatever it was would be well hidden, Mendrano began to think of unlikely places.

But despite every effort there were no signs of anything. He was irritated and frustrated. There was no way to prove what he had seen and he knew Drake would never listen to mere suspicion.

He picked up the book and the table and returned to the dig site.

When he gave the book to Sir Richard their eyes met for a moment and Mendrano wondered if he saw amusement there. Had Sir Richard expected to have his tent searched? For a moment he imagined that Sir Richard knew about his suspicions . . . and was laughing at him.

"They've been down there over an hour, Mendrano," Sir Richard said. "I'm not sure it's wise for them to make their excursions so lengthy at first. The air has not had time to circulate."

"Senor Drake will know when the time is too long. He won't endanger his life . . . or Caitlyn's either. They will most likely be up soon."

"I suppose you're right. After all, you know Drake much better than I."

"Yes . . . I have known him a long while. He is not a man to ignore danger . . . of any kind. This dig is so important to him that I'm sure he's always aware of anything that can cause a problem."

"You do not approve of my presence here, do you, Mendrano?"

Mendrano shrugged, but refused to back down from a man he mistrusted. "It is not up to me to approve or disapprove. I work for Drake as all the other men do. I do not question his choices."

"But you don't think I need to be here?"

"No, Senor Macdonald, I don't. Senor Drake . . . he is very good at what he has chosen for his work. I believe he will prove his idea and discover a great find . . . with or without you."

"But he sent for me. So why do we not try to accept one another . . . for his sake? I'm sure you don't want him to have to make choices where his career is concerned. It would not be fair to ask him to do that, would it? If I am not here," he shrugged, "then I cannot claim that his find is so valuable. In fact . . . I might have to claim otherwise. Such a thing could ruin a young man in Drake's position. Living here, you don't quite understand how the civilized world is. They like the . . . ah . . . tried and true. They would hesitate to take what Drake said seriously. He would just be a lucky man who found a tomb. The museum would make out well. But Drake's dream . . . his theory would never get the attention it deserved."

Mendrano clenched his teeth. With a smile and a soft word he was being threatened and he recognized the power in the threat. Sir Richard was taking advantage of Mendrano and Drake's friendship, knowing Mendrano would never stand in the way of Drake's success.

"I understand your position . . . and mine."

"Good. Then we need not fight each other."

"No, of course not," Mendrano agreed, promising himself he would be much more careful in the future, guarding every move and every facial expression. It had also just occurred to him that Sir Richard had not trusted anyone enough to leave the object in the tent. Had he carried it with him in his wooden tool case? Was that why he had sent Mendrano back?

"Maybe," Mendrano said, "it would be better if I went below and checked on them."

"Good idea. They may be so caught up in the excitement that they've forgotten how long they've been working."

Mendrano nodded. He crossed the room to Antonio, who had been waiting with them. He knelt before him and spoke swiftly in their language, telling him where he was going and cautioning him not to leave the room under any circumstances.

"Even," he finished, "on the orders of this man. He does not run this dig. You are to stay here and watch that door. Do you understand?"

Antonio nodded and Mendrano rose and walked to the small door. Without looking at Sir Richard again, he knelt and went inside.

Drake and Caitlyn stood in a huge chamber. They could hardly determine its size because the single lantern they had did not throw light far enough. With Caitlyn's hand still in his, Drake began to move forward cautiously. As he moved he raised the lantern as high as possible and he and Caitlyn both paused abruptly. They could see the top of the walls and a section of the ceiling. Along the wall, at the height of a man, were several stone ledges spaced only a few feet apart. Each was a part of the wall itself and extended out about twelve to fifteen inches. Objects that rested on them were too difficult to make out.

"I wonder if they run the whole length of the room?" Caitlyn said.

"There's only one way to find out." Drake and Caitlyn moved forward, hand in hand, until they found the farthest wall. Then they turned and started back. They had their answer when they reached the opposite wall. The small stone ledges did run the length of the room . . . and there were thirteen of them.

"Can you see what's on top of any of them?" Caitlyn asked.

"It's hard to see the top. I can make out something, but they're only dark shapes. If I just had something to stand on."

"We can bring something down later, I guess."

"Yes, I'll have a scaffold built. We need to check and see if the opposite wall has the same shelves. Have you noticed the floor?"

Caitlyn hadn't, but now she paused to look down. The floor seemed highly polished, as if it had been cared for only the day before, and was made up of small squares forming an intricate pattern they would not be able to identify until there was enough light to see the entire room. She knelt and brushed her hand across it. It was smooth and cool to the touch. "It's beautiful."

"Yes, look at the colors. Bright red . . . gold . . . green, mixed with black. I'd bet my life the full mosaic will picture a warrior in full regalia."

"You sound like you've seen it before."

"No, but I've seen this kind of design on Moche art. If I'm right, this might help date the entire tomb. I'll have to search through all my books tonight, but I think there's a picture of just such a warrior."

"Then maybe this tomb, if it is a tomb, is dedicated to a particular warrior."

"I want to see what's on those shelves and at the same time get a good look at this floor." He raised the lantern as far as he could, and from her kneeling position Caitlyn looked up at him. She was caught by the magic of their surroundings. To Caitlyn, Drake looked as if he, too, were a descendant of the once-mighty warriors who ruled the valley.

"Drake," she said softly as she stood up beside him. "What do you really believe we'll find below?"

"I have a lot of theories . . . one of which almost scares me. But I don't want to hope because I'm afraid it won't happen. We have a lot of work ahead of us, you and I. If we're right, this could be the find of the century."

"I'm so happy for you."

"For me?"

"Yes, it's a great discovery."

"It could very well be *our* discovery, Caitlyn," he said softly.

In the pale glow of the lantern, surrounded by the intense black of the darkness, it was suddenly as if they were alone in the world.

He bent to kiss her. They didn't touch . . . just their lips and the moment was brief . . . but almost overpowering. Both could feel the current that leapt between them.

"Senor Drake!" Mendrano's voice came from the top of the stairs.

Drake cursed softly and Caitlyn smothered a giggle.

"Senor Drake!" Mendrano called again.

"I hear you, Mendrano. Stay there, we'll be right up."

Again Drake took Caitlyn's hand and they moved slowly back across the room to the bottom of the steps. Caitlyn started up, preceding Drake.

"I did not know you were going down to another level," Mendrano said. "For a minute I thought the floor had opened and swallowed you."

"We were getting a little carried away. This room has some material we'll need to bring up this afternoon. There are some large jars on the level above, but they're too heavy because they're full. Caitlyn and I will take some of the artifacts out, then you'll need several men to carry them up."

"Si, I will take care of it."

"Set up a special tent, Mendrano, with round-the-clock guards. This is too important to take any chances. There's a fortune in those jars, not to mention the jars themselves. And keep a close watch during the moving. This should keep Sir Richard busy for the next couple of weeks. Later

Caitlyn and I have to arrange for more lighting. I don't know how many more levels there are, but if they're as good as this we've had miraculous luck."

"I will be very careful. Sir Richard waits impatiently for word."

"Then let's go tell him. Caitlyn, do you still have that piece of jewelry?"

"Yes, it's in my pocket."

"Give it to your father to catalogue and identify. That ought to keep his mind spinning for a while."

They joined Sir Richard in the upper room and he was, as Drake had said, extremely excited by the exquisite jewelry.

"It's time to take a break," Drake said. "Let's eat a light lunch and then get back to business."

"Just what are the plans for this afternoon?" Sir Richard asked.

"I thought you could supervise the bringing up of the jars."

"Do you want them carried back to camp?"

"That would be advisable. Mendrano will set up a tent where we can put them, and he'll arrange for the guards. That way you can categorize at your leisure."

"And you and Caitlyn?"

"We're going to see just how deep this tomb goes—and what other treasures are down there." Drake went on to tell him about the shelves and floor of the room they'd just found. "I have a strong hunch about the floor and I intend to look into it when the day's over, just as I intend to find out what's on those shelves. We're going down as far as we can."

"You're really intense," Sir Richard laughed.

"You're probably right. But you weren't down there. It's the most fascinating . . . awe-inspiring thing I've ever seen.

And to know there could be so much more . . . well, actually it's hard to stop."

"He's right," Caitlyn agreed. "I'm afraid I could stay there until someone dragged me out, which is pretty much what Drake did."

Drake called out to Mendrano, who was in conversation with the other men. He turned at his name and then started toward Drake. "Tell the men to wait here and keep a close guard. I'll see that food is sent over," Drake said.

"Why do I not just go and bring the midday food here?" Mendrano suggested. "That way you will not have to make the trip back and forth."

"Good idea," Drake said, laughing. "Now why didn't I think of that?"

"While you're gone they can start bringing up whatever's inside those jars so we can start looking it over," Sir Richard suggested.

"I'd like that," Caitlyn said. "Especially the mate to that earring. They must be worth a fortune."

"Not to mention possible matching pieces," Drake grinned. "You can be an empress for an hour or so."

"Then I shall be back in a short time," Mendrano said.

"Oh, Mendrano," Caitlyn said, touching his arm, "would you go in my tent and bring the box at the foot of my bed? I have some cleaning material there—we might be able to restore a smaller piece or two. It's a small wooden box, plain and kind of weatherbeaten," she went on.

Mendrano left, leaving Drake, Sir Richard, and Caitlyn to relax for a while. They sat together on an outcropping of rock that afforded an excellent view of the entire valley.

"It's so very beautiful here," Caitlyn murmured as she inhaled the cool air with obvious pleasure.

"I can just imagine how this valley was when it was bustling with life," Drake said.

"It's amazing that a civilization ends so abruptly—somewhat like the disappearance of the dinosaurs," Sir Richard added.

Drake regarded Sir Richard with a puzzled frown. This man, above all others, should know the theory about what happened to the Moche. Drake case a quick glance at Caitlyn who was watching her father with admiration. Obviously she had not *yet* digested what he had said. Maybe I'm picking at shadows, Drake thought. After all, a man of Sir Richard's age and experience gave him the right to be forgetful occasionally.

"If you remember, the controversy was ended when Reinhold came up with his theory, which is now generally accepted. He thought natural cataclysms struck the country periodically. First a calamitous earthquake that buckled the land, then a sporadic weather disruption known as El Nino unleashed torrential rains. Finally there was a decade-long drought that shriveled the harvests. Somewhere between A.D. 650 or 700, another massive earthquake created more disaster, then the fury of El Nino struck again and the combined tragedies destroyed the buildings. The loss must have been catastrophic. By that time, the Moche seemed to have disappeared. It was the end of a golden era."

"A terrible tragedy," Caitlyn said softly. "How sad . . . how devastating it must have been."

"I wouldn't want to have any part of an earthquake in these mountains," Sir Richard said firmly.

"That's one of the reasons I'd like to bring the tomb and all its glory to light. It would be a magnificent epitaph for a very remarkable people who met a fate they didn't deserve."

"That's a noble idea," Sir Richard said, "and I concur heartily."

"Drake . . . do you think there are other important sites in this valley?" Caitlyn questioned.

"Indeed I do. A civilization the size of this one would leave behind more than one tomb. There have to be city walls, houses, well and cisterns . . . and countless other signs of their presence."

"And you'll go on working here until you find the entire city?" she asked.

"That's too uncertain even to imagine. I hope to. It depends on more than me. If it were just me I'd give an unqualified yes."

"You'd like to stay year round?"

"At least part of the year."

"Isn't one find like this enough to make you a rather . . . famous archaeologist? I mean, you could most likely name your own price at the finest university. You could teach . . . write a book, and be quite comfortable."

"My future can't be measured in physical or monetary comfort," Drake replied. "Sir Richard . . . I'm sure you understand what I mean. After all, it's only been the past few years that you've agreed to teach. And I believe your first book came off the press around the same time."

Sir Richard was about to answer when Mendrano hailed them. He was accompanied by five men, all burdened with bundles.

The three rose to join them and partake of the meal Mendrano and the others prepared.

Mendrano gave Caitlyn the small case she'd requested. She sat it between her and Sir Richard, where it remained. Mendrano tried to keep his eye on it, but there were too many things to be done. It was out of his sight too often for him to be sure who opened it first. When he caught sight of it again, it was already open and Caitlyn was preparing the equipment so her father would have as little trouble as possible cleaning what was brought to him.

It took Drake only minutes to realize Mendrano was deep in thought, that something was really bothering him. But the preparations for the care and storage of the artifacts took a great deal of his time.

He looked up from his work once to see Caitlyn and her father some distance away in animated conversation while they worked.

He smiled as he wondered if Sir Richard was foolish enough to try to convince Caitlyn not to go back down. He knew her too well by now, and how much she enjoyed her work. Sir Richard would have little luck if he tried to talk her out of it. He returned his attention to his work and ignored the conclusion of the discussion.

Mendrano, too, watched the couple, a worried frown knitting his brow.

Once they had started the seven workers on a rhythmic pattern designed to remove the jugs and their contents, Drake and Caitlyn started down again.

This time they carried several lanterns, hoping to illuminate the entire room.

At Drake's orders, Mendrano had brought enough material back with him for several men to whip together a temporary form of scaffolding. Once it was carried down, Drake and Caitlyn would have to wait a short time for it to be assembled. As Drake walked past Mendrano he could see his attention was focused on Caitlyn and that surprised him.

"Mendrano?" he said quietly.

"Senor?"

"Something wrong?"

"I do not know."

"I don't understand."

"I would prefer, Senor Drake . . . if we could talk some things over . . . later, when we are alone."

"Mendrano, this mysterious business is getting out of hand. If you have something important to say that affects this dig, then tell me now."

Caitlyn had turned to look at Mendrano and Drake, which seemed to upset Mendrano even more.

"Senor Drake . . . can we move far enough away that we can speak privately?"

"Come . . . we'll walk over there."

Mendrano followed Drake a short distance from the dig site. In a few moments they were sheltered by the thick jungle—only then did Drake turn to Mendrano.

"All right. From the look on your face, this must be very important. Suppose you tell me just what could have upset you so much more in the past couple of hours than you were before?"

"This troubles my mind and makes me very uncomfortable. I do not want things to be as I feel they may be."

"Mendrano, I don't have any idea what you're talking about."

"You remember that I told you Sir Richard was leaving his tent at night and at times when you were not in camp?"

"Yes, but what . . ."

"Please, just hear me out. The other night I decided to watch carefully. It was very late when he left his tent. I followed him and watched him meet two men. I recognized them as two who had deserted us when we first came. I could not get close enough to see what it was they gave him. But I had the feeling it was one of the green stones."

"An emerald?" Drake said sharply. "How do you know?"

"I *don't,* Senor Drake, but I felt it was. I followed Sir Richard back to camp. Then I waited for the first opportunity to present itself for me to find out for certain."

"And?"

"I went back to the camp and searched his tent carefully, but I could find nothing."

"That should convince you we're jumping to conclusions. There could be a logical reason for what he's done."

"No . . . but there is a possible reason I could find nothing."

"What?"

"He could have given it to someone else," Mendrano said quietly.

"Someone else? But there's no one . . ." Drake paused. There was someone . . . someone very close to Sir Richard. "I don't believe it."

"I didn't want to, either. Not until I went back to camp today. I was asked to bring a box to her."

"The box with her equipment."

"Yes," Mendrano replied. "I looked inside. The small emerald was there. I left it there, thinking I could watch. But in the confusion it was opened . . . and I didn't see who opened it. I only know there was no mention of it, no surprise shown."

Drake didn't want to believe it . . . but Mendrano had never lied to him. The question was . . . who opened the box? If what Mendrano thought was true . . . if Sir Richard was really interested in emeralds . . . if he was not exactly what he claimed to be, then what did that make Caitlyn? After all, he had only their word that they had never seen each other before. Or could it be that Sir Richard, feeling guilty about the long separation, had a plan that was his alone? The worst thought of all struck him: was she really Sir Richard's daughter?

He was confused, and worse, he felt like a fool. Was Caitlyn involved in some plan to make a fortune in emeralds? If so, then he was only in her way, a tool, a means to an end.

Was anything she said real? Was what happened between them a way to keep him off-guard while she worked out whatever plans she had . . . or *they* had?

The questions, the doubts, and the pain the small green stone had caused was reflected in his expression only for moments. Then his face became grim and he slid the stone into his pocket.

"Say nothing, Mendrano. We'll see what happens when they find out the stone is gone. Maybe two can play the game."

Mendrano nodded and watched Drake walk away. Somehow he felt as if he had done something wrong. Something that could, in the end, cause more harm than good.

Thirteen

Ethan dismounted at the dock and welcomed the man who was disembarking, smiling and extending his hand. "Marc Livingston! Welcome to Fountainhurst."

"Thank you. I wasn't sure what to expect, but this," he gestured about him, "is remarkable. I cannot see why you need an engineer. I have a feeling you could have built your dam yourself."

Marc Livingston was one of the finest engineers in the field and that was exactly what Ethan wanted.

He was tall and powerfully built, the breadth of his shoulders and the muscles of his arms awesome. His hair was so blond it was nearly white and his eyes were crystalline blue. His craggy face was that of an ancient Viking king, with a square, rugged jaw and broad forehead.

"I'm afraid I couldn't do anything of the sort. If there's anything I know, it's when I don't know enough. Besides, I need most of my men for the harvest so they wouldn't be much use to you anyway. They're farmers, not builders."

"I've looked over the plans you submitted to the governor. He supports your idea enthusiastically. In fact, he seems to think you're a very positive force here. I don't think I've heard the old boy say anything so complimentary about many other white men."

"I'm grateful for his support. Come in, have a cold drink.

I'll introduce you to my other houseguests. Then I'll show you the model of the dam I have in mind."

After Ethan had acquainted Marc with Lettie, Bill, and George, the men went directly to Ethan's study. He ordered drinks, then the three watched in anticipation while Marc examined the scale model of Ethan's dam.

As Marc accepted his drink he said, "It's well done, very well done. I see no flaws."

"I'm sure you're being generous," Ethan replied, smiling. "But after dinner I'll show you the blueprints and the specifications. Then you'll be able to pinpoint the flaws I'm sure must be there."

"This is quite an expensive project," George said.

"It's worth it to me. Crop control alone will repay me over a period of five years or so."

"Well, you might be interested to know that the governor has asked me to tell you that the government will absorb half the cost. After all, it's not just for you, but will benefit every man, woman, and child along the river," Marc added.

"That's a piece of good news. I'd begun to tighten my belt."

"I'm looking forward to going up to the site."

"I think I've chosen a pretty good place. The lake it will form won't restrict anything—the farms, Bogota, the dig, all of them will be out of reach."

"The dig?" Marc raised a curious eyebrow.

"The governor didn't tell you?" Ethan asked.

"No . . . what is it?"

Ethan went on to explain about Drake and his project. "I talked it over with him a long time ago and he's agreeable. The water will come within eight or nine miles of his place, but Drake says it won't be a problem."

"Then it seems everything is ready to go."

"We can't do anything today, but we can start out in the morning, get the lay of the land, and be back by nightfall. The jungle is no place to be alone. When we go out to work it'll be en masse."

"Once we clear some of the area, the danger won't be so bad. I have plenty of men and we're pretty well armed."

"You'll have to be, and you'll have to keep constant watch. Some of the animals can be quick and mean."

"We can handle it."

"Well, since that's settled, what do you say to a guided tour of my little empire?"

"My pleasure. I'm looking forward to it."

"While you take Mr. Livingston on a tour," George said, "Bill and I'll partake of a libation and wait for your return."

They took a quick tour of the house. Marc was respectfully awed, but the ride around Ethan's land left him totally amazed. "You said *empire* facetiously, but you damn well have one here. It must have taken a lot of work."

"It was a labor of love—I'm pretty proud of it. Now we go back to the house. You're in for a culinary treat."

"All this and a good cook, too. Ethan . . . you must have lived right."

"No . . . I worked hard," Ethan replied, laughing. "At first it was fifteen to twenty hours a day. After a couple of years I got it down to ten. It's only been the last year that I've worked a nice, comfortable eight-hour day . . . seven days a week."

Marc was shaking his head and laughing as they returned to the house for dinner.

The work on the dam began slowly, with careful measurements and even more careful planning. It was only a week later that the clearing of the jungle covering the dam area was begun.

Marc had brought at least two dozen skilled workers, some of whom guarded the perimeter of the site carefully and all of whom carried rifles, pistols, and ammunition.

Ethan spent a great deal of time moving from his plantation to the dam site, his excitement and pleasure obvious. There was a rapport among Marc's men that made the work progress smoothly. The relaxed and fun-filled atmosphere made work easy and it looked as if the project would go smoothly. That was why the accident came as such a shock to everyone.

When they found the body at the edge of the jungle, every man in the entire group was totally stunned.

"Snake bite!" one said.

"What kind of snake?" another asked. The dead man had been well liked and each of them regretted not being able to help.

"I'd say a coral snake."

"Like hell," another man broke in.

"You don't think it was a coral snake?" Marc questioned.

"Look," the disbeliever said, "coral snakes are real poisonous . . . but they hate people. They're secretive and unaggressive. Carl would have had to go after it to get bitten and Carl was an old hand; he knew better than that. I ain't never heard of a man being bitten by a coral unless he hunted it up and tried to catch it."

"I know what it was, Joe," Ethan said softly.

"What?"

"A fer-de-lance. At least, that's what they were called in Martinque . . . here they're called Jararaca. Very aggressive . . . very deadly." The men were quiet as Ethan stopped speaking. "I'll see to the arrangements," he finished.

Because of the death of a co-worker and friend, none of the men seemed able to concentrate on work. Ethan saw that the body was taken back to the house and sent for the authorities. Then a wooden coffin was made and the man was wrapped carefully and put in it. It would have to be shipped at once to Barranquilla and, after a medical examination, be interred there.

He never told anyone that he could find no sign of a snake bite, that what he did find was one small hole in the artery of his neck . . . and he knew no snake had made it. He was a little scared—he could find no logical reason for what had happened. He knew by the time a professional examined the body there would be no sign of what really killed him.

Maybe he was wrong, he thought. He *had* to be wrong.

Tana knew from the very active grapevine that the work on the dam had started. Every night she dreamed of Ethan, knowing he was with the men laboring in the jungle.

She wanted to see him and since her father and brother were so involved in their work for Drake Stone, she felt she was quite capable of finding her way on her own.

She knew her father and brother would be furious, just as she knew the trip was dangerous. She had traveled the distance from her father's house to Drake's before. If she were careful she could take a canoe from there to the place where the dam was being built. Her only problem was finding a reason to be there. Ethan was too close a friend of her father's and Drake's not to ask a million questions. Still she was determined, so she set out alone, certain that a good reason would come to her along the way.

Taking the overgrown path that led down to Drake's

house, she arrived to find Maria, occupied, as usual, with her house cleaning.

"Ah, Tana," Maria smiled in greeting—then her smile faded as she realized Tana was alone. "You have not traveled here alone? Your father will be very angry. The jungle is a very dangerous place."

"I know its dangers, Maria," Tana replied. "And you know I have come here many times."

"Not alone. Always you have had your father or brother or one of the men come with you, and they were always armed." Maria placed her hands on her ample hips. "Now you will have to stay until someone comes."

"I can't do that, Maria. I have to go on. I . . . I have a very important message for Senor Ethan and I know he is not very far away."

"His plantation is miles away!" Maria argued.

"But he is not there. He and many men are working at the dam he is beginning. It is an easy and very safe trip by river." Tana lied very convincingly.

"I cannot understand why your father would send you alone on such a journey. And all those men! You will not be safe there."

"I'm afraid it was necessary, Maria." Tana held herself erect and tilted her chin in stubborn arrogance. "There was no one else free at the time and I am not a child. Besides, you know none of Ethan's men would dare harm me."

"I know you are not a child. Have I not watched you grow? But men are men, whether they are Ethan's or not. How soon will you be returning?"

"I shall be returning . . . tomorrow." Again Tana's eyes did not betray her. She did not have the strength to paddle a canoe *against* the current. Her hope was that Ethan would bring her back . . . he would not trust another man to do so.

Maria was far from convinced, but she knew Tana—it was very unlikely she could stop her. But she was suspicious.

"I must go now, Maria. I don't want it to be dark before I get there. Is Senor Drake's canoe by the river?"

"Yes."

"Then I must hurry. I'll stop and help you for a while on my way home."

Tana walked away quickly, knowing that Maria's doubtful gaze was following her. She wondered how long it would be before Maria would figure out that Tana was too small and her muscles far too weak even to paddle the canoe upstream.

At the riverbank she found Drake's canoe. It was a good sturdy one and she had a struggle to push it into the water. When she could feel the rush of the current she jumped in, remembering it was Ethan and her father who had taught her where to sit and how to paddle. Soon she was headed downstream.

Tana had been up and down the river many times, enough times to recognize landmarks. The trip was long, but lushly scenic.

Still she knew that behind the lavish green border of the river lay dangers beyond most people's dreams.

Screaming fights were the way, and the least damaging way, for monkeys to defend their territory. They heralded her passing as a warning of danger to those who occupied the thick branches hanging over the water.

A monkey the white visitors referred to as a howler greeted her with a cacophony of sound. She could see him on a branch, a gnome-like old male who held his ground and howled as she passed.

A large eagle found a nest in a high tree, and a million colors ran rampant on a cock-of-the-rock, a startlingly beautiful bird that had been, at one time, worshipped by the natives. Toucans and macaws added their voices to the melody and hummingbirds flashed through the forest like brilliant gems. All their raucous cries rang through the jungle, carrying a great distance.

Tana admired the colorful display, but it was not these she feared. It was the long fish that could shock a human and often kill him, a stranger-than-fiction creature whose long body composed of electricity-producing tissue. This and the crocodiles that broke through the tall grass and slipped into the river with a frightening swiftness. Some of them remained on the banks, motionless, their open mouths showing rows of teeth that gleamed white in the sun. Tana paddled faster.

Keeping her eyes open and watching carefully, Tana saw the cluster of canoes at the bend of the river just before the dam site. Curiosity made her wonder why they were there and not at the camp.

Gently she used her paddle to steer the canoe toward those on the bank. Still no one appeared. She grazed the shore, stepped out of the canoe, and dragged it further onto the bank.

Evidence was all around her that this area had been occupied for a while. There was a circular place, well trampled, and several paths leading from it into the jungle . . . and toward the dam site.

The puzzle grew deeper. Why would Ethan have men camp here, so far from the dam, and have to walk the dangerous jungle path every day? It did not make sense.

Carefully she chose a path that led in the direction of the main camp. She walked slowly, her eyes darting about, watching for predators.

Because of her silence, she came upon a man without

him knowing. She would have just taken him for a curious native if she hadn't seen something in his hand. She had never seen any native use binoculars. Even as she watched his squatting figure, he raised the binoculars to his eyes and she realized he was watching Ethan's camp.

A man who watched this way could not be a member of the camp. She could not fathom the puzzle.

But whether she understood or not, she knew it would be best to tell Ethan. Her only problem was how to get past the man to Ethan without being seen or heard. Every instinct told her that the danger from this human could be greater than from any animal.

Slowly she left the trail and stepped into the shadowy undergrowth. Its warm, moist heat curled about her as she began to move toward Ethan's camp as fast as the thick greenery and hidden vines and brush allowed.

She kept moving as directly as possible, and after an hour of heart-stopping movement she could hear the voices of the men in the camp.

She paused to listen, then started forward. Tana had taken only a few more steps when a sixth sense told her she was no longer alone. She didn't want to turn around. The hair on the back of her neck stood erect and a shiver of fear went through her. Whatever was behind her . . . she had to know. Was it human or animal?

She stood immobile for a moment, fighting the desire to run. If it was a swift animal she might not be quick enough. She had to know for certain.

Very slowly she turned around and her heart froze. Forty feet or so on the path behind her, a huge puma was crouched. She knew she might find temporary safety in nearby trees. But what paralyzed her with unreality was the fact that on the same path, some distance behind the huge cat, she saw the man with the binoculars. Only now he held a rifle and she could tell from the relaxed way he stood that he had no intention of using it. He meant to let the huge cat do the job for him. She knew the man was a trespasser on Ethan's land, was not welcome there, and didn't want his presence known. He could see the cat sensed she was helpless, and did not know he was there at all.

She felt rooted to the ground as she and the puma stared at each other. She inhaled deeply and backed up several steps. The huge cat remained motionless, its dark eyes locked on her.

The cat was a pale, sandy brown with a white tuft on its chin. It was a beautiful animal . . . but not at the moment. At the moment, Tana knew, it was stalking its next meal.

When Tana backed up another step, the big cat inched forward and moved into a lower crouch. At the same time it emitted a guttural growl. The man remained still.

She had no time and few choices. She glanced about feverishly and saw a tree that she might be able to get to— the race would be close . . . if she made it at all.

She tensed every muscle, judged the distance, eyed the poised cat, then broke into a run.

She could hear the puma's scream, the rustle of the jungle growth, and the sound of its approach. The tree seemed a million miles away. She didn't have to look back to know the cat was gaining on her.

Tana's breath was growing short, and she almost stumbled as she reached the vine-entwined trunk. She had climbed many trees in her youth but she was certain she had never climbed one this fast before.

She was only inches out of reach when the cat leapt, its great claws skimming her leg as she pulled herself up. For a moment she could only cling to the branch, her eyes closed and her breath coming in huge, gasping sobs. One second slower and she would have been too late.

Tana's father had told her long ago that the great cats were more afraid of humans than humans were of them, and that they did not generally attack unless they were old, feeble, or hurt in some way that made hunting difficult.

She looked down at the pacing cat and realized it limped. That could have been why Tana reached safety—and why it preyed on her.

Tana looked up and could see no sign of the man. Obviously, he felt reasonably sure she had been taken care of.

She sat on the limb, her back resting against the trunk of the huge tree, and let her ragged nerves rest for a minute. She was shaking and it was beyond her ability to contain her tears. Then her will took over. She did not intend to die here!

She remembered that the voices from Ethan's camp had carried well on the warm air. Would her voice carry as far if she cried out for help? And if it didn't reach Ethan . . . would it carry to that strange man and bring him back to finish the job?

Ethan and Marc posted guards in pairs. They did not want the fatal accident to instill fear in the men. Ethan didn't tell Marc he was certain it wasn't a snake that had killed Carl because he could not answer the obvious questions: what had killed him? And why? He would have to wait and see what the authorities said.

The clearing of the area on either side of the river was going reasonably well and soon Ethan would return home to have building supplies brought in.

Ethan had been fighting a strange feeling for several

days—a feeling that he was being watched closely from a distance. He looked around him. The men were so busy they were oblivious to him. Still, the feeling created an itch between his shoulder blades.

He carried a high-powered rifle and a pistol nestled in the holster on his hip. He hoped he could handle whatever danger presented itself.

He was so attuned to the sounds of the jungle that most often he could filter them out. After all, he'd been working amid this cacophony for years. He could name every animal whose call he heard above the sound of the river.

He wasn't prepared for the shrill, piercing scream that cut the air like a knife. He snatched up his rifle and in that minute Marc was at his side, his own rifle in hand.

"What the hell was that?"

"It was no animal," Ethan said. "I can tell you that. It was a woman." He was gazing at the jungle about him, trying to pinpoint exactly where the sound had come from.

"A what? Out here? This heat is getting to both of us."

"No, it was a woman. Maybe a native woman has wandered near. Something's scaring her."

"I'll go . . ."

"No, you stay here. We don't want any more *accidents*. You keep a close watch. I'll go."

"You better be careful."

"I will."

"Do you know where it came from?"

Before Ethan could answer the scream pierced the air again. He nodded and started toward the edge of the jungle at a loping run.

The scream ricocheted through the air again and finally Ethan focused in on it. When he came upon the huge puma it startled the cat as much as it did Ethan, who raised his rifle.

Unprepared for interference and shaken by the suddenness of Ethan's appearance, the cat decided there might be a better chance to acquire its dinner elsewhere. He disappeared in the foliage. Ethan put the gun over his shoulder and walked to the base of the tree. He might have expected a lot of things, or a lot of people, but Tana was not one of them.

"Tana! What in God's name are you doing up there?"

Tana regained her composure as soon as she realized the cat was gone.

"I'm running away from that cat," she said as she smiled down at him.

"I know that," he replied, unamused. "I mean, what are you doing here? Where's your father?"

"If you will help me down I'll answer your questions."

Ethan stood the rifle against the tree and aided Tana in her descent. When she was safely beside him he scowled down at her.

"What do you mean by this? You could have been killed! Did you come all this way alone?"

"I came alone."

"Why?" he demanded. The shock of her brush with an ugly death unnerved him.

"Don't shout at me," she said calmly.

"Who's shouting?" he cried, raising his voice another octave. "And don't dodge the question."

"I am not dodging the question. I came alone. My father is working with Senor Drake . . . and he does not know I have come."

"What possible reason could you have for coming here . . . for taking such a chance? That's a dangerous trip."

"It's a good thing I did come. There is something going on around your camp you should know about."

"What would you know about what's going on around my camp?" He finally grinned. "You're too busy playing tag with pumas." When he smiled Tana was caught in his golden aura. Like the great cat that had nearly caught her, Ethan exuded strength and power. To her he looked like a brilliant, golden-haired son of the sun god himself.

"Not too busy to know what I see." She was pleased to see his humor return. She went on to describe the bunch of canoes and the man with the rifle and binoculars.

"He was watching every move you made."

"A white man?"

"Yes."

"What did he look like?"

"I wasn't close enough to see his face really well. He was tall . . . like you, but he wasn't as handsome," she added quickly.

At this Ethan laughed. "You weren't that close but you know he wasn't handsome?"

Tana's dark eyes held his without smiling.

"He would have killed me. He wanted that cat to kill me. He was an ugly man."

Catching her meaning, Ethan nodded. "All right, come back to camp with me and I'll see that word gets to your father. I hope he understands this was all your idea."

Tana wasn't about to be sent home like a wayward child. In fact, she had no intention of being treated like a child at all anymore. She definitely had other plans. Her quick mind spun and she started to move toward Ethan, only to give a soft cry and collapse.

Ethan was beside her immediately, lifting her. "What is it? Are you hurt?"

"I . . . I am afraid my swift climb was not without harm. My leg . . . I cannot seem to walk . . . it hurts."

Ethan knelt to examine her ankle and leg, trying to ignore the fact that it was enticingly slim and smooth, the skin like gold and cream.

"I'll carry you back to camp where we can look it over better. You might need a doctor."

He slung the rifle strap over his shoulder, then bent to lift her easily into his arms.

Tana was delighted. She wrapped her arms around his neck, then rested her head on his shoulders, feeling thoroughly contented.

It felt like the fulfillment of the dream Tana had had since the first day she met Ethan. She remembered when her father had brought him home to stay with them until his house was built. She had loved him then, and she had grown to love him more every day. She knew quite well how her father and brother felt, but nothing could change the way she felt about Ethan.

She had faced the truth a long time ago, but she would not deny her feelings and if the day ever came that Ethan looked at her as a man looks at a woman, she would go to him—without a care about what the world had to say about it.

Ethan was having his own problems. Having known Tana since she was fifteen, he had always thought of her as Mendrano's child or Antonio's sister. In fact, he had always thought of her as a little girl. Now, with her body pressed close to him, he was suddenly discovering the little girl had grown into a woman—a delightfully curved and even more delightfully soft and warm woman. It came as a shock.

He was astounded by his reaction and grimly forced his mind away from her . . . but his body and senses refused to cooperate.

He was grateful to reach the clearing. Marc raced to his side at once, accompanied by several men . . . none of whom looked at Tana with the remotest idea that she was a little girl. Ethan could read their minds easily, and he realized this camp was no place for Tana.

He ignored a feeling of annoyance when their eyes swept over her in appreciative silence.

"Who is she?" Marc questioned. "What happened?"

"Puma," Ethan answered shortly. "She got a pretty good scare, and I think her leg is hurt. This is Mendrano's daughter. You remember him?"

"Yes, I do. You can take her to my tent," Marc offered.

"I think she's going to need a doctor. I have to get one of my men to go upriver and let Mendrano know where she is. I'll take her back to my place—it's not that far. Marc, I'm not sure just when I can get back. Then . . . you and I have something pretty serious to talk about."

"Trouble?" Marc said softly.

"Looks that way," Ethan replied. "I'll tell you all about it later. In the meantime, pull the guards in closer. I don't want anything else to happen before I get back."

"You think it will?"

"I hope not. Just be careful," Ethan said, lowering his voice so the others couldn't hear. "I think we have uninvited—even dangerous—company. From what Tana tells me we're under surveillance. I don't know who or why but let's not take any chances. I'll bring more men back with me— men who know the jungle."

"All right. I'll triple the guard and bring them in closer. But I can't figure why anyone would want to watch us."

"Neither can I. That's what scares me."

Ethan walked to the canoes that lined the river and gently

placed Tana in one. Then he pushed it away from the shore, jumped in, and began to ease the canoe downstream.

Marc watched as he slowly disappeared. One of the men walked over to him.

"Now I know for certain what this camp is missing."

"Huh? What?" Marc said as he turned to him.

"Pretty women," the man grinned, "and that was about one of the prettiest I've ever seen. Your idea of supplyin' a camp falls pretty short of the mark, boss. You need to send Ethan into the jungle more often if he can come back with something like that each time."

"Yeah?" Marc laughed. "Well, if I tried to bring that one here, we might all find our heads mounted on a spear. Her father's the head man up at the dig and her brother's a man to be reckoned with. So cool off, my friend."

Both men laughed as they turned away, but Marc's laugh didn't last long. He began to worry about Ethan's last words.

Quickly he gave orders to triple the guards and draw in the perimeter of the camp. Then he ordered the men back to work. But he could not control the way his eyes kept going to the rim of jungle, as if he expected something or someone at any time.

What was the reason for this? Why would anyone want to watch them? The dam was useful to everyone, so they were not causing anyone a problem. So the questions would remain unanswered . . . at least until Ethan got back.

Tana was quite aware that Ethan was eyeing her during the entire trip down the river. Try as she might, she could not think of a single excuse for coming to his camp that she felt he would accept, so she gathered her nerve and her courage. She was going to tell him . . . the truth.

She knew Ethan was worried about the men who had his camp under surveillance—what she didn't know was that he was wondering if those men were in any way connected to Carl's death. It was one thing to be watched, it was something else entirely when it included murder.

The sun was nearing the horizon when the canoe bumped against the dock. Ethan stepped on the wooden planks, then bent to grasp her hands and lift her up beside him.

"Can you stand for a minute?"

Tana nodded and watched him kneel to secure the canoe. Then he swept her up in his arms.

The walk to the main house was a long one, a distance usually covered on horseback. Ethan walked easily, marveling at the fact that Tana felt so light . . . and so right in his arms.

"Ethan?" Tana spoke softly.

"Yes?"

"You . . . you must put me down. I can walk."

"Don't try to be brave, Tana. You might have hurt yourself . . . and it's a long walk."

"I . . . I have not been hurt."

Ethan stopped and looked at her. In the light of the dying sun he was aware of how beautiful she was. He was also aware of what she had just said.

"You're not hurt?"

"No."

He slid her legs to the ground to test what she was saying, feeling certain she was just trying to save him the effort of carrying her. She walked a few steps away and turned to him.

His first sensation was a feeling of emptiness when she left him, but it was followed by a puzzled half-anger.

"I don't understand what you're up to, Tana."

"I . . . If you will promise not to be too angry, then I will explain."

"I won't be angry," he replied. "But standing out here until it's dark is foolish. We'll go on to the house and talk. This had better be good, Tana, because after me, you have to explain this to your father and brother."

"I know you will not believe me," Tana replied softly, "but my father and brother will have no problem understanding what I have done. They know my heart already. I have only to explain it to you . . . and hope you will understand."

Ethan was mystified. He took her hand in his and they started for the house together.

Fourteen

Ethan sent for food and cool drinks. He could see that Tana was very tired. He still couldn't imagine any woman making the often frightening and always long trip to his house from hers.

"Tana, do you realize how dangerous this really was? Anything could have happened and none of us would have known about it."

"I've made the trip before," she said defensively.

"But never alone. I hate to think about what Mendrano and Antonio are going to say. I'll bet they're worried sick. I'm sending a runner first thing in the morning. By the day after tomorrow someone should be here to take you home."

Tana bowed her head and Ethan stood studying her. "What is it, Tana? What brought you down to that camp? I've known you for a long time—I know you're not the kind of girl to be drawn to a camp full of men."

"No," Tana whispered softly.

"Then why?"

"It was not men . . . it was one man."

Ethan stood in stunned silence. Marc and his men were new to the area. She didn't know any of them. There was only one man in that camp she knew.

He couldn't believe his ears, but when she lifted her eyes to his there was no mistaking the feeling there.

"Tana," he said softly.

She stood and turned her back to him. She could not stand to see rejection in his eyes.

"My brother has told me over and over that we are worlds apart. That you would not *want* to be a part of my life, and I *could not* be a part of yours. He says I am not the kind of woman you would want."

"Your brother loves you, I'm sure. He doesn't mean to hurt you—he just wants what's best for you."

"I know. But . . ."

"He wants you to be happy."

"He does not know what will make me happy!" She turned to face him. "I know," she cried, pressing a closed fist against her breasts, "I know what I think and what I feel and what I want!"

"Tana," he began cautiously, "you must understand . . ."

"Don't speak to me as if I were a child!"

"I . . . don't think you're a child, but you have a young and romantic heart. You've never had any experience. You just don't know . . . you've been so well protected. I mean . . . Tana, maybe you're dreaming of something that could be a disappointment and a mistake."

"And again, like my family you are wrong. Everyone seems to think they know what is best for me. But no one knows what is best for me . . . *except me,* and no one cares how I feel. I am the only one who knows. Why does a woman have to kiss many men to know that she desires one man's kiss? Why does a woman have to seek the love of many men to know she wants the love of only one? I believe a woman who has to love many is foolish. It is the wise one who can see what is true, and an even wiser one who refuses to deny it."

Ethan felt as if he were seeing Tana for the first time in

all the five years he had known her. It was true—he had thought of her as a little girl and had just gotten a rather startling awakening.

It was a shock, and he wasn't quite sure how to handle it. It was also very flattering. But he had to consider what a grave mistake it could be, especially for Tana. He also knew that, as sweet and inviting as she was, touching her could create a reaction he hadn't bargained for.

"Look, Tana. You're tired and a bit overwrought. Have something to eat and get some sleep. Tomorrow we can talk this out. I don't want to argue with you . . . and well, to be truthful, this has been kind of a shock. I'm flattered, sincerely flattered."

"Sleep and food will not change my mind."

"Now's a good time to find out how stubborn you are," he said gruffly. "Please, Tana, if this isn't too much for you it sure is for me. It's not every day a beautiful woman pops into your life and tells you she's in love with you."

To Ethan's surprise, Tana smiled shyly. "You think I am beautiful?"

Ethan swallowed heavily, his attention riveted on her face. Her smile was devastating and he was suddenly very aware of her presence in his house . . . alone. He certainly appreciated a beautiful woman as much as the next man, but this was out of bounds for a lot of reasons. The first was that she did not fit into his plans at all . . . not at all.

"Yes, you are a beautiful woman. And that's another reason to put an end to this. Now have something to eat and drink. Then I'll show you where you can sleep."

They had been standing in the dimly lit entranceway; Ethan took Tana's arm as they walked into the spacious living room.

Bill Holmes was seated before the huge fireplace, engrossed in a book. He looked up when Ethan and Tana walked in, then his face brightened when he saw Tana. He rose and smiled.

"Ethan, I hardly expected you back today." Bill spoke to Ethan, but he could not pull his eyes away from Tana. He was very curious about the connection between these two.

"Bill, this is Tana. She's Mendrano's daughter."

"Hello, Tana." Bill smiled and she responded with a shy smile. Neither noticed Ethan's frown.

Before either man could speak again the sound of footsteps could be heard on the stairs and in moments Lettie appeared.

"Ethan, you're home . . ." Lettie stopped to appraise the girl with Ethan. Then she smiled. "Hello."

"Hello," Tana answered quietly.

Ethan again introduced Tana, who was beginning to wonder about the number of people in Ethan's house. She had hoped to be alone with him. She looked up at Ethan and it took a very astute Lettie to figure out what was going on.

While Ethan explained as much of the situation as he could, Bill listened and Lettie observed. Then George returned from a walk and said, "Ethan, it's good to see you home, but at this time of day I'm really kind of surprised."

"Well, I had a little problem." To Tana's annoyance, Ethan explained the situation again.

George said nothing more, carefully keeping his thoughts from reflecting in his eyes. He liked Tana, had met her several times before, and he didn't want to do or say anything tactless in a situation he could sense was . . . to say the least, delicate.

"Ethan was just telling us that someone is spying on the camp at the dam," Bill announced. "What on earth for? And who are they?"

"I don't have an answer to either question," Ethan admitted. "But I sure intend to find out as soon as I can. But now, I think Tana is hungry, and I know I am."

"You're not going back to camp tonight?" Lettie asked.

"No," Ethan replied, carefully keeping his eyes from Tana. "It's too late. I'll probably see to some things around here, then go back up after I've seen Tana safely home."

"Tana," Lettie said, "if you'd like to get cleaned up before dinner, come up to my room. In case there's anything you might need, I'd be glad to supply it."

"You've very kind."

Ethan smiled. *You've very curious,* he was thinking, but he said nothing. Tana and Lettie walked up the stairs together.

"Wow," Bill said softly. "That is one gorgeous woman. If I'd known she was part of Drake's dig I might have been persuaded to stay a while longer."

"She is lovely," Ethan admitted, more to himself than to Bill. Then he grinned. "And she has a rough, tough father and a very protective brother."

"What in God's name is a creature like that doing moving about this wild place unaccompanied?"

"It wasn't the time to ask her," Ethan said. He went on to explain the circumstances under which he'd found Tana.

"She could have been a meal for that cat," Bill said.

"She sure could. I've already given her a lecture. I'm sending a runner for her father . . . or someone to take her back."

"Why don't you take her back? It would save a day," George mentioned casually, a merry twinkle in his eye that Ethan missed completely.

Yes, Ethan thought, why didn't he take her back? But the answer slipped into his mind just as easily. He didn't want to camp overnight in the jungle alone with a woman who looked like Tana and had told him she loved him. He wasn't a dishonorable man, he thought, but this could push any man a bit too far.

"I'm afraid I haven't the time. It's better if someone comes for her. Lord, I'm famished. I hope those two come down soon."

Bill could see Ethan wanted to change the subject so he complied. But it only served to rouse his curiosity even further.

Lettie and Tana became friends almost at once. Within minutes they were chattering as if they had known each other for years.

"That skirt and blouse could certainly use some attention. It's torn and dirty," Lettie said as she studied Tana's clothes objectively.

"I'm afraid I had to climb that tree so fast I didn't have time to think about clothes," Tana laughed.

"Well, don't worry about it. I have a lot of things—you can wear anything you like."

"Oh, no . . . I couldn't." Tana was aghast.

"Don't be ridiculous. All those dresses are just hanging there and I can't wear more than one at a time. So go ahead, choose whatever you like."

Lettie swung the closet door wide and Tana's eyes filled with awe. She had never had more than three dresses at one time.

It took her only minutes to settle on a dress of black lace.

"Umm," Lettie chuckled. "You have good taste. If that dress doesn't take Ethan's breath away I'll be surprised." She watched Tana flush. "Oh, Tana, it's all right. I'd have to be pretty blind not to see how you feel about him. Come on, let me fix your hair and help you dress. Dinner ought to prove very, very interesting."

Ethan, Bill, and George enjoyed a drink while they waited for Lettie and Tana to come downstairs.

"I suppose Lettie and I ought to go up to the dig with you and see how Caitlyn's getting on. I'm sure you didn't count on your houseguests staying this long."

"Don't even think that way. My house is open for as long as you care to stay. I have a feeling yours and Lettie's interest is not really in archaeological digs."

"No. Quite frankly, I'm more interested in what you've done here. I should think this would be an interesting challenge."

"Well," Ethan said with a smile, "there's a lot of land out here, and it is a challenge . . . an invigorating one. I don't think I'd care to live anyplace else."

"I can understand that," George said. "I've gone away a million times and I still find myself coming back again and again. I suppose it's a bit because I admire you and what you've done. And I've come to admire Drake as well. This is wild, beautiful country and it requires strong men . . . and women, I might add."

Before anyone could respond, they could hear women's voices. All three turned toward the door.

Ethan was prepared to be as kind and gentle with the shy and childish Tana as he possibly could . . . but the Tana who walked through the door was so unexpected that he stood, his glass raised halfway to his mouth, his eyes reflecting a very profound shock.

Tana appeared—tall, elegant, and breathtaking. The black lace dress fell from her tawny shoulders, caught at her slender waist by a ribbon. It caressed slim hips and then fell to her ankles with a handkerchief hem. Her gleaming ebony hair had been drawn atop her head in a mass of soft curls. She wore no jewelry, but no jewelry could have enhanced her beauty as she stood framed in the gleaming wood of the doorway.

Tana's eyes went to Ethan at once, hoping to see more in there than before. She watched him, Lettie watched her, and George noticed Ethan struggling to maintain his control.

After a moment Ethan realized he was as speechless as the other men. He took a deep gulp of his drink, set the glass aside, and walked slowly toward Tana.

"Tana, you look absolutely beautiful," he said honestly, helpless against the surge of pleasure he felt at the brilliance of her eyes or her dazzling smile.

"Thank you," she replied, a little breathlessly.

"I should say you do," George agreed enthusiastically.

"Well, I'm starved," Bill said as he walked over to Lettie. "No matter how long I have to wait you always make it worth it," he whispered softly.

"Now that the ladies are finally here," George announced, "I think it's time to get fed. I happen to be extremely hungry."

Everyone laughed and Ethan held out his arm to Tana as Bill did for Lettie. The five walked to the dining room. Ethan was shaken—it promised to be a long, long evening.

It surprised Ethan how much he enjoyed Tana's company. Dinner was an extremely merry affair and Ethan fought the feeling that Tana could easily belong right where she was.

He built strong defenses and managed some semblance of control for the rest of the evening. When he escorted Tana to her room, he was calm and considerate.

"Good night, Tana. Pleasant dreams."

"I wish you pleasant dreams as well, Ethan, and thank you."

"For what?"

"For being so . . . so nice." He was unprepared for her to suddenly stand on tiptoe and kiss him. Then she was gone and the door was closed between them.

The next morning Ethan was already at the breakfast table when Tana came downstairs. She had been delighted with the soft bed and the spacious room. A hot bath first thing in the morning made her giggle with pleasure as she sank into it.

She walked into the sunlit dining room and smiled at Ethan, who rose as she approached.

"Good morning, Tana. Did you sleep well?"

"Yes . . . oh yes. I have never slept on a bed so soft—and to have a hot bath brought to your room . . . how terribly spoiled you must be."

Ethan laughed, her excitement and enthusiasm making him feel good. "Sit down and eat. Everything on this table was grown right here."

Tana could see Ethan's pride in what he had accomplished, so she ate lustily and complimented him on everything.

"What will you do with your day, Tana?"

"Be with you," she replied quickly and honestly.

"Ah . . . Tana . . . I'm afraid that's not only impossible, it's hardly wise."

"Why is it impossible?"

"Because I have to go back to the camp sometime today, but even when I'm here I work most of the day on horseback and I know you've never ridden. Now, you have the run of my house, the grounds, garden, anything you choose.

If there's anything you want, the housekeeper, Ama, will see that you get it."

"You've sent someone for my father?"

"I'm going out to talk to Perez right now. He can make it up to the dig by tonight."

"You will be in to eat the afternoon meal?"

"I don't know," he lied cautiously. He had no intention of spending more time with her than necessary. He didn't ask himself why she was presenting him with such a problem. "It depends on how the day goes and how much I have to do."

He watched her eyes as she lowered her lashes and bent her head, and felt a strong sense of regret. He didn't want her unhappy—and he knew somehow his words had made her so.

He wanted to say more, say something to make her smile again. But he didn't get a chance.

"Good morning, you two," George said as he approached the breakfast table. "You're the first up, I see."

"I have a great deal to do," Ethan said, annoyed at the almost apologetic tone in his voice. He stood. "I'm sorry to leave so quickly, but since you're here, George, you can keep Tana company until Lettie and Bill get up. I have to make sure Perez gets off with the message to Tana's father."

"I'd be delighted," George announced with a warm smile at Tana.

"I . . . I'll most likely see you both at dinner. Have a good day. Remember, my house is your house. If there's anything you need or want don't hesitate to ask."

Ethan turned and walked away and George and Tana remained silent for some time while George's breakfast as served. They ate in silence for several minutes.

"Tana," he said quietly, "the world is never quite as black

as it seems sometimes, and believe it or not, time has a way of changing things."

"Time . . . time should never be wasted."

George laughed. "You have everything ahead of you." He paused and studied her face for a moment. Then his voice was gentle. "Tana . . . how long have you been in love with Ethan Marshall?"

Tana looked up at him quickly, but she could see that he was no longer laughing.

"I think, from the first time he came here. My father was one of his friends. I was very young . . . but he . . ."

"I know," George smiled, "first he was too busy building his home, then he could only see you as Mendrano's daughter . . . Antonio's sister . . . or a child."

"Yes, and what can I do?"

"Nothing, Tana . . . this is something that cannot be forced. Whatever is meant to happen will happen, and if it is not meant to be, then truly it is time wasted. It is best that you return home."

Tana did not want George's advice, since it did not fit into her plans, yet she knew he was being kind. She smiled and nodded. "I know . . . but, I shall enjoy this day, even if I do not have any others. I'm sure my brother will come for me and he will be very angry."

"Does that frighten you?"

"Antonio?" She laughed. "no, Antonio does not frighten me. His bark is much worse than his bite and I know that his anger only means he loves me. I would never be afraid of Antonio."

"And your father?"

"Most certainly not. My father is very kind. Maybe," she admitted with a smile, "a little too kind at times. But . . . he knows I would never do anything to shame him. I would not betray his trust. Of course, he will growl for a while . . . but at the same time he will try to understand." She sighed deeply. "The only man whose moods and feelings I do not understand is Ethan's."

"Maybe . . . maybe it's just not the right time for you to understand him, or for him to realize what a truly appropriate gift you might be."

"Thank you," she said, looking at George in surprise.

"Tana, you belong to this country, and one day Ethan might realize that is the only kind of woman who could make his place her home and truly be part of it. Frankly, I think he got a little lesson in your . . . appropriateness last night." He reached out to pat her hand. "Now, why don't you give him time to adjust to that? Use that phenomenal patience your people seem gifted with, and wait until he comes around."

Tana looked at George with a new kind of understanding. Perhaps he was right.

"Do you think I have made a complete fool of myself?"

"Hardly. Last night was remarkable. I'd bet my life you're on Ethan's mind this minute."

George was not far from wrong. Ethan took care of the morning's work and resisted all thought of going back to the house for lunch. He tried to deny the fact that Tana had had a profound effect on him . . . but his denials had no effect on his memory.

He had told a very startled Perez to make sure the word got to Mendrano and Antonio at once.

"They're probably frantic with worry, Perez, so make the trip as fast as you can."

"You would like, maybe, for me to take Tana back?"

"No," Ethan said quickly, and refused to think of why he refused. He justified it by thinking he was being considerate of Tana. He did not want her wandering in the jungle with anyone outside her family. It would upset Mendrano, he thought . . . but in truth it would upset him as well. To Ethan, Tana was an innocent who needed protection—he would look no further than that. "Just take word to her father about where she is. Tell him she's fine, perfectly safe."

"Si, senor." Perez seldom questioned Ethan's orders.

Now Ethan was looking for any excuse that would keep him away from the house until dinner. He would not go back to the camp at the dam until Tana was taken care of.

Ethan was enjoying his guests. Bill and Lettie were amusing and George was a good conversationalist and an exceptional chess player. Besides that, he knew, understood, and loved this country as much as Ethan did. Ethan knew he'd been rather lonely and hungry for stimulation from the outside world, and it had made him happy that Caitlyn's friends had decided to stay.

But it also made him realize that when they did decide to go, the house would seem even larger and emptier than ever before.

If this brought his thoughts back to Tana he did his best to fight them.

Ethan managed to fill the balance of his day with strenuous activity, but the evening inevitably drew near. As the sun was just meeting the horizon he rode toward the house.

Mendrano stood with the tablet in hand and wrote down each piece that was taken from the jars. After he had done so they were taken to Sir Richard, who was working to identify and make notes about each piece.

Sir Richard sat at a small table with Caitlyn's box of cleaning tools and fluids that Caitlyn had put near his feet.

Drake was helping with the cleaning and wondering just who had opened the box. If it had been Caitlyn, she was an excellent actress, and if it had been her father . . . then maybe she did know about the stone. These questions roiled within him. He didn't want to hear them and he didn't want to answer them . . . but he couldn't just ignore them.

Drake was puzzled, for Caitlyn seemed so intent on her work that she never even glanced toward the box.

By the time they stopped for a late afternoon break, Drake was tense. When he'd told Mendrano what had happened, or rather what had not happened, he was just as puzzled.

"Do you think someone else could have put the stone in that box, and neither of them knew about it? After all, Mendrano, you weren't really close enough to see what happened."

"I suppose you are right. There was no reaction from either of them?"

"Not even the blink of an eye. If they're acting, they're doing a fine job. I just don't understand . . . unless we're jumping to conclusions. Whatever, we can't do anything now. Let's just get back to work. The dig is more important than our suspicions."

Mendrano nodded. He wasn't really sure of Caitlyn's guilt; after all, someone could have placed the stone in the box without her knowledge. But he did not doubt what he had seen, and he meant to keep Sir Richard Macdonald under a very watchful eye.

"Mendrano," Drake said, "I want to get down to the next level this afternoon. I'll take Caitlyn with me and you stay close to Sir Richard. That way you can keep records and keep your eyes open at the same time."

"Don't worry. Go on with your work. I will see to the rest."

"Good."

When Drake and Mendrano joined the others at the table it was to take part in an animated discussion with Caitlyn. Drake watched her and wondered if she could be two people . . . or if she was a really experienced actress. How far did the act really go? Did it include him?

"Caitlyn, I'm going to leave some of the cataloguing and cleaning to Mendrano and your father this afternoon. How would you like to give that next level a try?"

"I'd love to," Caitlyn exclaimed. He could see the excitement sparkle in her eyes, and he found it hard not to pray that this was the real Caitlyn.

"Good, we'll go right after we finish eating. Sir Richard, you don't mind taking over some of the tedious work?"

"Of course not, my boy. I've already made it very clear that those steps and the physical work are not exactly my cup of tea. I'd be pleased to sit right here and finish as much of this as I can today. These are remarkable pieces."

"Yes, and beautiful. But do you realize they must have been left over . . . not of enough value to put below? Just discarded?"

"Junk," Caitlyn whispered. "Invaluable, fabulous junk. It's hard to believe. It meant so little to them, and means so much to us."

"It's hard to believe, isn't it?" Drake said. "I only hope there's a lot more."

"I'm sure there is and I can't wait to get at it," Caitlyn exclaimed.

"It's going to be a long afternoon," Drake grinned. "I've already had lanterns placed along all the steps on the first two levels, but we'll still have to carry two apiece to get light below that. It ought to be a bit thick down there so be prepared to work slowly."

"I'm prepared for just about anything," Caitlyn said, smiling. Her laughter and excitement were contagious to Drake.

"Well, anything is just what's liable to be there."

"So," Caitlyn retorted, "let's go see what anything is."

"Let's," he chuckled.

"Drake, don't you want to see what's up on those shelves at the second level first?" Caitlyn asked.

"I've had some of the men build a bit of scaffolding. We should be able to climb up and get a good look."

"What do you suppose . . ."

"It doesn't do much good to suppose. Let's go see."

Caitlyn rose quickly and she and Drake walked toward the tomb. Sir Richard watched them go, his face passive and unreadable.

Inside the second level, Mendrano was just seeing to the last of the jars, placing the record in the notebook and closing it so he could follow the rest of the men out. He was about to leave when he saw Caitlyn and Drake coming in.

"Everything out and accounted for, Mendrano?" Drake asked.

"Yes. I'll put the notebook in your tent."

"Good. Caitlyn and I are going to take a look at those shelves, then we're going down to the next level."

"As you go deeper it becomes more dangerous," Mendrano said. "It might be better if you take some of the men, or me, along."

"No, Mendrano," Drake said quietly. "I want you topside . . . just in case. There's a lot you need to keep your eye on. We'll be careful."

"See that you are," Mendrano grinned. "This is the tomb of a king, I am sure. I don't want it to be yours as well."

Mendrano went up quickly. He had no intention of letting Sir Richard out of his sight any longer than necessary. Despite the lack of proof, he knew what he had seen, and he had his own ideas about what was going on.

Drake and Caitlyn went down to the third level quickly to find the scaffold erected and ready for their use.

The shelves were at least eight feet from the stone floor and a little over two feet from the ceiling. It was clear that some kind of an object sat on each of them, covered with centuries of dirt and grime. Given the discoloration of precious metals over time, it was difficult to see what they were.

A rough pair of steps had been hastily nailed together to provide Drake and Caitlyn with access to the platform, but the entire apparatus was a bit unsteady so they had to move carefully.

The hastily built scaffolding only extended the length of three of the shelves, so they examined the objects on each of them as closely as they could without touching them. Then Drake took the object from the first shelf. It was green from exposure to the air, which confirmed Drake's opinion that it was made of gold.

The shape was that of a large crab, and perched atop it was the face of a man wearing an ornamental crown.

"It's gold . . . pure gold and when it's clean I think you'll find those red eyes are rubies and the stone in the center of the crown is an emerald."

"It's beautiful even all corroded like that," Caitlyn said. "But I don't understand . . ."

"What don't you understand?"

"This is obviously a deity . . . and if every shelf holds some form of deity, then maybe whoever is buried here is someone so utterly unique," she looked up at Drake, "that they have surrounded him with golden gods."

"And thirteen . . . thirteen," Drake spoke half to himself. "Something . . ."

"Something rings a bell, doesn't it?" Caitlyn suggested.

"Yes . . . but I can't quite grasp it. A legend, I think, an old legend I must have heard . . . or read."

"Maybe my father will remember."

"Maybe. Maybe Mendrano will have some ideas. We'll ask them tonight. Let's look at the next shelf."

Drake replaced the first object and they moved the few feet to the next shelf.

The next object supported their theory. It too was a deity, a feline carving of gold with a crown that was also studded with what looked like small diamonds. Wordlessly they replaced it and moved to the next. It was the figure of a tiny warrior-lord mounted on a tarnished silver plate. He wore a headdress of thinly hammered gold with a ruby in the center. His turquoise eyes had pupils of small diamonds. He carried a war club and a spear.

"There's very little doubt about it. We do have something here that'll require a little research. I have a feeling it's something I should know and just can't remember."

"In time it will all fall into place.

"I suppose." He smiled. "It's just annoying to have a memory in the back of your mind and not be able to get hold of it."

"Yes, I know what you mean. But maybe if we go on to

other things it'll come to you. Besides," she laughed, "this scaffolding is making me a little seasick."

"You're right. It is a little rickety. Come on." He preceded her to the edge of the scaffold and went down the few steps. Once on the ground he turned to help her, grasping her by the waist and lifting her down.

But letting her go was not easy—memories of another sort took over. Caitlyn felt a little humor might break the tension.

"The gods are watching us, Drake Stone," she sighed. "And I don't think they'd take it kindly if we didn't keep their sanctuary sacred."

"Maybe you're right," he grinned, "but if they're unhappy, in my opinion it's sheer envy."

He brushed her lips with a quick kiss, then took her hand and started toward the steps to the next level.

"I wish I knew how many levels there really were," Drake said, "and I sure wish I could remember that legend or folk tale or whatever. I have a feeling it might tell us something important."

"I think we're about to find out at least part of the answer," Caitlyn said as they reached the top of the steps.

Drake chuckled. "If I go down there and find out this is just the tomb of somebody's grandmother I'm sure going to be disappointed."

"Maybe," Caitlyn laughed in response, "unless someone's grandmother happens to be a queen. Then you might get more than you bargained for."

"Leave it to a woman to come up with an idea like that," he teased.

"I think it's a brilliant idea, and I hope, Mr. Stone, that you find a lady goddess down there surrounded by a whole lot of other lady goddesses. That'll make you eat your words."

He enjoyed the banter and it eased their nerves as they looked down into the depths of the darkness below.

"Frankly," he said seriously, "I hope we find something that justifies my theory. That alone would make me a very happy man."

"Drake," Caitlyn squeezed his hand. "I hope so, too."

"Then I guess we'd better find out."

Hand in hand and holding the lanterns aloft, they began to move slowly down the steps.

Fifteen

After breakfast Tana took the opportunity to wander through Ethan's house alone. George had invited her to ride with him for an hour or so.

"I cannot," she smiled. "I have never been on a horse, and to tell you the truth, I'm very much afraid of them."

"Well, I want to take one last fond look. I'm afraid I have to be on my way."

"You're leaving Fountainhurst?"

"I have to pack later tonight. Day after tomorrow I will be leaving for Barranquilla. I have some work to do."

"I'm sure Ethan will miss you. He speaks of you often. I think you two are very good friends."

"I'm glad to say we are. I've known Ethan almost from the first day he came here." George smiled down at her. "And I'd like to consider you my very good friend as well."

"Thank you."

"I'll most likely be back this way next year sometime," he said, his eyes twinkling. "I hope I find you right where I'm leaving you."

"I want you to know," she laughed softly, "that I share your hopes."

"Good girl," George said as he kissed her cheek. Once he had left the house, Tana's smile faded. She found it hard to survive on illusion.

Slowly she wandered about, examining everything. Each time she touched something she thought of Ethan and the fine things with which he had surrounded himself.

She sat down before the beautiful ebony Steinway and gently let her fingers touch the keys. She liked the sound . . . but as she continued to touch one key after another, frustration began to grow. She would never be able to make anything beautiful come from the piano. Anger made her slam both hands down on the keyboard, emphasizing her rage and helplessness.

"You're not mad at the piano, are you, Tana?" Lettie's voice came from the doorway. Tana turned quickly.

"I'm sorry. I didn't mean to do that. It was just . . ."

"Just a little frustration, I know. I've felt the same thing a few times. But the poor piano isn't to blame. Why don't we take a walk?"

"All right," Tana rose and she and Lettie walked out into the garden.

"I've taken a walk here almost every morning since Bill and I arrived," Lettie said. "I can hardly believe that Ethan has built such a paradise in the middle of the jungle."

"Yes . . . it is beautiful."

"I'm a city girl," Lettie said with a laugh. "I've never seen this much greenery in my whole life. I like it, really. And the sounds . . . I've never heard anything like them."

"I guess I am so used to it that I don't always hear it."

"It's like a kind of music . . . very erotic."

"Erotic . . . what is erotic?"

"Erotic," Lettie laughed softly, then her laugh stilled. Tana was an innocent and that was precisely what was scaring Ethan away. He would not hurt her. In fact, Lettie wondered if Ethan wasn't just scared to death. "Erotic," Lettie added softly, "is sort of a way to describe how you feel about Ethan."

Tana's cheeks grew pink. "I cannot describe to anyone how I feel about Ethan."

"You needn't describe it to any woman who's been in love. You've run across a rare breed of man, Tana, the kind who thinks of consequences, and doesn't want to cause any harm. He's put up barriers between you that you'll have to take down piece by piece."

"I don't understand you . . . and I wouldn't know where to begin."

"I would say the first place would be to go home with no fuss . . . with pleasure."

Tana turned away from Lettie. "You don't understand, either. If I go home it will be over. My father will keep his eyes on me. I'll never . . . you don't understand."

"Oh, but I do. More than you think. If you want Ethan Marshall you're going about it in all the wrong ways."

Tana turned to look at Lettie again, trying to see if Lettie was teasing—or laughing at her. She was doing neither.

"If I go home I may not see Ethan for weeks. He is so busy with his home and his dam that he doesn't even visit Drake as often as he used to."

"Tana . . . let's sit here," she suggested, pointing to a low, white bench that sat partially surrounded by well-clipped hedges. "I think it's time we had a woman-to-woman talk . . ." Tana sat.

Ethan had not returned at midday and no one was sure that he would even return for the evening meal.

Wearing a rose-colored dress of Lettie's, Tana came down the stairs just after seven. She could hear Lettie, George, and Bill talking, but before she could enter the living room the front door opened and Ethan came in.

Trying his best to ignore her exquisite beauty, Ethan smiled. "Evening, Tana. Sorry I'm so late for dinner. I'll go and wash up quickly. Do you want to tell the others I'll be down as soon as I can?"

"Yes, I'll tell them," Tana replied. She waited on the bottom step for Ethan to cross the entrance floor. When he paused beside her, she tried to make her smile friendly and warm. It brought Ethan to a stop. "And Ethan, I really regret all the inconvenience I've caused you. I'm sorry. I guess it was just a foolish thought on my part. It won't happen again." As she said the last words, she touched his arm gently. Then she turned and walked toward the living room, aware that he had not moved and that his puzzled gaze was following her.

The dinner was, thanks to George, filled with interesting conversation. Ethan kept up with it, at the same time becoming very aware of a subliminal change in Tana. She laughed softly and took part in easy conversation, but her attention seemed to be on everything and anything but him. If it did nothing else it roused his curiosity and shook his ego a bit.

Of course, he rationalized, Tana had come to her senses and realized that what had happened had been only a passing thing. He was more than ten long and eventful years older than her twenty short and well-protected ones. He was aware of her sweet innocence more with every word, every move she made . . . and he refused to recognize or acknowledge in any way the sensations that filled him when he looked into her lovely dark eyes.

When the meal ended Ethan was quick to claim an excess of paperwork that needed his attention.

"I'm sorry, but it has to be done. I hope you all understand. Please, enjoy your evening. I shall see you all at breakfast, since I intend to work late."

He was surprised when Tana displayed not even the slightest hint of interest.

"Of course we understand," George said. "This is your business and you must care for it. We'll be fine. I intend to teach Tana how to play chess. I suspect the lady has a very quick mind behind that beautiful face."

"I wouldn't be surprised," Ethan answered lamely, annoyed by the realization that teaching Tana anything might have been both challenging and exciting.

"We'll see you in the morning," Bill said.

Once at his desk, Ethan tried his best to keep his mind on the papers, but a soft smile and a pair of dark eyes danced between him and them. Three hours of struggle might have warned him he was getting nowhere.

Logic told him this would never do, that he had to have more control.

"Like a schoolboy," he muttered as he rose from his desk and walked to a sideboard that held a decanter of brandy and several glasses. He poured one drink, tossed it down and poured a second which he carried with him to a comfortable chair before the fireplace.

He lectured himself while he nursed the second drink. The French doors stood open and the moon was bathing the garden in mellow gold light. He rose, refreshed his drink, and carried it with him.

He crossed the patio and walked down the stone path into the garden. He'd always felt such peace and contentment there.

He sat and sipped his drink slowly, trying to recapture his equilibrium. He'd not been lonely! He didn't need more than he already had! There would be time! When his dream was fully realized. Vaguely he wondered why he felt everything was slipping away from him.

He looked about him with a good bit of pride. It had been a fierce struggle, but he had carved something worthwhile out of the wilderness. Then why did he feel so strangely empty? Why did he have this feeling of urgency, as if he were racing after something that was just beyond his reach . . . and what was he reaching for when he had the world in the palm of his hand?

He drank the last of his drink and stood, preparing to go back inside. He might not be able to sleep but he could work and that might just be good medicine for whatever ailed him. Tomorrow he would go back to the dam and try to figure out who was spying on the camp and why.

He had not taken a step when a sound drew his eyes up. He stood quite still, not sure of what he was seeing.

She wore white, the dress flowing about her as if it were mist. Her ebony hair hung loose and caressed her shoulders.

Tana stood on the balcony of her room looking up at the moon, quite unaware of his presence. Unable to sleep, she had come out for a touch of night air. She raised her arms to lift her hair in a sensuous gesture, then released it to fall about her shoulders.

She considered what she had done and had realized both George and Lettie had been right. George, with his advice that what was meant to be would be, and Lettie telling her that she was a woman who need not pursue. Lettie had tried to awaken Tana to her own power.

Both were right, she thought, and both were wrong. She knew she had made a mistake in being so blunt with Ethan. She had felt both young and foolish and yet as if she had crossed some kind of a bridge. Now she needed time to consider herself and her newfound sense of maturity.

Her feelings for Ethan had been unformed and uncontrolled, a dreamer's wish. She had begun to realize that there was so much more to a relationship than passion.

Ethan's life . . . and what he wanted, were so different from hers, and for the first time she understood what her father and her brother had been trying to say.

She needed time now to reconsider her feelings and test this new facet of herself. Tana was grateful to Lettie, for she had opened new and vital doors in Tana's mind and heart.

Tana knew that she had to talk to Ethan—and this time she would listen to everything she had obstinately ignored before.

As if to answer her thoughts, a sudden movement in the garden below drew her attention.

Ethan had stood breathlessly still, feeling much like a voyeur, yet unable to take his eyes from the exquisite picture. Her tawny skin glowed in the soft moonlight.

She was obviously deep in contemplation and he wondered if he were part of her thoughts. That idea had a surprisingly strong effect on his emotions. He began to wonder if he didn't really like the idea of being uppermost in Tana's thoughts.

His steady gaze must have made her suddenly aware of his presence, for she turned her head and saw him in the shadow of a wide-branched tree.

For a moment, in the clear light of the brilliant moon, their eyes met. Ethan knew his voice would carry well in the clear air.

"Can't you sleep?"

"No. I . . . I have a great deal to think about. Ethan, wait there, I must talk to you."

Before Ethan could protest, Tana had stepped back into her room. There was little he could do but wait.

As she passed the bed, Tana put on her robe and ran barefoot down the carpeted steps.

When she approached Ethan her steps slowed a bit. Then they were standing only inches from each other.

"I was just having a drink before I went to bed, and it's such a beautiful night I thought I'd bring it out here." Ethan knew quite well he was only saying words to fill the space and time.

"Of course," she answered softly, unsure of how to begin. "You sent Perez for my father yesterday?"

"Yes. My guess is he'll be here tomorrow. I imagine he's relieved to know where you are and that you're all right."

"I suppose," Tana said, walking a few steps away. She closed her eyes and inhaled a deep breath. "You are right, it is a very beautiful night." She turned to face him again. "You've made this place very special. I suppose you are a very happy man."

"I guess I've enjoyed the battle," Ethan admitted.

"I was walking through your house today. It's the first time I've really seen how it is."

"How is it? I don't understand."

"I mean . . ." she shrugged helplessly. "It is so much another world . . . different from this, than mine."

"You mean it doesn't belong here?"

"No! No, that's not what I meant. It's perfect where it is. It's just . . ."

Ethan took a step or two toward her, filled with a sort of helpless confusion. He found himself wanting to say more than he'd planned to.

Her unusual beauty drew him like a magnet until they were standing close. He could smell the clean scent of her, like the fragrant breeze that whispered about them. His equilibrium took another gentle blow.

"It's just . . . ?" he prompted.

"It's just," she looked up at him, completely aware of his masculinity. Dressed in tan breeches that hugged his muscular legs, knee-high dark brown riding boots, and a white shirt open at the throat to reveal a mat of soft gold hair, Ethan was as powerful as an aphrodisiac. Tana could feel the tug of an emotion she was not equipped to fight. "I don't know."

She backed away a step and turned her back to him. But Ethan reached out and took hold of her arm and turned her to face him, pulling her close.

"Tana, I don't want you ever to believe the things I said were meant to hurt you. I never thought of my home as a barrier for the people I care about. You're welcome here. You, your father, Antonio, all of you have been special friends." He watched as crystal tears formed in her eyes and felt his words were miserably inadequate. Every word he said seemed to make matters worse, and besides that, he was feeling things he had no right to feel.

Her skin was like velvet, and her soft mouth was only inches away. He began to lose his fragile grip on all the arguments he'd memorized earlier. He drew her even closer and whispered her name moments before his lips touched hers.

It was a soft kiss, a whispered touch, yet it seemed to unleash something so powerful that he almost gasped from the force of it.

He raised his head to look into her eyes and saw the same look of surprised wonder that must have been in his.

Then he took her in his arms and this time the kiss was deeply shared.

She wanted his kiss, wanted it with the fear that it might be all she would ever have. She returned the kiss with a fire that shook Ethan to his depths.

But the force of her own emotion had the power to frighten her as well. Because—if Ethan didn't share it, what was the point? She tried to pull herself together. For the time being, she had to retreat.

Then, as suddenly as she had come, she was gone. He watched her run to the door and enter the house. At that moment his arms and his heart felt excruciatingly empty.

Tana felt she could bear no more of the overwhelming need building inside her. She hadn't planned on this, yet she knew if she stayed in Ethan's arms one minute longer she would beg him to make love to her. And all the wisdom of a lifetime warned her that this could be a big mistake. She wanted Ethan . . . but only if he wanted her, too, not just passion on a moonlit night. And only if and when she knew it would be with no regrets.

Uncertainty and desire raged within her the rest of a sleepless night. She knew it was better if her father came for her. Maybe she could talk to him. All her life he'd helped her with her problems. Maybe he'd have a solution to the biggest problem she'd ever had . . . the one that scared her more than anything ever had.

But it was not Mendrano who came, it was Antonio. Ethan, George, Bill, Lettie, and Tana had just finished breakfast. George had just announced that in the morning he wold be leaving first for Barranquilla, then London where he had some business to settle.

"I hate to see you leave so soon, George," Ethan said. "It's always years between visits."

"Ah, but not this time," George chuckled, his sparkling eyes on Tana. "I have decided to return next year . . . just to see if there are any changes around here."

"Well, if you have to go—and you'll make that a promise to be back next year," Ethan grinned, "I have a list of things I'd like you to purchase for me in London."

"I'll see to it."

"I suppose you'll be going out to that dam of yours this morning," George said.

"Yes, just as soon as . . ." his eyes moved quickly to Tana, then back to George. "I'm . . . ah . . . expecting someone to come for Tana. When that's taken care of I'll be on my way."

"I see."

"I wonder," Lettie said, "if Bill and I should go on back up to Drake's dig and see how Caitlyn is getting on."

"Do you really want to, Lettie?" Bill asked humorously.

"Actually," Lettie laughed, "I'm as cozy as can be right here. But Caitlyn . . ."

"I have a feeling Caitlyn is getting on famously. You know how caught up she gets when she's digging. She probably hopes we're content so she can go on," Bill replied.

"I suppose," Lettie laughed.

"So why don't you just relax and enjoy my version of civilization," Ethan urged. "When I've checked on the dam, if you'd still care to visit I can see that you get there."

"Tana," George said, "I'm afraid I'm going to have to bid you a very reluctant farewell. You're a most charming lady and I do hope to see you again."

"Thank you," Tana smiled. "I hope to see you again as well."

Ethan had the vague feeling there was more in the conversation than was being said, but before he could try to decipher it Antonio appeared in the doorway. Ethan saw him first and rose.

"Antonio, welcome. Come on in and join us. I kind of expected your father."

"There's a lot going on at Drake's dig and my father was needed, so I have come for Tana." He had not looked at Tana yet and she, who knew him so well, realized he was very angry.

"You seemed to have traveled fast, Antonio, to get here this morning," Tana said. "I did not expect you until much later."

"You did not expect me at all," Antonio stated firmly. "And I traveled day and night so no time could be wasted."

"That is true. I expected our father, and traveling at night is very dangerous." Tana was teasing but the flash of anger in Antonio's eyes made her contrite.

"Tana, I would like to start home today . . . now." Antonio turned his attention back to Ethan. "I am sorry to seem ungrateful for the hospitality you have shown me and my sister, and I wish we could stay longer, but there has been much discovered at the dig and I am needed there."

"Drake has found what he was searching for?" Ethan asked excitedly.

"I'm not sure it was all he was looking for, but he has discovered many levels to the tomb." Antonio went on to give a quick description of what Drake had found. "So you see why I must get back."

"Of course," Ethan replied.

"I will be ready to go whenever you wish, Antonio," Tana said.

Bill and Lettie had remained silent and George had kept

his eyes on Tana. She had seemed subservient, but he had begun to see the spirit and the will behind her quiet demeanor.

"Then it would be best if we left now. We will go upriver as far as Drake's home." Antonio and Tana said as pleasant a farewell as either could manage. When they were gone, George chuckled.

"I'm afraid Tana's brother is quite angry with her."

Ethan frowned. "What Tana did was dangerous, but after all, she was safe here. He should be relieved instead of angry. I hope it doesn't cause her a problem."

"Oh, I doubt it," George replied. "His anger is just a reaction. It's because he loves her. That's not hard to understand . . . is it?"

Ethan looked quickly at George to see if his question was as pointed as it sounded, but George's expression was completely neutral.

Antonio and Tana traveled for two hours in complete silence, both deep in thought. Tana was bothered by the fact that her brother had had to leave when Drake must have needed him. She felt contrite and wanted to make peace with him and her father.

But Antonio was more puzzled than angry. He could see clearly that nothing seemed to have happened between Tana and Ethan. And he was a bit surprised at Tana's sudden willingness to come home with no argument.

"Antonio?"

"What?"

"I am sorry for what I have done. I shall never do such a thing again."

"It was a foolish thing, Tana. Has it really changed anything?"

"Yes. In a way it has changed a great deal for me."

Antonio was silent for a long moment and Tana sensed the question that was on his mind. She answered before he could voice it.

"No, I did nothing to bring any shame to my family. Ethan and I . . . we talked with each other, and I began to realize that what I did was wrong in many ways."

"He . . . he said nothing to . . ."

"He was kind . . . and did nothing to hurt me. I am afraid my coming was quite a shock to him, too. But my mind is much clearer now, Antonio, and the trip was worth that, if nothing else."

Antonio was not sure this was the complete truth. Tana seemed to have changed in more than one way since he had last seen her.

Tana sat in the native dugout canoe and watched her brother's broad back and muscular arms as he paddled rhythmically against the current. For him it was easy, but she knew her slight strength could not have done it. She wondered for the first time about Antonio's life. They had been inseparable as children, he the leader and she the admiring follower.

But she had not noticed he had grown into a very handsome man. It made her wonder if she would see everything in a new light from now on.

They moved slowly upriver, letting the hours pass as smoothly and silently as the water beneath the canoe.

If Tana wanted to say more, Antonio's silence made it hardly possible. She wished she knew what he was thinking. They traveled on, each caught in their own thoughts and each promising themselves that the days to come would make a difference.

* * *

The sun was only a pale gold rim on the horizon when Antonio brought the canoe against the dock below Drake's house.

"We'd better tell Maria we will stay here for the night."

"It is only a few more hours and we will be home."

"I thought . . . maybe you would like to rest before . . ."

"Before I faced Father?" Antonio had reached down to help her onto the dock. "No, what I have said to you I shall say to him—both of you will have to choose whether you trust what I say or not. Come, Antonio, let's go home." He started to walk away and she reached out to stop him. "Antonio . . . I am very grateful . . . because you care, you try to understand." She turned and walked away.

A puzzled Antonio followed Tana to the small house. After a few words and a rather severe scolding from a worried Maria, who embraced her before she would let them go, Tana and Antonio started home.

Ethan filled his day with as much work as he could cram into it. He would have gone to the dam but George's announcement that he was preparing to leave made Ethan postpone his departure until after George had gone.

He found himself thinking of Tana at the strangest moments. When the sun reflected through the trees he could remember the gold of her skin . . . it was more than aggravating, it was setting his teeth on edge and straining his nerves. The battle raged within because he refused to acknowledge his real feelings.

When he came to the house that night it was long past dinner and he was exhausted.

He apologized to his three guests and told them, just to reassure them, that he would get something to eat and find his way to bed.

"I'll see you all in the morning. George," he grinned, "I hope you don't plan on leaving too early."

"No I don't have to leave at the crack of dawn. I'll wait until you manage to crawl out of bed. I'm not in any great hurry."

"Good. Good night, all."

The three bade him good night, and as soon as he left the room Bill spoke up.

"What's going on with Ethan? He's not coming down with something, is he? For the past couple of days he seems . . . different somehow."

"Oh, I don't think there's anything wrong," George said. "He's just a little preoccupied. After all, he does have several projects going at once. Just running this place would be enough."

"It's quite possible," Lettie added, "that he has things on his mind that we know nothing about."

George glanced at her in time to see her abort a smile and he thought to himself: Here I am, taking the credit for the change and I do believe our little Lettie is much more responsible than I. We shall have to discuss this at a more opportune time.

"I suppose," Bill replied.

"Well, I think I'll go outside and enjoy my pipe for a while," George said. "It'll be a long time before I get the opportunity again. I shall miss this place. I always do."

"Why don't you stay?" Bill asked.

"Oh, I guess in a few more years I'll have to find a permanent abode. Maybe then I can convince Ethan to sell me a small piece of land somewhere nearby. I would enjoy having him for a neighbor in my waning years."

"In the meantime you'll come back here occasionally," Lettie added, "sort of to renew yourself."

"That's a fine way of putting it. I guess I'm a uncivilized man who enjoys only the veneer of civilization. When I feel crowded by it, I run to a sanctuary."

"Bill and I are beginning to feel almost the same way. Do you think it possible that if Drake has discovered something really important and Caitlyn's father decides to go home, Caitlyn might want to stay?"

"I'm sure if Sir Richard leaves, Caitlyn will as well. You know what a field day the newspaper would have over that situation. Drake needs all the credibility he can get. No, I'm afraid Caitlyn would have to leave."

"That would be a shame. She's so good at it and so enthusiastic. She could only be a help to Drake."

"It would do very little for her credentials. She's somewhat of a beginner and could not afford to stay . . . alone."

"You two talk as if you had some kind of control over Caitlyn," Bill laughed. "Lettie, you ought to know better than that. I have a feeling Caitlyn will do exactly what she pleases and if that's staying, then she'll stay."

"I guess you're right," Lettie answered, smiling.

"How about one last drink before you go out, George?" Bill asked.

"A brandy would cap the evening rather well," George agreed.

"Lettie?"

"Yes, I'll join you."

Bill poured the drinks and handed snifters to George and Lettie. Then he raised his.

"A toast. To Drake and Ethan. May they both have continued success in their endeavors."

"Hear, hear," George replied.

When they'd finished, George set his glass aside and wished them both a good night. In the garden he puffed contentedly on his pipe for a while, then he went to his room and to bed.

By eleven o'clock the next day Ethan had the last of George's baggage loaded on the boat. They stood together and watched the final preparations.

"I'll miss you, George."

"And I you, my friend. But time will, I hope, pass rapidly. I have meant to speak to you about a more permanent situation and I was reminded of it last night in a conversation with Bill and Lettie."

"Permanent?"

"I would like to purchase a small piece of land from you. Nothing much," George said with a laugh. "I don't want to be enticed into being a planter. I just would like enough to retire and tend a small . . . very small garden."

"George! I'd be delighted."

"How much land do you have here?"

"Over fifteen hundred acres."

"Good heavens! Well, an acre or two is quite enough for me. I intend to be very lazy in my old age."

"You know you're welcome to make your home with me."

"Thank you, Ethan. But I imagine, one day, there will be a lady gracing your home, and I don't think I should be here then."

Ethan's face clouded momentarily. It seemed this idea was

in everyone's mind lately, and he didn't feel too comfortable that despite his best efforts, Tana flitted into his mind.

"Possibly. But I'm far from finished with this place, so for now consider my door open to you at any time. On your next trip back we'll talk about that land."

"Fine. Well, I think I'd best be on my way. When you see Drake and Caitlyn and her father please extend my best wishes."

"I'll do that."

They shook hands and Ethan stood on the dock and watched the boat pull away and start downriver. He watched until it disappeared. He really would miss George's company.

George enjoyed the slow trip down to Barranquilla. It gave him time to think and begin to make his own plans.

The trip down was much faster than the trip up, since they were moving with the current rather than against it. The six days it took to come up were cut to three since they didn't bother to stop at night, but just moved along with the current. One man remained awake at night to stand watch.

When he arrived in Barranquilla he went to the hotel he had always frequented and acquired a room. Then, once his baggage was delivered and he was settled, he went out to find a good meal.

Satisfied and quite comfortable, he decided to go to bed early. In two days he was scheduled to sail for London.

When he returned to his room he read for a while, smoking his beloved pipe. Then he began to prepare for bed.

He was taken totally by surprise when someone knocked on his door. But the surprise turned to total shock when he opened the door and the man on the other side smiled, extended his hand . . . and said his name.

Sixteen

As Drake held the lantern aloft, he and Caitlyn could see that the room was even larger than the one above it. But the same polished stones made up the floor.

Drake told Caitlyn to stand at one end of the room with her lantern while he walked to the other, measuring as accurately as he could. Standing at opposite ends of the room with their lanterns held high was an eerie experience. Pools of light from each end narrowed in the center, giving the room an elongated look. It also made Caitlyn feel Drake was much farther away than he actually was.

"It's about thirty feet, give or take a couple," Drake's voice echoed through the chamber. Then he walked to her end.

"Look—up around the ceiling," Caitlyn cried, pointing.

About a foot from the ceiling ran a frieze, its colors still vibrant. It was completely intact, running the entire circumference of the room.

The intricate design depicted warriors, each carrying a war club diagonally in one hand and a ceremonial goblet in the other. Each warrior was fashioned in red, while the goblets and clubs were black. The background was white. The heavily-adorned remnants of what must have been men lay on low shelves cut deeply into the walls.

"Look at the ornaments!" Drake exclaimed. "Each of these must have been important men in their own right."

Drake picked up one artifact from atop the disintegrated remains. It was a miniature figure, worn as a nose ornament.

"Considered in terms of craftsmanship, this is a spectacular find," Drake said.

"It will take months just to identify and label what's here. There must be an enormous number of artifacts."

"Have you noticed the use of emeralds?"

"Emeralds? No, I hardly noticed."

"They use them for eyes, and for various designs . . . as if they had an unlimited supply."

Caitlyn looked at Drake with a puzzled frown. "What do emeralds have to do with anything? We've found a treasure that could never be compared to such things. Drake, the emeralds might have a monetary value, but look at the exquisite workmanship of the masks and the other ornaments. The archaeological value far outweighs anything else. I never thought you, of all people, would even be interested in the monetary worth."

Drake smiled. He'd wanted to hear her say it. Caitlyn's reaction seemed sincere, and he felt reassured. If emeralds had been what she had come for, surely she would show some interest, some excitement at finding so many used so casually.

"We're making good progress," Drake said, trying to divert her attention. "Now I think we'd better concentrate on the deities above us. They might enable us to date the entire dig."

Caitlyn had been looking around and suddenly spoke in a quiet voice. "Drake."

"What? Do you see something special?"

"No . . . I've just counted the remains," she said and looked up at him. "There are thirteen."

Drake paused a moment to count, then returned her gaze. "Thirteen," he confirmed. "Well, that seems to settle that question. There is no coincidence. The number thirteen had a great deal of significance here. We shouldn't go on much further until we trace it down."

"How do we do that?"

"I have a room full of research books down at my house. We can go down after dinner and see what we can find. I'd planned on asking you to come down there anyway. I want you to see it."

"I'd like to. Besides, it may help us discover who's buried here."

"Well, from the fact," he pointed to a shadowed area, "that there's another flight of steps, we're safe in concluding there's at least one more level."

Drake moved toward the next flight of steps, Caitlyn right behind him.

"Do you hear something?" she questioned.

"Sounds like . . . water, rushing water. This gets more complicated by the minute."

"Let's go down and see . . ."

"No. We have no idea what's there, and we'll need a lot more light. Our lanterns aren't having much effect in this room. If the one below is bigger, these two lanterns will be practically useless. Besides, we're running out of time." Drake took his watch from his pocket. "It's going on four. Time to go up. We'll start early in the morning. If we want to go over those books, we'll need the time."

"I suppose you're right," Caitlyn agreed. "My curiosity was getting the best of me. Besides, it might prove helpful if we ask Mendrano and my father a few questions."

"You're right. Legends sometimes lose a bit over the years but the essence is usually intact."

"Whatever the legend was or whoever this king was, he

must have been someone very important. Maybe . . . it was a tragedy of some sort."

"What makes you think that?"

"I heard of an ancient Egyptian legend where a king was accused of some ugly thing. They entombed him, then surrounded him with a ring of gods and soldiers with weapons." She looked at Drake seriously. "To keep his spirit *inside,* so he would not be unleashed on the world again."

"King Tunken Ra."

"Yes, you know the legend?"

"I've heard it."

"This is a lot like that. Those deities above us, surrounding the exits. The thirteen warriors . . . protecting the world from the spirit locked below."

"We're dancing with shadows, Caitlyn. And in a place like this it can get out of hand. Let's not jump to any conclusions until we can prove who and what he is . . . or was."

"Let's hope there's something in those books of yours. This can drive you crazy."

"Before we go down to my place, I'd like to ask your father what he knows of Tunken Ra."

"And if he knows of anything about a thirteenth king . . . or a thirteenth son or . . ."

"Or a thirteenth daughter," Drake grinned. He shrugged at her surprised look. "You were the one who suggested this might be someone's grandmother."

"Or granddaughter."

"We keep this up and the puzzle will just get more complex."

"I agree. But it's exciting, isn't it?"

"Come on," Drake chuckled, "let's get you some fresh air before you get carried away."

They went up into the late afternoon sunshine to find

Mendrano and Sir Richard concluding the counting and sorting of the contents of the jars. The jars themselves were set carefully on a blanket Drake had spread out for this purpose.

Supper was already prepared so they sat down to eat before they explained what had happened. At the end of the meal, Drake addressed Sir Richard.

"What do you know of the ancient Egyptian king Tunken Ra?"

"Tunken Ra? Hmm . . . Tunken Ra." Sir Richard seemed puzzled. "I'm afraid the name escapes me. Why? Does it have some significance here?"

Caitlyn looked at her father with deep surprise bordering on disbelief. He was an internationally-respected expert in Egyptian history.

"Tunken Ra had a pretty nasty reputation, so nasty that they entombed him alive," Drake added. "Caitlyn seems to think this is something like that."

"Tunken Ra, Father, was buried with all his wealth. They found an unbelievable treasure when they opened the tomb. I guess the legend was created when they put what are known as spiritual guards around and in the tomb to make sure his spirit didn't wander back into the world."

"I guess getting a glimpse of all the emeralds in this tomb caused Caitlyn to think of that," Drake remarked.

"Emeralds?" Sir Richard asked with obvious interest. "I had no idea you found emeralds down there. Did you bring any up?"

"No . . . we brought nothing up with us."

Caitlin grew silent. She didn't like the uncomfortable feeling her father's interest in emeralds gave her.

Mendrano had remained silent as well, but suddenly spoke up. "There is no need to search further for a legend. I have just remembered one—and it might be what you're looking for."

"You know a legend that fits here?" Drake asked, a touch of excitement in his voice.

"More than that. I think I know now whose tomb you have found."

"Oh, Mendrano," Caitlyn breathed, "tell us."

"Many centuries ago there was a young king who came to the throne when he was only twenty years of age. Hunsahua was trained and determined to be a good king. Hunsahua was too young for such a rank, but he governed more wisely than anyone thought he could. He led his people bravely in battle. He might have ruled a long time, respected in life and forgotten in death, but he sinned greatly and so exchanged longevity for immortality. The young king was consumed by a passion for his own sister, who was considered the most beautiful woman in the empire."

"How terrible," Caitlyn whispered.

"Yes," Mendrano said and continued. "He was called to a distant part of his realm, took her with him, and made her his wife. The legend does not say how or where the wedding took place, but if the ceremony followed the usual procedure, the priest stood before the couple and asked the girl if she would love the gods more than her husband, her husband more than her children, and her children more than herself. And when she had sworn, the priest would ask if she would promise never to eat if her husband were hungry, and to this condition she would again agree. Then the king would testify that he desired this woman for his wife, conferring on her alone all the rights of the position—and the marriage was official."

"But that's a travesty of any religion or any society," Drake said.

"Yes. But that is not the end of the story," Mendrano continued. "When the lovers returned home they told no one what they had done. But maternal eyes are sharp; the time came when their mother guessed the secret and confronted them. Even the king was not powerful enough to openly flout the laws he had created. But he tried. He tried to stop judgment of what he had done and used his powers with stunning brutality until his people began to see the evil growing inside him. They brought him to trial. Within his treasure room he had a huge casket filled with green fire."

"Emeralds," Sir Richard said softly. "A whole casket full of emeralds."

"Yes, he tried to use these to bribe the men who would judge him. It didn't work and the king became enraged and called down a curse from the world beyond. The curse filled the judges and the people with fear. In their fear they made a decision. The king and queen were entombed . . . together. But the people were still afraid, afraid of the curse. So they set warriors and gods to guard them . . . and all the treasure the king possessed."

"So . . . this may be the tomb of the young king and his sister-wife," Drake said.

"What a remarkable treasure they must have buried with them," Sir Richard added.

"Think of all the artifacts that must be buried down in that tomb," Caitlyn said.

"If you can find it," Mendrano said.

"But we've found the tomb," Drake responded questioningly.

"Yes . . . but if this is the one, there is another secret inside. For the legend says the king and the queen were 'shut away,' even from the guards set to contain them. When you go down to that final level, who knows what you will find . . . and what will still remain a secret."

"Well secret or no secret, legend or no legend, and curse or no curse, tomorrow I'm going down to the next and maybe last level. We'll see just what kind of secrets it holds," Drake said firmly.

"Drake, maybe if we go down to your home tonight we could read up on this. Whatever information we find can only be beneficial," Caitlyn offered.

"You're right. If you're finished eating, would you like to go now?"

"Let's go."

"Sir Richard, would you like to come along?"

"No, thank you, my boy. That's a considerable distance and I'm not sure my legs would make it. I think I'll retire early. I'm afraid I've not been quite up to par the past few days."

"You're not sick, are you?" Caitlyn asked worriedly.

"No, my dear," Sir Richard said, "I'm just feeling the pinch of time. You two go and do your research. I'll go through the books I brought. Maybe tomorrow we'll have all the answers."

"Well, don't push yourself," Caitlyn cautioned.

"I won't. I'll go to bed early. You two run along. At this rate it'll be evening before you get there. I wouldn't want you to be out after dark."

"I guess we'd better get going, Caitlyn," Drake said. "Mendrano, you'll keep things moving here?"

"Don't worry. I'll take care of everything."

Caitlyn and Drake went to their respective tents, and re-appeared a few minutes later. Caitlyn carried her notebook and had put on a jacket to protect her from the brush. Drake wore a jacket, too, and carried a rifle with an ammunition belt looped over his shoulder. "Ready?" he asked Caitlyn.

"As ready as I'll ever be. I'll see you later, Father."

"Take care," Sir Richard said. He watched them walk into the jungle, then turned to look with new interest toward the site of the tomb.

Drake walked with a relaxed, easy stride, shortening his steps so Caitlyn would have no problem keeping up. They moved down the hillside with Drake in the lead.

If there was any kind of a path Caitlyn couldn't see it, yet Drake seemed to have no trouble. He must have been up and down this path a hundred times in the time he'd been here, she decided.

Nothing moved. The landscape, so full of trees and entwined with vegetation, seemed empty of life, yet the sounds all around them told a different story. There was the steady, metallic whine of cicadas—from time to time a staccato birdsong managed to be heard above it.

It was eerie and primordial, heavy with humidity and shadowed by luxuriant growth that transformed the brightness of day into a green twilight.

Somewhere high above, gibbons and monkeys crouched unseen in the treetops and chattered angrily at the trespassers. In the same mighty trees lurked giant flying squirrels the size of house cats.

Entwined around the leafy boughs and thick vines were sleek arboreal snakes, lying in wait for prey.

The trees, some as tall as five hundred feet, impressed Caitlyn and she found herself constantly looking up in admiration.

Almost an hour later Caitlyn thought she could hear another sound slowly taking precedence over all the others.

"Drake, what is that?"

"It's a surprise I want to show you. Be patient—we'll be there in a couple minutes."

As they walked the sound grew louder and louder and she realized it was the roar of falling water. But what she thought she knew and what she was about to see were totally different.

Drake stopped walking, waiting for her to come up beside him and when she did her eyes widened in awe.

They stood facing a horseshoe-shaped escarpment, fully three hundred feet high. From the top roared a stream of clear water that glistened silver in the dying sun. Beneath it was a wide pool, and where the falling water touched the pool rose a fine mist. It was enough to take Caitlyn's breath away.

"I come down here occasionally to swim," Drake said. "The water is crystal clear and even tastes sweet."

"How do you get down there?"

"There's a path. We don't have time to take it right now. We still have over a two-hour walk." Drake turned to face her, his dark eyes warming as they gazed down into the emerald glow of Caitlyn's. "But I would like to share it with you . . . soon."

Caitlyn could feel herself respond to his gaze—she wished the time were now.

"We'd better go," she managed to say, but Drake's eyes were still locked with hers and for the life of her she couldn't seem to move.

Drake knew it was urgent that they keep moving. Being caught in the jungle after dark was not exactly smart, but he couldn't resist the need to touch her.

He put his free arm around Caitlyn and drew her against him, then bent to brush her willing lips in a gentle kiss that stirred every nerve in her body. He hadn't meant it to grow into passion, but it was like an unleashed storm, quickly slipping from his control. Even when the kiss reluctantly ended, he couldn't seem to let her go.

Drake inhaled a ragged breath—it was hard enough to control himself without reading the willing warmth in her eyes.

"You're right. We'd better go," Drake released her and they stood for a minute before either moved. Then he turned and took the lead again with Caitlyn a few steps behind him.

Caitlyn had to admit she was a bit tired when they entered the clearing near Drake's house. She was not paying attention to what he was doing and nearly collided with him before she realized he'd stopped.

"Drake?"

"That's funny," Drake said, almost to himself.

"What?" Her heart leapt. "What's funny?"

"It's getting dark and there's no light in the house."

"Maybe Maria hasn't gotten around to lighting them yet."

"You don't know Maria. She's afraid of the dark. She lights the lamps at the first sign of darkness."

"I hope she's not sick . . . or hurt."

Drake nodded and started across the clearing to the house. He went up the four front steps in two quick bounds, crossed the porch, and opened the door. Darkness and silence.

"Maria!" Drake shouted. But there was no answer. A quick examination of the four small rooms made it clear that no one was around.

"This is strange," Drake muttered. "I wonder if . . ." Then he suddenly snapped his fingers. "Bogota! Maria's gone to Bogota. There's a big festival of some sort. She told me last week her brother was going to come for her but I forgot. Oh well, let me light a lamp or two and we'll get at those books."

He set his rifle in a corner and hung the ammunition belt

on the back of a nearby chair. Then he removed his jacket and draped it over the belt. Only then did he realize that Caitlyn had been standing inside the doorway and was watching him with a half-smile.

He chuckled. "I didn't plan it this way and I swear I didn't remember Maria wasn't going to be here. But I do have to admit that it couldn't have worked out better."

"We're here to do research," she replied.

"Of course we are." He struggled to keep an innocent look on his face as he added softly, "But you know there's no possible way to get back to the dig until morning, don't you? We have to stay here tonight."

"You're serious?"

"Absolutely. I'm afraid of that jungle at night. So, we don't have any choice . . . no choice at all."

"Drake Stone, you're one devious man."

"I swear. I . . ."

"Don't swear," Caitlyn laughed. "The gods around could be listening and you might be cursed or something for telling such stories . . . and I have a suspicion you're no more afraid of that jungle than you are of going down into that tomb." Drake was watching her closely, trying to read her thoughts. Then with a sparkle in her eyes she smiled. "Of course, since there's not much we can do about it now, we might just as well make the best of it."

Drake crossed the distance between them so quickly Caitlyn only had time to gasp his name before his arms were around her and nearly lifted her from the floor. His mouth found hers and stopped any other words she might have said.

The kiss was lingering and heated, until Caitlyn felt as if she were melting. It took considerable effort to break it.

"I think we'd best do that research, or we may never get to it."

"All work and no play," Drake murmured as his lips found a sensitive spot and tasted the warmth of the flesh of her throat.

"Drake . . . please, I can't think."

"I don't want you to think. I want you to feel what I feel."

"I know . . . and I do. But . . ."

Drake held her a few inches from him and looked down at her, sensing what she felt—and understanding. Gently he cupped her face between his hands and touched her mouth with a feather-like kiss.

"I'm sorry, Caitlyn, I didn't mean to make it feel that way. It's just . . ." He paused as if he were choosing his words very carefully. "It's just that I'm very much in love with you, and it's pretty hard to control the need to hold you . . . make love to you. Suppose we start this whole thing over."

Caitlyn nodded and Drake kissed her again, then released her. "Welcome to my home," he gestured, waving her inside. "You're welcome, humble as it is."

Caitlyn walked inside and began to look around, with Drake following close behind. She could see at once that although it was small, it was owned by someone who cared about it. The house told her a lot about Drake.

He had moved away to make sure a lamp was lit in each room and soon the house was filled with mellow, golden light.

Maria kept the whole house immaculate. The kitchen contained a table and chairs clearly cut and designed from the trees that surrounded the house. There was a small cupboard in one corner and marvelously woven carpets of native design, patterned in brilliant colors, were scattered across the wood floor. As all natives did, Maria kept a profusion of multicolored flowers about.

The next room was obviously one in which Drake had worked. Bookshelves lined the walls and were filled to capacity. The desk was cluttered with papers. An oversize chair sat near a window, covered with a large throw that had obviously been woven on the same loom as the carpets, for it bore the same bold pattern.

The third room seemed to be for storage, containing boxes and chests, some of which were left open.

The fourth room was a bedroom—its obvious comfort took Caitlyn a bit by surprise.

It was dominated by a huge bed that looked as if it had been hewn from a very large tree. It supported a thick mattress and was covered by the same multicolored cloth, only this time it was soft to the touch. A chest of drawers stood in one corner and on it was a native pottery piece of elaborate design filled with bright red blossoms. Once again the patterned carpets appeared on the wood floor.

The window was covered with fine mosquito netting, which allowed the scented breeze to fill the room. Caitlyn turned to face Drake.

"Your home is lovely. I can't see why you go on living up there in that tent when you have this."

"Up to now it's just been easier. Sometimes I work until the wee hours. It's too much to come here and get there again by dawn. Now . . . I wouldn't mind coming back here . . . if I had someone to share it with." He smiled. "You see, a tent says . . . *this is not permanent, don't get attached. This is easy to walk away from.* But a house . . . a house should be permanent, it should say *stay . . . belong.* And a house that's lonely," he shrugged expressively, "well, sometimes the things it says are hard to live with. Caitlyn . . . you fit here very well. I'd like you to . . . to like it."

"I do," her voice softened and her eyes grew warmer.

He stood, hands in his pockets, one shoulder braced against the door frame.

"If you keep looking at me like that," he said softly, "there's no way you're going to leave this room."

Caitlyn walked to him and slowly slid her arms about him. "I suppose we'll have to look through any number of books."

"Uh-huh," he agreed.

"And I suppose it's going to take hours and hours."

"Uh-huh," he agreed again, but there was a twinkle in his eyes.

"Then . . . don't you think the trip down here was tiring?"

He chuckled softly and his arms slid easily around her. "Is this a bit of teasing just to punish me or are you serious?"

"Oh," Caitlyn said softly as she reached up to slide her fingers into his thick hair and draw his head down. "At this minute I couldn't be more serious," she murmured as their lips met.

His lips lingered against hers, tasting again and again until the soft sound she made echoed his own need. Then, he bent and lifted her in his arms and held her against him. The kiss deepened, growing in intensity until Caitlyn could only cling to him and return it with all the passion within her.

Drake stepped inside the room and used his foot to kick the door shut.

When he finally let her feet touch the floor they were close to the bed. Weakness flooded through her and she felt dizzy. His hands trembled a bit as he began to slowly undress her. Looking up into his eyes she felt as if this were somehow the completion of something.

"Do you believe in reincarnation?" she asked suddenly.

"Because we know each other so perfectly . . . because it is so right?"

"Yes," her answer was a whisper. He knew what she was thinking. She felt as if she had known him forever, had stood here with him, had loved him before. From now on their lives were inextricably woven together . . . did he know that, too?

Drake tilted her chin up toward him, and covered her mouth with his, the warm wetness of their mouths intermingling. She felt his heartbeat drumming against hers, felt him weaving her into his being. The dizziness left her and strength surged through her. She felt stronger and more alive than she ever had.

She began to help him undress. She wanted him, wanted her breasts against the hardness of his chest. She yearned for their bodies to touch, to feel his legs entwined with hers. She began to feel a ferocious heat.

She watched as he tossed aside the last of his clothing. What a beautiful body, she thought. Lean, tall, strong. For a few precious moments they absorbed each other. Then, very slowly he took her into his arms and held her against him, his hands gently caressing her back.

"Do you have any idea," he said softly, "how painful it's been to work with you, to touch you in passing, to sit for hours and talk about our research and our ideas, to look at you and not reach for you? Not kiss you? Have you any idea how worthwhile you make my life?"

Caitlyn closed her eyes as he drew her down onto the bed. It amazed her how slowly and gently he began to make love to her. His lips found sensitive spots while his hands began to memorize every inch of her.

"When I'm lonely at night, and that's most of the time since you came, I try to imagine you like this," his voice shook a bit. "I've imagined the velvet of your skin . . . I've dreamed of how you taste and how it would feel if you touched me. I've wanted to explore you, be inside you. I've wanted all of you."

He began to heat her blood with kisses, increasing the intensity of her need to the boiling point. But she discovered that when she touched him it was a distinct pleasure; his skin was surprisingly warm and smooth. If she nibbled here, stroked there, she would get a response that made her feel surprisingly powerful.

Their passion grew, each holding on until their need was unbearable. When he thought he couldn't endure the exquisite pain, when he knew by the soft sounds they were making, only then did he plunge into her. His mouth locked with hers as they rocked to the age-old rhythm that matched the primeval fire of the jungle all around them.

Caitlyn could feel his fierceness and she wanted it, lifting her body to meet his, wrapping herself around him as if she could hold him forever. More than once he teased her close to climax, then stopped. He did this again and again until she went wild with desire, until she wanted him as she could not remember wanting anything in her entire life. By this time they were completely immersed in a cauldron of passion.

What elated him most when they reached the pinnacle together was that he felt he'd given her as much pleasure as she'd given him.

For a while they lay still, holding each other. Then Drake moved and lay by her side. He rested on his elbow, his hand supporting his head, so he could look down into her eyes.

Caitlyn reached up and brushed a wayward strand of hair from his forehead, and he turned to kiss her palm. The night sounds filled the air and Caitlyn smiled.

"It's like being alone in the world."

"Eden," he said huskily. "This has to be Eden and you're my Eve."

His hand rested lightly against her thigh and his fingertips slowly began to caress her.

"Drake?"

"Hmm?"

"I love your home." She laughed softly at his frown. "That's not what you wanted to hear?"

"Not exactly," he responded. "I'd like to hear something more."

"That I love you?" she replied. His eyes grew serious and deep with warmth.

"Do you?" he said with quiet urgency.

"Yes . . . I think I do."

"Think? I haven't convinced you yet that this is as near perfect as you can get?"

"It might take a bit more practice."

Laughter rumbled deep in his chest. "Just how much do you have in mind?"

"Oh . . . it might take years . . ."

"And years and years . . . maybe a lifetime," he murmured just before he bent to kiss her again. "That sounds like a reasonable length of time."

Caitlyn stretched luxuriously in his arms and then turned full against him, nuzzling his neck. "All we need is music," she murmured, "and this would be heaven."

"You need only ask," Drake said. When he started to get up from the bed Caitlyn blinked in surprise. She was even more surprised when he moved to a shadowed corner.

Drake lifted the lid of the victrola and cranked the handle. When he placed the needle on the record soft music filled the room. He turned to Caitlyn and smiled, then held out his hand. "Shall we dance?"

It was deliciously erotic, Caitlyn thought as she slipped from the bed, crossed the room, and moved into his arms. Dancing naked in a moon-washed room in the middle of the Colombian jungle, the music accompanied only by mysterious night sounds and their own heartbeats.

They moved only slightly, feeling remarkably sensuous as their bodies slowly caressed each other. Drake's arm was around her while his other hand caressed her shoulder, the curve of her back, and her buttocks, drawing her snug against him.

She could feel his passion grow again. He was hard against the flatness of her belly, yet he made no move. Wordlessly they continued their slow, undulating movement to the music. The pleasure was intoxicating.

Only when the music stopped and they stared at each other did they give way to their need. Caitlyn looped her arms about his neck and with one easy move Drake lifted her and filled her at the same time. She gasped with the force of it as he backed toward the bed; she could feel the movement of his body deep within her.

Then she was astride him, still holding him deep inside her. She began to move as his hands slid from her hips to her waist, then reached to cup her breasts. She bent forward and he raised his head to capture her mouth. Her hair fell around them and she could hear his muffled groans mingle with hers.

Exhausted, she collapsed against him and he held her tight. After a while they slept.

Seventeen

Mendrano took a short walk through the sleeping camp to make certain all was well. Sir Richard's tent had grown dark long hours before. As far as Mendrano could see, there was no sign of any movement.

He had posted guards around the dig and would change them every few hours. For now, he had to get some much-needed rest. He went to his makeshift accommodations and curled up beneath a blanket. The ground was not his usual sleeping place, and although he wasn't comfortable, he was tired enough that sleep came quickly.

The moon reached its zenith and began its descent. Only then did Sir Richard's tent flap open slowly and cautiously. He stood in the opening several minutes, then left his tent, walked around behind it, and vanished silently into the surrounding jungle.

He had only gone a short distance when a familiar sound made him stop. "Carlos?" he whispered.

"Si," came the reply.

"Where is he?"

"About a hundred feet ahead. I told him you said you had to speak to him. It took a great deal of effort for him to be here. I need not tell you he is not pleased."

"Well, right now I don't care how *pleased* he is. Besides, I have some information that might interest him."

"Then go on." The voice was less than sympathetic. "He's waiting for you."

"This jungle is too dangerous to be . . ."

"It's only a few feet," the voice urged, amused. "Don't worry, we're watching. We won't let anything eat you."

Gritting his teeth, Sir Richard continued down the path until he reached a clearing. He could see a man, and he recognized him even in the darkness. The man had been standing with his back to Sir Richard, but now he turned. The two men stood a few feet apart.

"Mr. Monroe," Sir Richard said without his usual control. His manner was subservient and nervous.

Slade Monroe smiled benevolently . . . but Sir Richard knew it meant nothing; the eyes were like ice.

"This is very dangerous. I hope it's important."

"Carlos told me about the *accident* at the dam," Sir Richard began.

"Yes . . . tragic."

"It was no accident and you know it."

"Some accidents are necessary . . . it might take more than one. You're not losing your nerve, are you?"

"No . . . no, I'm not. Look . . . they've found very few emeralds here in the dig, and if what they think is true there are only historical artifacts left down there. Why don't we just concentrate on what we can dig here and go?"

"We intend to take whatever they come up with, but right now the spot where our men are digging has proven productive."

"Then you still have to stop that dam?"

"Of course. The lake it will form will inundate our mining place, flood it. The emeralds that might be lost under there is an intolerable thought. We must stop that dam. In the meantime, do what you've been paid to do. If there are any emeralds there . . . I want them."

"Their head man . . . that Mendrano, he suspects me." Sir Richard's voice was sullen and a bit frightened.

"So? When the time comes we will eliminate him as well. I don't want you losing your grip. Do those emeralds mean nothing to you?"

"I . . . I can take care of myself."

"Look, when Sir Richard Macdonald came to me to try to find his wife, I knew what he had, Paul."

"Why the hell didn't you tell me about that girl showing up!"

"How did we know he had a daughter who'd show up on your doorstep? It doesn't matter now."

"You killed him?"

"No. We don't want to get Scotland Yard into it. Let's just say we . . . detained him until this is over. Then we'll see to him, and no one will be able to trace us."

"I was just supposed to read a few books and do an acting job for a share of the emeralds. I didn't count on . . . murder."

"It's only a couple more weeks, Paul. If we can keep that dam from being built and find enough emeralds, we'll be able to leave this godforsaken place and live like potentates the rest of our lives."

"They've found a few emeralds so far, but the tomb looks well looted," Paul lied, hoping he sounded convincing. "But the legend says . . ."

"Legend?" Monroe asked, suddenly interested.

"Yes." He went on to explain the story Mendrano had told, and then quickly inserted the idea that Drake and Caitlyn both felt they were about to find a huge treasure. "Of course, those two, Caitlyn and Drake, are so caught up in the history and artifacts, it doesn't matter to them that there's very little treasure left."

"You think there's any truth to the legend?"

"I'm not an archaeologist, as you well know. Nor do I have much interest in history. All I know is that they've found no emeralds so far, and the ones they did find are inferior decorations."

"What have they done with them?"

"They're in a box in Drake's tent. Why?"

"Because . . . we don't want to leave any behind when we go."

"Drake will never . . . part with anything unless he's . . . you do plan to kill him, don't you?"

"Imbecile! This dig could take four or five years. We have to bring it to a halt before we go. And we have to do it so no one causes any problems."

"The men . . . the workers . . ."

"That can be handled. Once the others disappear you'll pay them a huge bonus . . . and send them home. There'll be no questions."

"You'll . . . all of them!" Sir Richard cried, his voice nearly breaking.

"Do you want to quit now? Go back to being Paul Macombe and act in second rate plays the rest of your life? Or live like a king. How do you want it?"

Paul licked his lips, balancing three lives against his own future. Greed won out. He could not go back to his nearly destitute former life. And Slade Monroe would never really have to know about all the treasure in the tomb.

"All right, I'll finish what I started."

"Good. Then it's time you got back to the camp. You wouldn't want anyone to discover you're missing."

"No . . . no, of course not. About the dam. I . . ."

"Don't worry about that. You have your end to think about. Me and the others will take care of stopping that dam . . . at least for as long as we need it stopped."

"Yes. Yes, of course."

"You'd best go."

He turned and walked away heading back to the camp—and his role as Sir Richard. No need to worry now about predators lurking in the jungle—he knew there were worse predators . . . and he was suddenly afraid they might not be too discerning about their prey. He would have to play his game carefully. And if he did . . . he could have it all.

George Frasier had a profound shock when he opened his hotel room door and came face to face with a man who resembled Sir Richard Macdonald so closely it was staggering. He must have gazed at him in open-mouthed surprise for several moments before the man spoke.

"You are George Frasier?"

"Yes."

"I'm sorry to disturb you, but it's important that I talk to you. I'm told you're the best guide upriver."

"Ah . . . no . . . no, you're not disturbing me. It's just . . . well, you resemble someone I know so well that it's rather upsetting."

"By George," the man laughed, "I didn't know there was anyone else with a face like this. My name is Sir Richard Macdonald. May I ask who my double might be?"

"Sir Richard . . . I can't believe . . ." George paused to clear his head. "Would you come in, please? Something needs clearing up here."

Once the door was closed George faced his visitor. "Can I get you something?"

"No, but you look as though *you* could use something."

"I can at that. Please sit down. We have a great deal to discuss."

Sir Richard sat down while George poured himself a generous shot of whiskey. He drank a hefty swallow, then pulled a chair close to a now very curious Sir Richard.

"Sir Richard, can you tell me, did anything . . . untoward happen before you made this trip? I mean, were you delayed somehow?"

"Now, it's strange that you should ask me such a thing. I had a terrible run-in with some thugs. Grabbed me right off the streets, held me locked in an old house. I imagine they thought that because my name was in the paper recently, they could ask for ransom. I tried to tell them I wasn't worth that kind of a fortune, but that I would give them all I had if they set me free. But they refused to listen."

"And they finally let you go?"

"The devil they did! Got out of that little predicament by myself—not the easiest thing I've ever done, I might add. Went straight to the police but they must have thought me a bit balmy. Anyway I had agreed to come here and meet a young archaeologist named . . ."

"Don't tell me," George said resignedly. "Drake Stone."

"Ah, you know the fellow?"

"Yes . . . I do."

"Well, I owe him an apology. I told him I would come to authenticate a dig he's working on. I hate not to do what I've agreed to do, and the young man seemed so sincere and enthusiastic in his letter, not to mention the fact that his find sounds intriguing."

"And now I have to tell you the other side of the story. I don't think your kidnapping was for ransom. You see . . . not too long ago I took three people up to Drake's dig.

When we arrived we were greeted by Drake and his very honored guest . . . Sir Richard Macdonald." Sir Richard's face was a study in total amazement. He couldn't quite grasp what George was saying.

"But . . . that's impossible! I don't understand."

"Someone wanted to take your place for a reason I can't fathom right now, but if it involves the need to kidnap you for a period of time, it can't be very savory."

"What on earth would someone have to gain from doing such a thing?"

"I don't know. But there's a whole lot more to this."

"I've jolly well heard more than enough for now."

"I'm afraid this part will be a bit more of a shock. You see . . . the people I brought up to the dig . . . one of them was a young lady named Caitlyn Emmerson. She came because she was looking for you, looking for the man she claimed was her father."

Sir Richard's face grew pale and George was sure he saw tears well in his eyes. "Caitlyn," he murmured. "She had a child and named her Caitlyn." He grew momentarily silent. "She . . . she must be my my daughter. I never knew . . . I've never seen her. The night I was kidnapped I was on my way to find her and her mother. It took me so many years . . . when I finally got away from those fiends I went to the address, only to be told that Rose was dead. Now, it seems I've been given a second chance."

"But don't you see? She believes this other man, this impostor, is you. She thinks he's her father and God only knows what advantage he'll take of that . . . as well as your reputation."

"You're quite right," Sir Richard answered. "We must get up to that dig and expose this man."

"I'm afraid we can't do that just yet."

"But . . . you're a guide. You know the way."

"Yes, but I won't have access to a boat until late tomorrow."

"And how long will it take to get there?"

"Traveling at our best speed against the current, four to five days I'd say. Of course, if I take along an extra man or two for protection, we can travel straight through. Once we get to Ethan Marshall's plantation, we'll get all the assistance we need."

"Then we must go at the earliest possible moment."

"Right. In the meantime we'll have to be patient."

"Then let's have a drink, and I can ask you questions about my daughter."

"It's amazing. You've never seen her?" George said as he rose, refreshed his drink, and poured one for Sir Richard.

"No," Sir Richard said softly. "It's a long and difficult story about the stubborn pride of two people who never should have separated. Please," Sir Richard said, reaching into his pocket, "let me show you a picture of Rose. Tell me if Caitlyn is as beautiful as her mother was."

George took the small folded wallet. It contained the picture of a very lovely woman.

"Yes, yes," George said softly. "Caitlyn does resemble her mother very much, yet," he cast a quick look at Sir Richard, "she looks like you as well."

"Tell me about her."

"I'll tell you everything I know."

They spent the evening talking about Caitlyn, Drake and his dig, and Ethan and his plantation until Sir Richard felt as if he knew everyone in question almost as well as George.

"But what puzzles me is the motive. There's nothing but hard work involved in a dig. Why did they want to impersonate me?"

"There's no real treasure there?" George asked.

"It's unlikely. Most tombs have been thoroughly looted over the centuries. And I'm sure if Drake did find anything he'd guard it well until it was turned over to the museum. No, there must be another motive."

"People don't resort to kidnapping and impersonation for nothing. But I can't imagine what they had to gain."

"We won't learn a thing until I find this impostor and get the truth out of him."

"I'll go down to the docks in the morning and see if I can find some transportation. I'll also leave a message for Emil Josiah—he's off on business but he should be back in a couple of days. We'll need all the help we can get. This is also a matter for the Colombian authorities."

"We'll take whatever we can find."

"I'll do my best. Do you have a room, Sir Richard?"

"Yes. I was just getting one when I asked about you . . . or rather asked about a guide. You were very highly recommended."

"Thank you. It's best we get some sleep—maybe we'll be lucky if we're at the docks early."

"Good idea," Sir Richard said as he rose. "I'll see you early tomorrow."

"Good night, Sir Richard."

"And thank you." Sir Richard extended his hand and George took it in a firm grip. "I'll be eternally grateful for your help. Good night."

George watched Sir Richard walk to the door. It was still such a mystery. Why would anyone want to kidnap and impersonate an archaeologist? They would find out in time—he just wondered how much time they had.

* * *

When George returned from Emil's office he and Sir Richard walked to the docks before sunrise—the sky was still washed in deep violet from the waning night.

George questioned one person after another and for a while it looked as if there was no hope for an early departure. Then luck came their way.

The boat was not the best, but it would, in George's opinion, get them as far as Ethan's. The price was exorbitant since the owner sensed at once this was some kind of an emergency.

"That's ridiculous!" George blustered.

"George, please," Sir Richard said. "The cost is not as important as whether we get there in time to foil these brigands and get my daughter to safety."

"You're right," George admitted, and reluctantly allowed Sir Richard to pay for the boat.

By the time the sun was overhead, Sir Richard and George had stowed their baggage on board and were on their way upriver.

Drake stood in the doorway and watched Caitlyn with fascination. She sat cross-legged on the floor of his workroom, a stack of books beside her and a few open on the floor. She was industriously making notes and had no idea he was there.

She wore only a bright piece of red fabric wrapped about her, sarong-style. Her long, tan legs were bare, as were her shoulders. Her hair was a tangled mass of gold. She looked more inviting than she could have imagined.

"Good morning," he said and was rewarded with a quick smile and a warm glance. "Do you have the remotest idea how empty that bed is when you aren't in it?"

"Oh, Drake, come over here quickly! You've got to read this. It's the answer—I know it is."

Drake chuckled as he walked over and got down on his knees beside her. "I knew it. You're the love 'em and leave 'em type. I've been deserted for a king who's been dead for a couple of thousand years."

Caitlyn laughed and got to her knees to fling her arms about him and kiss him with uninhibited abandon. "I'll take you over a dead king any day. You're much warmer and I love kissing you."

"You're the most unpredictable . . ." he began, but the lure of her warm body and inviting lips was hard to resist. He held her close and kissed her deeply. But before one thing had a chance to lead to another, she was out of his arms and reaching for her notebook. Her eyes were aglow as he watched her with pleasure.

"I've found him," she said elatedly, waving the notebook.

"Found who?"

"Our king, that's who!"

"Not *our* king, love, *your* king. I'll take a princess instead." He reached for her again but she moved just out of his reach.

"Drake, listen to me. I've found the thirteenth king and guess what his name was?"

"King lust," he leered playfully. But Caitlyn wasn't having any of it.

"King Hunsahua—the king of Mendrano's legend. Listen to what it says about him." Drake knew he wasn't going to defeat Caitlyn's enthusiasm, so he found a comfortable place and sat down.

"King Hunsahua," Caitlyn began, "the thirteenth king under the god of the sun, did not reign for many years. Little is known of his rule except for ancient legends that have been handed down for generations. He was, as the legend goes, punished by entombment for a transgression against the very laws he had laid down for his people. The location of his tomb has been a mystery for centuries. But much has been told of the great riches buried with him and watched by the thirteen guards of honor and the thirteen gods that were worshipped in his day." Her brow furrowed and her voice deepened as she tried to sound ominous. "It is said," she went on, "that a curse followed him into the other world and that he will never rest until he has atoned for his sin."

"That's all there is?"

"That's it."

"I guess he really was being punished—there's been so little written about him."

"Oh, Drake, we've found his tomb, I know we have!"

"Aren't you afraid of the curse?" Drake grinned.

"It says the curse follows him, not those who dig him up. Who knows, maybe we'll do something to help release him," she laughed.

"Well, if that's all there is, I guess our research is over," Drake said suggestively.

"Yes, and it's time to get dressed and get back to our dig."

"Oh, so it's *our* dig now."

"Drake, I've worked it with you and I've done the research and . . ."

"Some research—you read one book," he scoffed.

"Come on, darling, it wouldn't hurt to share."

"So," he grinned, "coax me a little."

Caitlyn laughed and launched herself at him so suddenly he was taken completely off guard. She sat astride him and bent to hold his arms to the floor, a position she knew quite well he could change at any minute. She bent down and kissed his forehead, his eyes, his cheeks, then his lips and while she kissed him she moved her hips seductively.

She was driving him crazy. Suddenly he pulled his arms free and she squealed as he reached up and caught her and rolled sideways. Suddenly she was beneath him and the sarong had somehow fallen away. "Now," he said, "let's discuss this."

"Unfair!"

"Why unfair?" he laughed. "You had your turn."

"All right. I give up. It's your dig."

"No," he said, his eyes growing serious. "It's *ours.*" He bent to kiss her.

"You don't have to do that, Drake. I don't mind."

"Why not?" he said softly. "You own everything else . . . including me."

When he bent to kiss her again Caitlyn was lost in her need for him. They made love slowly—and it was another hour before they left the house and started back to the dig.

They walked single file again, each deep in thought. They were walking for what seemed to Caitlyn an interminable time—then she realized the trip from the dig had mostly been downhill. She breathed deeply as sweat began to bead on her forehead. Every muscle was protesting.

She must have heard the roar of the falls long before she realized they were drawing close. Drake stopped and Caitlyn moved up beside him.

"Think maybe this is a good time for that swim?"

"Why not? How far are we from the dig?"

"About another hour's walk," he estimated.

"Then we have plenty of time."

"I'll lead the way. Be careful, it's a little steep."

"Okay."

Drake started down the winding path to the crystal pond below. Mist from the falls was in the air and when she looked back up it was amazing.

They stood at the bottom by the pond for a few minutes, catching their breath and admiring the beauty around them.

They were nearly surrounded by the huge, lush green walls of jungle growth as sunlight glittered on the falling water.

"What a beautiful place."

"Yes, isn't it?"

"Is the water warm?"

"Comfortably cool. You won't realize how hot and sweaty you are until you get in."

"After you," she said.

"Oh no, that's my treat." He folded his arms and watched her. With a sultry laugh she began to slip out of her clothes. Leaving on her sheer underwear, she ran to the edge of the water and paused.

"Go ahead, it's deep enough to dive."

She did—and came up with a gasp and a shriek.

"It's cold!"

"No, not really," he said, grinning. "You'll be used to it in a minute and it'll seem warm."

"Come on in."

"I intend to." He stripped down and dove in beside her.

He'd been right—suddenly the water felt warm and invigorating. They splashed and played, stopping to kiss and touch each other, knowing that their time alone was growing short.

Standing in water to his waist, he picked her up out of the water and into his arms, sliding her out of the wet clothes. Then he entered her; his body surged within her, his mouth enveloped hers, his arms held her tight. She wanted to keep him inside her forever. They rocked back and forth in the water, sensing the wonder that had invaded their lives.

George sat watching Sir Richard, knowing he was deep in thought. The boat seemed to be moving at a snails's pace and he knew it was as much of an irritant to Sir Richard as it was to him.

He also knew that Sir Richard's situation must be very difficult. He'd been too late to see the wife he had never stopped loving, and now he was not sure he would be in time to save his daughter from this mysterious threat.

It puzzled George, this strange situation. No matter how he tried, he just could not imagine what the impostor's motive could be.

Sir Richard came to sit beside him.

"It's astounding, is it not?"

"Sir?"

"This place. The sounds, the sights, the smell—all seem to be larger than life. It's as if every breath is deeper, cleaner, more invigorating. I have a feeling it would be a pleasure to work here."

"And . . . to work with your daughter?"

"Yes. We've missed so much, she and I. We have so many things to make up for—birthdays, school days, trips."

"I know Caitlyn will want to share those memories as much as you do."

"Lord, I wish this boat could go faster."

"The condition it's in, I'll be grateful if it gets there at all. It's a long trek through some pretty nasty jungle if it doesn't."

"We'll make it. We must," Sir Richard said softly, "We must."

Caitlyn and Drake arrived at the dig by mid-afternoon and were welcomed by her father and Mendrano. When they told them that they had found information about the tomb, both men started asking questions.

"Hunsahua was the thirteenth king who reigned among these people. That's why everything is done using the number thirteen," Caitlyn said excitedly.

"And he's guarded by the deities and the warriors, but for the sole purpose of keeping his spirit *in,* not to keep anyone out," added Drake.

"Then there's supposed to be a great deal of treasure there?" Sir Richard questioned.

"Yes, he was buried with everything he owned," Caitlyn replied.

"Then . . . the final level must contain all that wealth. There has been no sign of looters anywhere, on any level."

"Yes," Drake agreed. "None of the levels has been touched in any way as far as I can see. I want to give that last level a quick look today before it's too late. I'd really like to see if the young king is really down there."

"Where else could he be?" Caitlyn asked.

"According to Mendrano's story there's more than one secret down there. This whole thing might not be as simple as we think it is."

"That is true," Mendrano added. "When they said a king was 'locked away' or 'sealed away' they meant exactly that. He was barred from any contact, even with those left alive."

"Left alive?" Caitlyn repeated. "I know the king and queen were alive and that's barbaric enough. But the others were left alive as well?"

"Not the warriors," Drake said. "They were . . . killed and their blood put in goblets. Then they were laid to rest inside."

"Then the ceremonial drinking of blood was recognized here, too," Caitlyn said.

"It looks like it. Did you notice the goblet at the head of every warrior? It's a sign."

"It's also an Aztec ritual," Caitlyn added.

"And Inca."

"So . . . maybe that's one sign that this ceremony was woven into this culture from outside."

"That and the worship of the sun."

"I've not seen much of that," Sir Richard said.

"I still hope to find evidence below," Drake replied.

"It looks as if your theory was true," Caitlyn said. "It's kind of interesting that it was proven with such a story as the young king's."

"I guess if he hadn't been blinded by passion he might have proven to be a better king than any of his predecessors."

"It's really a sad story," Caitlyn agreed.

"I think . . . this time, I should like to go down with you two, if you don't mind," Sir Richard said.

"Of course, you're more than welcome. I'm sure all the levels will be of interest to you," Drake replied. "Especially the one with the warriors. They must have been buried in full, and, I might add, very rich regalia."

"Did you count on any of this wealth . . . I mean, do you intend it all to go to one museum?"

Sir Richard missed Caitlyn's quick glance again and focused his attention on Drake.

"Everything down there belongs to the world. I'm sure you know that even better than I. At your dig in Cairo I was fascinated by the attention you paid to the inventory. If a man were free to keep all this, he'd be rich beyond his dreams."

"Well," Caitlyn said softly as she looked up at Drake, "there's rich . . . and then there's rich. There are some things you just can't measure in terms of money."

"I couldn't agree more." Drake smiled. "It's a wise man who knows when he's got the best of the two."

"I have a feeling," Sir Richard chuckled, "that there is much left unsaid here."

"Sir Richard," Drake said happily in response, "I'd like to turn this into a formal announcement . . . if Caitlyn will agree."

"I do," Caitlyn nodded.

"Caitlyn and I are making plans to share our lives together if you have no objections. We're very much in love. Of course," Drake laughed, "I don't know if it's me or the magic of the dig that's gotten to her, but I'm going to grab her while I can. Before she has a chance to think about it."

"I could think about it for years, Drake Stone," Caitlyn said, "and I wouldn't feel any different."

"I couldn't be happier for you both," Sir Richard said as he shook Drake's hand enthusiastically. "I hope you're both very happy."

"I'm sure we will be," Drake said, "at least I'll do everything I can to make Caitlyn happy."

"It's a good thing," Mendrano said. "This place has brought the two of you good luck. Perhaps it is fate's answer to the unhappy young king."

"What a wonderful thought, Mendrano," Caitlyn said. "I

would love to think that our love could help heal a terrible tragedy."

"We'd best get going. I'm anxious to find out if we've solved the puzzle—or just found another piece."

"I agree, Drake," Sir Richard added. "From what Mendrano says we may just find another empty, or nearly empty, room."

"Lord, I hope not," Caitlyn said with a frown.

"There's only one way to find out." Drake rose and reached for Caitlyn's hand. "Let's take a look. Mendrano, will you see to the lanterns? We're going to need a lot of light. That room is pretty big."

"I'll do it right now." Mendrano went to gather the workers, while Sir Richard, Caitlyn, and Drake headed for the tomb.

Eighteen

Most of the lighting was arranged to illuminate the way down to the last level. From there the three of them would again carry two lanterns apiece and return for more should they need it.

Drake gave Caitlyn a quick wink and a smile before he started down the steps. As the light moved ahead of them and they neared the bottom, an almost fantasy-like panorama began to appear.

The floor was as smooth as the ones above and extended almost eighty feet in length and over fifty feet in width. But on one side a flight of steps ran the entire eighty feet and led down to water that flowed swiftly past the room. Where it came from and where it went it was difficult to discern for it seemed to appear and disappear from solid rock. The wall on the opposite side of the forty-foot-wide stream looked as if it had been chipped away to make room for the tomb.

The room had three smooth stone sides that contained brilliantly painted murals that obviously depicted the life of the young king who had spent his last days here. The pictures were as clear and well preserved as if they had been painted the day before.

One wall depicted the young king hunting. His arm was drawn back as if preparing to use his spear. If the painting was anywhere near accurate, the king was a very handsome young man. Another depicted him judging or accepting tribute, sitting on a throne as a number of figures knelt before him.

There was a great many pictures, each depicting a different aspect of the tragic story. There was one with him standing with his head bowed before a group of men. The next was of him and his beloved sister-wife. The rest of the pictorial story was clear, and below each picture was a chest carved from stone.

On the far end of the room the wall was almost completely taken up by a huge affair that looked much like a three-tiered altar.

What caught their eyes quickly were stone carvings placed against the wall between each mural. There was no doubt it was a stone relief representing the sun god.

There were several carved idols on the steps leading up to the altar, with a chest near each one. It was hard to tell what they were made of, but all of them were in the same excellent state of preservation. Drake guessed they'd been carved from stone as well—it was obvious they were meant to last.

"There's something rather large on top of that altar," Drake observed.

"If the king and his wife were buried alive," Caitlyn said, "where are they? There's no sign of their remains anywhere that I can see."

"Do you suppose that in desperation and fear they might have drowned themselves?" Sir Richard asked.

"I don't think so," Drake said thoughtfully.

"What *do* you think?" Caitlyn asked. "There doesn't seem to be anyplace they could go."

"Unless . . . are you sure they were alive? Maybe that

object at the top of the altar is where they were sealed up," Sir Richard suggested.

"No," Drake countered.

"Drake, they have to be somewhere," Caitlyn said.

"I know. But I don't think that somewhere is here in this room."

"There are no other levels," Caitlyn observed.

"No."

"Then this is the last and only room."

"I'm not too sure. That mechanism at the first level shows a lot of ingenuity. People who could manage that a century or two ago could have a lot of other nice little tricks up their sleeves."

"Very comforting thought," Caitlyn said dryly.

"Well, that can come later. We'd better look over what we've got here."

"I agree," Sir Richard said. "It's an immense room. Why don't we each take a separate section and see what we can put together."

"Good idea," Drake said. "Look, Sir Richard, why don't you and Caitlyn see if you can get one of those stone chests open? I'll try to go up on that altar and see what that thing is."

"All right. Choose one, Caitlyn," Sir Richard said, smiling, "and we'll see what we can find."

Caitlyn and Sir Richard moved to the nearest stone chest, the one closest to the bottom step and one of the lanterns. They knelt beside it to study it for a minute to see if they could get it open.

Drake walked to the foot of the altar and stood looking at it and the objects on it for several minutes. Then he approached the first tier, which was almost two feet from the floor. He stepped up on it and knelt to examine the idols on each side.

The first was an exquisite carving of a woman standing with her arms raised toward the top of the altar, as if she were offering a prayer. The one opposite her was of a man, standing in the same pose. Both had been carved out of a very hard material Drake couldn't recognize, but he meant to examine them more closely later.

He moved up the second tier, another two feet, and gave a cursory examination to two more elaborate and beautifully carved forms he suspected were gods.

There was another tier a good three feet from the second. Drake put both hands on it and propelled himself up until he stood on the top platform.

He stood looking down on what, if he had been in Egypt, he would have called a sarcophagus. But he knew instinctively it wasn't. The only question was—what was it?

It was approximately six feet in length and four in width. The shape was oval and it was made of the same ebony stone from which the figures had been carved. As far as he could tell, there was no line of demarcation to prove it was a chest of any sort, yet Drake had a feeling the thing was not solid. He just had no idea of how to get it open.

He put that problem aside to examine the carvings. In the center was a sun, a round golden globe with rays extending from it to the edge of the chest, except for the two edges on each end of the oval where two squares had been cut into the stone. There was a figure of a woman in one, and a man in the other.

The legend was here and so was the evidence, but there was no sign of where the royal couple might be. He knew the secret had not been discovered.

"Drake!" Caitlyn called urgently. He turned to look

down—she was some distance from him but even from there he could see she was excited. He jumped from one tier to the next to reach the floor, then joined Caitlyn and Sir Richard by one of the stone chests. He thought they hadn't managed to get it open because the lid was so heavy and they had brought no tools.

But when he reached them he could see he'd been only half right. The lid to the chest had to be slid off and they had managed to slide it far enough to see inside . . . and what they saw was enough to take anyone's breath away.

The glitter of gold . . . the sparkle of diamonds . . . the blaze of rubies . . . and the fire of emeralds.

"Good Lord," Drake breathed as he knelt beside Caitlyn and Sir Richard.

"There has to be a fortune in this one alone," Caitlyn said, "and believe it or not, there are thirteen."

"Thirteen chests filled with treasure," Sir Richard said softly. "There has to be a vast fortune here. I've never seen anything like it." He reached one trembling hand into the chest and picked up an emerald almost the size of his palm. He held it up and it reflected the glow of the lantern, burning with a deep fire. "Magnificent," he whispered, "just magnificent."

Watching him, Caitlyn again felt a strange, uncomfortable feeling. They were impressed by what they had found, but they knew there could be no personal attachment to anything. And yet personal attachment was what Caitlyn distinctly saw in her father's eyes. Something inside her stirred, but she could not let herself believe it. Her father was famous for his dedication to the furthering of the field of archaeology. He had never been interested in any kind of personal wealth. But lately he had seemed to be very focused on the treasure. She could never believe that a man with his reputation could behave as if this find was really as important as the tomb, the legend, and the artifacts of the young king.

Drake, too, was looking at Sir Richard with a puzzled frown. "We have a lot to figure out, but we can't take the time to do it now. I imagine all the chests contain the same things."

"My God, it's hard to fathom such riches," Sir Richard said.

"Well we have other problems to 'fathom'. Like, where's the burial place, what's in that . . . object up there . . . and how we get all this stuff dated and catalogued and still go on searching."

"It's obvious to me that this part of the legend might have been exaggerated," Sir Richard said. "You can see as well as I—there's no evidence here. If they'd been entombed alive we would have found remains of some sort. I think this was some sort of temple."

"A temple?" Drake repeated. "With thirteen *warriors* and thirteen *deities* to guard it? You don't believe they would go to all this trouble just to guard a treasure?"

"I believe what I see . . . and what I don't see. I don't see the remains . . . or the burial place of the king. It is just not here."

"Well, I can't give up that easily," Drake replied. "I believe we're not seeing a lot of things we should see and that's why we can't find the burial place. It's going to take a lot of study, especially that thing up there on the altar. It's like nothing I've ever seen before."

"I'd be delighted to make a record of what's in the chests. I could also list the deities and the objects on the remains of the warriors."

"That's a big job, Sir Richard," Drake said. His face was

expressionless—even Caitlyn couldn't read it. "We'll have to do it together, because . . . under no circumstances do I want any of these things moved."

If Sir Richard wanted to argue, he suppressed it. Drake was in charge of the dig, and he gave the orders.

"Of course," Sir Richard said, "you will forgive my over-abundant enthusiasm . . . for a minute I was somewhat overcome by the magnitude of your discovery."

"Of course," Drake said casually.

"What's our next step?"

"Let's go up on that altar. I have a hunch there are clues but I haven't found them yet."

With Drake's help, Sir Richard and Caitlyn slid the heavy stone lid back on the chest and then the two men walked toward the altar. For several minutes Caitlyn stood watching them, her face immobile, but her eyes reflecting the painful questions in her mind and heart.

Mendrano came cautiously down the steps. He realized that the sun was close to setting and there was still no sign of the three. He found them engrossed in a discussion about the statues and murals and the drawings Caitlyn and Drake had made of them. Drake looked up in surprise when he saw Mendrano.

"Something wrong?"

"No," Mendrano said, "except you have been down here more hours than you know."

Sir Richard took his watch from his pocket and snapped it open. "Good heavens, Mendrano's right. It's after six."

"No wonder my stomach has been putting up such a fuss," Caitlyn said with a laugh.

"Think noble thoughts," Drake responded with a grin. "It helps."

"You really believe that?" She gave him an arch look.

"You mean you don't want to sacrifice a mere meal for archaeological progress?"

"Nope. I want to eat."

"Then I guess we'd better go. I wouldn't want to lose my best worker."

They started toward the steps, Mendrano leading the way with Drake behind him, followed by Caitlyn and Sir Richard.

Caitlyn was halfway up the steps and Mendrano and Drake had already vanished into the upper level when she realized her father was not right behind her. She turned and looked back. Sir Richard had paused and rested his hand on one of the stone chests—he seemed lost in thought.

Suddenly he realized how quiet it was and became aware of someone observing him. He jerked his hand from the chest when his eyes met Caitlyn's. For a long moment they looked at each other, then Caitlyn said his name softly. Sir Richard didn't answer but simply walked toward her.

Caitlyn had already decided to have a long talk with her father later . . . when the camp slept and they could have some privacy. His reputation was at stake and she wouldn't let him be hurt . . . he was her father and their life together had just begun.

They ate supper amid conversation about the hows and whys of what they had discovered and the best way to deal with the problems.

After the long trek from Drake's house and the work and excitement of the day, Caitlyn found she was really tired. She tried to remain alert, but Drake knew she needed rest.

Still, she had her mind set on talking to her father, so when Drake suggested she go to her tent and get some sleep she smiled and shook her head.

"If I go to sleep now I'll be up at three in the morning. Then I'd really be exhausted tomorrow."

"Well, I don't know about you, but this has been a pretty tiring day for me. I think I'll go to bed," Sir Richard said.

"Good night, Sir Richard," Drake said. "We'll see you in the morning. Our real work is about to begin."

"I wouldn't be surprised. Good night all." Sir Richard left the tent and Drake and Mendrano settled back to talk a bit about plans for the next day.

Caitlyn tried to concentrate on the drawings and notes before her, but all she could think of was those last few minutes in the tomb. Her father had seemed so changed . . . something was different and she couldn't understand it.

She knew she had to talk to him. She had to hear his side of it, for surely she was misinterpreting it . . . she had to be. Caught in her thoughts, she didn't know Drake had been watching her. When she realized the conversation had ceased, she looked at Drake quickly and he smiled.

"You're exhausted."

"I am a bit tired."

"I'll walk you back to your tent. You need some sleep— Mendrano and I have a few arrangements to make for tomorrow. Come on, Caitlyn," Drake stood and reached out for her. She took his hand gratefully.

"I'll be back in a few minutes, Mendrano. Wait here."

Mendrano nodded. "Good night, Caitlyn."

"Good night, Mendrano. See you in the morning."

As they left the tent, Drake put his arm about her waist and they walked in comfortable silence.

In front of her tent he took her in his arms and kissed

her. Not a passionate kiss, but infinitely gentle. She relaxed in the warm security of his arms.

"You pushed yourself pretty hard today. I'm sorry. I forgot the walk back was almost all uphill and you're still not used to it. Besides that, all this excitement is enough to wear you down."

"It is exciting, isn't it?" She smiled up at him. "You seemed a bit overcome, too."

"A bit," he grinned. "I thought everyone could hear my heart pounding."

"Oh, Drake, I'm so happy for you. You'll find all the clues you're looking for. I know you will."

"Thanks for the confidence." He took her face between his hands. "But this whole thing is second to something much more important—us. I love you, Caitlyn, very much."

"And I love you, Drake," she whispered as their lips met.

After a moment he held her gently away from him. "You need your rest and if this goes on another minute I won't be responsible. Good night, love, and sleep well."

"Good night, Drake."

He kissed her again, then turned back toward his tent. Caitlyn watched him go. Maybe because of her love for Drake and her commitment to his dream . . . maybe because she was afraid to lose the love of her newly found father . . . or maybe because she needed to understand, she turned and walked toward her father's tent. She had to clear this up. Everything of value in her world depended upon it. As she walked, she was quite unaware that no one saw her. The workers were camped along the edge of the dig and Sir Richard's tent was nearly on the edge of the surrounding jungle.

A light still glowed, so she was sure he was still up . . . perhaps doing some research, or just reading.

She tapped lightly on the tent pole, and when she got no result she called out softly. Again there was no response. She pushed aside the flap and stepped inside . . . the tent was empty.

It took her so totally by surprise that for several minutes she stood immobile. He had claimed weariness, had said he was going to bed. Since he was not with Drake or Mendrano, where had he gone?

She sat for a moment on the edge of his cot and looked around her. Her tent and Drake's were both cluttered with work tools, books, notebooks, drawings, and fragments of artifacts. This tent was devoid of all these things. In fact, it was very nearly barren. If a note of alarm deep within was beginning to sound, she was doing her best to ignore it.

She would not judge him by what she didn't know, or was quite possibly just imagining. She would wait and see what he had to say.

She was prepared to leave when she noticed the book. It protruded a few inches from beneath the cot, as if he had been reading it. It looked like a photograph album and she grew a bit excited. Maybe it was a record of his life, of the years they had been separated.

She bent and lifted the book onto her lap. It was heavy and seemed rather old. The edges of the cover were frayed. This book was most likely the story of her father's life, a life she could happily share from now on. It brought tears to her eyes and she hesitated, then with a trembling hand she opened it.

The first page was a newspaper clipping. It was a large picture of Sir Richard, quite a bit younger. She smiled . . . until her eyes fell on the words printed below it: Paul Macombe Impresses Audiences in Shakespeare's *Hamlet*.

She gazed at it, dumbfounded. This was not possible.

This was her father. This was not Paul Macombe. Quickly she turned the page, then another and another. The book was full of news clippings, all of them critiques of the work of one Paul Macombe. The pictures portrayed Paul Macombe in *King Lear* . . . Paul Macombe in *Romeo and Juliet* . . . it went on and on.

Toward the end, only a few of the clippings were complimentary about Paul Macombe's acting . . . some were a bit critical, yet the book covered a lifetime of acting . . . *acting!*

This man, this man who claimed to love her, who came here to work with Drake, who professed to be Sir Richard Macdonald, was an *impostor!*

Her intuition had been right, she thought bitterly. Surely she should have seen through his guise before this. Looking back, she realized there had been so many things.

"Oh, God," she groaned. His lack of knowledge should have been obvious to her and to Drake, but they had both been blinded by their need to have him be what they wanted him to be. "I should have known," she whispered. "Oh God, I should have known."

"Should have known what, my dear?" His voice was deceptively soft and Caitlyn gasped in surprise. She'd been so intent on the book and its painful revelation she had not heard the tent flap open.

Grasping the situation at a glance, Paul withdrew his pistol and when Caitlyn slowly rose to her feet he aimed it at her heart.

"I see you've found my clippings. Rather eventful career, wouldn't you say?" Caitlyn took a step toward him. "Don't, Caitlyn. I'd hate to shoot you . . . because," he added, reading her expression, "it would mean I would have to kill your lover and his friend and I'd hate to have to do that."

"Why?" Caitlyn asked. "Why did you do this?"

Paul reached into his pocket and took out the emerald he had found in the stone chest in the tomb. "I went back to get it. It was too beautiful to leave it there any longer."

"You can't get away with this."

"But I can."

"The men . . . the workers . . ."

"Can be handled easily. They're ignorant and believe whatever I tell them."

"Drake will never let you do this."

"He'll have no choice. I have you, and he'll do anything to keep you safe—just as you will do anything to keep him safe."

"What . . . what are you going to do? Don't hurt Drake and Mendrano. I'll do whatever you want, only don't hurt them."

Paul seemed to be mulling his options, and Caitlyn could feel her heart beating furiously. She was the only one who knew the truth about Paul, and she would do whatever was necessary to keep Drake and Mendrano from harm. She needed to play for time—time to see if there was a chance to convince this man to come to his senses.

"You and I are going to take a short walk. Be very quiet, because if we are seen Drake and Mendrano will be finished. I guarantee you, Caitlyn," he said firmly, "I will kill them." He motioned toward a small trunk. "There's some rope in there—bring it along."

She didn't know what he planned to do, but she knew Drake would come running if she created a fuss—running to his death.

She knelt and opened the trunk and took out the coiled length of rope, then stood and faced Paul.

"We'll circle behind the tents and hide in the shadows of the trees."

"Where . . . ?"

"Walk ahead of me. Walk toward the tomb."

Caitlyn felt her entire body quiver. She'd never been so frightened in her life and Paul Macombe knew it.

She could do nothing to alert Drake and Mendrano—she couldn't see them die. Yet she was confident that when she was found missing tomorrow, Drake would find her. And if Paul was going to force her down into the tomb, he had to know that would be the first place Drake would look.

Time, she needed time to try and find a way out of this. Maybe she could convince Paul he was making a big mistake. After all, he had done no one real harm yet . . . unless . . . her father! Her real father! Surely Paul had been the one to switch their identities. She prayed her father was not dead.

They moved slowly through the night shadows in the shelter of the jungle. When they reached the tomb Paul forced her inside.

She continued on ahead of him down through the levels until they reached the last room. There he came up behind her.

"Stand still," he ordered, his command harsh. "Put your hands behind you." Obediently she did as he commanded as he grasped her hands and tied them tightly. Then he forced her to sit on the bottom step of the stone altar, and bent to tie her feet together.

"My father? My *real* father. You didn't . . ."

"No, he's very much alive. He's just being temporarily detained. No one would have been hurt if you had minded your own business." He stood and looked down at her.

"Now I'm afraid it's too late—there's much too much at stake."

"Don't you understand? If you commit murder you'll be found out. There is no way to get away with this. Too many people are involved. Give it up now, and I swear I'll convince Drake to let you go."

"Let me go?" He chuckled softly. "When I leave here it will be with more wealth than one man could possibly have dreamed of."

"That's impossible. One man alone can't get all of this out of here."

"Oh, I don't expect to even try."

"Then you're not alone in this?"

"That's beside the point," he replied, angry that he'd revealed more than he meant to. "You see, I don't intend to take it out now. I'll simply seal the tomb and get rid of the workers. I have an excellent map. When the right time comes I'll return to redeem my treasure."

She wondered just who was really behind this, for now it seemed abundantly clear that Paul Macombe had been hired to act a part.

"You should have talked this over with your boss before you did this. He might not take kindly to murder."

"Murder? I won't kill you . . . or your lover and his friend. And I'm my own boss."

Caitlyn breathed a premature sigh of relief.

"I'll simply let nature take its course."

She looked at him blankly for a minute. Then the truth of what he was saying struck her like a blow.

"You . . . you can't . . ."

"Caitlyn, my dear," he said smoothly, "I can . . . I have to. Look around you. With all this wealth in here, do you think I won't do whatever I have to, to make it mine?"

"Paul . . . please."

"I'm sorry. I'd grown rather fond of you. But you have such a sense of morality. I cannot comprehend locking all this inside a museum. It's such a waste. If only you had stayed out of my business there would have been no need for this."

"You . . . you're going to leave me here?" Her face was white. There were only two lanterns lit and the shadows against the muraled walls seemed to make them come to life.

"This conversation bores me," he said coldly. He removed a white handkerchief from his inside pocket, shook out its neat folds, and gagged her. "Don't worry, you won't be alone. You will have company soon enough. Then the three of you will have time to contemplate the mystery of the young king. All the time in the world, for you will share his fate."

Her eyes widened in horror as he stood, looked down at her for a minute, then turned and walked away. She could hear his footsteps diminish as he went up the steps.

Caitlyn looked about her. She realized the terror the young king and his wife must have felt when they were closed away here. She knew that they must still be somewhere nearby and that she and Drake might really share their fate as Paul had said. She closed her eyes for a minute, trying to muster courage. She was utterly terrified.

Paul moved swiftly, heading for Drake's tent. This time so much more depended on his ability to make his acting believable.

As he neared the tent he heard the muffled sound of voices. Mendrano was still there. He could kill two birds with one stone.

He inhaled deeply, then concentrated on the look of fear and anguish he wanted on his face. Then he burst into the tent.

Drake and Mendrano were as startled as he'd wanted them to be. It would keep them from thinking before they acted.

"Sir Richard, what's wrong?" Drake asked.

"Caitlyn . . . Caitlyn and I . . ." he gasped.

"Good Lord! What happened!"

"I went to talk to her and we were discussing an idea about where the actual tomb might be. It's terrible. We, we just decided to take one more look . . . just to see if our theory might be good enough to present to you. We went to the tomb."

Drake's face had gone gray and he stood abruptly, his gaze piercing Paul.

"Where is she! What happened?"

"She fell! It was terrible! As we reached the bottom room she fell! . . . all those steps! I tried to grab her and jerked my arm. She . . . she lay so still and I couldn't carry her up . . . oh God, she lay so still!"

Drake couldn't wait to hear any more. Visions of Caitlyn lying in that stone room pushed every other thought from his mind. It would take time to get to her and time could be a killer if she was badly injured.

He ran the entire distance to the tomb with Mendrano right behind him and Paul bringing up the rear.

Once inside, Drake and Mendrano raced down one flight of steps after another, but Paul stopped inside the first room. When the sound of their steps faded he ran to the sack of stones weighting the door. It took all his strength, but he dragged the sack away and listened to the stone door roll back into place.

* * *

Mendrano and Drake raced down one flight after another until they reached the steps to the last room. Both men expected to see Caitlyn lying at the bottom, but there was no sign of her.

Drake ran down the steps, his heart pounding furiously, his thoughts on Caitlyn and Caitlyn only. But Mendrano paused to look back the way they had come. Then he turned and raced back up.

Drake grasped a lantern as he passed it on the steps and held it aloft. Only then did he see Caitlyn. He thought she was lying still because she was hurt and he moved toward her with a silent prayer on his lips.

The prayer turned to an exclamation of surprise when he found she was bound and gagged, her eyes filled with terror.

He ran to her and undid the gag at once.

"Drake . . . oh, Drake," Caitlyn sobbed as she leaned against him. He reached around her, holding her and loosening the bonds at the same time. "It's Sir Richard . . . he's not Sir Richard! He's not my father! Drake, please, we've got to get out of here! We've got to stop him!"

"Are you all right, Caitlyn? Can you walk?"

"Yes. Please, Drake, you can't stay down here! He's insane!"

"Caitlyn, it's all right. Come on. Let me take you out of here. You're distraught." He helped her to her feet and she swayed for a moment, then clung to him.

Realizing that fear had taken its toll, he bent and lifted her in his arms.

He had only taken a few steps when Mendrano reappeared, his face grim. He was trying not to show the fear that gripped his heart.

He had raced up all the steps, only to find his worst fears confirmed. The doorway to the outer chamber was sealed. The mechanism had been arranged so that it would only work from the outside. They were completely entombed.

"Mendrano?" Drake questioned, but he knew with a sinking heart what Mendrano was going to say. Caitlyn uttered a helpless cry and buried her face against Drake's shoulders.

"The door is closed," Mendrano said. "There is no way out. And the air shaft, it's been jammed from the outside. There will be very little air in here after a few hours."

Drake held Caitlyn tight against him and fought the fear. Not for himself . . . but for her.

Nineteen

The day was heralded by a brilliant sun that glistened off the mist-touched trees and caressed the shadows among the hills, turning them into a sparkling, colorful mosaic.

As the light reached the sleeping camp, the men roused themselves sluggishly. They prepared a quick morning meal and waited for Mendrano to bring the orders for the day. Antonio rose early. He saw that his father was not in his bed, but Mendrano often slept at the dig so his absence did not alarm Antonio.

Tana had prepared a large breakfast, and as usual for the past few days, she was quiet—too quiet to suit him. She had changed, and Antonio didn't like it. He wanted her back the way she was, his sparkling, smiling sister. He instinctively felt Ethan Marshall was the cause of it all and it angered him.

"The breakfast was excellent, Tana."

"Thank you," she smiled. "I see Father has chosen a hard bed again. I wonder if he has had a good meal this morning. Find out, Antonio. You know how he is."

"I will, Tana . . ." Antonio began.

"Please, Antonio," Tana said softly. "Ask me no questions. I know the ones that are on your mind. But I have no answers for myself yet, much less for you. Be patient with me."

"I never meant for you to have such unrest."

"I cannot forget him," Tana whispered. "Leave me in peace. I know it is useless. I am trying to remember who I am and where I belong."

"Tana . . ."

"Go and find our father," Tana said. "I worry about him, as you and he worry about me. He devotes himself so completely sometimes."

"It's a trait he handed down to his daughter."

"And his son," Tana laughed. "Do not act as if you weren't having the same thoughts. Go . . . go find Father and I will make you both something special for supper."

Antonio rose from the table and walked toward the door.

"Antonio?" He turned to face her and she walked to him and stood on tiptoe to kiss his cheek.

"I do love you both, Antonio." He smiled and left the house. Tana stood quietly for a minute. "And I shall always love him as well."

Antonio walked to the dig site, and as soon as he approached it he had an instinctive feeling something was wrong.

Men were working at the original dig site and he knew many of them should have been with his father, Drake, and Caitlyn at the tomb.

He looked about for someone to tell him what was happening, but none of the three was in sight.

It was then that Sir Richard stepped from his tent. Antonio smiled and walked toward him. At least someone was here who could answer questions.

"Good morning, Sir Richard."

At first Paul looked at him with a puzzled frown, then

he registered recognition, accompanied by something else that Antonio had no way of understanding.

"Ah, yes, Antonio?"

"Where is my father?"

"He and the others were called down to the plantation. Ethan sent a message. Some affair or other required Drake's presence and, of course, he insisted Caitlyn and your father go along. I'm sure they'll be back in a few days. I hated to see them trek off into the jungle like that. I know how dangerous it is. But Drake was sure they'd be fine. He said to expect them back in about five days. It has something to do with the dam, I believe."

Antonio nodded and retained his pleasant expression, but instinctively he knew something was not right. Drake may have been called away, he may have sent his father on an errand, but he would not have taken two of them from the dig at the same time.

The men were simple—they would never have known what to do with something valuable if they found it. The responsibility would have been Mendrano's and he would notify Drake. Antonio found it hard to believe Drake would have taken Mendrano to Ethan's.

Also, there was an atmosphere that bothered Antonio. But he did not question Sir Richard. Instead he thanked him, tried to act as if nothing were wrong, and moved toward the men.

He began to work, subtly inquiring, asking what had been discovered . . . and if anyone knew the reason his father was not there.

The answers he got were unsettling. When the men had awakened, Drake, Mendrano, and Caitlyn were gone. No, they had not seen the messenger from Senor Ethan's and no, they had not been left any orders. They were doing what Drake's friend, Sir Richard, told them to do.

Antonio's worry grew into alarm when he saw Sir Richard watching him, narrow-eyed. He tried to remain calm and not rouse more suspicion than he already had. Finally Sir Richard went into his tent and came out with a rifle in hand. He stood it nearby and then sat at the small table near his tent where he was ostensibly cleaning and cataloguing artifacts. Still, Antonio knew he was being watched.

Unable to identify his suspicions, yet aware that alarms were going off in his head, Antonio kept himself under control. He tried to approach the situation logically, but the more he thought about it the less sense it made. He didn't want to question Sir Richard any more, so the only place he could seek information would be at Ethan's.

Paul was cursing his carelessness. He had forgotten completely that Mendrano had a son and a daughter. If they posed a problem before he was ready to move he would just have to find a way to eliminate them.

When it came time for the noon meal, Antonio casually informed the man he still knew as Sir Richard that this sister always cooked for him and he would go home to eat.

"There's plenty of food here in the camp," Paul said. "I don't see the necessity."

If nothing else solidified his instincts, that did. Antonio was certain there was something amiss, and he meant to find out what it was.

He agreed with a smile and drifted among the men who sat around eating, obtaining enough food for a meal which he ate with one eye on Sir Richard.

If he wanted to avoid Sir Richard's suspicion, he knew he would have to finish the day's work. What worried him was the idea of traveling the jungle at night. He also knew he could not leave Tana at home alone.

If he and Tana ran to Ethan, it would have to be with little or no preparation. And it would most likely be the most dangerous trip they had ever made.

Paul was sure of himself and just a bit too smug. He felt Antonio did not have the intelligence to figure out what was going on—until it was too late. Nor did he have the courage to travel the jungle at night.

Slade Monroe had assured him a few days' work would bring them a king's ransom in emeralds. But that was not the reason he remained. Somewhere in the depths of that tomb lay a cache of jewels that would make what they had already dug seem insignificant. And he did not intend to share the wealth that lay buried below.

He could see the outline of the mound in the distance, and struggled with his greed and the knowledge that three people were entombed there . . . a day had already passed and they were without food and water. Soon the air would be gone as well and they would die. If the horror of this penetrated his thoughts at all, it soon lost out to a conscience consumed by material desire.

Toward sunset Antonio was preparing to go home when Paul approached him, rifle in hand.

"In your father's absence, Antonio, you're in charge of the workers. It's best you stay here until he gets back."

Antonio kept his reaction to himself. If he hadn't been certain something was wrong before, he was now.

"If you wish," he said calmly. "I'd best settle the camp and get to bed then."

"Yes. Good night, Antonio," Paul replied. He turned and walked back to his tent.

Antonio had nothing definite to accuse Sir Richard of,

he thought. But still, there was something wrong and he knew he had to find Ethan Marshall.

Quite possibly he would arrive at Ethan's and find Drake, Caitlyn, and his father there and make a complete fool of himself. Quite possible, but he was going to do something anyway because if his instincts were right, he was the only person who *could* do something.

Antonio waited until the campfires died and the moon began to descend; then he rose and slowly and carefully made his way out of camp.

It would be a difficult trip to Ethan's and he knew he'd travel faster alone. But for some reason he could not leave his sister. If something were wrong, attention might be focused on an unsuspecting Tana.

He moved silently down the path to his house. It was dark when he arrived, since Tana had gone to bed sometime before. He moved toward her room, with no need of a light.

He stood for a minute to let his eyes adjust. Then he made out Tana's slender form, a darker shadow against the bedcover. He went and sat down on the edge of the bed, shaking Tana's arm slightly.

"Tana," he whispered.

"Ummm," she muttered and tried to turn away from the irritating interruption.

"Tana," Antonio spoke a bit louder. This time he shook her more firmly, and her eyes blinked open. For a moment she was disoriented and surprised, then she sat up abruptly.

"Antonio! What's wrong? What are you doing here? It's not . . . Father . . . ?"

"Don't be so alarmed, Tana. As far as I know, Father is all right. Get up and get dressed. We have to go down to Ethan's at once."

"At once? Now? In the middle of the night? Antonio, there *is* something wrong."

"There's no time to explain anything now. Tana, please do as I ask. I'll explain everything on the way."

"We're going to travel in the jungle . . . at night?"

"Only to Drake's house. We'll take a boat from there."

"It's dangerous, Antonio. You know that. Father has always forbidden us to go even when the sun was not yet set."

"It's dangerous, I know. But I'm afraid there just might be more danger here. Tana, we have to take the chance."

"All right, all right." Tana rose from the bed.

While she dressed Antonio tried to gather some things they might need. A canteen of water, a jacket to protect him from the cold air and tangled brush. Then he took the rifle that had been a gift from Ethan, even though he had only a pocketful of shells. At least it gave them some protection.

When they came together at the door Antonio scrutinized Tana carefully. She had dressed in soft leather boots and a heavy jacket.

"All right, let's go. Until we get far enough away from the camp so that no sound travels we should move as quietly as possible."

"All right," Tana agreed. "If you say this is important it must be. But you'd better have a good explanation when we get there."

"I will . . . I hope."

"Antonio!"

"Come on." He gripped her arm and pulled her out the door behind him. In a few minutes they blended with the jungle shadows.

* * *

Ethan was both exhausted and frustrated. The day Antonio had come for Tana, Ethan had gone to the dam. From that day on his life seemed filled with accidents and bad dreams. Well, he reconsidered the last. The dreams had not been all bad, but they'd been quite difficult for his logical mind to accept—as had the accidents.

"*Accidents,*" he muttered. There was no reason to call them anything else, yet his instincts told him it was something different. Ropes were found frayed and broken. Logs had been loosened from their restraints and sent floating down the river. One thing after another, until he'd begun to think the whole idea was jinxed.

And the dreams—the dreams were hard to cope with because his waking mind told him they were impossible. Tana. He'd had her on his mind from the moment she'd gone. Tana, and what she had said to him . . . and the effect that last touch . . . that kiss had had.

He remembered as if it had only been a moment before. Tana was a part of this country, like the beautiful flowers that bloomed in profusion. She was like the clear morning air and the brilliant sunsets. He began to wonder if any other woman could belong here.

Even though he had made the house into something unique and comfortable, a woman would still have to give up so much. This place he had chosen for his empire was hardly one that most women would fit into.

But then there was Tana . . . yes, Tana. Lately he'd envisioned her in his house, her wide-eyed innocence absorbing everything. With a touch of surprise he found himself thinking how delightful it might be to teach her about his world—music, art, books. He could show her so much. But was it fair?

"Damn," he muttered. Of course it wasn't. He was the

wrong man for Tana. He was ten years older and their backgrounds were so different. Her family—Mendrano and Antonio—would never agree. Still he could not get the taste of her lips and the feel of her in his arms out of his mind.

He'd been standing on the bank of the river, deep in thought, and he didn't hear Marc come up beside him.

"Ethan?"

Ethan turned, wondering if something else had gone wrong. Marc read his expression and laughed.

"No, nothing's wrong, except we're over a month behind."

"What's going on?"

"Message came for you."

"Message? Nothing wrong at my house?"

"No, Perez says there's a boat coming upriver. Says its passenger is your friend George Frasier."

"George! But he's not due back for a year."

"Well, he's on the way. Perez thinks maybe you ought to come home."

"There must be something up for George to make this trip so soon. I know he had some business to take care of, something about a new client. If Perez says I should come back, then maybe I should. His instincts are pretty good."

"Don't worry. I'll take care of things here. You better go and take a look."

"Yeah, I'd better. In the meantime, be careful, Marc. This dam is important, but so are you and the men who work for you. If it comes to making choices, take care of yourselves."

"I'll do that."

"See you in a couple of days."

"Take care."

During the trip back to his house Ethan tried to think of what could possibly bring George back so quickly. It worried him because he knew it would have to be extremely important. George wouldn't make the trip for nothing.

It was late in the day when Ethan arrived and Perez was there to meet him.

Lettie and Bill were a bit surprised to see him, and as worried as he was when he explained the unusual circumstances.

"You mean George usually comes here only about once or twice a year?" Bill asked.

"Sometimes I don't see him for more than a year."

"No wonder you're upset."

Ethan turned to Perez. "Think the boat will be in now?"

"No, senor. But the boat does not come slow as usual. It comes fast."

"You mean they aren't stopping at night?" Perez nodded. "This has really got to be serious," Ethan said with a dark frown.

"Soon they will be here, senor. Then all your questions will have answers."

"Let's go down to the dock. I want to be there when they get in. God, I hope George is all right."

Perez and Ethan rode down to the docks, taking an extra horse with them. Ethan spent the next couple of hours alternately pacing the dock and sitting on the edge of it. The sun was only a bare line of scarlet when the boat came into view.

Ethan watched impatiently as the dark speck grew larger. It seemed hours before the boat approached the dock.

Ethan was at the bottom of the rickety plank when it was pushed out to the dock. He knew at once that it was not the sturdy boat George had always used.

Ethan studied George's face as he approached. It was not his usual smiling countenance. There was another man walking behind him, one Ethan had never seen before, yet whose appearance rang some kind of bell.

"George," Ethan said as he extended his hand, "I hadn't thought I'd see you again so soon. This is a surprise. I hope nothing's wrong."

"I'm afraid a great deal is wrong, Ethan," George said seriously. "I have someone with me that I felt you should meet as soon as possible. That's why I took this boat."

"I'd say," Ethan laughed, "the boat looks a bit unsteady. What was the hurry, George . . . and who's your friend?" Ethan's voice faded slowly as he got a closer look at the man. "He looks just like . . ."

"You should recognize him."

"He's the mirror image of . . ."

"Sir Richard Macdonald."

"Yes, he could be his double."

"No," George said. "In this case, the other one could be his double. Ethan, let me introduce you to Sir Richard Macdonald."

For a minute or two Ethan could not quite digest what George was saying. He was speechless.

"Well, it's getting dark, and I could use some brandy," Sir Richard said. "George and I can fill you in on what we know. Then we can take a little trip to the dig and see what kind of a game this blighter is trying to play."

"Yes, yes, of course." Ethan suddenly found his voice. "I'm afraid we only brought one extra horse. I thought it was just George. Perez can ride behind me. But I can promise you some excellent brandy and I'm sure looking forward to this explanation. Come, let's go."

A short time later George, Sir Richard, and Bill joined Ethan in his study, brandy snifters in hand. Sir Richard began his story as Lettie, too, sat quietly and listened.

"Of course, my knowledge of the affair is limited to my experience in London. I didn't know someone was impersonating me until I arrived here and had the deuced good luck to try and hire George as my guide."

"But none of this makes any sense," Bill said. "What could a man possibly have to gain by making people believe he's you? He only let himself in for some hard work, no glory and no gain."

"Unless," Ethan said with a puzzled frown, "the dig is a guise and he's here for some other reason."

"Like what?" George questioned.

"I've no idea," Ethan admitted.

"His attention must be focused on something, some other activity," Sir Richard added.

"Some other activity?" Ethan said. "But there's no other activity going on around here except Drake's dig, my plantation . . . and the dam. I wonder . . ."

"You wonder what, Ethan?" Bill asked.

"I wonder if this dam is interfering with someone's plans in some way. Maybe there's something altogether different going on and no one wants anyone to know about it."

"It must be something so profitable that it makes men stoop to some pretty dastardly deeds," Sir Richard said.

"Profitable," Ethan repeated softly. He stood quietly for a minute as if he were reaching for something locked deep in his memory. Then with his sudden intake of breath they all realized Ethan had remembered something . . . and he had. "Emeralds," he said in a half-whisper. "By God, it's got to be. It's emeralds. They think there are emeralds at Drake's dig . . . and maybe other places, too."

"Emeralds," George repeated, a touch of worry in his voice. "What do you know about that, Ethan?"

Ethan went on to explain about the huge emerald Drake

had found. He told them how Drake and Mendrano were the only two, besides himself, who knew about the stone, and that, because of its threat to the dig, they had decided to keep it a secret.

"But now it's pretty obvious that someone knew about it. That's what brought the fake Sir Richard here . . . to see if there are emeralds at Drake's dig." Ethan's eyes widened as he considered other possibilities. "There must be other places where they're digging. I'll stake my life on the idea that this dam and the small lake it will form is interfering with someone's plans. There must be several men involved," Ethan added coldly, "who don't mind killing for what they want."

"Killing!" Lettie was shaken. "You mean there has been a . . . a . . ."

"A murder," Ethan said grimly. "Yes, I thought it was an accident at first, a snake bite. But there was no way to find out. But now I believe he stumbled on someone's illicit activity and they had to do away with him." Anger flashed in Ethan's eyes. "That's a score I'll have to settle with someone."

"In the meantime we have to get up to Drake's dig," Bill said.

"Not tonight, you don't. Nobody in their right mind would tackle that jungle at night. I hate to waste time, but we just can't do anything until daylight."

"Well, we have one thing on our side," George said as he took a sip of his brandy.

"What?" Sir Richard asked.

"Whoever they are, they have no idea we know anything. The element of surprise is on our side."

"Yes, you're right," said Ethan. "Now a lot of things come together. The man who threatened Tana in the jungle. The man or men we never could find. All the 'accidents' we've had. They were right under our noses all the time. They must be having quite a laugh at our expense."

"All of this could have become quite a disaster if we hadn't discovered it," Sir Richard said. "I'm surprised they didn't kill me."

"Maybe they planned to, and someone turned out to be weak-hearted," Ethan replied. "They don't stop at murder. I can attest to that."

"If the others are digging . . . somewhere," Bill said, "why would the impostor be at the dig?"

"Because that's where the first rumor of emeralds came from. They're greedy. They'll take what they can from wherever they are, and if there are emeralds at Drake's dig, they want them, too."

"Where do you suppose they're digging?" George queried.

"Let's take a look at some maps. I've marked the area where the lake will be and I can pinpoint the place where Tana ran across the man who tried to kill her. Maybe if we put the two together we can come up with something."

"Good idea," George agreed.

It took only minutes for Ethan to get the maps out and unroll them on a table.

"Here," he said as he circled an area with his finger. "Here's where the lake will be . . . by God, the place where Tana ran across them is nearly in the middle. No wonder they're playing games with the dam."

"What an operation," Sir Richard exclaimed. "Destroying a dam, murder, deception . . ."

"And profit," Ethan said quietly. "Tremendous profit."

"There must be millions at stake here," George agreed. "And there are men to whom the benefits of the historical find and the dam . . . and even the deaths of people . . . mean very little in comparison to the wealth."

"Drake, Caitlyn . . . they're so unsuspecting," Ethan said. "I hope no harm comes to them," he added, his voice growing grim, "or I'll take care of whoever is responsible, one way or the other." He paused as another thought came to him. If Drake and Caitlyn and Mendrano had to be eliminated . . . so did Antonio and Tana. The thought almost knocked the breath out of him.

Tana . . . he could not cope with the idea that something could happen to her. It made him see that she meant much more to him than he realized.

"We should start for the dig first thing in the morning," Ethan said, "and circle around the camp. That way we can corner this fake Sir Richard and maybe get some information out of him before the others realize we're after them."

"I agree," George replied. "He's alone and we have no idea how many others there are. But he must have all the information."

"I can't wait to get my hands on him," Ethan said grimly.

"Can you imagine how Drake is going to feel?" George said.

"Betrayed, at the very least. Furious at most," Ethan said. "I just hope he doesn't have a problem before we get to him. He'll be taken so off-guard he won't know what's happening, or why."

"How is Drake at . . . handling situations?" Sir Richard asked.

"Drake can handle just about anything. He's pretty calm in most situations. He's a man I'd like to have with me if I ran into trouble."

"That's good news. He'll need a cool head if anything should go wrong before we get there," George added.

"I hadn't asked you two if you're hungry," Ethan said quickly.

"I'm starved, actually," Sir Richard said, laughing.

"I'll see to some food. Make yourselves comfortable. I'll be right back."

When Ethan had gone, George poured everyone another brandy.

"Terrible situation," Sir Richard said as he accepted his. "I do hope we're in time."

"I do, too," George replied. "I do, too."

Ethan went to the kitchen and ordered some food to be prepared, then returned to the study. When the food arrived they ate together, but the conversation remained on Caitlyn, Drake and the fake Sir Richard and his friends.

"George, I think I should take Marc along, at least. We have no way of knowing how many of the workers at Drake's are in cahoots with these men. We might run into a trap of some kind."

"Good idea, Ethan. We'll take one boat and the fastest rowers we can get. The element of surprise might just tip the balance toward us."

"I'll see to it first thing in the morning."

"It would be wise for us all to get some sleep. Tomorrow might prove to be a bit hectic," Sir Richard offered.

"Yes, not counting the upriver rowing, but from Drake's dock to the dig is a nice little trek. We'd better get some rest."

Ethan showed both men to their rooms and Bill and Lettie retired. But Ethan was too overwrought to go to bed. He returned to his study to try and work, but his mind couldn't concentrate on figures. He paced the floor for a while, trying to get some kind of plan straight in his mind.

Caught up in his thoughts, he was astonished when he heard someone pounding on the front door. He glanced at the clock. It would be dawn soon.

Ethan went to the door. He had no idea what to expect—it turned out to be a breathless Antonio and a badly shaken Tana.

He looked at them for a moment in complete surprise, but combined with the knowledge of what might be happening at the dig, fear edged out all other emotion.

"Antonio, Tana, what's wrong?" Ethan said as he urged them inside and closed the door.

"We don't know, Senor Ethan," Antonio said. "Please, we must know—are Drake, Caitlyn, and my father here?"

"Here? No, they're not. They should be at the dig. What makes you think they could be here? And what are you two doing traveling at night? Don't you know how dangerous it is?"

"Yes, Ethan," Tana said. "We know. But Antonio felt it was less danger than we would face if we remained."

"Something very strange is going on up there," Antonio concluded. "Drake, Caitlyn, and my father . . . well, it seems they've just vanished."

Ethan's heart began to pound. Were they going to be too late to prevent a disaster. Quickly he explained about the arrival of the real Sir Richard and their worry over what was happening.

"You two need to rest for a bit. It's only an hour or so until dawn. We're heading back upriver. Antonio, do you think you'll be missed right away?"

"I'm not sure. I suppose Sir Richard's mind is on other things, but I don't think it will be too long before he realizes I'm not among the workers. Once he does, he might go and check on Tana; then he will know we're both gone."

"Antonio, you and Tana get something to eat, then rest a while. If you're up to it, I want to be on our way at the first light of day. Tana, you really look exhausted."

"I am tired, but I cannot rest until I know my father is safe."

"I can understand that, but you have to get a little rest at least until we're ready to go. Come on, I'll get you something to eat."

They followed him to the kitchen where the three of them put together enough food for Antonio and Tana. Then Antonio left to get some rest, leaving Tana and Ethan alone in the semi-dark kitchen.

"Come on, Tana, you should go upstairs and try to sleep a bit."

"Ethan, please, I cannot sleep." She walked to him and stood close. "I . . . I'm so frightened. Antonio and I . . . we had nowhere else to go."

Her eyes were filled with fear for her father and thoughts of her frightening trek with Antonio to Ethan's place.

"You're a very courageous woman, Tana," Ethan said gently. "I'm glad you came to me."

For a moment Tana was breathlessly still. There was a change in Ethan and she wasn't sure what it was. Ethan understood her hesitancy. After all, she had poured out her feelings to him once and been rejected.

He reached out and gently touched her cheek.

"Tana, after this is over . . . when we've found your father and the others and know they're safe, you and I have some important things to talk about."

She wanted what she thought she was reading in his eyes to be the truth. But was her heart seeing more than just kindness and consideration?

"What have we to talk about, Ethan?" she asked softly. "When I came here before . . . well, what you felt, or did not feel, you made very clear to me."

"I suppose," Ethan said with a sigh, "but the whole thing

was a bit of a shock. You . . . you have to make allowances for the fact that sometimes a man who's too sure of himself can make a lot of damn fool mistakes. In this case, I think I made a very big one."

"Ethan . . . ?" she began, her eyes aglow with hope.

"To be honest about it, Tana, I was a fool. I almost let something very rare and beautiful walk out of my life. I should have realized when I saw the beauty of this place and decided to make it my home that the wisest choice would be a woman who belongs to it as much as I want to. Tana . . . can you forget what happened before? Can you forgive me for being so blind? And can you . . ." He paused as he watched her eyes fill with tears. "Tana," he said softly. He reached for her and she came into his arms.

Twenty

The kiss was as deep and breathtaking as the first had been, only this time he did not release her. As her body melted into his, for the first time Ethan felt the rightness of it. She seemed to fit against him as if they were two parts of a whole.

When he finally held her gently away from him they looked at each other in a kind of surprised wonder. Then Tana laughed softly, a laugh that he immediately matched. For both it was the laughter of disbelief—and of intense excitement . . . the excitement of discovery.

"It's kind of hard to believe," Ethan said.

"For you, Ethan, not for me. I have been in love with you for so long I can hardly remember when I wasn't."

"No, what's hard to believe," Ethan said as he drew her back into his arms, "is that . . . I've never really seen you before, never realized how beautiful you are. We have a lot of time to make up for."

"I wish . . ."

"What?"

"That the time began now."

"As do I . . . but we have to think beyond ourselves right now. But I've been a fool and I don't intend to remain one. Stay here, and when I get back, I want you to make this place your home. We can talk to your father when all of this is over."

"My father—Ethan, do you think . . . we will find him?"

"We'll find him and we'll put an end to all this deception and mystery."

"I can't stay here. I want to go with you."

"It's too dangerous."

"I don't care!" she pleaded. "Please, Ethan, I'll be safer with you than anyplace else . . . I'll feel safer with you than with anyone else. I want to be with you."

"Lord," Ethan chuckled, "do you think after this I don't want to be with you? Right now I want . . ."

Tana said softly, "I have waited so long to hear your words."

He slid his fingers up her arms, then took her face between his hands. "Tana, you're beautiful and you're very special. I want you very much and I intend to make you happy. Loving you," he added softly, "is going to be the easiest thing I've ever done. I'm grateful that you want me . . . and I won't let you regret it, not for a day . . . not for an hour. Come to my home . . . and to me and share your life with me. Stay with me, Tana." His voice became a whisper as he bent to kiss her so gently that it brought tears to Tana's eyes.

Slowly her arms slid about his waist and his arms tightened around her as the kiss grew deeper and deeper. Her mouth parted to accept his heated searching.

Time became a forgotten thing, and where they were no longer seemed to matter. The world consisted only of the two of them and the miraculous thing that had blossomed between them.

There was no longer any way for either of them to deny

their feelings . . . and when the kiss ended Ethan looked deeply into her eyes.

Tana was breathless with emotion. Her deepest longings were now becoming a reality. In Ethan's eyes, she saw what she had wanted to see for so long.

"Come with me now?" he asked gently.

"Yes." Her reply took no thought—she wanted him as much as he wanted her. Tomorrow was going to be difficult and frightening, so they pushed it away and held onto this night as if it were their last.

With Ethan's arm around her waist, they walked up the stairs to his room. Inside Tana paused while Ethan lit the lamps by the huge four-poster bed. She looked around her. The room was so like Ethan—a whisper of fear began to grow within her.

Ethan was wise enough to see her hesitancy. He came to her and gently took her in his arms.

"It's just a room, Tana. A bit different from what you're used to, but still just a room. None of these things is as important as you are. I'd give them up tomorrow and start over before I'd lose you."

"Do I belong here, Ethan? It frightens me that I can give you so little."

"So little! Sweet idiot." Ethan laughed. "Do you think anything I have compares to you? You love me, Tana, and that's worth more than everything I own. And I love you. You *do* belong here. What we have, what we do, and what we build from now on we'll build together. I don't think I knew how lonely I was until now. This house . . . it's been empty for a long time and now you're here and everything is going to be right. You belong, right where you are . . . in my arms," he added softly. He held her with one arm and gently tipped up her chin with the other hand. Then he bent his head and tasted her soft, willing lips and the emotions that claimed them put an end to any other thought. His quickened breathing joined hers as he pressed his body intimately to hers.

He trembled, and she could see his hands shaking a bit as he began to undress her. She began to unbutton his shirt. She closed her eyes when she felt their bodies touch and his hands come alive on her flesh. She hadn't known it would be likes this—every nerve ending so alive. She felt disembodied, as if she were floating. A wonderful feeling of opening every sense to something new to her, but something she instinctively knew would be the most memorable and precious moment of her life.

She felt him lift her gently in his arms and she pressed her lips to his throat, tasting the warmth of his skin and feeling the beating of his heart.

Carefully, slowly, his hands explored and his lips followed. She wanted to give as much as she was receiving and she followed his lead, her hands seeking out sensitive places, her lips teasing and tormenting as he was teasing and tormenting her. She felt a touch of both pleasure and power as she heard the involuntary sound he made deep in his throat.

He'd held off as long as his body would allow. Both were beyond control and both sought fulfillment of their need, a primeval force that consumed them.

With a passion so wild it had grown to a fury, he came into her, catching her startled cry and her murmur of intense joy with the same kiss.

They moved as one, taking and giving all, reaching a culmination that left them clinging to each other, their sweat-streaked bodies entwined.

Slowly, ragged breathing became controlled and trembling nerves relaxed and they held each other, deliriously happy and completely content.

Tana lay curled against Ethan, her head on his shoulder, too warm and sated even to speak.

Slowly he turned to face her and she looked up into his eyes. He held her gaze, a new intensity in his eyes; then he brushed her cheek lightly with his fingertips.

"What?" she questioned, a bit shaken by the look in his eyes. "Do you regret . . . ?"

"No! Tana . . . no! It's . . . it's just that it's hard to believe you came into my life almost out of the blue and changed everything. I've done so much, without realizing that all of it was worth nothing . . . and I overlooked the real treasure right under my nose. I . . . I've just begun to wonder what kind of an empty life I'd have had if I hadn't finally gotten some sense . . . I think . . . it might have become unbearable. I'm glad we found each other . . . even if I was pretty blind for a while."

"I love you, Ethan. I used to dream . . ."

"Dream what? Tell me."

"That I was here with you," she said, feeling her cheeks warm under his penetrating gaze, but she went on. "Here, in your bed, in your arms."

"God, I love you," he whispered. He kissed her gently, holding her close.

They were silent for a while, savoring the feel and the warmth of each other, enjoying the security and strength of the new and vibrant thing that united them. Ethan spoke first. "We only have a couple of hours until dawn."

"You'll let me go with you, Ethan? I want to find my father . . . and I want to be with you."

"Of course. I don't intend to let you out of my sight.

There's an off chance you might change your mind, and I want to be sure that doesn't happen."

Tana sat up and looked down at him. "You know I would never . . ."

"Tana," Ethan chuckled, "I was teasing." He caught her hair in both hands and drew her down to him. "It's another thing we're going to share, learning to laugh together. There's so much . . ." he kissed her almost feverishly. "There's so much to learn about each other. We'll get married as soon as we get this business over with."

"My brother will be surprised, I think," Tana laughed.

"Antonio is not a violent man, is he? I'd hate it if you were a widow before you're a wife."

"Antonio may roar like a lion, but he admires you. He will think I am very lucky."

"Lucky! The man's not too observant. I'm the one who's lucky. I'd better have a talk with Antonio first thing."

"He . . . he may not be . . . agreeable."

"You mean he might think this is all a game and I'll send you home when it's over?"

"Possibly."

"And you, what do you think?"

"I think that I love you more than the breath in my body, and if it's only for today, then I shall be happy for today. And if it's forever . . . I shall die happy."

"It's forever, Tana. It might take me a few years to convince you," Ethan grinned, "but I'm a patient man—I'll work at it."

"It's such a short time until dawn," Tana said, her voice husky with rising passion from his caressing hands.

"Yes . . . too short."

Tana laughed softly as he drew her to him. She wanted

him to kiss her again and again . . . to love her again . . . and he did.

Antonio had not been able to sleep. Worry about his father's mysterious disappearance weighed heavily in his heart. That—and the disappearance of Drake and Caitlyn—was mystifying. He had a feeling time was running out, but he had no way of knowing why. He just felt a need to be on his way and frustration at the fact that they could not travel in the jungle at night.

On top of everything else, he was worried about Tana.

He was aware of the strong chemistry between her and Ethan and it scared him. Ethan was from a different world and Antonio was certain that world could not accept Tana. He didn't want her hurt, and he didn't want her to want things she could never have. Antonio promised himself that once his family was reunited he was going to do all he could to prevent the outside world from touching them again.

He walked in the solitude of Ethan's garden and considered things he could say that might make Tana return with him and forget Ethan Marshall.

The moon slowly sank toward the horizon and a pale streak of white heralded the coming day—and still Antonio fought confusion and worry.

He heard a footstep behind him and turned to see Ethan walking toward him. This was the best time to try and make Ethan realize the way his sister felt and how futile everyone but Tana knew it to be. He paused and waited for Ethan.

Even after Tana slept Ethan had lain awake. The time was slipping away much too fast. He was filled with a million conflicting emotions. Worry about Drake, Caitlyn, and Mendrano, excitement about Tana, and troubled about what he would say to Antonio. He didn't want the situation to be any more stressful for Tana than it had to be, but he wasn't too sure Antonio's protective attitude would be penetrated so easily.

The worst thing was he could understand Antonio's point of view and was ashamed to say it was similar to what his own had been.

He turned slightly to look down at Tana, sleeping curled against him. Remembrance of the too-short night sent a surge of protective desire through him. He'd almost missed the joy of having Tana in his life and the gratitude he felt towards the fates made him want to crush her in his arms and make love to her until it eased the hunger in him.

He knew that day would come soon, but now he wanted Tana to get all the rest she could.

Gently he lifted her hand and pressed a kiss to the palm, then he carefully drew the covers over her and eased from the bed.

Quietly he gathered his clothes and went to the small dressing room off his bedroom. He washed, shaved, and dressed. There was still time before dawn but he wanted to make some kind of plans and be prepared before he awakened Tana. He had decided it was only fair to take her along. After all, it was her father who was missing. Besides, he admitted to himself, he just didn't want them to be separated any more than they had to be.

He walked downstairs and directly to the kitchen, where the scent of coffee was a welcome one.

"Nobody else awake yet?" he questioned his cook.

"None of the others except the young Antonio. He has

not slept, and even now he paces the garden like a caged puma."

"Antonio," Ethan sighed quietly, "I've a pretty good idea of what's on his mind." Ethan poured himself a cup of hot, dark coffee and carried it with him as he walked toward the garden.

Deep in thought, Antonio did not hear Ethan approach and it gave Ethan a few moments to study him. He'd known Antonio even longer than he had Tana and their father, and he knew Antonio had grown up with an unspoken yet rigid set of principles. He also knew those principles would have Antonio believe that Tana did not belong in Ethan's life.

Ethan had to be honest with Antonio because he was pretty sure Antonio would see right through any other approach. Besides, he wanted Antonio's respect and blessing.

"Morning, Antonio." Antonio turned to look at Ethan. "You didn't get much sleep, I take it."

"No, I didn't . . . did you?"

"Not much. I've made all the arrangements. In a short while it will be light. Then we'll get moving. George has told me he sent word to Emil Josiah. I have a feeling the Colombian authorities won't be too far behind us."

"That's a good idea. We don't really know what we're getting into."

"Are you ready?"

"That's not what you came out here for, is it? To ask if I was ready?"

"Not exactly. I think it's time you and I had a talk."

"I thought that might be so. Ethan . . . you and I know that things are not always what we hope them to be."

"Are we talking about our hopes . . . or . . ."

"Or Tana's," Antonio finished. "Tana is very important to me."

"I don't doubt that. But she has become very important to me as well. You're going to have to realize, Antonio, that Tana is not a child. She's the woman I want for my wife. You have a choice of believing that or not. But I don't intend to hurt her. One way or the other, Tana is staying with me. I'd like us to be . . . family . . . and friends. If it's to be enemies . . . then that will be *your* choice."

They stood a few feet apart in a silence pregnant with emotion. Antonio was trying to read Ethan's heart.

"You can't help but hurt her, Ethan. One day you will begin to realize she doesn't belong here. What will you do then?" Before Ethan could answer, Antonio spoke again. "I'll tell you. Tana will come back to us, but she will never be the same again. She will want your world and you can't give it to her."

"That's where we are . . . or were, both wrong. You see, Antonio, I used to think that way, but now I know. There is no woman in the world who belongs here more than she does. In fact, she belongs more than *I* do. I'm the alien. Tana *is* this country . . . I love this place . . . and I love her. If she'll let me I want to marry her. You're the only one who can hurt her, really. She loves you and if this separates her from her family, it will be painful. You plan to do that, Antonio? Make her suffer because you're blind, obstinate, and as stubborn as a mule?"

Antonio laughed softly. The rising annoyance in Ethan's eyes had just begun to make him realize he really was in love with Tana.

"I think you'll find out my sister can be as stubborn as I."

"I already know that," Ethan grinned in relief.

"And you still have my father to talk to."

"I need to know, Antonio. Do I have your support or not?"

"I'll consider it," Antonio chuckled, "but it will probably do you good to worry a bit."

"I hate to tell you, but I've been worried since Tana came here. Worried . . . but not dumb enough to let her go again."

"I hope for Tana's sake . . . and for yours, that it all works out."

"Well, our first step is to find Drake and Caitlyn and your father and see what this impersonator had in mind when he came here."

"Ethan . . . do you think . . ."

"I don't want to think like that. Drake is not a man easily taken advantage of. He might have stumbled onto the secret and gotten wise enough to take Caitlyn and your father and run."

"Then he would run here."

"That jungle is not easy, even for men as able as your father and Drake. With Caitlyn along they would have to be careful. I'd say they'd stay near the camp."

"I hope you're right."

"Well, guessing won't do any good. It's getting light enough to move." Ethan started to turn away when both men realized Tana was standing in the doorway. Her eyes were on her brother with a look of gentle defiance. But Ethan walked to her and took her in his arms. "I think," he smiled down at her, "it's time we go and look for the rest of our family."

Her quick smile was enough of a reward, and her brother's embrace assured her that he would not argue. Together the three left with George, Bill, and Sir Richard.

They made their way as rapidly as they could to the dam site, where they found a very angry Marc looking at a totally destroyed piece of equipment. His vocabulary was extremely colorful—only when he saw Tana did he get himself under control.

"Another problem?" Ethan asked as they joined Marc.

"Yeah . . . another one," Marc said angrily, "among a hundred."

"Well, we have to bring an end to this. We're not sure yet, Marc, but we think we have some new ideas about what's going on." As concisely as he could, Ethan explained everything they knew and all they suspected. "We'd like . . . no, we need you to come along with us. We've no idea what we'll find up there."

"Sure. We'll bring as many men as you need."

"Then let's get moving."

Soon they were on their way, each person offering their own personal prayers for those they loved.

They traveled by boat, each doing everything possible to make this the fastest journey ever made. They accomplished it in half the usual time. When they arrived at Drake's house the long trek to the dig still lay before them, but no one considered stopping to rest. Their imaginations were playing havoc with them.

They walked single file through the dense jungle in silence, worry heavy in their hearts.

When they came in sight of the dig Ethan stopped. Antonio, Marc, Bill, and George came up beside him, followed by Sir Richard and Tana.

"What's wrong, Ethan?" Sir Richard asked. He could tell by the look on Ethan's face that something was amiss.

"Something's not . . . it looks like the whole dig is deserted."

"Deserted?" George said. "Impossible."

"Well, impossible or not," Ethan said grimly, "there's not a sign of a soul. No workers . . . nothing."

"This doesn't make sense," Antonio said. "There were workers, a lot of them. Something is very wrong."

"We have to get down there," Ethan said. "Let's go."

Ethan led the group to the deserted dig. The area was ominously quiet. In fact, the entire place seemed exceptionally . . . clean. Tools were gone along with all signs of work in progress. There was a hollow emptiness in the place that frayed their nerves.

"Oh, Ethan," Tana said, "where do you suppose they are?"

"I don't know," he replied, "but no harm had better come to them or by God whoever our Sir Richard is, he won't be able to find a corner of this country to hide in."

"Ethan," Antonio said, "we've searched the tents . . . everything. There's no sign of anyone. And . . . Sir Richard's tent . . . everything's been taken."

"So he's gone . . . somewhere. But where?"

"And where is my father?" Tana said.

"And Drake and Caitlyn," Ethan added. "None of this makes a damn bit of sense. Surely if Drake had to take to the jungle he'd head for his house, the dam, or my place."

"Maybe," Antonio said thoughtfully, "maybe if they were forced to run . . ."

"Forced!" Tana cried.

"Well . . . maybe they took refuge from something . . . or someone."

"Refuge? Where?" Ethan asked.

"In the tomb, perhaps."

"If someone were trying to do you any harm surely that would be the last place to run. They could be trapped there."

"But," Antonio said stubbornly, "it is the only place we haven't looked, and I'm going to go and see—even if it is a foolish idea."

"Maybe you're right," Ethan said. "Let's go take a look."

Ethan led the others to the tomb. He took a deep breath before he could make himself step inside. Closed places made him very nervous. He had refused to go down no matter how many times Drake had coaxed him. A place like that made him physically ill . . . and it was a mental strain as well. He hated to admit it, but the thought of going down into the cavernous place below was terrifying. He could feel the sweat pop on his brow.

The entire group gathered at the first level. The room was semi-dark and empty, and it was Antonio who discovered the clue.

"The sack of stones."

"What?" Ethan asked quickly.

"There was a sack of stones holding the door open. It's been moved. Someone wanted that door closed."

"Oh, no," Tana gasped, her face white with fear. "You don't suppose . . ."

"Good Lord," Ethan muttered, stunned at the idea of anyone inhuman enough to enclosed someone in the deep caverns. He and Antonio dragged the heavy sack of stones toward the square where the weight would open the door that led below.

Paul had risen early, annoyed that what little sleep he'd had had been filled with the most unbelievable dreams—dreams of dark and airless places. He did not reason that the conscience he had smothered was giving its last gasp before it expired.

The knowledge that he had condemned three people to an ugly death was something he was able to push aside only when he was awake.

When he stepped from his tent he could see the men milling about, a group without a leader. Mendrano, he knew, would never be found again. But . . . Antonio. Where was Antonio? He'd ordered him to spend the night in camp. Maybe, he thought, the ignorant young savage had gone home to the comfort of his bed.

He walked to Mendrano's house alone. He didn't want to ask questions he could answer himself.

At Mendrano's house he found only silence. He knew Antonio had a sister. Someone should be there, but no one was.

"So . . . he was suspicious after all," Paul muttered. "We shall have to do something . . ." He paused, then turned and headed back to camp.

Paul was certain, since they had obviously left quickly and without preparation, that Antonio and Tana had little chance to make it to safety. Even then, their story would hardly be believed. Of course, even Antonio had no way of knowing where his father, Drake, and Caitlyn were and if they did return, it would be too late.

By the time they were found out, Paul and his friends would have escaped with a fortune in emeralds. Still . . . the jewels that lay below lured him. His greed was hard to satisfy. He had to leave for a while . . . but he would return. He wanted all that was buried here beneath his feet. He also knew he had to act his finest part—to convince Monroe that they had to leave soon . . . and that the tomb contained no treasure at all.

He returned to the dig, gathered the workers, and gave each more money than any of them had ever seen before. Then he told them they were to return to their homes until they were needed again.

"But, senor," one protested, "what will Senor Drake say? He will think we have deserted him and be angry."

"No. He has no reason to be angry. It is just that something has come up that he must tend to, and it will take a couple of weeks. When he returns to this spot he will call on you again."

"It will be soon?"

"Soon? I am not sure it will be soon, but don't worry, when the time comes you will work here again. That I promise you."

"Thank you, senor. We are good workers. My men are content to work here."

"Then I will call them again . . . when the time is right. For now, take the money and gather your men and leave. Rest assured, they will be . . . employed again soon."

Paul watched the workers drift away and felt a sense of satisfaction. One day they *would* dig again, but they would be digging for his treasure. By the time he returned here the three in the tomb would be nothing but skeletal remains, and who could identify them?

Eventually the men would carry the treasure up for him— a treasure that would make him wealthier than any king in history.

When Paul returned to his tent he gathered up his possessions. His body was warm with tension, and perspiration dampened his forehead and made his palms slick with sweat. He hated the jungle, was deathly afraid of it, but he knew what he had to do if his plans were to succeed. He took a path known to him alone, and within two hours he reached the place where his friends and their workers were digging up a fabulous cache of emeralds.

"Paul," Monroe asked quickly, "what are you doing here?"

"I'm afraid I've come out of necessity."

"Necessity? What has happened?"

"My identity is no longer a secret."

"Don't talk in riddles!" Monroe snapped. He was impatient with Paul's eternal acting. It was a trial to put up with the vain actor, and only the promise of a fabulous fortune enabled him to do it.

"I'm not talking riddles. It's a temporary setback, that's all. I'm afraid the inquisitive lady who was my so-called daughter has found me out. Since she and Drake were so . . . close, and since his interfering head man was much too suspicious, I had to do something about the three of them. But you needn't worry." He went on to explain what had transpired from the moment he'd walked into his tent and found Caitlyn with his scrapbook.

"You buried them in the tomb? You stupid, vain popinjay! Don't you think someone will be looking for them?"

"Not any of the workers. I've paid them off and sent them home."

"But the family of that head man, that . . . Mendrano. What of them?"

"You don't think those two, a boy and a girl, will reach that plantation alive, do you? Across that jungle out there? They're as good as dead. It'll be weeks before anyone comes up to look for them. By then . . . we will have all we want and be gone."

"You damn fool," Monroe growled, "I did not hire you to think! I hired you to play a part. What if those two *do* get through alive? What if they bring help back in time to set them free?"

"Impossible."

"No, I'm afraid it's not impossible. Now we have to protect ourselves." Monroe called one of his men over. "Go up and keep an eye on the camp. If anyone comes, bring me word."

The man left quickly and Paul remained silent, intimidated by the anger in the eyes of the man who had brought him here. No matter what Monroe said, Paul could think of nothing but the chests of treasure in the dark rooms of the tomb. He meant to have them . . . he had to have them. He would never be subservient to a man like Monroe again.

He found a comfortable place to relax and watch the small group of men as they dug for emeralds. He laughed to himself. Let Monroe have all these emeralds—he would have a fortune Monroe could not even imagine.

He spent the day dreaming about all the things he would do with his wealth. He stayed out of the way of Slade's angry looks. All he needed now was patience.

They ate a quiet and solemn meal and Paul took to his bed as soon as he possibly could. The dreams that plagued him were kept at bay during the day, but they ran rampant at night and Paul found himself jerked awake in a cold sweat.

He clung with desperation to the thought of the riches he would soon have. Wealth would mean freedom. Still he did not try to sleep again and refused to recognize his fear.

The next afternoon when Paul joined Monroe for lunch, he tried to overlook Monroe's look of disdain and ignore the uncomfortable feeling it gave him.

"The men are pretty busy today. They've found a lot of rather large stones. You should be pleased."

"Oh, I am, I am," Monroe said mildly. "And you're not pleased? After all, you get a healthy share."

"I'm satisfied," Paul answered smugly.

"I don't doubt that you are," Monroe chuckled. "I don't doubt it for a minute."

Paul was suddenly alerted to something in Monroe's voice he had not heard before. But he looked into his eyes and saw . . . nothing.

He was about to doubt his own suspicions when one of the workers came toward them. He recognized him and his heart began to pound. He had a feeling he was not going to like what he was about to hear.

"Senor, men come to the camp. Many of them. I think it is the friend of the one who was the leader. Also the young one . . . the son of Mendrano. They are at the camp now."

Monroe exchanged a grim but meaningful look with Paul.

"You see, Paul, you must learn to plan ahead." He turned to the worker. "Gather the men. We have some unfinished business to attend to." He stood up and looked down at Paul. "And then, when we have taken care of that . . . we'll have to find out for ourselves what's in that tomb."

Paul sat watching Monroe retreat and felt a virulent hatred well up. Monroe no longer trusted him . . . and it seemed he would have to work out a plan of his own to get what he wanted.

Ethan fought for breath, feeling that the walls of the tomb were closing in on him. He had only gone down a few steps into the second level and he knew there was still a cavernous distance between him and the bottom.

The lanterns were already burning so low that their shadows danced like specters in the flickering haze.

He was quite aware that none of the others was having any difficulty—it was his own personal hell. Yet he also knew he would go on, because he could picture his three friends below . . . if they were there. He hoped they were in time to find them alive.

He could envision that dark, empty, and airless place and it made his claustrophobia even worse. Still he pressed on.

He led the way with Tana right behind him. Antonio was followed by George, Sir Richard, and Bill. In fact, Ethan was grateful to be first. He wanted no one to be aware of his condition.

And no one was . . . except Tana. As Ethan paused at the head of the flight of steps she moved close beside him and slid her hand in his. He was grateful for her presence and squeezed her hand to let her know.

They went down to the next level. Everyone was silent—afraid for themselves and of what they might find.

A wave of nausea almost overpowered Ethan, but he clenched his teeth and grimly kept on. He was certain if he paused even for a moment he'd be overcome by paralyzing fear and no longer be able to move at all.

They finally reached the top of the steps that led to the bottom level. Everyone was praying silently.

"Drake!" Ethan shouted. They heard only the echo of his voice. It was difficult to believe that they couldn't hear him, but he shouted again, "Drake! Mendrano! Caitlyn!"

Still no sound in return, nothing but the dying echo as it faded into the darkness.

They couldn't look at each other. They didn't want to see the fear in everyone's eyes.

Step by step . . . they moved down to the last floor, and couldn't believe their eyes. The entire place was empty. Completely and totally empty.

Twenty-one

Drake could feel Caitlyn struggling to gather her courage; he was doing the same thing himself, as he knew Mendrano must be.

"Someone will be looking for us," Drake said. "By morning, when the workers gather . . ."

"No, Senor Drake," Mendrano stated firmly. He didn't want Drake or Caitlyn to have false hope. "The men are frightened of this place. They will only come down here *with* us."

"And . . . he's such a good actor," Caitlyn said bitterly. "I doubt if they will question whatever he tells them. Mendrano . . . what of Antonio, or Tana?"

"My son will not be fooled for long by this impostor. I'm sure he will be looking for us in a matter of hours."

"We'd better not kid ourselves," Drake said. "This man, as Caitlyn said, is a professional actor. He'll be able to convince them we've gone off somewhere, maybe to Ethan's. Once he does, it's only a matter of time until he can take control."

"There's no doubt about what he's after, either," Caitlyn said, half in anger and half in fear. "But . . . there is some doubt about how long we can last down here with that door closed."

"We can't panic, Caitlyn," Drake said firmly. "We have to use our heads."

"I don't understand you, Drake. There's only one way out of here and that's sealed. We're going to run out of air before we discover the secret of this place." There was a note of near-panic in her voice and he knew she was struggling for control.

"I'm not so sure there *is* only one way out."

"We don't have the time to find the way, *if* there is one. I don't see how you can believe that."

Drake took Caitlyn into his arms and held her, feeling her entire body shaking. "Caitlyn," he said in a comforting, caressing tone, "I love you, and I'm not giving up so easily." He looked into her eyes. "We're going to believe, and we're going to fight . . . and we're going to find a way, because I'm not letting anything happen to the most precious thing in my life."

The depth of his love for her was obvious in his expression and the gentleness of his voice. Caitlyn felt a new strength flowing from him to her.

"Drake," she whispered with renewed hope, and he smiled, knowing she would fight every inch of the way with him. He loved her more at that moment than he ever had. He drew her back into his arms and rocked her against him.

"We can't waste any time, Mendrano. You start at the far end and Caitlyn and I will start down here. Check every stone, every crack, anything that might look . . . I don't know, suspicious, or interesting, or out of place."

Mendrano turned and started toward the shadows at the far end of the room. Drake and Caitlyn moved in the opposite direction.

Laboriously and carefully, studying every minute detail, they examined the walls and the floors, running their fingers over every crevice, checking every separate square that made up the floor, testing every spot for weight or pressure.

They worked their way toward each other and, three hours later, met in the middle of the room again. All three were breathing deeply. Their perspiration made the dust cling and they were aware that the air had a decidedly musty odor.

Drake felt the first tinge of real fear. He could stand it if it were just he and Mendrano. But how could he stand by helplessly and watch Caitlyn die?

Mentally he cursed Paul Macombe and longed for a minute alone with him. From the moment Caitlyn had told him who Paul really was, the anger had been growing. Still, he knew that wasn't doing him much good. And besides, Paul Macombe was probably miles away by now.

Time ticked slowly on, pushing them relentlessly closer and closer to the moment when the air would be gone.

Drake sat on the bottom step of the altar. He had to think! He had to try and find a way. The royal couple had been entombed here, yet there was no sign of their remains . . . impossible! If they died here centuries ago, there would be evidence. So there must be a way out of this stone room . . . but where . . . how?

Caitlyn came and sat beside him. He drew her against him, feeling her exhaustion. She had not slept in over twenty hours.

"Caitlyn, you must rest for a while," he said firmly. He turned her around so she could lean against his chest, then he rested his back against the second step and cradled her in his arms. She was grateful for the solid beat of his heart, but sleep was an impossibility. She didn't want to sleep away the last few hours she might have with Drake.

Mendrano sat beside Drake with his back against the second step.

"There's something we're missing, Mendrano."

"I know, but what?"

"For all we know, we may be inches from freedom," he said as he tightened his arm around Caitlyn. "It has to be here," his voice softened. "It has to."

"There's hardly anything we haven't examined," Caitlyn said. "None of the stones seem moveable."

"Then let's consider what we haven't examined," Drake said positively. "There has to be something."

But it didn't seem that there was. There was silence . . . a silence deeper than the three of them had ever known. The only thing that echoed through it was the passage of time and the knowledge that the air was getting thinner every second.

Drake's mind was struggling, as was Mendrano's. Caitlyn, totally exhausted, had drifted into a light sleep. The lanterns were burning dangerously low and Drake was shaken by the thought that they could find themselves in total darkness.

He looked down at Caitlyn and the fear almost overwhelmed him. He couldn't let her die. She had not really slept, but had only retreated into herself a bit. She was afraid. She had never been so terrified in her life.

She opened her eyes and looked up into Drake's worried gaze. She tried to smile as she reached up to lay her hand against his cheek.

"I love you, Drake Stone," she whispered.

"Look where it's got you, Caitlyn. God, I'm sorry. I . . ." Her fingers touched his lips to silence him.

"Don't, Drake. There's no sense wasting our last hours together with recriminations. It's greed, it's lack of conscience, it's a lot of things . . . all of them that impostor's fault."

"You're very brave."

"No, I'm very scared. My only consolation is that I'm with you—and he's not really my father. Right now . . . that's all that matters."

Her eyes glittered with tears and Drake couldn't find words that came remotely close to telling her how he felt. He bent his head and kissed her deeply.

"Senor Drake?" Mendrano's voice interrupted and drew Drake's attention.

"What?"

"We have tried every stone and none moved . . . we have tried every small stone in the walls and floor. But we have not tried the largest stone in the room."

"The largest . . ." Drake paused, considering Mendrano's words. He looked around him. Caitlyn, too, sat up. Puzzled about what Mendrano meant, he saw Mendrano simply pat the stone step he was sitting on.

"Good Lord," Drake said. "I never thought . . ." He helped Caitlyn to her feet as he rose, and both of them turned to look at the huge altar. "Is it possible that the whole thing moves?" He was awed at the idea. "If it does, these people weren't clever . . . they were geniuses. The question is, if it moves . . . how does it move?"

The three of them began a close examination of the altar. Carefully, trembling fingers traced each crevice, each thin line of demarcation, every place where the huge stone might be moveable. Mendrano and Drake braced their shoulders against every spot that seemed like a possibility and pushed with all their strength. But nothing moved.

Exhaustion and the thin air made them finally come to a breathless stop. Despair hung heavily over them and they battled it silently. There seemed to be no way out.

Drake stood panting and gazing at the huge altar in frustration. Helplessness angered him. He dreaded looking into

Caitlyn's eyes because he knew he'd see a reflection of his own fear there. He *wouldn't* look in her eyes. He had to find the way.

Caitlyn was sitting on the bottom step of the altar, her elbows resting on her knees and her face buried in her hands. Drake swallowed the heavy constriction in his throat and went to her. He knelt before her and gently took hold of her wrists to draw her hands away.

She hadn't been crying, she had just been suddenly overwhelmed. She tried to smile at him, but her lips quivered. He drew her to him and put his arms around her. At that moment one of the lanterns flickered . . . and went out.

Drake knew Caitlyn was hanging on only a thin thread of raw courage. There was nothing he could say that would help. All he could do was try to share his own strength with her.

Caitlyn sighed and looked up at him. Gently she reached out and put her hand on his gun. She watched his face pale and his eyes register a new kind of fear.

"It . . . it might be easier, Drake," she whispered.

"No!" He gritted through clenched teeth. He could have used the gun on himself, but never on Caitlyn. "I can't," he said, his voice breaking at the sheer agony of the idea. To kill the one thing he loved more than anything in the world was beyond endurance. He had the courage to face many things, but not that. "We're not giving up, Caitlyn . . . we're not!"

"Drake, it's useless. In a few more hours there will be no air in here . . . the lanterns . . ." Her eyes were wide with horror. "They'll go out." Her voice trailed off to a sob.

"But we have time left," he said as he caught her face between his hands. "Look at me, Caitlyn." She raised her eyes to his. "The young king and queen got out of here. If they can find it, so can we. We have to believe there's a way."

"Drake, we tried everything."

"Then we'll keep on trying. We're can't let it end like this. You're too strong to give up. We'll go on trying." His voice was firm, and he kissed her fiercely. "We'll keep on . . . won't we? Won't we?"

"Yes . . . yes," she cried. Drake crushed her to him, wishing he believed as deeply as he wanted her to.

Mendrano had gone on with the search, climbing to the top of the altar and examining the ebony stone.

He knew he was close to death, but strangely, his thoughts were on his children. What stories would they be told about what had happened to him? He had never been so frightened in his life.

Some deep instinct made him ask the same question that Drake had. If the young king's remains were not here, in the airtight room, then had he found a way out?

He ran his hands over the huge stone, subconsciously marveling at the workmanship, contemplating a solution to a centuries-old puzzle.

He'd wanted to give Drake and Caitlyn time to talk, knowing the pain of watching each other struggle in this trap was very difficult. He also knew pity would not make anything easier.

He was still deep in thought when Drake came over to stand beside him.

"Anything, Mendrano?"

"No . . . it's just that I can't get past the idea that the solution is staring us in the face."

"Me, too," Drake said. Then he lowered his voice. "Mendrano . . . we're running out of time. It's five in the morning, which means we've already been down here eight hours. If my calculations are right, we'll run out of light in about two hours. And I'm afraid the air won't last much longer than that."

"Maybe we can make the light last longer."

"How?"

"If we empty the oil from all the lanterns into one we can add several hours."

"Good idea," Drake replied. "I'll put Caitlyn on that. She needs something to do. Then you and I can concentrate on finding clues."

"You'd best do it quickly. The air is already pretty bad."

"I'll get her on it right away." Drake rejoined Caitlyn while Mendrano continued searching for cracks in the stone.

Relieved to find something to concentrate on, Caitlyn gathered the lanterns quickly. The possibility of hours of extra light and the hope that they would not die in darkness appealed to her. Once she had gathered the lanterns at the foot of the altar, the rest of the room was shrouded in total darkness.

She poured the oil carefully into one lantern, casting a brilliant circle around her. As each lantern was extinguished the darkness at the top of the altar became deeper and deeper, until Mendrano and Drake could not make out the elaborate carving.

"Caitlyn," Drake called down, "bring that lantern up here. We need some light."

"I'm coming," she replied. She went up the two steps until she was standing beside Mendrano and Drake, the lantern hanging at her side.

"If you'll hold the lantern up over this thing maybe we can see," Mendrano said.

"Better still," Drake replied, "set it in the middle . . . on that flat area where the sun is carved. That way we can all look for something."

Caitlyn nodded and raised the brilliantly glowing lantern, then set it in the middle of the sun carving. She had hardly let go of it when she felt the tremor.

"Drake!"

"Don't move!" Drake said in a commanding voice. "That's not from outside this tomb—it's from in here!"

The tremor grew, accompanied by a muted rumble, as if stone was sliding against stone. The rumbling increased until it vibrated against the wall of the room and filled it with sound. The tremor grew as well, until the three had to grasp the stone to hold on.

Then the altar slid forward, away from the wall behind it. It moved about six feet, revealing a flight of steps that disappeared into a dark room beyond.

At first the three were too shaken to realize what had happened. They looked at the passageway in shock.

"Do you suppose . . ." Caitlyn began.

"Don't get your hopes up," Drake said. "It's part of the tomb . . . another room. I wouldn't be surprised," he added quietly, "if we found the burial place. But it's not necessarily a way out."

"How do you know?"

"Because," Mendrano said, "there's no fresh air there or we would feel the draft."

"You're right," Drake said, "but I think we'd better look it over anyway."

Mendrano reached out to pick up the lantern but as he did so the low rumbling began again. Drake reached out to stop him. "Put the lantern back."

Mendrano did as he was told and the rumbling ceased. "It's the light or the weight, or both," Drake said. "We should have known. We've seen a million references to the sun. Why would the sun . . . the light combined with the weight . . . not be the key?"

"But we can't leave the lantern here. How will we see what's in there?" Caitlyn questioned. "It's as dark as . . ."

"As a tomb." Drake chuckled mirthlessly. "We'll have to rob the lantern of just enough oil to light one of the other lamps . . . and hope that what we take isn't too heavy and this closes up again."

Mendrano went to fetch one of the other lanterns and they were careful to take only enough of the precious oil to create a dim light. Then, with Drake leading the way and Caitlyn's hand tightly in his, they descended the steps and entered the dark room beyond.

As the glow preceded them into the room, Caitlyn gave a startled gasp and the two men were stunned to absolute silence.

"Well," Drake finally said, his voice quiet, "I guess we finally found them." He turned to look at Caitlyn and saw the tears in her eyes.

The room was small, no more than ten feet by ten feet. But what it held was enough to make anyone speechless.

The remains of the two lovers were so close together it was obvious they had expired in each other's arms—amid a treasure of such opulence that it was staggering.

There were carved statues with ruby and emerald eyes, low tables covered with gold jewelry, and smaller figures molded in gold. Figures, obviously gods and goddesses, lined the room, all facing the same spot, the place where the remains lay.

It was hard to grasp the enormity of the treasure. The three remained silent because the atmosphere was one of deep sorrow.

The walls told the last of the tale in brilliant colors. The gods were painted weeping . . . bending their heads in despair. Caitlyn found herself in tears.

Drake and Mendrano were grim. They had found the secret to the tomb, they had found a treasure beyond belief . . . but they had not found a way to freedom.

Caitlyn stood close to Drake and, without speaking, he put an arm around her and drew her close. Their own fate seemed to lie before them. If these two desperate people had not found a way out . . . how could they?

For the first time Drake felt a sense of defeat. There was no way to stop the inevitable now. First the air would go . . . then the light, and they would meet the same fate as the young couple. He wanted to be angry, to find some emotion to help cope with the knowledge that Caitlyn would die here with him and he could not prevent it.

"If they had wanted to drown themselves they could have done so here," Mendrano said. He gestured toward the rapidly moving water that passed through this room as it did the others. It seemed to come from some unknown place and pass through the tomb to another.

Drake gazed at the water, wondering which death would be easier. He must have gazed at the water for some time before the thought struck him.

"Maybe," he said thoughtfully, "the water wasn't here when they were put here."

"It had to have been, Drake," Caitlyn said. "How else could it have . . ." She paused, realizing what he was saying.

"It's a law of nature," Drake said. "Water finds its way through the smallest of places and over time it can eat away the largest rock. I would say this water began as a trickle and grew as it ate away at the rock."

Mendrano was frowning, but Drake and Caitlyn were looking at each other with sudden hope.

"Mendrano . . . this water has to go somewhere. If it's found its way *under* the wall of the tomb, then it must come up on the other side."

At first Mendrano stared at them in disbelief, but soon the logic of the idea dawned on him. A small trickle of water, in its fall from the mountains, had turned into a river. A river that had to lead . . . *out of the tomb*.

"It would mean we have to swim down and see how deep and how far the wall goes," Drake said. "I'll test it out first."

"Drake! You could drown if that wall goes into rock and you can't get out," Caitlyn cried.

"Caitlyn . . . we can't just stay here and die. If there's any chance at all, we have to take it." He smiled and kissed her gently. "I can't let this be the end, love. I've got to try it. We'll just have to trust that fate provided a way for us . . . maybe to atone for the deaths of these two. Caitlyn . . . we have a lot of life ahead of us and I want to live it together."

He could see Caitlyn battle with her fear, and knew the amount of courage it took for her to smile a trembling smile. "All right, Drake."

"Good girl," Drake said and grinned. He was excited at the idea that they might have one slim chance to cheat death. He took her in his arms and held her for a long moment, then he released her and walked to the edge of the water. He sat down to remove his tools and his belt and gun. He needed to rid himself of any excess weight.

Caitlyn's face was white with terror as she watched him remove his shirt. Then he slid over the edge, clinging to the side of the stone floor.

"I was right," he said. "The wall is smooth, so this was

part of the tomb. I'll bet there's even more treasure at the bottom."

"Drake . . . please be careful," Caitlyn said as Drake maneuvered himself to the wall through which the water seemed to vanish.

He smiled at Caitlyn, inhaled several deep breaths to clear his lungs, then drew in a deep breath and disappeared below the surface. Caitlyn and Mendrano stood in silence, watching the place where Drake had disappeared. Both of them knew that in trying to find the outlet for the water, Drake might swim past the point of no return.

Drake dove down into the murky depths, trying to keep one hand close to the wall to see if it had a shelf bottom he could reach. It seemed as if the wall had no end. Then his hand slipped under and he could feel the water flowing outward. The question was, how far did the shelf run and was there an exit on the other side?

His lungs were already feeling the need for air as he ducked under the shelf and swam beneath it. He began to pray. His lungs burned and he began to see pinpoints of light caused by his oxygen-starved brain. Still the ledge went on. He felt as if he were breathing his last, as if he could contain the need for air no longer . . . and he knew he could never make it back. He kicked with every ounce of strength he had left and hoped for a miracle. Then he saw it. The water grew clearer and the shelf edge appeared. He followed it up with a last powerful kick and burst to the surface, gasping for air. Air! Sweet, precious, clear, clean air!

He grasped a rough rock that protruded from the edge of the wall and heaved a deep, rasping breath. Then he looked around him. He was in a cave and the water flowed outward. But all he could see, some distance ahead, was blue sky. Then over the rush of the water he heard the sound and knew he was at the top of a waterfall. The water left the cave and plummeted over the edge . . . he had no idea how far it fell. But for now he could see the sky and feel the air and he was grateful. He gathered his strength, for he had to swim back against the current. Caitlyn and Mendrano were still trapped and he had to get them out.

He breathed deeply, slowly, until he'd cleared his lungs and rested his muscles. Then he dove beneath the surface again.

Minute followed minute, and there was no sign of Drake. Caitlyn and Mendrano were afraid to look at each other, afraid they would have to face the fact that Drake was lost.

Caitlyn refused to give up hope. Drake was strong, and an excellent swimmer. He had to be safe, she prayed, he had to be.

But time told another story. No man, no matter what his strength, could hold his breath for five minutes. A sob caught in her throat and she could not stop the tears that traced lines down her cheeks.

"Oh, Mendrano . . ."

"He had to try," Mendrano said. "He was a man of great courage."

"I . . . I can't bear it," Caitlyn whispered. She closed her eyes, realizing she would have to face her fate without Drake.

She opened her eyes again, clinging to what strength she had. Mendrano and she would share the same fate, but at least she would face it as bravely as Drake had.

A painful resignation filled her and she dropped to her knees beside the swift-flowing water.

She shrieked as Drake suddenly burst to the surface,

grabbing for the edge of the stone floor and gasping for breath.

"Drake! Oh, thank God!" She was beside him as he pulled himself up on the ledge, putting her arms around him and kissing him wildly. Drake had little strength left, but he held her close and laughed softly.

"There's . . . there's a way . . . out," he panted. "It's not easy, but we can do it. Mendrano, you and I will have to help Caitlyn. It's a long, hard pull."

"It is certainly better than staying here," Mendrano said with a grin. "You'd best wait until you are rested if the way is so hard."

"You're right," Drake agreed. He went on to explain how they could swim out, describing the distance. Caitlyn grew quiet. She was not so sure, since it taxed every ounce of Drake's strength, that she could make it. Drake sensed her stillness and turned to her.

"I'm not letting anything happen to you, love," he said gently. "It's long and it's hard, and you have to trust me."

She looked into the soft grey eyes and her doubt and fear faded. "I love you, Drake. I do trust you."

"We'll make it, you and I," he said. "We're not going to end here, I promise you. When we go, hold on to Mendrano and me . . . we'll get you through."

"I will."

Drake held her close for a minute then brushed her lips with a light kiss. "Take off those boots and that heavy belt and jacket."

She obeyed instantly and Mendrano did the same, removing everything that could weigh them down.

Then Drake slid off the shelf and back into the water. Mendrano did the same, and stood beside Drake. Then they both reached up to help Caitlyn down.

She could feel the pressure of the water as it tugged at her feet. It was cold and for a moment she shivered in expectancy.

As they moved to the wall that disappeared below the surface, Drake turned to look at her again.

"All right?"

"Yes . . . I'm fine."

"Listen to me. Take a few deep breaths and let the air all out. On the last breath take in all the air you can. Understand?"

Both Caitlyn and Mendrano nodded, then they began to inhale and exhale until they could take a very deep breath.

"On the next breath," Drake commanded, not giving them time to think about it. "Deep!"

They inhaled and dove below the surface.

Caitlyn kicked with all the force she had, and she could feel Mendrano and Drake's strength as they helped pull her along.

Still, panic began to claim her as her body cried out for air, and her heart began to pound furiously. Still they swam.

Caitlyn could feel darkness closing about her and a sense of disorientation told her she was losing the battle. Consciousness slowly began to ebb.

She did not know when they began to surge upward and when they burst to the surface—she was nearly unconscious.

Drake and Mendrano brought her to the edge of the cave, then Drake heaved himself from the water and reached down to pull Caitlyn up beside him.

"Caitlyn! Caitlyn! Take a deep breath!" His voice was harsh with fear and seemed to Caitlyn to come from a great distance. She struggled to obey and Drake could have wept with relief when he heard her suck in a deep, ragged breath.

He sat with his back against the cave wall and held her shaking body against his until he could feel her respond.

"Are you all right?"

"Yes," she murmured as she inhaled another deep breath and smiled up at him. "We're out."

"We're out," he replied. "Now I have to find out where we are and where we go from here. We're not exactly up to a long jungle trek. Stay still while I take a look."

He left Caitlyn beside Mendrano and walked to the entrance of what had appeared to him to be a cave. But when he stepped out on the ledge and looked out he got a surprise.

He returned to Mendrano and Caitlyn, grinning broadly with a broad grin as he knelt beside them.

"I don't think either one of you will believe where we are."

"I'm too weary even to guess," Caitlyn said.

"We're at the top of an immensely beautiful and very familiar waterfall."

"Drake," Caitlyn said with a smile. "Our waterfall?"

"Our waterfall. And if I can find a way down, there's no question of where we're going first."

"I can't believe . . ." Caitlyn smiled through her tears, but this time they were tears of joy.

"Believe it," Drake grinned. "I'll find a way down. In a couple of hours we'll all have warm clothes, food, and we can get some rest as well. Then . . ."

"Then?" Caitlyn questioned anxiously.

"Then we'll see about Mr. Paul Macombe and his friends. We'll have to find out who else is involved and put a stop to their plans to rape this area of its wealth and its history. More important, I intend to make that man pay for leaving you to face an ugly death."

"We can report him to the authorities," Caitlyn said in

response to the anger she saw in Drake's eyes. "They'll make sure he's punished for what he's done."

"He tried to kill you, Caitlyn, in a merciless and brutal way. A few years in prison is nothing compared to what he deserves."

"And we've been through hell and we're together. Do you think I want something you do in anger to separate us again?" Caitlyn's eyes sparked like emerald fire. "We have our lives back, Drake . . . don't throw that away."

He looked deep into her eyes and realized she was right. He had thought of a hundred ways to punish Paul Macombe. Now he knew there was something more important.

"Your lady is right," Mendrano said. "Fate itself might have plans for him. You do not need to punish, just make him fail. Then . . . enjoy your lives together."

"I'm outnumbered," Drake said, "and maybe you're both right. Come on, it's a long trek to my house. We'd best get going."

He pulled Caitlyn up beside him and the three of them walked to the cave entrance to search for a way down.

Twenty-two

They were on the edge of a ledge. Beside and below them the jungle looked impenetrable. The drop was not sheer, yet the falling water made everything wet and dangerous. The water fell three hundred feet into the pool in which Caitlyn and Drake had swum.

"We have to be very careful," Drake said. "A fall from here might be pretty bad."

"It might be deadly," Caitlyn added. "It's also going to be quite a trek in our stocking feet."

Drake studied Caitlyn's face. Her eyes drooped with fatigue and she was pale, but she smiled at her own small bit of humor. He reached out to touch her hand and found it not only cold but shaking from exhaustion.

It was nearing midday and the sun was high and hot. Mendrano and Drake were already casting about for any kind of path that would lead them safely down, but what they could see wasn't encouraging.

"I should go first," Mendrano said, "with Caitlyn between us. I'm a little better at this, and if she should slip we would be able to help."

"Good idea. Go slowly and carefully. This would be a bad time for an accident—we're all too tired to get up if we should fall."

Tentatively, one slow, calculated step after another, they moved at a snail's pace down the rough terrain.

Caitlyn wondered if she had ever been more tired in her life. She felt numb and her head throbbed. She was losing her concentration and at one point her feet slipped from beneath her and only Drake's quick grasp kept her from tumbling downward.

She began to wonder if she would ever see the bottom and even when they got there she hardly realized it until the sound of the waterfall began to fade. And it was still some distance to Drake's house.

They kept moving, losing track of time and place. Drake knew if he was as tired as he was, Caitlyn had to be nearing the point of collapse. Their feet were sore, but they couldn't allow that to stop them.

When they broke from the jungle toward the clearing and Drake's house, Caitlyn was no longer aware of much. Drake was amazed at her fortitude and determination. He turned to her, stopping her in mid-stride.

"We're here, Caitlyn . . . we made it, love," he said tenderly.

"We're here? We made it?" Caitlyn repeated softly.

"We did. A few more feet and . . ." Drake saw her start to collapse seconds before she closed her eyes and sagged forward. He caught her as she fell and carried her into the house.

Mendrano stood in the doorway watching Drake as he placed Caitlyn gently on the bed and covered her. When Drake turned to Mendrano, both men smiled.

"You have yourself some woman there," Mendrano said.

"I couldn't agree more. She's wonderful and courageous. I know a lot of men who would have given out before this.

Let's let her sleep. You and I need something real strong to drink and some rest ourselves."

"That is another good idea."

"I have a bottle in the cupboard. Suppose you find it and pour a couple."

Mendrano nodded and left the doorway. Drake paused and looked down at Caitlyn, then he sat down beside her and took her hand, lifting it to kiss it. With his other hand he brushed her hair from her damp forehead and bent to kiss her.

"I love you, Caitlyn," he whispered. Then he rose and went to join Mendrano for the much-needed drink. They tried to search their tired minds for some kind of plan.

"What will we do next?" Mendrano questioned.

"I'm not sure yet," Drake admitted. "I hate the thought of not going back up there to get Paul Macombe."

"We don't even know if he's there."

"Mendrano, do you think we could get back up to your place and see if Antonio and Tana are still there?"

"I don't see why not. If we get some rest."

"Yeah. The shape we're in, we can hardly make it to our beds." Drake tossed down the last of his drink. "A couple of hours, Mendrano . . . a couple of hours. I've got to close my eyes—it's hard even to think."

"It's already late afternoon. It would be best if we rested until morning. Then we can decide what to do. Your idea of finding my children first is our best bet. We'll be safe at my house and we can study the situation there."

"All right. There's a cot in the back room. Get some sleep."

Mendrano nodded wearily and went into the back room. Drake walked slowly toward his bedroom. He lay down beside Caitlyn and drew her gently against him. In minutes he was asleep.

Caitlyn stirred uncomfortably, then opened her eyes to a dark room. For a moment she was so disoriented that she thought she was still in the tomb. She sat up with a cry of terror that jolted Drake awake.

He sat up beside her and could feel her whole body shaking. He put his arms about her. "Shhh, Caitlyn, it's all right. We're safe. I'm sorry, I should have lit a lamp."

"Oh, Drake," Caitlyn gasped as she clung to him.

"You're safe, Caitlyn. How do you feel?"

"Sore and hungry. I don't remember how I got into bed."

"I don't suppose you would. You almost made it to the door."

"And you carried me in and put me to bed?"

"Very uneventful," Drake replied with a chuckle. "There are, in my humble opinion, much better ways to go to bed."

"I'd give anything for a bath and some clean clothes."

"Caitlyn, it's four o'clock in the morning."

"We could go for a swim in the river."

"You forget where you are, lady," Drake replied, smiling. "A nice twelve-foot anaconda could give you a hug or two and maybe a croc would have you for breakfast, and . . ."

"That's enough," Caitlyn giggled. "I get the idea."

"I'll tell you what I'll do. There's a big tub Maria hangs on the wall out back to wash clothes." Drake rose and lit the lamp. "I'll drag it in here and heat some water on the stove. Then, I imagine Maria has some clothes hanging around. They'd be a little big but maybe you could improvise."

"Drake, I'd be so grateful."

"How grateful?"

"Very, very." Her laugh blended with his.

"Grateful enough to share the bath?"

She looked at him with a gaze that matched the warmth of his. "It seems the least I can do since you're being so generous."

"I'll be back in no time. While I get the water you might go through the drawers and that closet over there. You should find some of Maria's things and some of mine." Drake laughed as he rose from the bed.

"What's funny?"

"Do you think anyone back in civilization would believe this? A bath in a wooden tub at four in the morning in the middle of the jungle?"

"I don't know if any of my friends would believe it," Caitlyn replied, humor tugging at her lips. "But I bet they'd envy me if they did."

Drake turned to look down at her. She sat cross-legged on the bed, her hair tousled from sleep and looking like a little girl and a seductive woman at the same time.

Caitlyn watched the warmth of his thoughts turn his eyes from grey to a deep silvery blue. It touched her in a place only he had been able to reach, making her feel as if something deep within was melting.

"I'd better go get that tub," he said, his voice deep and husky.

"Yes . . . you'd better."

Drake reached out and pressed his hand against her cheek. "If I were ever looking for treasure, Caitlyn, I've found it. I'm glad you came into my life—I wouldn't have wanted to miss you." He bent and kissed her, then walked to the door. Caitlyn watched him leave, filled with an almost overwhelming love.

When he was gone she climbed off the bed and went

about finding clothes for the both of them. She found a white blouse, woven of some fabric she could not identify, but it was soft and looked comfortable. Then she found a matching skirt. It would be long enough to fall to her ankles and she knew she would have to belt it somehow to keep it on. Searching further she found a red scarf she could fold and tie about her waist.

She laid them on the bed, then set about gathering clothing for Drake. She had the most difficulty finding shoes and by the time she did, the door opened and Drake came in lugging a huge empty wooden tub.

"The water's almost hot. Find anything?"

"Enough to get by on until I can get my own clothes."

Drake set the tub down and left to return with two buckets of steaming water. He poured them into the tub, then left and returned with two more buckets of cold water. When he poured them in he tested the water. "Comfortable," he said. Again he left, only to return with towels and soap.

"I guess that's about it," Drake said, flashing a decidedly wicked grin. "I'll race you. Last one in has to do the backscrubbing." He eyed her quick smile. "Never mind—I'll get too much pleasure out of washing yours. See if the water is warm enough."

"I have a feeling," Caitlyn said with a soft laugh of pure sensuous pleasure, "that we'll be able to warm it in case it isn't."

"You can count on it," he promised. He stood very still, watching Caitlyn, who returned his gaze with a soft smile. Then she began to remove her clothes.

No pretended timidity, no shy teasing, her complete willingness and the smoky promise in her green eyes threatened Drake's control. Here was a woman who admitted she wanted him as much as he wanted her. His heartbeat began to pick up.

As her body emerged from her clothing, Drake caught his breath and held it until he was dizzy with longing.

Caitlyn watched Drake as he finally remembered to rid himself of his own clothes. She enjoyed his exceptionally tall, muscular body and his fine, well-made face. But even more, she warmed to his startlingly expressive gaze. It seemed to reveal everything he hadn't put into words . . . she could feel her whole being respond. She loved looking at him.

She went to him and he sighed with the pleasure of her firm young body against his. "I didn't think I could want anything as much as I want you," he said as he traced her fragile collarbone with the tips of his fingers. "When I hold you you're so much a part of me that I don't know where I stop and you begin."

Caitlyn could feel threads of heat that seemed to come from his gentle touch and streak through her. There was so much she wanted to say, and she knew mere words could never express the depth of her feelings. She took his face between her hands and drew it down to hers. She closed her eyes slowly as their lips met.

Then she felt him lift her from the floor. Still kissing her, he stepped into the tub and sat down with her on his lap. The feel of the warm water moving against her skin was suddenly so sensuous that she moaned softly against his mouth. Only then did he set her free. They looked at each other in a sort of breathless wonder . . . then Drake smiled.

He took the soap in his hands and lathered it. Then gently, beginning at her throat, he began to caress her skin. Caitlyn shivered. His hands moved slowly, making sure they missed no vulnerable, sensitive spot. When he cupped her breasts in his hands he massaged them, his thumbs circling the erect nipples until she wanted to cry out.

But his hands continued their journey, eliciting a flow of heat wherever they touched. She wanted him to feel what she was feeling. Following his example, she lathered her hands and explored the smooth warmth of his body as he had explored hers.

She like the feel of hard muscles beneath his skin as they rippled in response to her touch—it heightened her pleasure to know she was making him feel so much. She could see the pleasure dance in his eyes.

Cupping his hands and filling them with water he rinsed the soap from her skin, then bent to sample the warm, wet, salty taste of her.

She closed her eyes, giving herself up to pure joy.

Drake kissed her again and again as he drew her atop him and lay back against the tub. Then he felt her enfold him in her warmth. Sensations coursed through him.

He could hear, from the deepening of her breathing, that she had surrendered completely to her senses. He wanted to slow down, to prolong the sensation, but she reached to hold him, then moved against him and he felt her body tightening with anticipation. Suddenly it was there, in powerful, shuddering waves. He felt the exquisite ecstasy of her complete abandonment and surged to meet her. Then she heard his strong breathing, the uncontrolled groan of her name as he, too, found release.

He held her quivering body close to him, gently caressing her. The water soothed and cooled their heated flesh.

"The sun's coming up," Drake said softly against her hair.

"I wish I could stop time," Caitlyn sighed as she sat up.

"But I can't and we'll be wrinkled as prunes if we stay in here."

Drake sat up, too, and enjoyed watching her as she climbed from the tub and wrapped herself in a towel. He wondered at the fact that no matter how often they touched, each time only made him want her more.

Finally, he, too, rose from the tub and dried himself, then began to dress.

"Drake?"

"Yes?"

"What are we going to do?"

"Find a way to get you on down to Ethan's where you'll be safe."

"That's not possible, and I wouldn't go anyway. You want me safe while you do what?"

"I won't do anything foolish, Caitlyn, but that man not only tried to ruin my career, destroy my work, and kill me . . . worse, he tried to kill you. All for greed. I can't let him get away with it."

"I know," Caitlyn said miserably. "He deceived me in the worst way imaginable. I wanted so badly to get to know my father. I'd begun to care . . . I'd begun to love him."

"Then you see why I can't just let him get away?"

"I'm going with you."

"Caitlyn, he's a dangerous man."

"I know that. I was with you in that tomb, remember?"

"I'm sorry, I didn't mean to sound like that. Caitlyn, at least stay here until . . ."

"No. If you go back to the dig, and I know you mean to, I go with you."

Drake sighed deeply. He'd known he wouldn't be able to talk her out of it.

"We'd best talk to Mendrano and see what ideas he has. I know he's worried about Antonio and Tana."

"Then let's go talk to him," Caitlyn said with a smile. "The sooner we talk to Mendrano, the sooner we'll get started."

"Pretty sure of yourself, aren't you?"

"No, but I'm sure of Mendrano. He'll want to go back and make sure Antonio and Tana are safe. Besides, all your workers are there. Paul will be flabbergasted to find we're alive . . . and he'll be outnumbered. The three of us can handle him. You have arms here?"

"Yes. Several rifles, handguns, and plenty of ammunition. I guess you're right. We will be quite a surprise . . . unless . . ."

"Unless what?"

"Unless there are more people involved in this than Paul Macombe."

"I don't see how or why they're connected. We know it's emeralds, and treasure at the dig."

"I wonder . . ."

"Wonder what?"

"Well, perhaps Paul Macombe has confederates. Suppose . . . he's betraying them somehow."

"I don't understand."

"Suppose he's led them to believe there was no treasure at the dig. Maybe greed got the best of him and he decided he wanted it all for himself. Maybe he's playing a more dangerous game than we think."

"What would he do?"

"If that's his game, I'm afraid he'd get rid of the workers on some pretext or another. But he might get rid of Tana and Antonio in a more permanent way."

"And I suppose he'd be as cold-blooded toward them as he was to us."

"I wouldn't doubt it."

"Poor Mendrano."

"I'm sure Mendrano is already thinking this way. There is no question about what he'll want to do."

"And there's no question about what we have to do," Caitlyn said gently. "We have to return . . . for Antonio and Tana . . . and for us. This is our dig, our find, and we won't let a man like that ruin it. And we won't let him get away with murder."

"I guess we won't." Drake grinned. "You're a pretty tough lady."

"I'm not tough, I'm angry. I don't ever remember being so scared in my life as I was down there. I won't be able to get the fear out of my mind or my dreams until I know he's caught."

"Then we'd better get Mendrano up and find some guns and be on our way. It's at least an hour to the dig, and we have to have a plan. We just can't walk into what could be a trap if Paul Macombe has friends and we don't want to endanger other lives. We have to take him by surprise."

Caitlyn agreed. She started for the door, but Drake caught her arm and turned her to him.

Maria's blouse was a bit large and fell off the edge of her shoulder. The skirt was held by the red scarf and the whole affair, combined with her free-flowing hair, gave her a wild gypsy look.

"You were talking about fear before. I guess I was afraid down there, too. But I'm still a little afraid—of your courage. I couldn't stand it if something happened to you. So you're going to stick close to me and be very, very careful."

Caitlyn smiled, looped her arms about his neck, and

pressed her body to his. "I'll take a great deal of pleasure in sticking very close to you."

"I'm not joking, Caitlyn."

"No, I know you're not. But there's only one way for us to face our fear . . . isn't there?"

"I suppose you're right, but I'll tell you—this is the first time since we met that I wish you were somewhere else."

"I don't. I'd rather be with you, facing any kind of danger, than be without you."

"You have a very neat way of getting around everything I say." He put his arms around her and held her close. "But I want you to promise me you'll be careful."

"I'll be as careful as you are."

Drake heaved an exasperated sigh and kissed her. "Let's go get Mendrano."

When they left the bedroom it was to find that not only was Mendrano up, he had prepared breakfast. That didn't surprise them as much as the sight of several rifles and guns lying on the table. It was obvious they had been cleaned and loaded.

"How long have you been up, Mendrano?" Drake asked.

"It was very difficult to sleep. I worry about my son and my daughter. I know he would not hesitate to do them harm should they interfere, no more than he hesitated to try and kill us."

"We have to hope that Antonio was clever enough to stay away from him."

"Antonio is clever. But he would take many chances for Tana."

"Would he take her and leave?"

"If he had the chance. But we don't know if he did."

"We'll eat and get going," Drake said. "We'll do everything we can to find Antonio and Tana."

"I know." Mendrano smiled for the first time. "It is why I prepared food and the guns, so we would not have to waste time."

"Mendrano, do you know any other way up to the dig beside the main trail? Surely he would have someone watching it."

"You think there are others beside him?"

Drake went on to tell Mendrano how right he'd been about Paul Macombe and that he might have friends he meant to cheat out of the treasure. It didn't take Mendrano long to put the rest of the possibilities together.

"Perhaps these men cannot trust each other. It is obvious he watched us and kept us from finding out where the others dig for the green fire."

"Right."

"And in the meantime maybe he intends to keep the treasure in the tomb for himself."

"Right again," Drake said grimly. "He could take the emeralds they dig and come back to the tomb in a year or so—when he thinks we're nothing but dust—and take a fortune from it."

"But surely Ethan would never believe . . ."

"He would have a story well prepared for Ethan and he could convince him of his sorrow at the loss of the beloved daughter he'd just found. And since he *saw* us leave for Ethan's house, it would be easy to assume we were lost to the dangers of the jungle. Ethan would lead a massive search, I know, but he would have no reason to doubt Caitlyn's father—and he wouldn't think to look in the tomb."

"So diabolically clever," Caitlyn said, "and so merciless. I cannot believe anyone could be so cold and unfeeling as to walk away and leave three people to die in such a terrible way."

"Greed does strange things to people. What he saw in that tomb was not a rich historical legacy, but a life of luxury for himself. He couldn't balance one against the other."

"He told me he had not killed my father . . . my true father. But can we believe that? How will I ever find out if my father is really alive?" Caitlyn asked worriedly.

"I have my doubts about that as well," Drake agreed. "Someone who would leave us to die surely would order another man killed. When this is over, we can try and find your father."

"I do know another way to the dig," Mendrano said. "It will take us a little longer but it will be safer."

"We have to have some kind of plan for when we get there. If Paul Macombe is not working alone, we might run into more than we can handle if we're not careful."

"You are right," Mendrano agreed. "It's best we make a plan."

Caitlyn agreed and Mendrano began to explain the route they would follow. "We should come out at the back of my house," he added.

"How long would you say it will take?" Drake questioned. "The trip from here, by the usual route, is only one to two hours."

"It will be about four hours . . . providing we don't run into any unforeseen problems."

"Unforeseen problems?" Caitlyn repeated.

"Four-legged, two-legged, or crawling. We have to be prepare for anything," Drake added.

"And the traveling won't be easy," Mendrano said, looking at Caitlyn. "The trail, if you want to call it that, is a difficult one."

"Are you suggesting I stay here, Mendrano?" Caitlyn queried with a smile.

"It might be a wise idea."

"Wise or no, I'm going with you and Drake."

Mendrano cast a quick look at Drake who glanced upward helplessly. "Mendrano, forget it. I tried. The lady is very . . . firm. The two of us combined couldn't get her to stay."

"It is only for your safety . . ." Mendrano began.

"Wrong argument," Drake warned, but Mendrano had already seen the spark of fire in Caitlyn's eyes.

"All right, I will not speak of it again. Where we go, we'll go together."

Caitlyn smiled. "I don't mean to be so stubborn, Mendrano, but I would be frantic with worry if I had to stay here. I won't slow you down or be a burden. I just couldn't stand all the waiting and wondering. Besides, I must know what really happened to my father. My father has paid a price for something he knows nothing about. If . . . if he is alive he must be desperate to know why these things are happening."

"Caitlyn . . . I . . . I hate to cause you any more problems. But . . . if your father were still alive . . . if he were safe, why wouldn't he be here? This was, after all, his destination when he left London. If he left London at all . . ." Drake's voice was gentle. He hated to hurt her, but he felt she had to face the problem realistically.

"I know. But I *must* believe. Until I know what the real truth is, I must believe . . ." Her voice broke.

"I didn't mean to sound so harsh. Of course we must

believe." He comforted her, but in his heart he felt the father she'd never had a chance to know was already gone.

"I think it's time we leave here," Mendrano urged.

Each of them picked up a rifle and a small packet of ammunition. Mendrano and Drake put gunbelts about their waists. They each took a canteen of water and strapped the packs Mendrano and Drake had prepared to their backs.

There was no need for further conversation. They left the house and headed into the dark jungle, walking single file with Mendrano in the lead, Caitlyn in the center, and Drake bringing up the rear. Caitlyn knew just how dangerous the trek would be, but with Mendrano on one side of her and Drake on the other, she felt as safe as she could in this forbidding wilderness.

The sun climbed higher and higher and even through the thickness of the huge trees that arched over them the travelers could feel the heat, intensified by the almost breath-stopping humidity. Caitlyn could feel her clothes grow damp and tendrils of hair clung to her face.

She knew they were steadily going uphill—she could feel the strain on the muscles of her legs. The strap of the rifle cut into her shoulder and the weight of it seemed to grow with every step. Still she did not complain. She was certain if she did both Mendrano and Drake would quickly take it from her and it would make traveling harder for them.

To keep her mind off her growing discomfort she focused all her thoughts on Drake and the hours they had spent together. She thought of his courage in the tomb when she had almost given up. She wondered at the fate that had drawn her here to find love in the arms of a man like Drake.

Her thoughts continued to drift and she remembered, with

bitterness, the father she had never had an opportunity to know. No matter how hard she tried, she could not find an iota of forgiveness in her heart for the man who had caused what might now be a permanent separation. It was only Drake, and her love for him, that kept the rage from consuming her.

If Caitlyn was deep in angry thought about Paul Macombe, it was no less than the emotions that tore at both Drake and Mendrano.

For Drake it was fury at the man who had tried to destroy Caitlyn and all of Drake's dreams at the same time. He wasn't too sure of how much control he could maintain if and when they found Paul Macombe.

For Mendrano it was fear for the two people in the world who meant more to him than his own life. Tana and Antonio, innocent of the intrigue that swirled about them, could very well be victims of that same intrigue. His smoldering anger at Paul Macombe was no less intense than Drake's.

They continued their slow, steady progress over a trail that only Mendrano seemed to know, for if there was one Caitlyn couldn't find it. It seemed to her as if the jungle was slowly enveloping them, cutting off air and sunlight until every breath was labored.

Her legs ached, her back ached, her head ached, and still they moved on and on until Caitlyn was no longer able to think. She moved mechanically and had ceased feeling a long time ago. She was thirsty, but she was afraid to break stride and get a drink from her canteen, sure if she stopped she would never be able to start again.

Caitlyn did not realize that Mendrano had stopped until she bumped into him, nearly knocking both of them off their feet. Instantly Drake was beside her, taking the heavy rifle from her and urging her to sit on one of the huge surface roots of a nearby tree.

"We need to rest for a while," Mendrano said, and Caitlyn could see, to her relief, that he and Drake were panting from the exertion. "Drink slowly and carefully," he cautioned Caitlyn. Obediently she drank only a few swallows, but even that much water seemed amazingly cool and rejuvenating.

When Caitlyn looked up at Mendrano she could see the glint of respect in his eyes.

"How long . . ." she began to choke out the question.

"You have come a great distance," Mendrano smiled, "much farther than you think. Drake is right. You are a lady with a great deal of courage."

The words made her feel good and she smiled up at Mendrano. "Thank you, but I'm not sure it's courage. This heat and this jungle wiped every thought from my mind. I wasn't really thinking at all." She turned to Drake, who'd sat beside her and was taking a drink from his canteen.

"We have come more than halfway," Drake said. "I'm afraid it's the easiest half."

"Easiest!" Caitlyn gasped.

"We have a lot of high ground to cover now. It's steeper. Caitlyn, don't confuse stubbornness with safety. If you feel you have to rest, it's wise to stop. If you push too hard now, you just might not make it at all. Are you listening to me?"

"Yes, I'm listening."

"It's the truth. I'm not pampering you. If you feel dizzy or sick to your stomach I want you to stop."

"All right," she nodded.

Drake looked deep into her eyes, then brushed damp strands of hair from her forehead.

"I love you, Caitlyn Macdonald," he said softly. "I love you very, very much. Take care of yourself . . . promise me."

"I promise."

Drake bent and touched her lips with a gentle kiss.

Twenty-three

Ethan stood with the others gathered about him, stunned at what he saw. He'd been torn between wanting to find Drake and fear that he would arrive too late. He hadn't expected to see a vast treasure in a room devoid of any sign of life.

They had come down to the lowest level cautiously. Ethan fought claustrophobia with all the strength he could muster. He was doing his best to think of his three friends who might be undergoing a trauma he could never have lived through.

No one spoke; the treasure was one thing, but the absence of their friends was quite another.

"Look!" Sir Richard said. "The entire altar has been moved. Do you suppose . . ." He had been closely examining the room with experienced eyes. He walked up the steps and studied the affair, wondering whether it was the brilliance or the weight of the lantern that had worked some unseen mechanism. "Fascinating," he said, more to himself than anyone else. Then he came down to rejoin the others.

"Do you think it's a way out?" George questioned as they all moved rapidly toward the dark void beyond the altar.

"Lord, I hope so." Ethan prayed.

If they were shaken about the contents of the outer room,

they were awed by the smaller room that lay behind the altar.

But it was still obvious there was no sign of Drake, Caitlyn, or Mendrano.

Tana's eyes fell on the remains of the couple that lay together and she stood closer to Ethan, who put his arm around her.

"They've been dead for centuries," Ethan said soothingly.

"But . . . it was a terrible way to die," Tana whispered.

"I quite agree," Sir Richard said."But we've one consolation. Drake, his head man, and my daughter are not here."

"No, they're not," Ethan said, "and that scares me, too. Do you have the remotest idea of how many places in the wilderness one could . . . dispose of unwanted problems?"

"Drake is very resourceful," George said. "I don't think we'd better count the three of them out until we find some definite proof."

"You're right," Marc said.

"Isn't it strange," George asked, "that the entire dig is deserted? Where are the workers? Even if this imposter had gotten rid of Drake, Mendrano, and . . ." He held up his hand when Ethan cast him a dark look. "I'm sorry, Tana, but we have to face the possibility that he did. What I'm saying is, he didn't expect us, and he most certainly didn't expect you, Sir Richard. Why run? Why not just make up a story about their absence and remain here?"

"He panicked when he found Tana and I were gone," Antonio said. "Then he had to cover up his tracks as best he could and he didn't want anyone around to answer questions. I imagine he hoped Tana and I couldn't survive the jungle trek. He judged us by his own weakness."

"I'd say," George said thoughtfully, "that someone's plans got mixed up pretty badly."

"It appears to me," Sir Richard said, "that Drake, Caitlyn, and Mendrano ran across some evidence so he had to . . . to get rid of them. The workers, if they'd remained, might have begun to develop some ideas, too, so he also got rid of them."

"How?" George asked, frowning.

"Made up some cock and bull story, paid them off with promises, and sent them away."

"Then where is he?" Ethan was puzzled. "Where is he, and why did he leave?"

"Unless . . ."

"What, George, unless what?"

"Unless his friends are nearby. Suppose this man is not the mastermind of this whole affair. Suppose he acted before he thought, then had to answer to someone else."

"This whole thing sounds a lot more complex than I imagined," Ethan replied. "Our timing was bad. If we'd just gotten here sooner."

"There's no use crying over spilt milk," Sir Richard said. "We have to search until we find where they've gone. Ethan, you're pretty adept at traversing this jungle. How good are you at tracking?"

"I don't know, but I'll give it a try. You sound as angry as I feel."

"I am. That bloody blighter might have robbed me of a chance to know my daughter. He has upset a lot of lives and maybe done more than that, all because of greed. I'd love to have my hands around his throat. I'd choke the truth out of him."

Tana, pressed close to Ethan, was the only one who knew his whole body was trembling. She looked up and saw the ashen color of his face and the look in his eyes that spoke of barely controlled fear.

"It does no good to stand in this empty, ugly room and talk," Tana said firmly.

"Ugly room?" Sir Richard said in a surprised voice.

"Yes, there is death here, and the men responsible were brought here by greed. They will rob, steal, and kill."

"Tana, it's not the room that's ugly. This room and its contents can tell stories about the past. These men brought the ugliness within them," Sir Richard said gently. "For those like Drake and my daughter, the room was a chance to link us to our history."

"You're right, Sir Richard," George said. "We have an obligation to hunt these people down and see that they pay for . . . for whatever crimes they have committed here."

"Then Tana is right," Sir Richard added. "We ought to get out of here."

"Amen," Ethan whispered raggedly. The group headed for the stairs and—as Ethan was gratefully aware—clean, open air. He made a silent vow never to go down in a place like that again.

Outside he gulped in deep breaths of air. Nothing had ever felt so good.

They started the walk back from the tomb to the dig.

Tana put her hand in Ethan's as they walked and it only occurred to him then that she had remained very close to him from the moment they had entered the tomb. He stopped and turned to her.

He didn't see pity in her eyes, or amusement. He saw warmth and love and he knew that somehow she had understood the terrible thing he was going through and how ashamed he felt.

"Was it that obvious?"

"Only to someone who understands. It is not an easy thing to go down into that dark place. It takes even more courage to be afraid and do it anyway. You care deeply for your friend and for the others. Not many men would have done what you have just done. I have loved you always, Ethan . . . but this only makes me love you more."

"Well," Ethan said softly, "sometimes the gods do smile, and a man's given a special gift in life. I'm one of the lucky ones." He kissed her deeply . . . and promisingly.

Tana and Ethan knew that from that moment on their lives were sealed together . . . and neither could have been happier.

It took very little time for Monroe to gather his men and arm them well. He gave them instructions and cautioned them to follow his orders carefully.

"I don't know how many of them are there, but I do know I don't want any mistakes this time. We're going to make sure there's no one left to tell tales."

"We won't have time to get there before the sun sets," one of the men said.

"If we move quickly we can get there by nightfall. That's when they'll let their guard down. Caught by surprise, they'll know nothing about us."

Carlos came to Monroe when the other men were occupied, unaware that Paul was close enough to overhear their conversation.

"Senor Monroe?"

"Yes, Carlos, what is it?"

"From what my men say there are at least eight or nine of the intruders?"

"Their count is accurate?"

"They are careful. I would not doubt there is that many."

"It is good, Carlos, for it means everyone is there. Once

they vanish without a trace there'll be no witnesses . . . no one at all. Then we can relax and take our time."

"There are many of the green stones here."

"I know. But I have a feeling we might just be on the verge of finding many more."

"They do not dig for the green stones up there," Carlos said with a derisive sneer. "They dig for the dead. It is hard to believe men want to do such things. To disturb the dead," he went on, his deep superstition obvious, "is an evil thing. It could anger the gods. It is best we stop them."

"You're right," Monroe agreed smoothly. "I suppose none of your men would even consider going down in that tomb?"

Carlos's face blanched a bit and his eyes averted Monroe's close scrutiny. "I do not think any of them would agree to do that."

"Well, never mind," Monroe smiled. "There's no need for any of your men to go down."

Then Monroe said something that let Paul know Monroe realized he was listening. "I'm sure Paul and I can decide if it's necessary for anyone to go. I'm just as sure," Monroe chuckled, "that if there was anything of real value down there Paul would have told me about it already."

Paul felt the usual stomach-turning anger. Monroe was playing with him and he knew it. Bitter greed rose up in him like a huge black wave. He had taken all the risk! He deserved to have what lay buried in that tomb! He had to find a way to stop Monroe from snatching it from his grasp.

The men were ready, and Paul had his rifle, a loaded pistol in his gunbelt, and enough ammunition to handle any emergency.

He'd learned the best way to handle Monroe was to keep

a low profile. When the opportunity came to stop him, it wouldn't slip through his fingers.

They began to move toward the dig in silence.

With the heat of the sun still a fiery menace, Drake Caitlyn, and Mendrano decided to move on. Caitlyn knew the next part of their trip would be both difficult and dangerous. But memories of her time in the tomb and the knowledge that something else just as terrible could happen to Antonio and Tana kept her determination fresh.

Coupled with the fact that the three of them were all that stood between Paul Macombe and the desecration of the ancient tomb was enough to keep her moving.

She was well aware that Drake was watching her every move, so she tried to keep her stride firm and even. What she did not know was that Drake could read her better than she thought. He knew her strength was more limited than her determination.

Mendrano also watched her closely. The terrain was rugged and steep and would tax the strength and endurance of most men.

They knew they probably wouldn't reach the dig before nightfall—they would have to remain in hiding until dawn to be able to assess the situation.

Once they made it to Mendrano's house, Drake thought, once they knew Antonio and Tana were safe, they would go after Paul Macombe and his associates.

Drake thought back to the time Mendrano had tried to warn him by voicing his suspicions about Paul Macombe leaving the camp so often. Mendrano had certainly been right. It had been the name of Sir Richard Macdonald that had temporarily blinded Drake, and he regretted it now. He had always put a great deal of credence in Mendrano's opinion and he would have been much better off if he had done the same this time.

He berated himself, promising he would never again doubt Mendrano.

The mountains loomed ahead in ranks of indigo and purple. To Caitlyn there was something fascinating and horrible about the furious vegetation struggling in a frenzied will to live. Below the jungle roof, where the big trees fanned out to the sun, a tangled mass of shoots and parasites and creepers entwined each other in mortal embrace; all three travelers felt that the dense foliage would engulf them if they stood still for a moment.

Caitlyn walked between the two men as they swung their machetes with a kind of rhythm. The *jejenes,* minute and hungry flies, fell on the unexpected human provender with voracious delight, and the three were continually slapping at them. The trees rose from the ground, still as death; the only sounds were the occasional bird call, the chattering of monkeys, and the complaining cry of a lonely tree frog.

It was lovely beyond words, but they were under too much pressure to appreciate it—all three breathed lightly lest the spirit of the jungle take note of their puny presence.

None of them spoke. Caitlyn was terrified with a thought she absolutely refused to put into words: how could Mendrano find his way so unerringly through the dense, semidark jungle? Surely, she thought as she fought her panic, they must be lost.

Caitlyn was unaware of one sound mixed with all the others that had made Drake and Mendrano pause and exchange a quick look.

They knew they were being watched unseen from the safe screen of the forest. After a while, when both were more certain, they had to inform Caitlyn in case they had to defend themselves. They were at a disadvantage by being in the open. Both men stopped and Caitlyn could tell there was a problem brewing.

"What is it?"

"Mutilones," Mendrano said.

"Who?"

"Indians," Drake answered. "Not unfriendly, but not necessarily friendly either."

"How can they be both?"

"Well, they are," Drake said. "Most likely, since there are three of us, they probably won't bother us."

"Well, how do you know?" Caitlyn could feel the goose bumps on her neck and arms.

"Believe me, you get a lot of warnings. One after another. So far, I haven't seen any so maybe they just intend to watch us and see we're not up to any mischief. They might just let us pass right on through and we'll never see them."

"What . . ." Caitlyn began, then gulped back the rising fear. "What are the signs?"

"Arrows shot at random into the ground around us, or planted broken in the trail; catcalls and whistles from the forest. They have a whistle made from a nut about the size of a chestnut, which they call a *chokola;* no white man can raise anything more than a feeble chirp from it, but the Indians can produce a shrill sound that can scare the devil out of you."

"What are you going to do?"

"Keep moving . . . slowly."

Caitlyn needed no coaxing. She forgot all her other fears and her exhaustion, staying as close to Drake as she possible could.

They moved cautiously, yet with as much speed as they could without looking as if they were running.

At any second Caitlyn expected to see the telltale arrow or hear the shrill whistle. But as they moved, no sound, no threat, came from the jungle around them.

The hours seemed to melt into one another as they moved on. Caitlyn felt as if this nightmare would never end and she almost wept with relief and exhaustion when Drake and Mendrano came to a stop.

She noticed that the sun was low on the horizon. The awful thought struck her that they might have to spend the night in this frightening place.

"We're lost," she said with dismayed conviction.

"No, we're not lost. We're here," Drake said.

"Here?" As far as Caitlyn could see, they were still surrounded by dense jungle. Then Mendrano very slowly and carefully drew aside several leafy vines and Caitlyn could see, across a small clearing, the back of Mendrano's house.

Drake was grateful that the house was some distance away from the other tents and the general dig.

"I'd best go first," Mendrano said. "If there is no one in the house I'll signal you. If there is someone there, and you don't see me in a few minutes, you'd best not try it."

"What will we do if . . ." Caitlyn began.

"Don't think about it," Drake said firmly. "It means we have to go through the jungle back to the river and hope they've left the canoes so we can get back down to Ethan's and alert the authorities."

"It's not possible!" Caitlyn gasped.

"It's possible," Drake said grimly. "But I'm not exactly overjoyed at the prospect."

"Wait . . . be silent . . . watch for my signal, and most important," Mendrano cautioned, "be careful."

"You be careful, old friend. I've gotten pretty attached to you and I wouldn't want to lose you."

Mendrano grinned, gave a slight wave, and was gone before Caitlyn could second Drake's words. She, too, had come to care a great deal about Mendrano.

They watched from their leafy shelter as Mendrano moved cautiously across the clearing, then disappeared into his house through the back door.

What seemed to Caitlyn like long, agonizing hours were only minutes before Mendrano's head reappeared around the back door and he motioned them to join him.

Drake took Caitlyn's hand as they moved swiftly across the open area and into the relative safety of the house.

Mendrano said, "There is no sign of them and the house tells a story. I don't know if they were together or not, but Tana left this house in a hurry."

"How can you tell?" Caitlyn inquired, hoping Mendrano was mistaken.

"If you knew my daughter, you would know she would never leave the house in this condition. For whatever reason, she left in a hurry, and maybe that is a good sign."

"A good sign?" Caitlyn repeated in surprise.

"It means she fled. Tana is very quick and clever. If she was alarmed about something, she had the good sense to flee first and ask questions later."

"But . . . they . . . she . . . didn't go to Drake's house. If she fled . . . ?"

"She would run to Ethan," Mendrano said matter-of-factly. "She would run to the one she trusts the most outside of her family. Perhaps," Mendrano said thoughtfully, "to the one she loves."

Drake kept silent. He'd never voiced an opinion on the matter of Tana and Ethan even though he was pretty sure how Tana felt. In his mind Tana was a beautiful creature who should be able to make a man like Ethan deliriously happy.

"Now that we know they are not here, we must decide," Mendrano said, turning to look at Drake, "just what our next move will be. We can't afford a mistake."

Caitlyn and Drake knew a mistake could cost them their lives. One close brush with death was enough to last them a lifetime.

Ethan, Tana, and the others gathered in the tent that was used as an eating place, as it was the largest. More adaptable to so many.

They sat around the oblong wooden table and tried to decide what they should do next.

"I can't understand where they could be," George said.

"I'm afraid to try," Ethan said angrily. "But I hope they don't think we're letting them get away with it. If I have to track them halfway across this continent, I'll do it, but by God someone's going to pay a high price if anything has happened to Drake, Caitlyn, and Mendrano."

"We have to control our anger, Ethan, and keep our minds clear," Sir Richard said. "You and Antonio know this jungle best. You'll have to take the lead. Much as I understand how you feel, anger will only make us less able to outwit them . . . if we can."

"You're right," Ethan admitted.

"Then what's our next move?" Sir Richard asked.

"George is right," Antonio said. "I'm not as good as my father, but I know the jungle a bit better than all of you except Ethan. It would be foolish for him and me to be in the same group."

"Right, Antonio," Ethan said. "We'll split into two groups, one of us with each. One half-experienced person is better than none at all."

"Then it's settled. Now let's draw up some kind of plan," Sir Richard said. "We can't just go wandering around helter skelter."

"Let's stop to consider possibilities and alternatives," George offered.

"Good idea," Sir Richard agreed. "First . . . what were their motives?"

"We don't know them all," Ethan said. "I'm sure part of it is the fabulous wealth in the tomb, but . . . it hadn't been discovered when Paul Macombe came here. Drake knew a long time ago that there might be a king's ransom in this area. So, it seems to me that they have a dig going somewhere else. I have a feeling we could find it if we just figured out the place that would be destroyed by the dam that Marc and I are building. That's the connection. Emeralds and the dam. In fact, buried in the ground in Drake's tent is one of the largest emeralds he ever saw. He told me about it."

"Drake must have a map in his tent," Antonio said. "If we examine it closely we might not have to race all over this jungle."

"If Paul Macombe came here before that tomb was discovered he was most likely working with them trying to find emeralds here at the dig," Sir Richard said. "That could mean," he added cautiously, "that among those trying to get rid of all of us, he alone might know about the treasure down there. Is it possible," he added, "that the villains may be falling out with each other? I've heard it said there is no honor among thieves."

"Antonio, would you go to Drake's tent and see if you can dig up that map?" Ethan said.

Antonio left the tent at once and loped across the clearing to Drake's tent. In minutes he returned with the map.

Ethan spread it out and studied it carefully with the others. He and Antonio pointed at nearly the same spot simultaneously.

"I'd guess here," Ethan said.

"And I'd agree," Antonio added.

"My dam," Ethan said, "would have buried that spot under quite a bit of water—too much water to allow digging for emeralds."

"That's the reason for all the trouble at the dam," Antonio said.

"Right," Ethan said, nodding. "We were about to bury their treasure and I sat and explained it all to Paul Macombe that night. No wonder he went off the edge and set that group against us."

"And they didn't hesitate to commit murder," Marc said angrily. "My man . . . and maybe . . ."

"No," Ethan said vehemently, "I won't believe Drake, Caitlyn, or Mendrano are dead until I have proof."

"You're right, Ethan," Sir Richard said. "I have to have faith as well. I don't think I've ever wanted anything as badly as I want to see my daughter . . . to know she's safe."

Carlos and Monroe cautioned their men to move silently as they neared the dig. The sun was beginning to set and shadows were growing deeper. They didn't want to make a mistake that would reveal their presence to those they hoped to take by surprise.

Monroe motioned Carlos to come closer so the sound of

their voices would not carry. It worried Paul, who couldn't hear what they were saying.

He was growing desperate. He didn't want Monroe to find out about the riches in the tomb.

He could see the mound that covered the tomb from where he stood and he stared at it for several minutes. He thought of the three people who had long ago run out of light . . . and air. They were dead . . . they had to be, he thought, fighting the guilt that made him sweat.

He forced his mind back to the jewels that had justified it all. He wanted to put it out of his mind, and once he was gone from this unfriendly place he was sure he could do that.

Monroe bent close to Carlos. "We have to scout the area. I don't want them to know we're here until we pinpoint their location and how many there are. You take one other man and see if you can find out what we need to know."

Carlos nodded, turned, and motioned to one of the men to follow him. Then the two vanished into the forest like ghosts. Paul came over to Monroe.

"What now? I don't see anyone," he said.

"They're there," Monroe said confidently. "And they've played right into our hands. The very foolish group has gathered," he turned to smile at Paul, "all in one place. It should make what we have to do very easy."

"And what is that?"

"I don't have to explain that to you."

"No . . . no, of course not. You do plan on taking them away from here, don't you? If any of the natives return . . ."

"You worry too much, my friend. Put them out of your mind—just as you did the three you left in that tomb."

"It was necessary," Paul said sharply. "But I don't think

it's necessary to go there again. I'm not . . . not interested in seeing the remains."

Monroe smiled, but did not answer. He was certain there was more than remains in that tomb that Paul Macombe didn't want anyone to see.

Carlos returned as silently as he'd left.

"They are there," he said. "There are six of them, and they're all in the tent once used for eating. One of them almost spotted me. It was the young man, the son of Mendrano. He went to another tent and returned with a map . . . or something that looked like it."

Monroe smiled at Paul, who clenched his teeth in agitation. So Tana and Antonio had gotten to safety. There was no need to worry about that now. Their fate would be sealed with the others.

"All right, Carlos, separate the men into three groups. We want to make sure none of them slips through our fingers. It's time to move."

"Antonio," Ethan said, "it might be a good idea if you took a small group, and the map, to see if you can locate that exact spot. It should be obvious, if it's there. Digging for emeralds leaves a lot of scars on the land."

"And what about you, Ethan?"

"I'll take the rest, check the perimeter of the dig, and see if I can scare up a track or two. If they left this place on foot they had to leave some kind of trail. With any luck at all, we'll follow it and see what we come up with."

"If I find this camp, and they are there, what do you want me to do?" Antonio questioned.

"Get back here just as fast as your legs can carry you. Whatever you do, don't try to engage in any confrontation.

You'll be outnumbered and if you don't get back, we'll be outnumbered as well. You understand, Antonio, no heroes. We have to check our time." Ethan glanced at his pocket watch. "We'll meet back here in . . . say, two hours." He compared his time with George's and they nodded in agreement. "Remember, Antonio . . . don't get too brave and forget that a lot of other lives depends on you."

"Don't worry. I'm no hero. If I find them I'll get back as fast as I can."

"We have enough arms and ammunition if we catch them by surprise," Ethan said, gesturing toward the rifles and pistols stacked carefully against the edge of the table. Ethan's air of confidence gave them a feeling that things might work out.

George was about to speak when a cold voice coming from the entrance made them all look up in shock.

"There's no need to worry about arms, gentlemen. You won't be needing them."

There was a startled gasp from Tana and a muttered oath from Ethan as he put his arm around her protectively.

The others rose slowly as the intruders filed into the tent, rifles leveled.

Sir Richard rose, too, his eyes on the man who looked so much like him that it was like looking in a mirror. Paul returned his gaze with an arrogant sneer.

"So," Sir Richard said softly, "you're the man who stole my identity—and my daughter—from me."

"Quite a successful job of acting, you must admit," Paul said.

"Damn you," Sir Richard muttered. "You've destroyed lives so coldly and carelessly. And for what? For what?"

"For a fortune," Monroe interrupted, "a fortune we shall

enjoy most thoroughly . . . long after you have," he shrugged expressively, "left all your worldly cares behind."

"And you," Sir Richard said, glaring at Monroe, "I trusted you completely. You're a man with no honor. How could you be so heartless, so utterly without conscience? How can you commit murder so easily?"

"There's a price on anything and everything, Sir Richard," Monroe said with cold, ugly humor. "The price for you and your friends is quite high, but I'll make a profit beyond most men's dreams. Balancing that against what has to be . . . sacrificed . . . I feel it's worth it."

"Bastard," Sir Richard growled. "May you rot in hell."

Monroe only laughed.

The prisoners knew that the situation in which they found themselves was meant to prove fatal. They were also quite certain their captors would be merciless . . . and that it was likely that no trace of them would ever be seen again.

Twenty-four

"Just what do you plan to do with us?" Ethan asked angrily. He had one arm around a trembling Tana—his fear for her was stronger than anything else.

"Come now," Monroe said as he laughed a mirthless, ugly laugh. "You don't really believe we could just let you walk out of here and tell the world what we found? I'm terribly afraid the government of Colombia frowns on anyone taking emeralds from the country without permission. It's made things a bit inconvenient. No, my friend, I'm afraid at the moment you and your friends are most expendable."

"My God, you're a bloodthirsty animal," Sir Richard said. "you can't just shoot us down like dogs."

"Oh, Sir Richard," Monroe chuckled, "I hadn't even considered such a thing. There are so many efficient ways."

"Efficient?" Ethan repeated. He had an idea of what Monroe had in mind and nothing could have been scarier. He'd already fought one battle with the tomb and wasn't too sure he could manage another.

"Let us say . . . final," Monroe said, smiling, "as I'm sure you know. Of course, by now it must be rather mute testimony."

The implications of his words struck most of them to silence. It was obvious that Monroe was bragging about doing away with Caitlyn, Drake, and Mendrano, and that he was assuming they had seen the bodies.

"By this time, your friends must be, shall we say, *unable to explain what happened down there. But explanations are hardly necessary—they simply ran out of air.

"You buried them down there?" Ethan said through clenched teeth. He didn't want his relief to show. He squeezed Tana's shoulder relentlessly, warning her to keep silent. The others needed no such warning. Drake, Caitlyn, and Mendrano had to be free . . . and were, actually, their only hope.

"I'm afraid I'm not responsible for that. Paul was a bit precipitous but it was made necessary by circumstances. It seems, Sir Richard, your daughter was a bit too inquisitive for her own good. It forced our hand, you might say."

"All of this just to dig for emeralds," Sir Richard stated bitterly.

"Not exactly," Monroe replied. "You see, I knew there were emeralds where Mr. Stone was digging for artifacts."

"How?" Ethan demanded. "How did you know?"

"I suppose I can tell you now. The secret will still be safe. When Mr. Stone first arrived one of the workers found an emerald. A very clever man, he knew if he continued to dig he would be found out and lose his find. So, he and another friend brought it to me.

"Needless to say, I recognized its value and the fact that where there is one, there are many. I paid him so well he was overjoyed. Then you, Sir Richard, conveniently came to me and asked me to find your family.

"I knew exactly where the emeralds were, and I could see the remarkable resemblance between you and Paul. In no time Paul, with your identification, was on his way.

"His job was to find a way to remove the emeralds. Of

course, I didn't count on a tomb. It was a bit of a surprise. But artifacts don't interest me. So, we will leave you all among the artifacts you love so well and go on with our own kind of dig—for a fortune in rare jewels."

Ethan cast a quick look at Paul Macombe, whose face was pale, his brow slick with sweat. Suddenly he had an explosive realization. Monroe was not aware there were riches lying in the tomb! He had never been told that without digging at all, there was a vast fortune there for the taking. Paul's glance was narrow-eyed and furious when he saw Ethan's knowing smile. Ethan needed time, and he meant to get it any way he could. Causing trouble among the enemy might just do it.

"It seems your friend hasn't been quite as truthful with you as he might have been," Ethan began. Paul swung his rifle, placing the barrel only inches from Ethan's chest.

"Shut up!" he snarled. "Don't try playing for time by starting trouble. Nobody will believe anything you say."

"I wouldn't be too sure of that. In fact, I'd say your *partner* has been suspicious for a long time. What's the matter, Mr. Monroe? Can't you trust the people you work with?" Ethan's voice was mild, amused, and taunting—but his nerves were stretched tight. All Paul had to do was squeeze the trigger and it would be over. And Ethan wasn't too sure he wasn't about to do just that.

"I learned a long time ago never to trust anyone as greedy as I am." Monroe chuckled. "I'm sure there's a great deal you could tell me, Mr. Marshall."

"I wouldn't be surprised. But not with this gun in my belly."

"Paul, move away," Monroe commanded.

"Can't you see he's playing for time!" Paul was furious . . . and afraid.

"Yes, but the question arises—playing for time for what reason? Do you expect some help? Maybe we should dispense with you quickly. Just in case." Monroe watched any trace of amusement die in Ethan's eyes. "But rest assured," he chided, "I shall make every effort to find out what little secrets my dear friend Paul might have kept from me." He motioned to two of his men with an almost imperceptible nod and suddenly Paul was aware that they had silently moved up behind him.

But that realization came seconds too late as he was grasped, disarmed, and shoved away from the group.

Paul's face reflected fear—then panic. He, more than any of them, was aware of Monroe's ruthlessness.

"You can't do this!" Paul gasped. "I did everything you wanted me to do. Now you turn on me because of what he says. You know he just wants time."

"Paul, don't be ridiculous," Monroe said. "I most certainly *can* do this. You are no longer useful, so why should I tolerate your traitorous presence? I'm quite aware of what he's trying to do. But it will get him nowhere. I'm also aware that you haven't been exactly truthful. I can see the greed in your eyes, and I know how your devious mind works. I'm afraid," Monroe said as casually and evenly as if he were concluding a business deal, "that your employment is terminated . . . as of now. So stop sniveling."

Paul stood frozen, mute with fear. He watched as Monroe turned away as if he were nothing.

Monroe smiled almost benevolently at Ethan. "Suppose you tell me just what I can expect to find down there."

"A fortune that might take the rest of your life just to calculate," Ethan answered. "If you were a smart man you'd make use of us before you . . . did away with us."

Monroe gazed at him in silent contemplation. Then he

answered softly, "Yes, of course. To bring the treasure up. There is so much that it would take such an effort?"

"Why use men who will *share* in the fortune, when you can use those you intend to . . . eliminate."

Ethan had read Monroe well and the others knew it. He knew Monroe wanted *all* the fortune for himself; he intended to share it with no one.

"Very clever idea," Monroe agreed. He smiled, knowing his men were not aware that the ultimate betrayal was already part of his plans.

"A few of you men go down into the tomb and bring the treasure up. The lady," he chuckled, "will stay with me to insure that you will do nothing foolish."

This was something Ethan had not counted on. The last thing he wanted was to be separated from Tana. He knew as she pressed closer to him that she was terrified of the dark, penetrating eyes of the men with Monroe.

"How can we do anything from there? We are unarmed and there's no way out except past you and your men," Ethan protested. "Tana goes with me."

"Do you want her to die with you here and now? Or are you wise enough to at least give her a little more time. She stays with me. That way, I'm sure you won't jeopardize her any more than she already is."

"If you touch her," Ethan said in a deadly tone, "if one of them touches her, I'll kill you, Monroe. You can count on it."

"No one will touch her, providing you don't do anything to cause it."

The faces of all the men were filled with rage, especially Antonio's. There was not a man among them who did not second Ethan's threat, and Monroe knew it.

"Come, it's time to move."

Monroe, Carlos, and the other four men prodded the captives toward the door. Paul was pushed along with the other prisoners, despair rendering him beyond words.

The path that led to the tomb seemed so much shorter to all of them than it had been in the past. The six men paused at the head of the shaft that led down to the entrance to the tomb.

Ethan could feel the old fear clutch him and he wasn't sure he could step inside that dark place again.

Drake, Caitlyn, and Mendrano had been completely unaware that Ethan and the others were in the main tent. Drake walked to the small window and cautiously drew the curtain aside to scan the area between them and the dig. He was just in time to spot Paul Macombe and the others as they slowly closed in on the tent. There must be someone inside, he thought excitedly.

"Mendrano!" he hissed. Mendrano was at his side instantly, Caitlyn right behind him.

"What is it?" she asked softly.

Mendrano read the situation quickly—then Drake explained his idea to Caitlyn.

"Who do you suppose is still in there?" Drake asked, as much to himself as to the others. "Some of the workers?"

"Why would they hold them?" Mendrano asked. "No, I think not."

"I don't know who else it might be, unless . . ."

"Tana and my son," Mendrano said, his voice cold with anger.

"Oh, no," Caitlyn said, her voice breaking. She was all too convinced of the brutality of the men who had just vanished into the tent. "We've got to do something."

"I count Paul and six others." Drake glanced at Mendrano, who nodded in agreement. "Maybe we can get the drop on them."

"It is very dangerous," Mendrano said. "Maybe Caitlyn should stay here. Then, if we fail . . ."

"If you fail I'll be left in the middle of this jungle alone, or worse, a victim of that man again. No, I'll take my chances with you."

Drake smiled and drew Caitlyn close.

"We'll have to be very careful. Look, Mendrano, do you see that tree on the other side of the tent? The big one?"

"Yes."

"Can you work your way around to it?"

"I think so."

"We can't just approach that tent in the open. Caitlyn and I will work our way around to the back. Once we make it—if we make it—I'll signal you. We'll watch until they leave. If they have Tana and Antonio," he said, hating to be brutal, but he knew Mendrano was fully aware of the possibility, "nine chances out of ten, they have the same plans for them as they had for us."

"They are animals without hearts," Mendrano snarled. "If harm has come to my family . . ." he did not need to finish—Caitlyn and Drake's sentiments were much the same.

"What will happen if they don't all come out together?" Caitlyn asked.

"Then we'll have to do something to force them out," Drake replied. "A nice little fire at the back of the tent would suffice."

"Let's hope it doesn't come to that," Mendrano said.

"Mendrano, these men are dangerous. Be careful and don't let anger get in the way of common sense."

"Don't worry, I'll be very careful."

"Caitlyn and I will keep you covered."

Mendrano nodded. There was nothing left to say. All three of them knew they had to get Tana and Antonio free from the grasp of their cruel captors.

Mendrano slipped from the back door, Drake's expert eye following him as he made his way toward the tree.

Drake and Caitlyn waited with bated breath until Drake spoke softly. "He's there. Now it's our turn." He took Caitlyn's hand. "Stay low—we have to move quickly." He looked down into her eyes. "Scared?"

"Yes." She couldn't deny it, because she knew Drake would know anyway. "I'm so scared I can hardly breathe. But I'm just as angry."

Drake grinned and bent to kiss her. His eyes were tender. "Damn, but I love you. Let's go."

They slipped from the door and made their way rapidly from tree to tree until they were less than twenty feet from the tent.

Caitlyn could feel her heart pounding as she reached to lay her hand against Drake's arm. She could feel his strength and solidity—it gave her the confidence she needed.

Drake, Caitlyn, and Mendrano watched the tent, waiting for the right moment. All three were quite unaware that less-than-friendly eyes were watching them.

When the group of prisoners and their captors came out of the tent, the three onlookers weren't surprised to see Tana and Antonio—but the presence of the others came as a shock.

There was no doubt in any of their minds where they were headed. Drake didn't know why he didn't try to stop them. Some deep instinct told him this was not the right time. Instead, he, Mendrano, and Caitlyn fell in behind them, following carefully to make sure they weren't seen.

Drake wished for some way he could get a signal to Ethan. If he could let him know he was still alive then Ethan would realize rescue was imminent.

He waited for an opportunity, but it never came. The prisoners were forced ahead in a tight group, which made it impossible to contact any of them.

"They're going to the tomb, all right," Drake said grimly.

"Drake . . . if they go down they'll find out we're not there."

"I know. But there's not much we can do about it now, unless . . ." His whole body seemed to grow still and his eyes scanned the area about them. Then he laughed softly. "Good move, Mendrano."

"What?" Caitlyn questioned insistently.

"Mendrano's moved ahead of them. He'll go down. He has two rifles and a pistol—he can arm a couple of them. That ought to change the odds a bit."

"But if they seal them in . . ."

"Mendrano knows the way out. From now on we just play it by ear and hope the old gods are looking down on us."

They continued to move ahead and eventually Drake and Caitlyn could see them gathered at the mouth of the shaft leading down into the tomb.

Mendrano was certain they would be concentrating on the main shaft, because they were unaware they were being watched. He made his way to the narrow air shaft and, carefully and quickly as he could, unjammed it. Then he slowly maneuvered his way inside the first small room of the tomb.

He set the weapons aside in a dark corner, keeping one pistol. Then he went to the small opening to the outer shaft

nd waited. He had to be careful, just in case they sent a
uard or two down with the prisoners.

Drake and Caitlyn watched as the prisoners and their
uards seemed to get into an argument. Then Tana was
oughly pulled from Ethan's side and Drake knew what the
roblem was.

It would mean that even if the others went below and
vere armed by Mendrano, Tana would still be held captive.
t was up to him and Caitlyn now to see that she was safe.

Paul was totally distraught. Everything he had ever wanted
ad slipped completely from his grasp. He would end up
vithout his fortune, and, if he couldn't think of a way out,
is life as well. His hatred for Monroe was a boiling blackness
nside him. He would have liked nothing better than to see
lade Monroe dead.

The group paused at the opening of the tomb.

"I'm not leaving Tana here with you," Ethan said, en-
aged at this turn of events.

"You have very little choice in the matter," Monroe said
onfidently, "and if you cause me any problems now she'll
e the recipient of your punishment. Later, I will take her
vith me into the tomb for a while. I have a strange feeling
've been told a few lies and I want to see for myself."

Paul's gaze snapped toward him. His face flushed with
lismay. Monroe laughed softly as his suspicions were con-
irmed. "I've never really trusted you, Paul, but you've been
seful . . . up to a point."

Ethan's face was full of fury, but he was helpless for the
noment, and he had to do whatever he could to protect
ana. He turned to the six men with him. "All right, let's
o down."

"Carlos," Monroe said, "you go down with them. Mak
sure they don't try anything stupid. If they get out of lin
or cause you any problem," his eyes met and held Ethan's
"shoot one of them."

Carlos's grin faded. This was the tomb of his ancestors
There was an inbred fear of disrespecting it. Yet . . . h
knew how deadly Monroe could be. He prayed that the god
would not punish him for what he was *forced* to do.

Ethan's face looked as if it were carved from stone. The
he looked at Tana and every feature softened. "Don't b
afraid," he said gently. "We'll be careful."

Tana wanted to cry but she held herself in check so sh
would not make Ethan's fear for her any worse than it wa
She knew just going down in the tomb again was a cha
lenge for him. She tried to smile as she watched Ethan an
the others enter the tomb one by one.

Inside the tomb Mendrano pressed himself against th
wall and held his breath. He had no idea how many guard
would come and he knew he would have only one slir
chance. He waited in silence—then he heard the first fair
noise of someone approaching.

"There are five men and Tana," Drake whispered i
Caitlyn's ear. "Maybe we can get the drop on them and fre
Tana. If we do . . . and I'm sure Mendrano will get tha
guard they sent in, we can get out of this. Can you handl
that rifle if you have to?"

"After what they've done to us?" Caitlyn answere
grimly. "Don't worry, I'll do my part. I'd like to . . . shoc
him somewhere so he wouldn't die . . . just wiggle a bit.

"Bloodthirsty," Drake chuckled. "Remind me not to get you really angry in the future. You ready to give it a try?"

"I'm ready."

They inched their way forward cautiously. It was two against five—and the five had the added advantage of holding Tana.

Their attention was so focused on the five men ahead that neither heard the slight sounds from behind them until it was too late.

"Freeze where you are," said a firm, cold voice. Caitlyn gasped as she and Drake spun around to see two men pointing rifles at them. With a sinking heart, Drake realized that they had probably just lost their last chance.

"Since you're so anxious to see what's going on down there I suggest you move on ahead. The boss just might have something planned for the two of you. Consider yourself invited to the party." He motioned with his rifle—they were disarmed and forced to walk forward.

When Monroe saw them he was surprised at first, then pleased.

Paul's face went gray, his eyes wide with shock. He could feel Caitlyn and Drake staring at him. They did not speak but their obvious disgust made Paul feel as if he were shriveling inside.

"Well, well," Monroe chuckled, "so the dead have risen. Fascinating. How did you get out of there? Paul assured me you would be dead by now."

"Paul tends to count his chickens before they're hatched," Drake said with a sneer. "How we got out is our secret. Maybe," he grinned, "we're only apparitions sent back to get the ruthless man who killed us."

"Very amusing," Monroe said and smiled. "But you're very much alive, and very much prisoners. Did you think

I would be careless enough not to use guards? We will see if we can't be more thorough the second time around."

Tana had said nothing. She was the only one who had given thought to her father and where he might be. They might still have a chance.

Ethan was the first one into the room. He was jolted by the sight of Mendrano, who put his finger to his lips.

One by one the others entered, Carlos bringing up the rear. He was hardly inside when Mendrano brought the pistol butt down and sent him into oblivion.

"Now what?" Bill whispered.

"Mendrano, they still have Tana!" Ethan cried.

"They will not have her for long," Mendrano answered. He quickly told him about Drake and Caitlyn as he handed a rifle and one of the pistols to Ethan.

"How did you get out of here?" Ethan asked. "I thought . . ."

"I know, but it is a very long story, better saved for later when we are safe."

"Safe," Ethan repeated reverently. "How are we going to surprise them? They're only a few feet from that door, and with Tana . . ."

As if to silence their thoughts, Monroe's voice came from the distance.

"Carlos!"

"Answer him," Mendrano whispered to Ethan.

"Yeah?" Ethan called out, hoping the hollow echo of the tomb would disguise his voice.

"Bring them out. It seems we have two more guests."

Mendrano closed his eyes—Ethan knew with a sinking heart it could only be Drake and Caitlyn.

"Listen, Mendrano," Ethan said quickly, "they don't know you're here. Can you get back up that air shaft?"

"It will be difficult, and will take time."

"Then we'll have to buy you as much time as we can. Right now, you're our only hope."

"What about him?" Mendrano pointed to Carlos.

Ethan grinned. "The poor man tripped and hit his head. It's not our fault. We'll just drag him out."

"Monroe is clever. He will not take this with a great deal of humor."

"I'll be careful. You just get a move on. He's not a patient man."

"Carlos!" Monroe called.

"We can't answer for him again. Bill, help me drag him out. Mendrano, get going."

Mendrano nodded and disappeared into the shadows. Ethan and Bill, the others behind them, dragged Carlos out to face Monroe's wrath.

"What happened? I thought you were too clever to try and jump him."

"We are," Ethan snapped angrily. "He tripped and hit his head on something." Ethan was aware of Drake's intense scrutiny and he nodded imperceptibly.

Monroe was deep in thought and looking from one to the other. There were more of them than he'd bargained for and two were men of undisputed daring and courage. Things were getting out of hand and he knew it. He had to eliminate some of the opposition. When they looked into his eyes, Drake and Ethan could read his thoughts.

"I'm afraid it's time for us to part company," Monroe said with a sneer.

"What are you going to do with them?" Paul asked.

"Bury them with the dead."

"But there's another way out of there," Paul protested.

"One they'll be in no condition to use," he said as he

smiled. "Paul, you and one man go inside first. Keep an eye on them as they come in. This time . . . there will be no escape."

Paul smiled and motioned to one of the men to follow him. He stopped to pick up Carlos's rifle. A gun could make all the difference. He could still end up with everything if he was careful.

There was no opportunity to escape. They were forced down one level after another until once again they stood in the shadowy lower room. Only two of the men had lanterns, which cast very little light.

Mendrano struggled out, only to find the area empty. Certain that his friends had been forced inside, he knew time was running out. He entered the upper room again and started down as stealthily as he could.

Drake and Ethan began to wonder if their luck had finally run out. They would have given their lives to save the women they loved, but in their hearts they knew they wouldn't get that chance. Monroe only had to let them die here and everything he'd ever dream of would be his.

"And so it's time to bid you all farewell," Monroe said. "It's a shame you interfered with my plans. One day soon I'll come back here for the jewels. By then you'll be just a memory. Goodbye, my friends. Meet your lost civilization in another world." He raised his gun, as did the others. Caitlyn moaned softly and pressed her face against Drake's chest. He held her tight. Tana clung to Ethan. All hope was gone. Mendrano could not help now . . . it was all in the hands of fate—and the gods.

It began with a low, throbbing rumble. Monroe looked down at his gun in surprise. It seemed to have a life of its own. Then the quivering could be felt beneath their feet and stark terror permeated the room like a tangible force. EARTHQUAKE!

The rumble grew to a soul-jarring roar and they could feel the ground undulate beneath their feet. The walls began to shake and a cloud of dust filled the room.

Guns were tossed aside as fear blotted out everything but the need to escape.

Drake grasped Caitlyn's hand and raced for the steps with Ethan and Tana. The walls shook violently and broken stones fell all around them. The steps vibrated as if they intended to tear themselves from the walls.

Mendrano had been on his way down when he was jerked from his feet by the massive tremor—it was the first time he had ever tasted such fear . . . not fear of death, but fear that those he loved would be trapped below.

Bill, George, Marc, and Sir Richard raced up the steps, followed by Antonio, Ethan, and Tana. Drake and Caitlyn were last, and as Drake pushed Caitlyn ahead of him he looked back.

Monroe, crushed by a huge stone from the ceiling, lay beneath it, a trickle of blood slowly staining the floor. Paul was in a traumatic state, alternately looking at Drake, then back toward the riches in the tomb.

"Paul," Drake shouted above the roar, "get out of here!" He could not hear what Paul said—he could only see his lips move.

"The emeralds . . . all that treasure . . . I can't . . ." He looked at the chests. If he could only grasp a handful . . . just a handful. He could not leave that gleaming, beckoning fortune behind.

"Paul! No!" Drake cried. The whole room seemed to shudder. Caitlyn turned to see Paul race toward one of the chests and push the lid up.

Greedily he grasped the glittering stones and filled his pockets and stuffed his shirt until it bulged. Then he turned.

Drake knew there was very little time left. He spun Caitlyn around and pushed her ahead of him. Then he turned at the top of the steps and looked down.

Paul raced for the steps. He was nearly at the top when the stairs shuddered and began to disintegrate. Drake tried to grasp Paul's arm seconds before the steps crashed to the floor below. Paul was hanging by one arm and it took every ounce of Drake's strength to hold onto him. Slowly his grip began to slip.

"Paul, drop the stones! Empty your pockets! Get rid of the weight! I can't hold you!"

"No! No! I can't . . ."

"You've got to let go."

Faced with this choice, Paul could not let go of the jewels. Slowly Drake's grip weakened. There was no room in the narrow doorway to shift positions and everyone was gone but Caitlyn. She refused to leave Drake's side, despite the rumbling and the shaking walls and floor.

"Paul, please," Caitlyn called over Drake's shoulders.

Paul struggled even harder to pull himself up, but his burden weighed too much. Drake clung to the doorway with one hand and to Paul with the other. His arm was pierced by excruciating pain. He could feel his grasp growing weaker and weaker—he knew he could not hold on much longer.

But Paul's greed outweighed his reason. He looked up at Drake in total disbelief as Drake's hand began to slip from his. Drake inhaled deeply as Paul disappeared into the blackness below.

The thundering roar was now deafening and Drake knew the tomb could not stand much longer. He turned, surprised to see Caitlyn still there.

"Get out of here!" he shouted.

"Not without you!"

He grasped her hand and they raced up the stairs. It seemed as if they would never reach the top. The air was filled with dirt and falling debris. The floor felt as if it would vanish beneath their feet at any moment.

When their lungs seemed ready to collapse and their strength was all but gone, they reached the upper room.

Anxious hands pulled them to safety and they all made their way to the top of the shaft.

It seemed as if the world had gone insane. The trees shivered and quaked, some of them leaned from the ground, roots and all. The earth rose and fell as if it were alive. In one place a huge rent appeared with a tremendous sound, swallowing everything in its path. Trees, boulders . . . all fell into what seemed like a bottomless amber-colored hole while flames leapt from its center, accompanied by hissing sounds.

Terror gripped them all as they clung to one another. Then with a thundering boom they could hear the walls of the tomb collapse.

Then as suddenly as it had begun, all was still. Silence filled the air so completely that none of them dared breathe for fear it was not over.

But the silence continued and finally Caitlyn looked up at Drake.

"I think . . . it's over," he said.

"Thank God."

"Yes, thank God. It seems as if it took divine help to get us out of this one."

"But we're here. We're safe." Caitlyn looked up at him with tears of love and relief in her eyes.

Caitlyn felt a light touch on her shoulder and turned to see George.

"Caitlyn," he said gently, "I think it's time you met your father . . . your *real* father."

Sir Richard stood just behind George, his grey eyes glistening. Caitlyn could hardly swallow the heavy lump in her throat. Suddenly she did not seem to have command of her faculties. Words seemed beyond her capacity. Sir Richard, speechless himself, held out his arms to her.

"Caitlyn . . . my child," he said, his voice thick with unshed tears.

Caitlyn could feel the heat of tears on her cheeks as she stepped into the loving comfort of her father's embrace.

Sir Richard looked at Drake and smiled. "It seems the three of us have a great deal to make up for. And so much to talk about." He looked down at Caitlyn, "You've given me back all that I lost. You look so much like your mother. Life has given us a second chance."

"Yes," Caitlyn whispered. She clung to her father, but reached out a hand to Drake who took it in a firm grip. "Let's go home."

Epilogue

Three Months Later

The sounds of the jungle and the rush of the river accompanied the boat as it chugged its way upstream.

Caitlyn and Drake stood together in the bow, Drake resting one arm on the rail, the other around Caitlyn's waist.

"It's still so beautiful," Caitlyn said. She closed her eyes and leaned against Drake.

"Compared to you," he murmured as he kissed her cheek, "it doesn't stand a chance."

Caitlyn turned to look up at him. "Thank you, my dear husband. But I'm glad we're going home and so are you."

"I didn't want to cut our honeymoon short," he protested.

"Of course you didn't," she said, laughing, "but I could see your face every time I mentioned how much progress Father was making at the dig."

"Was I that obvious?"

"Absolutely."

"Then in self defense I have to get you to admit you were a bit anxious to get back home."

Caitlyn slid her arms around him and smiled at him. "Maybe you should ask me why."

"Why?"

"Because I remember that old victrola and dancing with

you. I remember our pool . . . Drake, I want to go back there again."

"That old wooden tub."

"Ummm, sounds exciting."

"You're exciting," he said, tightening his arms around her. "I can still taste the fear I felt when I almost lost you."

"It was a terrible time. But when I think of all that came from it I can hardly regret it. Ethan and Tana are so happy. I'm glad we stayed long enough to see them get married. And my father, he's in heaven having a family and sharing the dig with you. As for me . . ."

"As for you?"

"I don't think I've ever been so happy."

"Are you ready to get back to work?"

"Drake . . . are we going to try to reopen the tomb?"

"I don't know. It sounds crazy, Caitlyn, but . . . I still think there was more to that situation than we'll ever know. That earthquake . . ."

"No, I think it's something else."

"What?"

"Don't laugh. I think we were being saved . . . or protected. Either way, the lovers owed a debt . . . and I think our lives were their payment."

"How lovely to think they might finally be at peace, that they found a way to atone for whatever sin they committed."

"I'd like to feel that was true."

"What a romantic man you are. Archaeologists are supposed to be dull and boring."

"Rumor," Drake said and grinned.

"I intend to keep it a secret. I want this archaeologist all to myself."

"Well, we'll be all to ourselves for a long time. The museum almost fell over themselves when they heard what we

und and read that letter your father wrote. Looks like that
ttle house will be our home for the next few years."

"And I couldn't be happier," she said softly. Drake bent
is head to kiss her—a deep, lingering kiss.

When they turned again to look out over the river, the
ocks of Fountainhurst had just come into view.

Even from the distance they could see three people await-
ig them. Ethan raised his hand in a welcoming wave, as
id Tana, who stood beside him.

Sir Richard Macdonald waved enthusiastically, welcom-
ig Caitlyn back. She smiled up at Drake, who returned it
ith warmth. "We're home, love," he said softly. "We're
ome."